JUDAS

Books by Amos Oz

AMOS OZ

JUDAS

Translated from the Hebrew
by
Nicholas de Lange

HOUGHTON MIFFLIN HARCOURT
Boston   New York
2016

First U.S. edition, 2016

Copyright © 2014 by Amos Oz
Translation copyright © 2016 by Nicholas de Lange

www.hmhco.com

Library of Congress Cataloging-in-Publication Data is available.
ISBN 978-0-544-46404-9

First published in Hebrew as *Habshura Al-Pi Yehudah*
First published in Great Britain by Chatto & Windus, 2016

Book design by Kelly Dubeau Smydra

Printed in the United States of America
DOC 10 9 8 7 6 5 4 3 2 1

To Deborah Owen

See the traitor run in the field alone.
Let the dead not the living now cast the first stone.

— Nathan Alterman, "The Traitor,"
from *The Joy of the Poor*

JUDAS

I

——

HERE IS A STORY from the winter days of the end of 1959 and the beginning of 1960. It is a story of error and desire, of unrequited love, and of a religious question that remains unresolved. Some of the buildings still bore the marks of the war that had divided the city a decade earlier. In the background you could hear the distant strains of an accordion, or the plaintive sound of a harmonica from behind closed shutters.

In many flats in Jerusalem you might find van Gogh's starry whirlpool skies or his shimmering cypresses on the living room wall, rush mats on the floors of the small rooms, and *Doctor Zhivago* or Yizhar's *Days of Ziklag* lying open, face-down, on a foam sofa bed that was covered with a length of Middle Eastern cloth and piled with embroidered cushions. A paraffin heater burned all evening long with a blue flame. In a corner of the room a tasteful bunch of thorn twigs sprouted from a mortar shell casing.

At the beginning of December, Shmuel Ash abandoned his studies at the university and decided to leave Jerusalem, because his relationship had broken down, because his research had stalled, and especially because his father's finances had collapsed and Shmuel had to look for work.

Shmuel was a stocky, bearded young man of around twenty-five, shy, emotional, socialist, asthmatic, liable to veer from wild enthusiasm to disappointment and back again. His shoulders were broad, his neck was short and thick, and his fingers, too, were thick and short, as if they each lacked a knuckle. From every pore of Shmuel Ash's face and neck curled wiry hairs like steel wool: this beard continued upward till it merged with the tousled hair of his head and downward to the curling thicket of his chest. From a distance he always seemed, summer and winter alike, to be agitated and pouring with sweat. But close up, it was a pleasant surprise to discover that instead of a sour smell of sweat, his skin somehow exuded a delicate odor of talcum powder. He would be instantly intoxicated by new ideas, provided they were wittily dressed up and involved some paradox. But he also tended to tire quickly, possibly on account of an enlarged heart and his asthma.

His eyes filled easily with tears, which caused him embarrassment and even shame. A kitten mewling by a wall on a winter's night, having lost its mother perhaps, and darting heartrending glances at Shmuel while rubbing itself against his leg, would make his eyes well up. Or if, at the end of some mediocre film about loneliness and despair at the Edison Theater, it turned out that the bad guy had a heart of gold, he could be choked with tears. And if he spotted a thin woman with a child, total strangers, coming out of Shaare Zedek Hospital, hugging each other and sobbing, he would start weeping too.

In those days, it was usual to see crying as something that women did. A weeping male aroused revulsion, and even faint disgust, rather like a woman with a beard. Shmuel was ashamed of this weakness of his and made an effort to control it, but in vain. Deep down he shared the ridicule that his sensitivity aroused, and was reconciled to the thought that there was some flaw in his virility, and that therefore it was likely that his life would be sterile and that he would achieve nothing much.

But what do you do, he sometimes asked himself with disgust, beyond feeling pity? For instance, you could have picked that kitten up, sheltered it inside your coat, and brought it back to your room. Who would have stopped you? And as for the sobbing woman with the child, you could simply have gone up to them and asked if there was anything you could do to help. You could have sat the child down on the balcony with a book and some biscuits while you and the woman sat side by side on your bed discussing what had happened to her and what you might try to do for her.

A few days before she left him, Yardena said: "Either you're like an excited puppy, rushing around noisily—even when you're sitting on a chair you're somehow chasing your own tail—or else you're the opposite, lying on your bed for days on end like an unaired quilt."

She was alluding, on the one hand, to his perpetual tiredness and, on the other, to a certain choppy quality in his gait, as if he were always about to break into a run. He would leap up steps two at a time. He rushed across busy roads at an angle, risking his life, not looking right or left, hurling himself into the heart of a skirmish, his bushy, bearded head thrust forward, his body leaning with it, as if eager for the fray. His legs always seemed to be chasing after his body, which in turn was pursuing his head, as if they were afraid of being left behind when he disappeared around the next corner. He ran all day long, frantically, out of breath, not because he was afraid of being late for a class or a political meeting but because at every moment, morning or evening, he was struggling to do everything he had to do, to cross off all the items on his daily list, and to return at last to the peace and quiet of his room. Each day of his life seemed to him like a laborious circular obstacle course, from the time he was wrenched from sleep in the morning until he was back under his quilt again.

He loved to lecture anyone who would listen, particularly his comrades from the Socialist Renewal Group: he loved to clarify, to state the facts, to contradict, to refute, and to reinvent. He spoke at length, with enjoyment, wit, and brio. But when the reply came, when it was his turn to listen to others' ideas, Shmuel was suddenly impatient, distracted, tired, until his eyes closed and his tousled head sank down onto his shaggy chest.

He enjoyed haranguing Yardena too, sweeping away received ideas, drawing conclusions from assumptions and vice versa. But when she spoke to him, his eyelids drooped after a minute or two. She accused him of not listening to a word she was saying, he denied it, she asked him to repeat what she had just said, and he changed the subject and told her about some blunder committed by Ben-Gurion. He was kindhearted, generous, brimming with goodwill, and as soft as a woolen glove, going out of his way to make himself useful, but at the same time he was muddled and impatient. He never knew where he had put his other sock, what exactly his landlord wanted from him, or to whom he had lent his lecture notes. On the other hand, he was never muddled when he stood up to quote with devastating accuracy what Kropotkin had said about Nechayev after their first meeting, and what he had said two years later. Or which of Jesus' apostles was less talkative than the rest.

Though Yardena liked his bouncy spirit, his helplessness, and the exuberance that made her think of a friendly, high-spirited dog, always nuzzling you, demanding to be petted, and drooling in your lap, she had decided to leave him and accept a proposal of marriage from her previous boyfriend, a hard-working, taciturn hydrologist by the name of Nesher Sharshevsky, a specialist in rainwater collection, who nearly always managed to anticipate whatever she might want next. He had bought her a pretty scarf for her secular birthday, and two days later, on her religious birthday, he had given her a small green oriental rug. He even remembered her parents' birthdays.

2

——

SOME THREE WEEKS BEFORE Yardena's marriage, Shmuel finally abandoned his master's thesis, "Jewish Views of Jesus," a project he had embarked on with immense enthusiasm, galvanized by the daring insight that had flashed into his mind when he chose the topic. But once he began to check details and explore sources, he soon discovered that there was nothing novel about his brilliant idea, which had appeared in print before he was born, in the early thirties, in a footnote to a short article by his eminent teacher, Professor Gustav Yomtov Eisenschloss.

The Socialist Renewal Group also underwent a crisis. The Group met regularly every Wednesday evening at eight o'clock in a soot-stained, low-ceilinged café in a back alley in the district known as Yegia Kapayim. Artisans, plumbers, electricians, painters, and printers met occasionally to play backgammon in this café, which to the members of the Group made it seem a more or less proletarian location. The plasterers and radio repairers, however, did not join the members of the Group, though sometimes one of them asked a question or made a remark from a couple of tables away, or else one of the members of the Group would fearlessly approach the backgammon players' table and ask a representative of the working class for a light.

After protracted argument, nearly all the participants in the Group were reconciled to the revelations of the 20th Congress of the Communist Party of the Soviet Union regarding Stalin's reign of terror, but there was a resolute faction that demanded of the comrades that they reconsider not only their allegiance to Stalin but also their attitude toward the very principles of the dictatorship of the proletariat as formulated by Lenin. A couple of the comrades went so far as to use the ideas of the young Marx to challenge the ironclad teachings of the later Marx. When Shmuel Ash attempted to contain the erosion, four of the six members of the Group declared a split and announced that they were setting up a separate cell. Among the four who split off were the two girls in the Group, without whom there was no longer any point.

That very same month, Shmuel's father lost his final appeal in a series of lawsuits lasting several years against his old partner in a small company in Haifa (Shahaf Ltd., Drawing, Mapping, and Aerial Photography). Shmuel's parents had no choice but to discontinue the monthly allowance that had maintained him throughout his student days. So he went downstairs to the yard and found behind the dustbin shed some used cardboard boxes which he took up to his rented room in Tel Arza, and every day he randomly crammed more of his books and clothes and possessions into them. He still had no idea where he would move to.

Some evenings he would roam the rainy streets, like a bewildered bear roused from hibernation. With his lumbering gait he plowed the streets of the city center, which were almost deserted of human life because of the cold and the wind. Several times after nightfall he stood stock-still in the rain in one of the narrow streets of Nahalat Shiva, staring at the iron gate of the building where Yardena no longer lived. Sometimes his feet led him wandering through remote wintry parts of the town that he did not know—Nahlaot, Beit Yisrael, Ahva, or Musrara—splashing though puddles and avoiding dustbins overturned by the wind.

Once or twice he nearly hit his head, thrust forward like a charging bull's, against the concrete wall that divided Israeli from Jordanian Jerusalem.

He paused absent-mindedly to peer at bent signs warning him through the coils of rusting barbed wire: STOP! BORDER AHEAD! BEWARE, MINES! DANGER — NO MAN'S LAND! YOU HAVE BEEN WARNED — YOU ARE ABOUT TO CROSS AN AREA EXPOSED TO ENEMY SNIPERS! Shmuel hesitated between these signs as if they were offering him a varied menu from which he had to make a choice.

Most evenings, he wandered like this in the rain, soaked to the bone, shivering with cold and despair, his unruly beard dripping, until at last he crept wearily back to his bed and curled up in it till the next evening: he got tired easily, perhaps because of his enlarged heart. In the twilight he heaved himself out of bed, put on his clothes and his coat that was still damp from the previous evening's excursion, and wandered again to the edge of town as far as Talpiyot or Arnona. Only when he was stopped by the gate of Kibbutz Ramat Rahel and a suspicious night watchman shone a flashlight in his face did he turn on his heel and head for home with nervous, hurried steps. After hastily consuming two slices of bread and some yogurt, he took off his wet clothes and burrowed under his quilt again, trying in vain to get warm. Eventually he would fall asleep, and sleep till the following evening.

Once he met Stalin in a dream. The meeting took place in a low back room in the grimy café where the Socialist Renewal Group convened. Stalin told Professor Gustav Eisenschloss to relieve Shmuel's father of all his troubles and his losses, while Shmuel, for some reason, showed Stalin, from the roof of the Dormition Abbey on Mount Zion, a distant view of a corner of the Wailing Wall beyond the border, in the Jordanian sector. He failed to explain to Stalin, who was smiling under his mustache, why the

Jews rejected Jesus and why they still stubbornly continued to turn their backs on him. Stalin called Shmuel Judas. At the end of the dream the flickering skinny figure of Nesher Sharshevsky offered Stalin a whimpering puppy in a metal box. At the sound of the puppy's whimpering Shmuel woke up, with a vague feeling that his rambling explanations had only made matters worse, because they aroused in Stalin not only suspicion but also contempt.

The wind and the rain battered the window of his room. Toward dawn, as the storm grew stronger, a metal laundry tub attached to the balcony railing banged with a hollow sound against the balustrade. Two dogs, far away from his room and possibly far from each other, did not stop barking all night long, and sometimes the barking turned into howls.

So it occurred to him to leave Jerusalem and find some easy work somewhere a long way off, perhaps as a night watchman in the Ramon Hills, where he had heard that a new desert town was being built. But in the meantime, he received the invitation to Yardena's wedding: apparently she and Nesher Sharshevsky, her compliant hydrologist, the expert on rainwater collection, were in a great hurry to get married. They couldn't manage to hold on until the end of the winter. Shmuel made up his mind to surprise them, to surprise the whole gang, by accepting the invitation: breaking with convention, he would simply turn up, loud and cheery, wreathed in smiles, patting shoulders; the unexpected guest, he would walk into the wedding ceremony, where only family and close friends were supposed to be present, and then he would throw himself wholeheartedly into the party afterward, contributing to the merriment and the program, his famous imitation of Professor Eisenschloss.

But on the morning of Yardena's wedding, Shmuel Ash suffered a severe attack of asthma and dragged himself to the clinic, where they tried in vain to help him with an inhaler and various allergy pills. When his condition worsened, he was taken from the clinic to Bikur Cholim Hospital.

Shmuel spent the hours of Yardena's marriage in the emergency ward. Then, for the whole of her wedding night, he was breathing through an oxygen mask. The next day he decided to leave Jerusalem without delay.

3

AT THE BEGINNING of December, on a day when sleet was beginning to fall in Jerusalem, Shmuel Ash announced to Professor Gustav Yomtov Eisenschloss and his other lecturers (in the Departments of History and Religious Studies) that he was abandoning his studies. Outside in the wadi, patches of fog drifted like dirty cotton wool.

Professor Eisenschloss was a small, compact man with thick beer-bottle lenses in his spectacles, and movements that reminded you of a cuckoo darting busily out of a clock. He exploded on hearing Shmuel's news.

"But how can this be! What nonsense is this! What has come over us suddenly? Jewish views of Jesus, indeed! Obviously, a fruitful field without parallel opens up before us! In the Talmud! The Tosefta! The Midrash! In our folklore! In the Middle Ages! We must surely be about to make an important breakthrough here! Well? But supposing we continue our researches one step at a time? Without a doubt we shall very soon find ourselves reconsidering this negative idea—to defect in midcourse!"

Having said which, he breathed on the lenses of his spectacles and polished them vigorously with a crumpled handkerchief.

Abruptly extending his hand, he said in a different, slightly embarrassed voice:

"If, however, we have encountered—heaven forbid!—some difficulty of a financial nature, there might be some discreet manner of mobilizing, one step at a time, some modest assistance." He pressed Shmuel's hand again, so hard that the bones made a faint cracking sound, and declared fiercely:

"We shall not give in so quickly! Neither over Jesus, nor over the Jews, nor over you! We shall bring you back to your inner sense of duty!"

In the corridor, after leaving Professor Eisenschloss's office, Shmuel was smiling at the recollection of those student parties where he himself had starred in the role of Professor Gustav Yomtov Eisenschloss, popping out suddenly like a cuckoo from a clock, and always speaking so pedantically and pontificating in the first person plural, even to his wife in their bedroom.

That evening Shmuel Ash typed out a notice offering for sale, cheaply, on account of "unexpected departure," a small Philips radio (made of Bakelite), a Hermes Baby typewriter, and a record player with a couple of dozen records: classical music, jazz, and French chansons. He pinned the notice to the corkboard next to the stairs to the cafeteria in the basement of the Kaplun Building at the university. Because of the accumulation of announcements, advertisements, and posters, he had to put it up in such a way that it completely covered an earlier, smaller notice of five or six lines on blue paper, written—Shmuel managed to observe while he was burying it—in delicate, precise feminine handwriting.

Then he cantered, with his disheveled ram's head thrust forward as if trying to break free of the thick neck it sprouted from, toward the bus stops outside the campus gate. But he had taken only forty or fifty steps, and was passing the Henry Moore sculpture of a heavy, greenish bronze woman lying draped in a shroud

of rough cloth, when suddenly he turned and rushed back to the
Kaplun Building, to the notice board next to the stairs leading
down to the cafeteria. His short, thick fingers hurriedly rolled
up his own note so he could read and reread what he himself had
hidden from his eyes just a couple of minutes earlier:

COMPANION SOUGHT

Offered to a single humanities student with conversational
skills and an interest in history, free accommodation and
a modest monthly sum in return for spending five hours
per evening with a seventy-year-old invalid, an educated,
widely cultured man. He is able to take care of himself and
seeks company, not assistance. For initial interview, please
present yourself Sunday to Thursday between 4 and 6
p.m. at 17 Rabbi Elbaz Lane, Sha'arei Hesed. (Please ask
for Atalia.) Owing to special circumstances, the successful
candidate will be required to commit himself in writing to
complete confidentiality.

4

RABBI ELBAZ LANE led down the slope of Sha'arei Hesed toward the Valley of the Cross. Number 17 was the last house at the bottom of the lane, at the spot where in those days the neighborhood and the city ended, and the boulder-strewn fields that extended to the ruins of the Arab village of Sheikh Badr began. Immediately after the last house the potholed roadway turned into a rocky path that slithered hesitantly toward the valley, veering this way and that as if it regretted continuing onto this wasteland and was attempting to turn back toward the inhabited regions. In the meantime, the rain had stopped. Above the western hills there was a whisper of twilight, a gentle gleam, beguiling as a scent. In the distance, among the rocks on the opposite hillside, a small flock of sheep appeared; their shepherd, wrapped in a dark cloak, sat upright between rain showers in the cloudy evening light, staring immobile from the desolate hillside toward these last houses on the western fringe of Jerusalem.

The house itself seemed to Shmuel Ash basement-like, lower than street level, sunk almost to its windows in the heavy earth of the slope. At a glance, from the street it resembled a squat, broad-shouldered man wearing a dark hat who had gone down on his knees to search for something in the mud.

Both the rusty iron gates had long ago buckled their hinges

and sunk in the soil under their own weight, as if they had struck root. So the gates stood ajar, neither open nor closed. The space between was just wide enough to squeeze through without scraping one's shoulders. Above was a rusted iron arch with a Star of David engraved at its top, and these words hammered out within it in square letters:

AND A REDEEMER SHALL COME UNTO ZION
MAY IT BE SPEEDILY REBUILT 5674

From the gate, Shmuel went down six cracked, uneven stone steps into a small courtyard that enchanted him from the first glance and stirred a pang of yearning for somewhere that he could not recall. A vague, shadowy memory flitted through his mind, a hidden reflection of other inner courtyards, many years before, and he had no idea where they were or when he saw them, but he knew indistinctly that they were not wintry courtyards like this one but, on the contrary, flooded with summer light. This memory brought him a fleeting feeling between sadness and delight, like a single note played on a cello at night from the depth of the darkness.

The courtyard was surrounded by a stone wall about the height of a man and was paved with stone slabs polished by the years to a brilliant red with gray veins. Here and there, spots of light flashed. An old fig tree and an arbor of vines shaded the courtyard. So dense and intertwined were their branches that even now, their leaves shed, only a handful of capering gold coins managed to filter through the canopy and flicker on the flagstones. It seemed not so much a stone courtyard as a secret pool, its surface ruffled by myriad rippling wavelets.

All along the wall and the front of the house and on the windowsills blazed little beacons of geraniums in red, white, pink, and purple. The geranium plants sprouted from a mass of rusty pots and disused pans, paraffin stoves, buckets, basins, tin cans, and even a cracked lavatory bowl, all filled with soil and promoted to the rank of flowerpot. The windows were protected with iron grilles and shaded with green metal shutters. The walls of the house were made of Jerusalem stone that turned its untamed, undressed face toward you. And beyond the house and the wall of the courtyard was a dense screen of cypresses, their color in this evening light closer to black than green.

Over all this lay the silence of a cold winter's evening. Not the kind of limpid silence that invites you in, but rather an indifferent, age-old silence that turns its back on you.

The roof of the house was tiled, and in the middle of the façade there was a small attic gable, a triangular structure that reminded Shmuel of a truncated tent. The gable, too, was roofed with faded tiles. He suddenly wanted very much to live in that attic, to curl up inside it with a pile of books, a bottle of red wine, a stove, a quilt, a record player and some records, and not go outside for lectures, debates, or love affairs. To stay there and never leave, at least while it was cold outside.

The front of the house was covered with a tangle of passionflower that clung to the roughness of the stone with fierce tendrils. Shmuel crossed the courtyard, paused to take in the dots of light trembling on the paving stones and the network of gray veins on the reddish stone. Then he was standing in front of a double iron door painted green, adorned with a knocker in the form of a blind lion's head. The lion's teeth were fastened on a large iron ring. In the center of the right-hand leaf of the door was the following legend:

RESIDENCE OF JEHOIACHIN ABRAVANEL WHOM G-D
PROTECT, TO SHEW THAT THE LORD IS UPRIGHT

Beneath this inscription there was a small, practical note stuck to the door with two delicate strips of sticky paper, on which Shmuel recognized the same handwriting he had seen on the notice in the Kaplun Building, a meticulous and pleasing feminine hand. There was no "and" between the two names, which were separated by a large space:

ATALIA ABRAVANEL   GERSHOM WALD
CAUTION — BROKEN STEP IMMEDIATELY
BEHIND THE DOOR

5

KINDLY WALK STRAIGHT AHEAD. Then turn to your right.
Please advance toward the source of light. Then you will find
me," said the voice of an elderly man from the depths of the
house. It was a low, slightly amused voice, as if the man had been
expecting this guest and none other, at this time and no other,
and was now celebrating his foresight and taking pleasure in having his expectations realized. The front door was unlocked.

Shmuel Ash stumbled as he entered the house, because he expected a step up, not a step down. And in fact it was not even a
real step, but a makeshift, low, rickety wooden bench. The moment a visitor trod on one edge, the other end rose up like a lever
and almost overturned whoever had put his weight on it. It was
Shmuel's haste that saved him from a bad fall—while the bench
was tipping up and rising into the air, he had already reached the
stone floor with a big leap, his curly head surging forward, drawing him along into the passage, which was almost completely
dark.

The farther Shmuel penetrated into the house, his forehead
forcing its way like the head of a fetus advancing along the neck
of the womb, the stronger grew the feeling that the floor of the
passage was not level, but sloped downhill, as if it were a river-

bed rather than a dark corridor. Meanwhile, his nostrils caught a pleasant smell, a smell of fresh laundry, of cleanness, of starch and ironing.

Another corridor branched off from the end of this passage. It was shorter, and from its end came the light that the voice had promised him. The light brought Shmuel Ash to a warm, high-ceilinged library. Its iron shutters were tightly closed and a paraffin heater burned with a pleasant blue glow. The single electric light was a gooseneck desk lamp that stooped over a heap of books and papers, focusing on them to the exclusion of the rest of the library.

Beyond this ring of warm light, between two metal trolleys laden with books, files, folders, and notebooks, an elderly man sat talking on the telephone. A plaid was draped around his shoulders like a prayer shawl. He was an ugly man, broad, crooked, and hunchbacked. His nose was as sharp as the beak of a thirsty bird, and the curve of his chin suggested a sickle. His fine, almost feminine gray hair cascaded down the back of his head and covered the nape of his neck. His eyes were deep-set beneath thick, craggy white eyebrows that looked like woolly frost. His bushy Einstein mustache was a mound of snow. Without interrupting his telephone call, he eyed his visitor with a penetrating, quizzical glance. His sharp chin tilted toward his left shoulder. His left eye squinted while the right one was open wide, round, blue, and unnaturally large. The man's face wore a sly, amused expression, as if he were winking or making a sarcastic denunciation: he seemed instantly to have understood the young man before him, as if reading his mind and understanding what he was after. A moment later he switched off the searchlight beam of his gaze, acknowledged the visitor's presence with a nod of his head, and looked away, continuing his telephonic debate all the while:

"Someone who is always suspicious, someone who always assumes that everyone is lying to him, someone whose whole life is nothing but an unending procession of traps to be avoided—excuse me a moment, an emissary has suddenly appeared, or maybe it's a workman I never sent for." At this, he covered the mouthpiece with one hand, its pink fingers looking almost transparent, ghostly, in the light of the desk lamp. His gnarled features, which resembled the trunk of an olive tree, lit up in a fleeting mischievous smile under his bushy white mustache, as if he had succeeded in trapping his visitor before the victim even realized what had happened.

"Sit. There. Wait."

He removed his hand from the mouthpiece and continued, his head still tilted toward his left shoulder:

"A persecuted man, whether he is persecuted because he himself has turned everyone into persecutors or whether he is persecuted because his wretched imagination swarms with throngs of scheming enemies, one way or another such a man has, besides his wretchedness, a moral flaw: surely there is a fundamental dishonesty in the enjoyment of persecution as such. Incidentally, such a man is dogged by suffering, loneliness, accidents, and ill health more than others—that is, more than the rest of us. By his nature, the suspicious person is destined for disaster. Suspicion, like an acid, corrodes the vessel in which it is put and eats away at the suspicious man himself: guarding oneself day and night from the entire human race, constantly devising ways of avoiding evil schemes and conspiracies, and sniffing out snares laid for you— these are what the Talmud calls 'primary categories of damages.' And these are the things that, as the rabbis say, take a man out of the world. Please excuse me for one moment—"

Again he covered the mouthpiece with his corpse-like fingers and addressed Shmuel Ash in a soft, ironic, almost charred voice:

"Kindly wait for a few more minutes. Meanwhile, feel free to listen to what I am saying. Though a young man like you no doubt inhabits a totally different planet."

Without waiting for a response, the old man removed his hand
from the telephone and resumed his homily:

" . . . Although, fundamentally, suspicion, enjoyment of persecution, and even hatred of the entire human race are all much
less lethal than a love of humanity, which reeks of ancient rivers
of blood. In my view, gratuitous hatred is less bad than gratuitous
love: those who love mankind, the world-reforming knights-er-
rant, those who rise up against us in each generation to save us,
with none to rescue us from their power, surely, in fact, they—all
right. All right. You are right. Let us not embark on that subject
now. While you and I are elucidating all kinds of salvations and
consolations, a corpulent young man with a caveman beard has
appeared before me, in a military greatcoat and probably military boots. Maybe he has come to enlist me in the army? So let
us pause at this point. We shall speak more of this subject, you
and I, tomorrow and the day after. Yes, my friend, we shall definitely speak more. Inevitably. What should men like us do if not
speak? Hunt whales? Seduce the Queen of Sheba? And by the
way, apropos the Queen of Sheba, I have my own personal, anti-
romantic, rather transgressive, in fact, interpretation of the verse
'Love covereth all sins.' Whereas the verse 'Many waters cannot
quench love, neither can the floods drown it' always puts me in
mind of the ominous wailing of a fire engine's siren. Please give
my regards to dear Zhenia, embrace and kiss her for me, embrace
and kiss her in my fashion, not in your bureaucratic way. Tell her
I miss her radiant face very much. No, not your radiant face, my
heart's desire—your face is 'as the face of the generation.' Like a
dog's. Yes. I look forward to seeing you one of these days. I do not
know when Atalia will return. She minds her own business and
she minds mine as well. Yes. Goodbye. Thank you. Amen, just as
you say, so be it."

And with that he turned to Shmuel, who had seated himself in the meantime, after some hesitation, very cautiously, on a frail-looking wicker chair that seemed to rock under the weight of his body. Suddenly the man roared:

"Wald!"

"What?"

"Wald! Wald! My name is Wald! And what are you? A pioneer? From a kibbutz? Have you favored us with a visit from the heights of Galilee? Or on the contrary, have you come up from the plains of the Negev?"

"I'm from here. From Jerusalem. That is, I'm from Haifa, but I'm studying here. Or rather, I've been studying here."

"Now, now, my young friend, let's get this straight. Are you studying or aren't you? Are you from Haifa or Jerusalem? Out of the barnfloor or out of the winepress?"

"I'm sorry. I can explain."

"And what is more, I assume you are a positive character? An enlightened, progressive person? A world reformer? A proponent of morality and justice? What I call an ideophile, an idealist like the rest of you? Am I right? Speak up and let us hear what you have to say for yourself."

Having said which, he waited meekly for an answer, his head tilted toward his left shoulder, one eye closed and the other open wide, like someone waiting patiently for the curtain to rise on a performance of which he has no high expectations and all he can do is resign himself to whatever the characters may be about to do to one another: how they will plunge each other into the depths of misery, if such a place exists, and by what means they will all arrive at their own disastrous self-inflicted destinies.

And so Shmuel began again, this time with great care: he announced his first name and his surname, no, to the best of his knowledge he was not related to the well-known writer Sholem Asch, his family were functionaries and land surveyors, from

Haifa, he studied, or rather he used to study, here in Jerusalem, history and religion, though he himself was not at all religious, definitely not, quite the contrary in fact, one might say, but somehow the figure of Jesus of Nazareth ... and Judas Iscariot ... and the spiritual world of the Chief Priests and Pharisees who rejected Jesus, and how quickly the Nazarene, in Jewish eyes, went from being a persecuted figure to a symbol of persecution and oppression ... and how this was somehow connected in his view with the fate of social reformers in modern times ... well, it was rather a long story, he hoped he was not intruding here, he had come in response to the notice, the one about a companion, that he discovered by accident on the notice board in the Kaplun Building. At the entrance to the student cafeteria ...

At this, the invalid stiffened, letting his tartan plaid fall to the ground, raised his long, distorted frame from the chair, twisted the upper part of his body in a series of complicated movements, gripped the arms of the chair with both hands, and stood up at a strange angle, though it was clear that it was not his legs but his strong arms grasping the chair frame that bore his weight. He chose not to touch the crutches that leaned against the edge of his desk. He was strong and bent, hunchbacked, yet so tall that his head nearly hit the low light fixture that hung from the ceiling, and when he stood he seemed twisted like the trunk of an old olive tree. He was big-boned and stiff, with large ears, and yet almost regal with that gray mane flowing down the back of his head, the snowy mounds of those eyebrows, and the striking whiteness of that thick mustache. When Shmuel's eyes met the old man's, he was surprised to observe that, in contrast to his amused and ironic tone, the blue eyes were clouded and mournful.

Then the man placed both hands on top of the desk and, again resting his whole weight on the muscles of his forearms, advanced slowly along the edge of the desk, with a mighty effort, like a large octopus thrown up on dry land and struggling to crawl down the seashore to the water. So the man moved, dragging himself with the strength of his arms from his chair along the whole length of his desk until he reached an upholstered wicker couch, a sort of chaise longue that awaited him beside the desk, beneath the window. Here, outside the ring of light cast by his reading lamp, he began to execute a series of bends and twists, shifting his weight from hand to hand, until he managed to lay his large body down on this cradle of his. And at once he declared in the same derisive voice:

"Aha! The notice! So there is a notice! And I said in my haste —well, but in fact, all that is between you and her. I have nothing to do with her mysteries. And meanwhile, please feel free to sit there and wait to your heart's content. And what hidden treasure are you concealing there? Under your beard? No. I was only joking. Forgive me now if, with your permission, I take a little nap. As you can see, I have a degenerative disease. I am degenerating. And you, young man, please sit, sit, fear not, no ill will befall you here in my home, you may even select a book or two to read until she returns, unless you, too, prefer to take a nap. Sit. Sit."

Then he fell silent. And perhaps he really did close his eyes, stretched out on his couch, wrapped like a huge silkworm cocooned in another tartan blanket, identical to the first and waiting for him in his new place. And at once he was transformed into a vague, silent range of hills.

Shmuel was surprised by Mr. Wald's repeated exhortations to sit, because he had only to glance at his visitor to realize that he had remained sitting all the time and had not gotten up or stirred even once. A valley, hills, olive trees, a ruin, and a winding mountain path appeared in a drawing by the artist Rubin on a calendar that hung, slightly askew, on the wall facing the desk, between the bookcases. Shmuel was gripped by an irresistible urge to get up and straighten the picture. Then he returned to his place and sat down again. Gershom Wald said nothing: perhaps he had dozed off and not seen. Or perhaps his eyes were not yet entirely closed under the thick white brows and he saw the adjustment, but accepted it in silence.

6

—

SHE APPEARED THROUGH another door, one that Shmuel had not noticed. It was actually not a door but a concealed entrance, hiding behind a bead curtain in a corner of the room. As soon as she entered, she reached out and switched on the ceiling lamp. At once the whole library was flooded with bright light. The shadows were banished behind the rows of books.

A woman of around forty-five, she held herself erect and moved around the room as if well aware of her feminine power. She was wearing a plain, light-colored dress that reached her ankles and a simple red sweater. Her long, dark hair flowed softly down on one side of her neck to land on the mound of her left breast. Beneath the hair nodded a pair of large wooden earrings. Her clothes hugged her body. Her high heels enhanced the lightness of her step as she glided from the entrance toward Mr. Wald's wicker cradle. There she stood, with one hand on her hip, waiting. When she raised her elongated brown eyes to Shmuel, she was not smiling, but her face wore an expression of curious sympathy with a faint hint of challenge. As if to ask: So? How about you? What can I do for you? What little surprise have you brought us today? And also as if trying to tell him that even though she was not smiling, a smile was definitely possible and should not be ruled out.

She brought with her into the room a faint scent of violets, but also a whiff of the pleasant smell of laundry and starch and ironing that his nostrils had caught as he was advancing between the closed doors along the passage.

"Have I come at an inconvenient time?" Shmuel asked.

And he hastened to add:

"I've come about the notice?"

She turned those eyes on him again, so sure of their power, and scanned his appearance with interest and possibly pleasure. She did not turn her gaze away until he was compelled to lower his eyes. She contemplated his unkempt beard as one takes an unhurried look at a crouching animal. And she nodded, not to him but to Mr. Wald, as if confirming her initial conclusion. Shmuel Ash, meanwhile, peeped at her once or twice, then hastily looked down again, though he managed to notice the well-defined furrow that descended firmly from her nose to the middle of her upper lip. It seemed unusually deep, yet fetching and delicate. Removing a pile of books from a chair, she sat down, crossed her legs, and straightened the hem of her dress.

She seemed in no hurry to reply to his question as to whether he had come at an inconvenient time, appearing to consider it from every angle until she was in a position to deliver a responsible and authoritative answer. Finally she said:

"You've been waiting a long time. You must have been talking, the two of you."

Shmuel was surprised by her voice. It was resonant and languorous, yet practical at the same time. Self-confident. She did not seem to be asking a question so much as summing up the results of various calculations.

"Your husband told me to wait for you," Shmuel said. "I gathered from the notice that—"

Mr. Wald opened his eyes and interrupted. He addressed the woman:

"He says his name is Ash. Without an initial *H*, we must hope."

And turning to Shmuel he corrected him, a patient teacher correcting a pupil:

"But I am not the lady's husband. I do not have that honor and pleasure. Atalia is, in fact, my mistress."

He allowed a little time for Shmuel to wallow in his astonishment before deigning to explain:

"I am not using the word in the vulgar sense, of course, but rather as in the famous saying of the first Queen Elizabeth of England: 'I will have here but one mistress and no master.'"

Atalia said:

"Well, just you carry on with this as long as you like, the two of you. You seem to be enjoying it."

She uttered this without a smile, but in a voice that seemed to promise Shmuel that all options were open so long as he did not overdo it or make a fool of himself. She put four or five short questions to him, repeating one with emphasis and in simpler language because she was not satisfied with his answer. She paused for a moment, then added that she still had a few questions left.

Mr. Wald intervened cheerily:

"Our guest must surely be feeling pangs of hunger and thirst! He has come straight from the heights of the Carmel! A couple of oranges, a slice of cake, a glass of tea might work wonders!"

"I'll leave the two of you to work wonders. I'll go and put the kettle on."

The smile that had had difficulty reaching her lips now rose from her voice.

She turned and left the way she had come in. But this time, as she went out, her hips stirred the bead curtain. Even after she disappeared, it did not settle at once, but continued to make waves and produced a trickling, rustling sound that Shmuel hoped would not die away too soon.

7

THERE ARE TIMES when the pace of life slows down, stuttering like water running from a rain gutter, cutting itself a narrow channel in the earth of the garden. The stream encounters a heap of soil, is checked, forms a small puddle, hesitates, and reaches out to nibble at the mound blocking its way, or tries to tunnel underneath. Because of the obstacle, the water sometimes shudderingly splits, groping its way along three or four fine threads. Or it gives up and soaks away into the dust. Shmuel Ash, whose parents had lost their entire life savings in an instant, whose own research had stalled, who had dropped out of university, and whose girlfriend had suddenly married her former boyfriend, decided to accept the position he had been offered in the house on Rabbi Elbaz Lane. Including the conditions of "board and lodging," and including the monthly salary, which was modest: for a few hours each day he would keep the invalid company, and the rest of his time would be his own. And there was also the presence of Atalia, who was nearly twice his age, yet he felt a pang of disappointment every time she left the room. Shmuel fancied he noticed a certain distance, or disparity, between her words and her voice. Her words were few and sometimes sarcastic, her voice was warm.

———

A couple of days later he moved out of his room in Tel Arza and into the house surrounded by a paved yard shaded by fig and vine, the house that had attracted him from the first glance. In a couple of cardboard boxes and an old kit bag he transported his clothes, his books, his typewriter, and two rolled-up posters, one showing the Pietà and the other the heroes of the People's Revolution in Cuba. He carried his small record player under one arm, his collection of records under the other. This time he did not stumble over the loose plank inside the front door, but carefully stepped across it.

Atalia Abravanel explained to him the scope of his duties and the rules of the house. She showed him the spiral iron staircase that led up from the kitchen to the attic. Standing at the foot of the staircase, she instructed Shmuel in the details of his work and the routine of the kitchen and the laundry, one hand resting on her hip with fingers outspread while the other fluttered for a moment on his sweater, pulling from his sleeve a wisp of straw or a dead leaf caught in the wool. She spoke precisely, practically, yet in a voice that conjured up a warm, dark room:

"Look. It's like this. Wald is a nocturnal creature. He sleeps till midday because he stays awake every night until the early hours of the morning. Every evening from five until ten or eleven you will sit and talk to him in the library. And that, more or less, is the entire job. Every afternoon at half past four you will fill and light the paraffin heater. You will feed the fish in the aquarium. You don't need to make a special effort to prepare subjects for conversation—he will have already equipped himself with an abundance of topics, and it won't take you long to discover that he's one of those people who talk mainly because they can't stand a moment's silence. Don't be afraid to argue with him. In fact, he really comes to life when people disagree with him. Like an old dog who still needs a stranger to appear now and then to give him a reason to bark, and occasionally to give a little nip. Though only a playful one. On the other hand, you can both drink as much tea as you wish: here's the kettle, and here's the essence and the sugar, and over there is a box of biscuits. Every evening at seven o'clock you will warm the porridge that will be waiting for you, covered in tinfoil, on the electric hotplate, and you will place it in front of him. He generally devours his food with gusto, but if he only eats a mouthful or two, or refuses to eat altogether, don't force him. Just ask him if you can take the tray, and put it just as it is on the kitchen table. He can get to the toilet by himself, on his crutches. At ten o'clock you must always remind him to take his pills. And at eleven, or a little earlier, you must leave him a thermos full of hot tea for the night, then you're free to go. After you've left him, come out to the kitchen and wash his plate and cup, and leave them to dry on the drainer above the sink. At night he usually reads and writes, but in the morning he tears up everything he's written. When he's alone he sometimes talks to himself or even argues with himself out loud. He talks for hours on the telephone with one of his three or four old enemies. Occasionally he sobs in the night. Don't go to him. Leave him alone. As for me"—for an instant a crack of hesitancy opened in her voice, but was immediately closed—"never mind. Come here. Look: here is the gas. Here is the dustbin. The hotplate. The sugar and coffee are here. Biscuits. Cakes. Dried fruit. There's milk and cheese and some fruit and vegetables in the refrigerator. Up here there are tins of preserves, beef, sardines, peas, and corn. We've had some of them since the siege of Jerusalem. This is the crockery cupboard. Here are the electric fuses. The bread is here. There's an elderly neighbor living across the street, Sarah de Toledo, who brings Mr. Wald a vegetarian lunch every day, and every evening she leaves a saucepan of porridge on our hotplate. It's a paid arrangement. There should be enough porridge for you too. You can take care of your own lunch: there's a little vegetarian restaurant nearby, on Ussishkin Street. Here's the laundry basket.

The cleaner, Bella, comes every Tuesday. If you like, Bella can do your laundry and clean your room at no cost to you. For some reason, one of your predecessors was terrified of Bella. I have no idea why. Your predecessors were trying to find themselves, apparently. What they found I don't know, but none of them stayed more than a few months. At first they were enchanted by the prospect of all that free time in the attic, but later it became a burden. I expect you've also come here for solitude and to find yourself. Or perhaps to write a new poem. You may think that bloodshed and atrocities have come to an end, you may think the world has been purged and cleansed of suffering and is just waiting impatiently for a new poem. There are always clean towels here. That is my door there. Don't even think of coming to look for me. Ever. If you need something, if some problem crops up, just leave me a note here on the kitchen table and in due time I'll supply you with whatever you need. Only don't come running to me out of loneliness or whatever, like your predecessors. This house apparently makes people lonely, but that's not my department. I have nothing to offer. And one other thing: when he is alone, he not only talks to himself but he sometimes cries out. He calls for me in the night. He calls out to people who no longer exist. He begs and pleads with them. He may even call out to you. It mostly happens at night. Pay no attention. Just turn over and try to get back to sleep. Your task in this house is well defined: it lasts from five to eleven. Wald's crying out at night is not part of your job. The same goes for some other things that may happen here sometimes. That is none of your business—steer well clear of it. Oh, I almost forgot: take these keys. Don't lose them. This one is the front-door key, and this is the key to your attic room. Naturally you are free to come and go outside your working hours, but on no account are you to bring any visitors here. Male or female. This is definitely not an open house. And how about you, Ash? Do you ever cry out at night? Do you sleepwalk?

No? Never mind. Pretend I never asked. And another thing: you
will sign here for me, to agree that you hereby undertake not to
talk about us. Not to pass on any information. Not even to your
nearest and dearest. You are simply not to tell anyone what work
you do here. If you have no alternative, you can always say you're
looking after the house, and that is why you're living here rent-
free. Have I forgotten anything? Have you? Is there anything
you'd like to ask? I haven't alarmed you, have I?"

A couple of times while she was talking, Shmuel tried to look
into her eyes, but each time he had encountered a glimmer
of wry warning, and he had been compelled to avert his gaze
quickly. This time he decided not to give up. He knew how to
smile at women with a charming, childlike innocence, and he also
knew how to imbue his voice with a certain shy, helpless quality, which contrasted strikingly with his overgrown body and his
unruly, Neanderthal beard. This shy approach, combined with
boundless enthusiasm and a kind of perpetual melancholy, often
worked for him.

"May I ask just one question? A personal question? What is
the relationship, or the connection, between you and Mr. Wald?"

"He has already given you the answer. I am in charge of him."

"And another question? You really don't have to answer."

"Ask. But that will be the last question for today."

"Abravanel? Such an aristocratic name. I don't like to pry, but
is there any connection with Shealtiel Abravanel? I seem to recall
there was someone called Shealtiel Abravanel here in Jerusalem
in the forties? A member of the Executive of the Jewish Agency?
Or a member of the National Council? If I remember rightly
he was the only one to oppose the creation of the state? Or else
he was only opposed to Ben-Gurion's approach? I remember
vaguely: He was a lawyer? An Arabist? A ninth-generation Jeru-
salemite? Or was it seventh-generation? I have an idea he was a
kind of one-man opposition. And afterward Ben-Gurion ousted

him from the leadership, so he wouldn't get in his way. Or maybe I'm muddling up two different people."

Atalia did not reply immediately. Instead, she gestured to him to climb the spiral staircase, and followed him up to the door of his attic, where she stood leaning against the railing, her left hip raised and curved into a little hillock, her outstretched arm holding the other railing, her body blocking his escape. And, as if breaking through low clouds, an inward-looking, pained smile spread from the corners of her eyes, but—it seemed to Shmuel at that moment—there might have been in her smile a hint of surprise and even gratitude. But at once the smile was shut off and her face went blank, like a door being slammed.

She seemed beautiful and attractive to him, and yet there was something strange, something hurt, in her face, something that reminded him of a pale theatrical mask or the whitened face of a mime. For some reason, tears welled up in Shmuel's eyes and he hurriedly looked away, because he was ashamed.

With her back to him, as she started to descend the iron stairs, she said:

"He was my father."

Several days passed before he saw her again.

8

A<small>ND SO A NEW CHAPTER</small> opened in Shmuel Ash's life. There were times when he felt a sharp urge to run and find Yardena, to snatch her for an hour or two from her rainwater-collecting husband Nesher Sharshevsky and lecture her passionately about his present monastic existence, so different from his previous life, as if he had been reincarnated here. He was keen to prove to her that he had now succeeded in overcoming all his defects—his feverishness, his garrulousness, his unmanly tendency to weep, and his impatience—and that he was turning into a calm, solid man like that husband of hers.

Or not just to tell her about it but to take her by the arm and show her the wintry stone courtyard with its polished flagstones, and this dark, inward-looking house, shaded by cypresses, fig tree, and vines, to bring her up to the little attic room where he now lived a solitary, meditative life beneath the bearded faces of the leaders of the Cuban Revolution, and to Mr. Wald's library . . . where we sit and chat for several hours a day and where I am gradually learning to be a patient listener. It would be good, too, to present to Yardena his didactic invalid, tall and stooping, with the Einstein-like mane of white hair and the snowy mustache; and the beautiful, distant woman whose piercing eyes mock you but whose voice, which is far from mockery, wells up slowly from deep in her chest.

How could Yardena not love us?

She might even have a sudden urge to leave her rainwater collector and come and join us.

But Atalia had made him sign an agreement forbidding him to bring visitors here or to tell anyone about his business in this house.

His eyes filled with tears again, and because he felt angry at himself on account of his tears and his fantasies, he decided to take off his shoes and get into bed fully dressed. There were so many free hours. And outside there was nothing but wind and rain. You wanted deep solitude, you wanted inspiration, you wanted endless expanses of silent free time, and here all your wishes have been granted. You've got it all. And on the ceiling of your attic room, directly over your bed, oceans and continents take shape in the cracking plaster: you can lie on your back for hours on end gazing at the archipelago of peeling plaster, islands, reefs, gulfs, volcanoes, fjords. And every now and again some little insect wriggles between them. Maybe this is the place where you can return to "Jewish Views of Jesus"? To Judas Iscariot? Or the common underlying reason for the failure of all revolutions? You could do some serious research, couldn't you? Or else you could start to write a novel? And every night, after work, sit over a glass of tea with Gershom Wald and an astonished Atalia and read installments aloud to them?

Each afternoon, soon after four o'clock, Shmuel got out of bed, showered, dusted his thick beard with fragrant talcum powder, descended the curling iron stairs, lit the paraffin heater in the library, and sat down facing Gershom Wald's black desk, on the wicker armchair padded with embroidered Arab cushions. Sometimes he fixed his eyes on the pair of goldfish that gaped at him almost motionless from behind the curved glass of the lit aquarium as he listened attentively to the homilies that Mr. Wald enjoyed delivering. From time to time, he stood up to serve some tea or to adjust the wick of the heater so that its flame continued to burn a soothing blue. Sometimes he opened the window a crack behind the closed shutters to let in a whiff of rain-drenched pine trees.

At five, and again at seven and nine, the old man listened to the news on the little radio on his desk. Sometimes he immersed himself in the newspaper and then explained to Shmuel what lay behind the latest news. Ben-Gurion was forming a new coalition. He might or might not include the Marxist-Zionist MAPAM Party and the Labor Union. "There's no one like Ben-Gurion," Wald said. "The Jewish people has never before had such a far-sighted leader as Ben-Gurion. Few understand as he does that 'the people shall dwell alone, and shall not be reckoned among the nations' is a curse and not a blessing."

Between news broadcasts Gershom Wald would talk to him about, for instance, the folly of Darwin and his followers:

"How is it possible even to imagine that the eye, or the optic nerve, came into being gradually, in response to the need to see, by means of what they term natural selection? Surely so long as there was no eye and no notion of sight in the world, nobody had any need or urge to see, and there was nobody and nothing that could even guess at the very need to see! It is inconceivable that within total sightlessness, an infinity of perpetual darkness that does not even have a clue that it is darkness, some cell, or some cluster of cells, suddenly appears and begins, *ex nihilo*, to blink and to start making out shapes, colors, and dimensions. Like a captive releasing himself from prison. Hmm. And, moreover, the theory of evolution has no shred of an explanation of the appearance of the first living cell or grain of growth amidst the eternal silence of a totally inanimate world. And who was it suddenly sprang up, *ex nihilo*, and began to teach some stray molecule of inanimate matter that it had to wake up all of a sudden from its perpetual inactivity and begin to convert the light of the sun into carbohydrates and to employ these carbohydrates for the purpose of growth and multiplication?

"Hmm. And surely there cannot possibly be any Darwinian explanation for the amazing fact that a cat, almost from the day of its birth, knows it has to dig a little hole to do its business in, then cover that with earth. Is it conceivable that natural selection is at work here? Were all the cats that were not capable of performing this complex hygienic operation wiped off the face of the earth without raising progeny, and only the descendants of the cats that buried their droppings succeeded in being fruitful and multiplying? And why was it specifically the cat that escaped from the cogwheels of the machinery of natural selection and was blessed with this remarkable tradition of hygiene, rather than the dog, or the cow, or the horse? Why did Darwin's natural selection not choose to leave in the world not just a cat but also, let us say, a pig that can lick and groom itself? Hmm? And who on earth could suddenly have taught the earliest ancestor of the sanitation-fixated cats, the first cat to inter its feces, how to dig the first cesspit and how to cover it with earth? It is like the question posed by the rabbis of old: how was the first pair of blacksmith's tongs made?"

Shmuel watched the old man's lips moving under his thick white mustache, and observed repeatedly the contrast between the cheery wit of his words and the deep anguish that clouded the graying blue of his eyes: tragic eyes set in a satyr's face.

Sometimes the old man spoke, in his usual way, at length, with pleasure and power, about the dark fear that the image of the Wandering Jew has always inspired in the Christian imagination. "Not everybody can simply wake up one morning, brush his teeth, drink a cup of coffee, and kill a god! To murder a deity you need to be even stronger than the god, as well as infinitely mali-

cious and evil. Whoever murdered Jesus, a warmhearted deity
radiating love, must have been stronger than he and also shrewd
and abominable. Those accursed god-killers were only able to
kill a god on condition that they really possessed monstrous re-
sources of strength and wickedness. And so that is indeed what
the Jews possess in the deepest recesses of the Jew-hater's imagination. We are all Judas. Even eighty generations later we are still
Judas. But the truth, my young friend, the real truth we can behold before our very eyes here in the Land of Israel: the modern
Jew who has sprung up here, just like his ancient predecessor, is
neither strong nor malicious but hedonistic, with an ostentatious
veneer of wisdom, boisterous, confused, and consumed by suspi-
cions and fears. Yes indeed. Chaim Weizmann once said, in a moment of despair, that there can never be such a thing as a Jewish
state, because it contains an inbuilt contradiction: if it is a state
it will not be Jewish, and if it is Jewish it will certainly not be a
state. As it is written in the Talmud, this is a nation that resembles
an ass."

At another time, he would expatiate on the migration of birds
or schools of fish. Both rely on mysterious powers of navigation
which scientific logic cannot begin to take the measure of. For
the most part, the cripple's hands were spread out calmly on the
glass surface of his desk, hardly moving as he spoke to Shmuel,
his white mane ringed with a halo of light from the desk lamp.
Now and again, he emphasized his thoughts by raising his voice
or lowering it almost to a whisper. Sometimes his fingers picked
up a pen or a ruler, and his strong arm cut all sorts of shapes in
the air. Every hour or hour and a half he rose and dragged his
twisted body, using the muscles of his arms, along the edge of the
desk, picked up the crutches, and limped toward the toilet or to a
bookshelf. Sometimes, dispensing with the crutches, he maneu-
vered his body by the strength of his arms alone, from the desk
to his wicker couch. He refused to allow Shmuel to help. His

awkward movement now was reminiscent of a wounded insect or a gigantic moth with burnt wings struggling vainly to fly.

As for Shmuel, he made them both tea. Occasionally he glanced at his watch, so as not to be late in serving the evening porridge, which was waiting in the kitchen, ready to be warmed on the hotplate. Once or twice, he tried to interest his host in the debate aroused by Dürrenmatt's *The Visit*, or by "Thoughts on Alterman's Poetry," a controversial article published recently by the poet Nathan Zach, in which he denounced mercilessly what appeared to him as the flamboyant artificiality that dominated the imagery of one of the leading Hebrew poets of his day. Mr. Wald, for his part, found in these debates a not insignificant element of acuteness, but also a strong dose of malice, conceit, and immaturity, and so he dismissed the subject with a witticism. On the other hand, he said nothing when Shmuel read him some poems by Dahlia Ravikovitch which had recently appeared. He merely inclined his snowy head and listened in attentive silence.

Because his neck was bent at a right angle, his face as he listened to the poems was turned to the floor, so that for a fleeting moment he looked to Shmuel like a hanged man with a broken neck.

9

FLAVIUS JOSEPHUS, THE EARLIEST extant Jewish source to mention the existence of Jesus, recounts the story of the Nazarene in two different versions. In his work *The Jewish Antiquities*, he devotes several clearly Christian lines to "Jesus, a wise man, if indeed one ought to call him a man. For he was one who wrought surprising feats ... He won over many Jews and many of the Greeks. He was the Messiah ... Pilate ... condemned him to be crucified ... On the third day he appeared to them restored to life." Josephus—how little he knew—concludes this short account with these words: "And the tribe of the Christians, so called after him, has still to this day not disappeared." Several contemporary scholars, however, including Professor Gustav Yomtov Eisenschloss, maintain that it is inconceivable for a Jew like Josephus to write in this way about Jesus, and it is almost certain, in Eisenschloss's view, that the passage was entirely rewritten over the years by Christians and was spuriously interpolated later into the *Antiquities*.

And indeed a totally different version of Josephus' remarks about Jesus appears in the writings of Agapius, a tenth-century Christian Arabic writer. According to Agapius, Josephus did not

consider Jesus to be a messiah, and he does not report his resurrection three days after his crucifixion as a fact, but he describes
objectively the belief of Jesus' disciples.

Josephus himself was born only a few years after the crucifixion, and perhaps the most interesting thing about what he says
concerning Jesus, whether in the *Antiquities* or in Agapius' version, is how tiny and almost negligible the whole episode of Jesus' advent seems to a historian who was his near contemporary.
In both versions, Josephus devotes fewer than a dozen lines to the
whole story of Jesus' life, his teaching, his miracles, his crucifixion, his resurrection, and the new faith of his followers.

Even after Josephus, the figure of Jesus aroused very little interest among Jews. The body of rabbinic literature, compiled
over many generations, contains only a small handful of scattered
allusions, which may possibly reflect denigration of Jesus on the
part of some rabbis, or else they may be totally unconnected with
him, and their mockery may be directed against someone entirely different, or against a number of different people. In general, the rabbis refrain from mentioning Jesus. In later times he
was alluded to, by way of a contemptuous *damnatio memoriae*, as
"that man."

There are a couple of passages in the rabbinic literature that
contain scornful remarks that can be interpreted in various ways,
such as when the early rabbi Simeon ben Azzai cites a genea-
logical scroll he found in Jerusalem, which said, "A certain man
is the illegitimate child of a married woman." This may reflect a
cowardly taunt at the followers of the rival faith, or it may simply
be a snippet of Jerusalem gossip whose subject is some unknown
"certain man," like those anonymous rumors that float around
Jerusalem today, even in the corridors of the university.

In Tractate *Sanhedrin* of the Tosefta there is a hostile refer-
ence to someone called ben Stada, who was executed in Lydda

for inciting people to idolatry, and there are scholars who insist on seeing some kind of allusion to Jesus here too. And elsewhere, in Tosefta *Hullin*, there is mention of a physician who could cure snakebites by uttering the name of Jesus ben Pantera. But who was that Jesus and who was Pantera? The matter is open to speculation which is no more than guesswork. Only much later, in the *Yalkut Shim'oni* on the book of Numbers, do we find an explicit warning against a human being "who tried to make himself into a god, and to lead the whole world astray."

However, in the Babylonian Talmud there are three explicit allusions to Jesus, who is variously described as a young scholar who strayed from the right path, or a sorcerer who promoted idolatry, or an apostate who repented but was not accepted back into the fold. But in the course of time, these three passages were deleted from almost all the printed editions of the Babylonian Talmud, because the Jews were terrified of what their Christian neighbors would do to them if they read such things.

The synagogue poet Yannai, who lived in Palestine in the fifth or sixth century, composed an anti-Christian hymn that mocks those "Who call the villain noble / Who choose the loathsome abomination / . . . Who address the hanged one each evening," and so forth.

When Shmuel brought his abandoned thesis to the library and began to read this convoluted hymn aloud to Gershom Wald, the old man sniggered and covered his eyes with his big ugly hand, like a man refusing to look at something disgraceful, and said:

"Stop, that's enough. Who can listen to such tasteless sophistries? I asked you to tell me about Jewish views of Jesus, not what all sorts of idiots think of him. This tea is too weak and too sweet, and it's also lukewarm. You are capable of compressing all the flaws of the world into a single small glass and then stirring them together. No, there's no need to make me a fresh tea. Just bring me a glass of tap water, then we'll sit quietly for a while. Who cares about ben Stada and ben Pantera? Let them rest in peace. As for us, we have only what our eyes can see. And even that, rarely. Now let's listen to the news."

10

His ATTIC ROOM was low-ceilinged and cozy, like a winter den. It was an elongated space, and the ceiling sloped like the sides of a tent. The single window looked out over the front of the house, the garden wall and the screen of cypresses beyond it, and the stone-paved courtyard shaded by the grapevine and the old fig tree. A charcoal-black cat, no doubt a tom, sometimes crossed the yard, slowly, imperiously, his tail erect, padding and gliding on velvety feet, as if each of his delicate paws did not step on the ground but languorously licked the polished paving stones that shone and glittered in the rain.

The window was set deep because the walls of the house were thick. Shmuel would drag his quilt over to the window ledge and make himself a kind of upholstered seat in which he liked to nestle for half an hour or so, looking into the empty courtyard. From this vantage point he discovered in a corner of the yard a cistern with a rusting iron lid. Such cisterns, he knew, were dug in the courtyards of old Jerusalem and served to collect rainwater before the British came and brought water from Solomon's Pools and the springs of Rosh Ha'ayin, spreading a web of pipes through the city. These old cisterns had saved the Jews of Jeru-

salem from serious drought in 1948, when the Arab Legion of
the Kingdom of Transjordan besieged the city and blew up all
the water pumps in Latrun and Rosh Ha'ayin so as to subdue
the populace. Was Atalia's father, Shealtiel Abravanel, one of the
leaders of the Jewish community at the time of the invasion of
the Arab forces, or had he already been stripped by Ben-Gurion
of the offices he had previously held? And why was he dismissed?
And what did he do afterward? And, in fact, when did Shealtiel
Abravanel die?

One day, Shmuel decided, I shall spend a few hours in the National Library and try to get to the bottom of this story.

But what good will it do you to know? Will the knowledge
bring you closer to Atalia? Or, on the contrary, will you only
make her shut herself away more than ever inside the shell of her
secrets?

Shmuel's bed stood between the corner where he made his coffee, and the toilet and shower, which were hidden behind a curtain. Beside his bed were a table, chair, and lamp, and facing it
was a heater and a bookcase, on which were arrayed an English–Hebrew dictionary, an Aramaic–Hebrew dictionary, a Bible
(including the New Testament) bound in black cloth embossed
with a gilded pattern, an atlas in a foreign language, a history of
the Haganah, and the volumes of *Parchments of Fire*, in memory of
the soldiers who fell in the War of Independence. Next to these
stood a dozen books of advanced mathematics and mathematical logic in English. Shmuel took one of them down, peered at
it, and failed to understand so much as the opening lines of the
introduction. On the shelf below these books, which belonged to
the house, Shmuel had arranged the few books he had brought
with him, as well as the record player and his records. There were
some metal hooks on the back of the door on which he hung

his clothes. And on the wall he put up with tape the poster of the heroes of the Cuban Revolution: the brothers Fidel and Raúl Castro, with their friend the Argentinean doctor Ernesto "Che" Guevara, surrounded by a crowd of other men, all with bushy beards almost like Shmuel's own, all of them in battle fatigues and looking like a group of poets and visionaries who had put on battle dress and fastened pistols to their hips. Shmuel's clumsy, disheveled image could have fit easily into this group. Each of them also had a submachine gun slung from his shoulder. Some of these dusty weapons hung by a rough length of rope rather than a leather strap.

Shmuel had also found in a corner of this attic room a metal trolley like the one he had seen downstairs in the library. Only up here, on his trolley, were carefully arranged in serried ranks, like soldiers on parade, pens, pencils, notebooks, folders, empty box files, a set of staplers and a heap of rubber bands, two erasers, and a gleaming pencil sharpener. Did they expect him to settle down here to copy sacred scriptures like a monk in his cell in the olden days? Or that he would plunge himself into research? About Jesus? Or Judas Iscariot? Or both of them? Or perhaps about the shady details of the rift between Ben-Gurion and Shealtiel Abravanel?

He lay on his back on the bed, trying to separate and join together complicated pictures in the plaster on the ceiling until his eyes closed. But even when they were closed, he continued to see the curved slope of the ceiling of the attic that had been allocated to him, something like a prison cell or an isolation room in a hospital for a patient with a rare infectious disease.

There was another object in the room, one for which Shmuel Ash found no use. He did not discover this object until he had been living in the attic for four or five days and nights, when he bent over and peered under his bed in pursuit of a sock that had gone absent without leave and hidden itself in the dark. Instead of the errant sock, his eyes were met in the darkness under the bed by sharp, shiny incisors set in the jaws of an evil-looking fox's head carved on the handle of a magnificent black walking stick.

II
—

Every day gershom wald made himself comfortable in the chair behind his desk or on his couch and delivered mordant lectures to his telephonic interlocutors. He larded his speech with quotations and allusions, witticisms and plays on words, aimed at himself as often as at the listener. Shmuel sometimes had the impression that he was piercing and wounding the person on the other end of the line with a fine needle, using the kinds of insults that only literati can be hurt by. He would say, for example: "But why must you prophesy, my dear? As the Talmud tells us, since the day the Temple was razed to the ground, the gift of prophecy was given to fools like you and me." Or: "Though you bray me in a mortar with a pestle, I shall not budge from my view." And once he said: "Well, my dear, it is assuredly the case that neither of us resembles any of the four sons mentioned in the Passover Haggadah, but it sometimes occurs to me that we are particularly unlike the first of the four, the wise son." Gershom Wald's ugly face at that moment radiated pugnacity and malice, and his voice trilled with glee and childish triumph. But his blue-gray eyes under his the bushy white eyebrows belied the ironic tone and expressed detachment and sadness, as if they had played no part in this conversation but were fixed on something too terrible for him to bear. Shmuel knew nothing about the people at the other end of the line, except that they were apparently prepared to put up with Wald's irony and forgive him for what seemed to Shmuel to verge on malicious mockery.

On second thought, it was not impossible that these various interlocutors, whom Wald invariably addressed as "my dear" or "my dear friend," were one and the same person, perhaps someone not unlike Gershom Wald himself; perhaps he, too, was an elderly invalid confined to his study, and perhaps he, too, had a poor student who looked after him and tried, just like Shmuel himself, to guess who was the imagined double at the other end of the line.

Sometimes Mr. Wald would wrap himself in a sad silence, lying on his couch cocooned in his tartan plaid, thinking, dozing, waking, then would ask Shmuel to pour him some tea and would sever the connection, humming some vague tune to himself, perhaps a snatch of a song, or else some kind of compulsive throat-clearing.

Each evening at a quarter past seven, after the news, Shmuel warmed up the old man's evening porridge, prepared for him by the neighbor, Sarah de Toledo. He sprinkled some brown sugar and ground cinnamon on it. There was enough porridge for both of them. At a quarter past nine, after the second news bulletin of the evening, he set before the old man a tray with six or seven pills and capsules and a glass of tap water.

One evening the old man looked up and scrutinized Shmuel's body from top to toe and back again, as if eyeing some dubious object or feeling the other man with his rough fingers, for a long time, greedily, until perhaps he found what he had been looking for. Without any attempt at politeness he asked:

"Still, it stands to reason that you've a got a girl somewhere? Or something resembling a girl? Or at least you have had? Haven't you? No woman at all? No girlfriend? Never?"

And at this he chuckled, as if he had been told a dirty joke. Shmuel stammered:

"Yes. No. I did. I've had several. But—"

"So, why did the lady desert you? It's not important. Forget that I asked. So, she left. Well, good luck to her. But our Atalia fascinates you, doesn't she? She can 'fascinate' strangers without moving a finger. But she's very fond of her solitary state. She lets men who are fascinated by her get closer to her, then she drives them away after a few weeks, or even just one week. 'There be three things which are too wonderful for me, yea, four which I know not . . . and more than the rest the way of a man with a maid.' She told me once that she's fascinated by strangers so long as they are more or less strangers. As soon as a stranger stops being a stranger he begins to bore her. And do you know the origin of the verb 'to fascinate'? No? Have they given up teaching etymology at the university?"

"I'm not at the university anymore."

"No, that's right. You have been cast into outer darkness, into weeping and gnashing of teeth. 'Fascinate' comes from the Latin and originally meant to bewitch or cast a spell upon. But did you know that the related Latin word *fascinus* means a male member in a state of erection? Now there is a thought! And how about parents? What? You do have parents? Or you have had?"

"Yes. In Haifa."

"Brothers and sisters?"

"One sister. In Italy."

"And that grandfather you told me about. The one who served in the Mandate police and was murdered by our zealots because he wore the king's uniform—was he also from Latvia?"

"Yes. And the truth of the matter is that he joined the British police so as to pass information and other things to the underground. He was really a kind of double agent, a secret fighter for the very organization whose members murdered him. They decided that he was a traitor."

Gershom Wald thought about this for a while. He asked for a glass of water. He asked Shmuel to open the window a crack. Then he remarked sadly:

"It was a great mistake. A great and fatal mistake."

"Whose mistake? The underground's?"

"The girl's. The one who left you. You're a soulful young man. That's what Atalia said to me a couple of days ago, and, as always, I know that she is right, because Atalia cannot be wrong. She was born being right. That's how she was created. But being permanently in the right is like being scorched earth—isn't that so?"

12

Sʜᴍᴜᴇʟ ᴀsʜ ᴡᴏᴋᴇ ᴇᴀᴄʜ ᴍᴏʀɴɪɴɢ at nine or ten, though he had promised himself time and time again to get up at seven o'clock the next day, brew some strong coffee, and sit down to work.

He woke but did not open his eyes. He curled up in his quilt and started to argue aloud with himself: "Get up, lazybones, half the day has gone already." And every morning he compromised with himself: "Just ten more minutes, what's wrong with that? After all, you came here to get away from the rat race. It's not worth feeling hunted again."

Eventually he stretched, sighed a couple of times, dragged himself out of bed in his underwear, shivering with cold, and went over to the window to see how this winter's day was different from the one before. The courtyard with its rain-polished flagstones, the fallen leaves blowing around on the ground, the rusty iron cistern lid, and the bare fig tree, the sight of all this filled him with peace and sadness. The bare fig tree reminded him of the fig tree in the New Testament, in Mark's Gospel, the one that Jesus, leaving Bethany, after looking in vain for a fig to eat among its leaves, cursed angrily and caused it instantly to wither and die. But surely Jesus knew very well that no fig tree produces fruit before Passover. Instead of cursing it, couldn't he have blessed it and worked a little miracle to make the fig tree bear fruit for him right then and there?

The sadness brought after it a strange, secret joy, as if someone inside him were glad to be sad. This joy gave him the impetus to thrust his frowzled head and beard under the tap and let the ice-cold water wash away the last traces of sleep.

Now he felt awake enough to face the new day. He grabbed the towel and dried himself vigorously, as if scraping the cold from his body. He brushed his teeth energetically, gargled, and spat with a snort from the back of his throat. Then he dressed and put on a chunky pullover. He lit the stove, boiled the kettle, and made himself a Turkish coffee. While the coffee was bubbling he cast a glance at the leaders of the Cuban Revolution looking down on him from the sloping ceiling, and said enthusiastically, "Good morning, comrades."

Holding the coffee cup in his right hand, he picked up the walking stick with the fox-head handle and stood at the window for a few more minutes. If he saw a cat gliding through the mist among the frozen bushes, he tapped the stick against the windowpane, as though urging the sharp-toothed fox to go a-hunting, or else sending distress signals to the outside world, to make someone notice them, the fox and him, and send somebody to rescue them from their attic prison. At times, he pictured Yardena sitting in the university cafeteria in a soft corduroy skirt, her fair hair pinned up on her head, liberally scattering laughter around her, because someone at her table was making fun of the way he, Shmuel, was coming down the stairs, his bearded head leading, his legs pursuing at the rear, and all of him gasping and panting.

After drinking his coffee Shmuel dusted his beard and his hair with baby talc, as if prematurely whitening them, then he descended the spiral staircase that led to the kitchen. He was careful not to make a sound, so as not to disturb Gershom Wald's morning sleep. At the same time, nevertheless, he gave four or five forced coughs, in the hope of attracting Atalia to come and spend a few minutes in the kitchen.

Usually she was not there, though his nostrils seemed to catch a faint whiff of her scent of violets. He was overcome again with his morning sadness. But this time it brought no joy in its train, but turned into an attack of asthma, and he hurriedly took two deep breaths from the inhaler he always carried in his pocket. Then he opened the refrigerator door and stared inside for a few minutes, without the foggiest idea what he was looking for.

The kitchen was always clean and tidy. Her cup and plate were washed and drying on the drainer, her bread was wrapped in tissue paper inside the bread bin, not a crumb on the oilcloth, and only her chair, drawn back from the table a little, stood at an angle, as though she had left in a hurry.

Had she gone out? Or was she closeted in her silent room again?

Sometimes he could not contain his curiosity, and he tiptoed down the passage to listen at her door. There was no sound to be heard, but after a few moments of concentrated attention he sometimes thought he caught a sort of humming or a low rustling through the closed door. He tried to imagine what was inside that room, where he had never been invited or ever managed to catch a glimpse, even though several times he had lain in wait in the passage for the door to open.

After a few moments he still had no way of knowing whether the rustling or humming sound actually came from the other side of the door or was entirely inside his own head. He almost succumbed to the temptation to try the handle, stealthily. But he stopped himself and returned to the kitchen, his nostrils twitching like a puppy's to catch a whiff of her perfume. He opened the refrigerator again, and this time he found a cucumber, which he consumed whole, skin and all.

He sat at the kitchen table for ten minutes or so, glancing at the headlines in the newspaper. In a day or two the new government would be sworn in. Its composition was still unclear. The leader of the opposition, Begin, had declared that there was no solution to the problem of the Palestinian refugees within the frontiers of the State of Israel, but there was a real and positive solution in the Greater Land of Israel, when the entire land was once again reunited. Meanwhile, the mayor of Safed had had a miraculous escape from death when his car tumbled down the mountainside. More rain was forecast all over the country, and in Jerusalem a light snowfall was possible.

13

Sometimes he would climb back up to his attic and read for a couple of hours. He would start at the table and continue lying on his bed, until the book dropped onto his beard and his eyes closed to the sound of the wind rattling the windows and of the rain in the gutters. He enjoyed the vague thought that the rain was falling only a few fingers' width away from his head, because the sloping ceiling of the attic slanted in such a way that he could touch it with his fingers as he lay in bed.

At midday he would get up, shrug on his shabby duffel coat, and put a *shapka* on his head, a type of Russian headgear introduced into the country by immigrants from Eastern Europe. He went out for a walk between one rain shower and the next. Skirting the new community center or continuing eastward toward Shmuel Hanagid Street, along the stone wall of the Ratisbonne Monastery, he passed the Yeshurun Synagogue and returned to Sha'arei Hesed along Keren Hakayemet Street and Ussishkin Street. Sometimes he took the fox-head walking stick with him without asking Atalia's permission, and as he walked he would tap the paving stones with it or test the iron railings. He desperately hoped that he would not bump into anyone he knew from his student days, so he would not have to mumble explanations: why he had suddenly disappeared as if the earth had swallowed him up, where he had vanished to, what he was doing nowadays, why he was wandering the wintry streets like a huddled ghost, and why he was carrying that splendid walking stick with a silver fox-head handle.

He had no answer, and no excuse. And besides, he had signed an agreement not to breathe a word to a living soul about where he was working now.

But why not, in fact? He was simply working as a companion to an elderly invalid for a few hours a day—in other words, he was a sort of part-time caregiver, in exchange for free room and board and a small salary. What exactly did Gershom Wald and Atalia Abravanel want to hide from the outside world? What was the point of their secrecy? More than once he had been overcome with curiosity and longed to ply them both with questions, but Mr. Wald's secret pain and Atalia's cold aloofness had silenced his questions before he could put them into words.

Once he saw, or thought he saw, Nesher Sharshevsky, the expert on rainwater collection, on King George Street, next to Beit Hama'alot. As he pulled down his *shapka* to hide his face, Shmuel smiled to himself at the thought that this winter was giving dear Nesher Sharshevsky plenty of rainwater to collect. Maybe one of these days he would come to check the level of the water in the cistern with the iron lid in the courtyard of the house on Rabbi Elbaz Lane.

Another time, on Keren Hayesod Street, he nearly collided with Professor Gustav Yomtov Eisenschloss, and it was only thanks to the professor's nearsightedness behind his pebble lenses that Shmuel Ash managed to slip into a courtyard at the last minute.

He ate his lunch in a little Hungarian restaurant on King George Street, always ordering the same meal: hot, spicy goulash soup with two slices of white bread, followed by fruit compote.

Sometimes he would cut briskly across Independence Park, at his usual awkward half-run, tousled head chasing his beard, body leaning forward and chasing after his head, and his legs scurrying after his body as though afraid of being left behind. He tramped through puddles without even noticing, sharp drops falling from the trees onto his face, his gait close to a run, as if he were being chased. Finally he reached Hillel Street, and continued to Nahalat Shiva, until he stood at last, puffing and panting, in front of the house where Yardena had lived before her marriage, gazing up at the entrance as though it were not Yardena but Atalia who was liable to emerge at any moment. He pulled the inhaler out of his pocket and took three deep breaths.

Jerusalem seemed quiet and thoughtful that winter. From time to time, church bells rang out. A westerly breeze stirred the tops of the cypresses and plucked Shmuel's heartstrings. Once in a while, a bored Jordanian sniper fired a stray shot toward the minefields and the wasteland that divided the Israeli from the Jordanian city. The stray shot seemed only to intensify the silence of the alleyways and the heavy gray mass of high stone walls that enclosed spaces concealing Shmuel knew not what—monasteries or orphanages or maybe military installations. Broken glass had been set in the tops of these walls, and sometimes coils of rusting barbed wire had been added. Once, as he was passing the wall that enclosed the leper colony in Talbiyeh, he asked himself what life was like behind that wall. Probably not much different from his own life, he told himself, shut away in a low-ceilinged attic in the last house at the bottom of Rabbi Elbaz Lane, at the end of Jerusalem near the deserted boulder-strewn fields.

A quarter of an hour later he turned and crossed Nahalat Shiva and returned home by a roundabout route through Agron Street, until he eventually reached the iron gate of the low stone house and arrived, puffing and panting, slightly late, at his post in Mr. Wald's library. He filled and lit the paraffin stove, fed the goldfish in their tank, and made tea. They exchanged pages from the newspaper. An old building in Tiberias had collapsed because of the winter rain and two residents had been injured. President Eisenhower had issued a warning against the machinations of Moscow. In Australia, a small settlement had been discovered of Aborigines who had never heard of the arrival of white men. And Egypt was building up stocks of modern Soviet weaponry.

14

One morning he came down to find Atalia in the kitchen, sitting at the oilcloth-covered table reading a book. The book was lying on the table, and she was clasping a cup of steaming coffee with both hands and all ten fingers. Shmuel gave a little cough and said:

"I'm sorry. I didn't mean to disturb you."

"Well, you have," Atalia said. "Sit down."

Her brown eyes scrutinized him with faint mockery, as if she were fully confident of her own femininity but slightly doubtful about the young man sitting opposite. Or as if wordlessly asking him, Well, have you finally got some little surprise for me, or are you just hanging around as usual?

Shmuel lowered his eyes and saw the tips of her black high-heeled shoes under the table. The hem of her green woolen dress which came down almost to her ankles. He took a deep breath and the scent of violets made him feel dizzy. Then he weighed his options, picked up the salt shaker in his left hand and the pepper pot in his right, and said:

"Nothing special. I just came down to look for the bread knife, or . . ."

"You've sat down. Why invent excuses?"

With this she looked at him, not smiling yet but with a gleam in her eyes that promised that a smile was definitely in the cards — all it needed was a little effort from him.

He put down the salt and pepper, tore a page from the notebook that was lying on the table, and folded it in half. He bent up two ears in the folded page, one on each side. Then he folded the page along the margin, pulled it and folded it again, making first a triangle and then an oblong, then folded it again into two congruent triangles, then into an oblong again, pulled it in both directions, and handed her a paper boat, with the words:

"A surprise. For you."

She took the boat from his hand and sailed it thoughtfully the width of the oilcloth, until it found a safe anchorage between the salt and the pepper. And she nodded to herself, apparently in complete agreement with herself. Shmuel looked at the deeply chiseled furrow that ran firmly down from her small nostrils to the center of her upper lip. Now he also noticed that she was wearing just a hint of lipstick. As if in response to his look, Atalia raised her cup and drained the rest of her coffee. Then, summing up her observations, she said to him in her rich, languid voice, seeming to caress each syllable before sending it on its way:

"You came here to be alone, and now after only three weeks it seems that loneliness is weighing on you."

She said this more like a diagnosis than a question. Shmuel heard that something in her words which reminded him of a warm, darkened room, with closed shutters and a table lamp with a dark shade. Suddenly he ached with all his being to touch her feelings, to stir some curiosity, or admiration, or maternal affection, or even mockery, no matter what, as long as he could prevent her from getting up and hiding away in her room. Or, worse still, going out. Sometimes when she went out she did not come back till late. Sometimes she did not return until the next day.

"I went through a slightly difficult period before I came here," he said. "And it still hasn't been entirely resolved. I had a crisis. Or, more precisely, a personal failure."

Now the smile trembled in the corners of her lips, as if she were trying to beg him to stop, not to tell her about it. As if she were embarrassed on his behalf.

"I've finished my coffee," she said. "How about you? You were looking for a bread knife, weren't you?"

She took a long, sharp knife from a drawer in the kitchen table and handed it carefully to Shmuel. As she did so, her smile finally broke out. This time it was not an ironic smile, but one that lit up her whole face with sympathy and affection.

"Talk," she said. "If you like. I'll sit and listen."

Shmuel absent-mindedly took the knife from her. He had forgotten to bring over the breadboard. Her smile dazzled him, and he told her, in seven or eight sentences, about his girlfriend Yardena who had suddenly decided, with no explanation, to marry her previous boyfriend, that dull hydrologist she had found for herself. Then he passed the knife from one hand to the other, waved it in the air, tested the blade on the tip of his fingernail, and said:

"But can we know anything at all about women's mysterious preferences?"

He was hoping to offer her—or their conversation—some fuel, or at least a signpost.

Atalia removed her smile and concluded with the words:

"There's no such thing as women's mysterious preferences. Where did you hear such nonsense? I have no idea why couples separate, because I have no idea how they get together in the first place. Or why. In other words, it's no use asking me about women's preferences. Or men's, for that matter. I have no womanly insights to offer you. Maybe Wald—maybe you should talk to him about this. He's an expert on everything, after all."

With that, she picked up four or five crumbs from the oilcloth, put them in Shmuel's paper boat, sailed the boat gently toward him, and stood up: a handsome woman in her mid-forties, her wooden earrings swaying slightly as she rose, her body caressing her dress from within. His nostrils caught a whiff of her delicate scent of violets as she passed him. But when she reached the door, she paused and said:

"Maybe, little by little, we'll anesthetize you, so it hurts less. These walls are accustomed to swallowing pain. Leave the cup— I'll wash it later. But don't wait for me here. Or yes, wait, if you've got nothing better to do. Wald would no doubt say, 'Blessed is he that waiteth.' I've no idea how long."

Shmuel brought the knife close to the oilcloth, but found nothing to cut, changed his mind, put it down carefully next to the salt shaker, and said:

"Yes."

After a moment he corrected himself:

"No."

But she had already gone, leaving him to cut the paper boat he had made for her into little pieces.

15

Sometime in the mid-ninth century, or a little earlier, a Jew whose name is unknown sat down and wrote a tract mocking Jesus and the Christian faith. There is no doubt that the author, who wrote his work in Arabic, lived in a Muslim country, for otherwise he would not have dared to deride Christianity as he did. The tract is called *Qissat mujadalat al-Usquf*—that is, *The Story of the Disputation of the Priest*. It tells of a Christian priest who has converted to Judaism, and after his conversion he addresses the Christians and explains to them why their faith is false. The author is clearly knowledgeable about Christianity and is familiar with its scriptures, as well as with some later Christian writings.

In the course of the Middle Ages this text was translated by Jews from Arabic into Hebrew and renamed *The Polemic of Nestor the Priest* (whether by way of allusion to the Nestorian Church, or to the Hebrew words for "contradiction" or "hidden," or perhaps simply because Nestor was the name of the converted priest). Over the years, various versions of the composition came into being. In some of them quotations in Latin or Greek were inserted, and some of them apparently migrated from Spain to the Rhineland and eventually reached Byzantine lands.

The main purpose of *The Polemic of Nestor the Priest* is to point out some striking inconsistencies in the Gospel stories, to refute the doctrine of the Trinity, and to challenge the divinity of Jesus. The book employs various means in the pursuit of these ends, some of which contradict one another. On the one hand, Jesus is described as an out-and-out Jew, who kept the commandments and never intended to found a new religion or to be considered divine, and it was only after his death that Christianity arose and distorted his image for its own needs and elevated him to the rank of a deity. On the other hand, the work does not shy away from deploying crude and ribald hints about the dubious circumstances surrounding Jesus' birth. The author even mocks Jesus' suffering and his lonely death on the cross. And, yet again, logical and theological arguments are advanced in the book aimed at refuting the principal tenets of the Christian faith.

Shmuel Ash examined these contradictory features carefully, and he wrote on a slip of paper that he attached to a draft of his notes that the anonymous Jewish author of this dubious polemic claims, almost in the same breath, that Jesus was a proper Jew; that he was the illegitimate offspring of his mother's adultery, and was necessarily tainted, like every human fetus, with the unclean blood of his mother's womb; that Adam was not born of a woman yet no one considers him divine; and that Enoch and Elijah, too, did not die but were taken up into heaven, and yet they are not thought of as Sons of God. Moreover, the prophets Elisha and Ezekiel worked more miracles and resurrected more corpses than Jesus did, not to mention the wonders and miracles wrought by Moses. Finally the author mocks and ridicules the crucifixion, recalling how the crowd scoffed at the dying Jesus on the cross and made fun of him with the words "Save thyself, and come down from the cross," and Nestor ends by quoting a verse from scripture showing that any hanged man bears a curse, as it is written, "He that is hanged is accursed of God."

When Shmuel told Gershom Wald about the claims advanced by Nestor the Priest, as well as about some other popular Jewish texts from the Middle Ages—the *Toldot Yeshu, Ma'ase Talui*, and other such scurrilous works—the old man brought both his big hands down hard on his desk and exclaimed:

"What filth! What disgusting filth!"

Gershom Wald was convinced that Nestor never existed and that there had never been any converted priest, but that all these foul texts were written by narrow-minded little Jews because they were afraid of the attractive power of Christianity and tried to exploit the protection of Muslim rule by attacking the figure of Jesus while sheltering safely beneath the cloak of Muhammad.

Shmuel disagreed: "But *The Polemic of Nestor the Priest* shows a certain acquaintance with the world of Christianity, a knowledge of the Gospels, familiarity with Christian theology."

Gershom Wald, however, comprehensively dismissed this familiarity—what familiarity? There is no familiarity here beyond a bundle of disgusting clichés bandied about by the crowds in the marketplace. The language of these Jews, when they attack Jesus and his followers, is identical to the foul language of anti-Semites when they attack the Jews and Judaism.

"Surely if you want to challenge Jesus the Christian," Wald said sadly, "you have to elevate yourself, not descend into the gutter. It is indeed possible and even fitting to take issue with Jesus, for example on the question of universal love. Is it really possible for us all, without exception, to love all of us, without exception, all of the time? Did Jesus himself love everyone all of the time? Did he, for example, love the moneychangers at the gates of the Temple, when in a fit of rage he violently overturned their tables? Or when he proclaimed, 'I came not to send peace on earth, but a sword'—did he forget at that moment his own exhortation to general love and his commandment to turn the other cheek? Or when he urged his apostles to be wise as serpents and harmless as doves? And especially when he said, according to Luke, 'But those mine enemies, which would not that I should reign over them, bring hither, and slay them before me.' What happened at that moment to the injunction to love even—and especially —your enemies? Surely anyone who loves everybody does not really love anybody. There. That's how you can argue with Jesus the Christian. Not with insults from the gutter."

Shmuel said:

"The Jews who wrote this polemic were certainly writing under the influence of their oppression and persecution by the Christians."

"Such Jews," Wald said with a contemptuous snigger, "such Jews, if they had only had the power, would certainly have oppressed and persecuted the followers of Jesus, probably no less than the Christian Jew-haters have persecuted the Jews. Judaism and Christianity, and Islam too, all drip honeyed words of love and mercy so long as they do not have access to handcuffs, grills, dominion, torture chambers, and gallows. All these faiths, including those that have appeared in recent generations and continue to mesmerize adherents to this day, all arose to save us and all just as soon started to shed our blood. Personally I do not believe in world reform. No. I do not believe in any kind of world reform. Not because I consider that the world is perfect as it is—certainly not, the world is crooked and grim and full of suffering—but whoever comes along to reform it soon sinks in rivers of blood. Now let's drink a glass of tea and leave aside these obscenities you've brought me today. If only all religions and all revolutions vanished from the face of the earth someday, I tell you—all of them, without exception—there would be far fewer wars in the world. Man, Immanuel Kant once wrote, is by nature a crooked piece of timber. And we must not try to straighten him, lest we sink up to our necks in blood. Listen to that rain outside. It's nearly time for the news."

16

Outside the closed shutters of the library, the wind suddenly died down and the rain stopped. A deep, damp silence filled the darkening city. Only two persistent birds tried repeatedly to punctuate the silence. Gershom Wald lay, angular and hunchbacked, on his wicker couch, covered in a woolen blanket, leafing slowly through a book in a foreign language with gilded curlicues on its cover. The desk lamp cast a warm yellow ring of light around him, from which Shmuel was excluded. The old man had already managed to have a long argument on the telephone this evening with one of his regular sparring partners: consistency, he had insisted, may not always be a quality one should be proud of, far from it, but inconsistency shames him who displays it.

Wald and Shmuel had drunk one tea and then another, Shmuel had fed the two goldfish in their glass bowl, and they had talked a little about the decision of the Jordanian authorities in East Jerusalem to delay the passage of the Israeli convoy to the encircled Hebrew University buildings. They had talked about the wave of attacks launched by young anti-Semites all over Germany and the decision of the Senate of the City of Berlin to outlaw neo-Nazi organizations. According to the newspaper, Dr. Nahum

Goldmann, president of the World Zionist Organization, had stated that Nazis were behind this new wave of attacks on Jewish institutions in Europe. Shmuel went out to the kitchen, picking up the empty biscuit plate on his way, and when he returned he handed the old man his evening pills, to swallow with the last sips of his tea.

Suddenly the man said:

"So, how about your sister? The one who has gone to study medicine in Italy? Have you told her about your present state?"

"My present state?"

"Yes, you came here to hide away from life and you have fallen in love: as if a man did flee from a lion and a bear met him. Have you ever thought, my young friend, how right the English were when they invented the excellent phrase 'to fall in love'?"

"Me?" Shmuel stammered. "But I—"

"And when the English were still living in the treetops, one of our own, the wisest of men, already knew that 'love covereth all sins'—in other words, that love is in fact bound up with falling down to the bottom stair, to the lower depths of the world of sin. And in the selfsame book it is also written that hope deferred maketh the heart sick. Is your sister younger than you or older?"

"Older. Five years older. But she wouldn't—"

"If not she, then who? A person like you does not turn to his parents at such a time. Or to his teachers. Perhaps your friends would stand by you? Have you got any friends?"

Shmuel, hoping to change the subject, replied that his friends had distanced themselves from him, or rather, he had distanced himself from them, because the whole socialist movement had undergone a great upheaval following the exposure of the deviations of the Stalin era, resulting in a rift developing between him and his friends. So as to prevent Mr. Wald from talking to him again about love and loneliness, Shmuel embarked on a detailed account of the Socialist Renewal Group which used to convene

weekly in the dingy café in a back alley in Yegia Kapayim until it
broke up recently on account of the split. From there he went on
to talk about the legacy of Lenin and what Stalin had done with
it, and he proceeded to muse aloud about the question of what
sort of legacy Stalin had left to his heirs: Malenkov, Molotov,
Bulganin, and Khrushchev.

"Should we really put an end to a grand idea and abandon
all hope of reforming the world just because the Party there, in
the Soviet Union, became corrupted and lost its way? Should we
condemn a wonderful figure like Jesus just because the Spanish
Inquisition claimed to be acting in his name?"

"So apart from your sister, and apart from Lenin and Jesus,
you have no close friends in the whole world? Never mind. You
are not obliged to answer. You are a valiant warrior in the army
of world reformers, and I am merely part of the corruption of the
world. When the new world triumphs, when all men are honest,
simple, productive, strong, equal, and upright, doubtless it will
be made illegal for deformed creatures like me, who only con-
sume but contribute nothing, and who sully everything with their
sophistries and sarcasm, to exist. So. Even she, I mean Atalia, will
no doubt be redundant in the pure world that will arise after the
revolution, a world that will have no use for single widows who
are not enlisted in the ranks of the world reformers but wander
here and there, doing all sorts of good and bad things, breaking
innocent hearts on the way, and enjoying a fixed allowance from
their father's estate plus a widow's pension from the Ministry of
Defense."

"Atalia? A widow?"

"And they won't have any need of you, my friend, not even
a shadow of a hint of a need, when the great revolution finally
becomes a reality. What will they care about Jewish views of Jesus? What will they care about dreamers like Jesus? Or like you?
What will they care about the Jewish question? What will they

care about any question? After all, they themselves will be the answer to every question. They will be the ultimate exclamation mark. And I'm telling you, my dear, pay heed and attend: if I had to choose a thousand times between our age-old sufferings, yours and mine and everyone else's, and their salvation and redemption, or indeed all the salvations and redemptions in the world, I'd rather they left us all the pain and sorrow and kept their world reform for themselves, seeing that it always involves slaughter, crusades, jihad or gulag, or the wars of Gog and Demagogue. And now, my dear, if you don't mind, we shall perform a small experiment on you. We shall ask you three favors: to be kind enough to close the shutters, to refill the heater, and to make us both some more tea. We shall ask you, and we shall watch the outcome of these three requests.

17

IN BED AT NIGHT he would wrap himself in his quilt, turn out the light, and watch the flickering flashes of lightning on the wall as he listened to the pounding of the rain and the rolls of thunder beating like iron chains on the tiled roof just above his head; he could reach out to touch the slanting ceiling and know that between his fingers and the forces of nature there was nothing more than a couple of inches of plaster and the roof tiles above.

The proximity of the cold, the wind, and the rain made him fall fast asleep, but after about half an hour he woke, because he thought he heard a creaking door downstairs or footsteps outside in the yard. At once he leapt across to the window, alert as a burglar, and peered between the slats of the shutter to see if she was going out into the night. Or coming back, and locking the front door behind her. Was she alone? Or not?

This possibility aroused a wave of blind rage in Shmuel, mingled with self-pity and a certain bitter resentment against her and her secrets. Her mysterious games. Her strange men who might be wandering around here, coming and going in these nights of wind and rain. Or maybe they did not come and sneak in here, but rather she went out to them?

But what does she owe you, in fact? Just because you told her all kinds of miserable stories about your disappointments, and about your having been left, and all sorts of things about hydrologist runts, is she obliged to tell you the story of her life or the details of her relationships in return? Why should she? What can you offer her, and what right have you to expect anything from her, other than your salary and the cooking and washing arrangements that were agreed between you and her the day you arrived here?

With this, he went back to bed and wrapped himself up well, listening to the rain or to the deep silence between rain showers. He dropped off for a few minutes, woke in a fit of despair or rage, turned on the bedside light, read three or four pages without taking in what he was reading, switched the light off, tossed and turned, struggled to stifle an agony of lust under his quilt in the dark, turned on the light again, sat up in bed, heard the snoring sound of a motorcycle in the empty narrow streets, was swept by a wave of furious hatred toward her and also to some degree toward her spoiled old man. He got up, paced the room, sat down at the battered desk or on the deep stone windowsill, seeing her before him, slowly removing her boots and her stockings, her dress rolled up, the line of her hips shining white in the darkness and her eyes teasing him: *Yes? I'm sorry? Did you want something from me? What exactly do you need or want this time? Is the loneliness getting too much for you? Or the remorse?* And he rushed to the window again, to the door, to his kitchen corner, poured himself half a glass of cheap vodka and drank it in one gulp, like bitter medicine, went back to bed, cursing his lust and her ironic smile, hating the greenish flicker in her brown eyes which mocked him and always trusted their own power, and her dark hair cascading down over her left breast, hating her bare feet and her white knees right in front of him as she removed her stockings one at a time. Once more the rain was beating on the tiles immediately above his feverish body, and the wind abused the tops of the cypress trees outside his window, and Shmuel had to discharge his lust between his fingers, and immediately a murky wave of shame and loathing swept over him, and he swore he would leave this house, the crazy old man, and the widow, if she was indeed a widow, who abused him so mercilessly. He would leave tomorrow, or the day after. Or by the beginning of next week at the latest.

But where could he go?

He woke at nine or ten in the morning again, all groggy and raddled from a bad night's sleep, his eyes full of tears of self-pity, cursing his body and his life, arguing with himself, get up, get up, you wretch, get up or the revolution will happen without you, pleading for another ten minutes, or five, turning over and dozing off, and waking again to find it was almost midday. And at four-thirty you have to be on duty again in the library, and as for her, the black widow, if by any chance she came into the kitchen and sat down to drink a glass of tea and spend a quarter of an hour there this morning, why, you've missed her again. Maybe you should get dressed and go out in search of some lunch, which will have to double as breakfast, and in fact supper too, because in the evening you will have nothing to eat except a couple of thick slices of bread and jam and the remains of the porridge that Sarah de Toledo brings to Gershom Wald every evening from her own kitchen across the road, in return for payment, according to whatever arrangement it is she has with Atalia Abravanel.

18

O NE EVENING GERSHOM WALD told him a true story about a band of crusaders who set off in the middle of the twelfth century from the region of Avignon to go to Jerusalem, to redeem the holy city from the infidel and to gain remission of sins and spiritual peace. On their way they traversed forests and plains, towns and villages, mountains and rivers. They were tested by various hardships, illnesses, quarrels, hunger, and bloody clashes with highway robbers and with other armed bands similarly making their way to Jerusalem bearing the cross. More than once they lost their way, more than once they were afflicted by plague, frost, and lack of food, more than once they were assailed by heartrending homesickness, but always, at every moment, they kept before their eyes the wondrous image of Jerusalem, a city not of this world, a city where there is neither evildoing nor suffering but eternal heavenly bliss with deep, limpid love, a city flooded with the everlasting light of mercy and compassion. So they made their way, crossing desolate valleys, scaling snowbound mountains, passing through windswept flatlands and grim regions of forsaken scrub-covered hills. Little by little their spirits fell, disappointment, weariness, and discomfiture gnawed at the fringes of the camp, some of them stole away by night and headed homeward one by one, some went out of their minds and others succumbed to despair and apathy as it gradually dawned on them that the Jerusalem they yearned for was not a real city but pure longing. But for all this, the crusaders continued to ride eastward toward Jerusalem, stumbling through mud, dust, and snow, dragging their weary feet along the bank of the River Po and the northern shore of the Adriatic Sea, until one summer evening, as the sun set, they came to a small vale, hemmed in by high mountains, in one of the inland regions of the land known as Slovenia. This vale seemed to them like the abode of God, full of springs with meadows and green pastures, woodlands and vines and orchards in blossom, and there was a small village built around a well, with a stone-paved square, with granaries and barns with sloping roofs. Flocks of sheep spread up the hillside, and patient cows stood dreamily here and there in the meadow, while geese wandered around. The peasants in the village seemed so calm and tranquil to them, and the black-haired girls so plump and smiling. And so it came about that these crusaders took counsel among themselves and decided to call the blessed vale Jerusalem, and there to bring their laborious journey to an end.

Thus they pitched camp on a hillside facing the village, watered and fed their weary mounts, bathed in the water of the stream, and after resting in this Jerusalem from the hardships of their journey, they set about building it with their own hands. They erected some twenty or thirty modest huts, allocated a plot of land to each man, paved roads, and built a little church with a charming bell tower. Over the years they married girls from the nearby village, and their children grew up paddling in the waters of their own Jordan, running around barefoot in the woods of Bethlehem, climbing the Mount of Olives, going down to Gethsemane, to the Kidron Valley and to Bethany, and playing hide-and-seek among the vineyards of Ein Gedi. "And so they live to this very day," Gershom Wald concluded, "pure and free, in the holy city and the promised land, and all without shedding any more innocent blood and without fighting endlessly against hostile infidels. They live peaceably and happily in their Jerusalem, every man under his vine and under his fig tree. Unto the end of time. And how about you? Where do you intend to go from here, if anywhere?"

"You're suggesting I should stay," Shmuel said, with no question mark at the end of the sentence.

"You're in love with her."

"Maybe a little, just with her shadow, not with her."

"But you spend your whole life living among shadows. As a servant earnestly desireth the shadow."

"Shadows, maybe. But I'm not so much of a servant. Not yet."

19

ONE MORNING ATALIA went up to Shmuel's attic and found him sitting at the desk, sorting through the papers he had put together when he was still hoping to complete his study of Jewish views of Jesus and submit it to Professor Gustav Yomtov Eisenschloss. She stood in the doorway with one hand on her hip, looking like a goosegirl in the meadow in Gershom Wald's story, standing by the river watching her geese. She was wearing an apricot-colored cotton dress with a row of big buttons down the front. She had chosen to leave the top and bottom buttons undone. She had a silk scarf tied in a bow around her neck, and a dark belt around her waist with a mother-of-pearl buckle. She asked him in a mocking tone what had happened to make him get up before sunrise this morning (it was a quarter past eleven). Shmuel replied that broken hearts cannot sleep. Atalia responded that the opposite is true: it is well known that the brokenhearted always take refuge in the arms of Morpheus. Shmuel said that Morpheus, like everyone else, had slammed the door in his face. Atalia said that this was the very reason she had climbed up here, to open a door for him, namely to tell him that this evening their old man was being collected by car and taken to visit friends of his in Rehavia, and so Shmuel could enjoy a free evening.

"How about you? Are you also liberated this evening?"

She looked at him with those green-flecked brown eyes until he was compelled to look down at the ground. Her face was pale, her gaze seemed to go right through him and fix on something beyond him, but her body was unmistakably there, and her breasts rose and fell with each calm breath.

"I am always liberated," Atalia said, "and I'm not doing anything this evening. Have you got a suggestion? A surprise? A temptation I cannot resist?"

Shmuel suggested a walk. Followed perhaps by a meal in a restaurant? Or maybe a film?

"All three suggestions are acceptable. Not necessarily in that order. I'll invite you to the early show at the cinema, you invite me to dinner, and as for the walk—we'll see. The evenings are cold now. Maybe we'll just walk home. Walk each other home. Wald will probably be brought back between half past ten and eleven, and we'll return a little earlier, be there to greet him. You come down to the kitchen at half past six this evening. And if I happen to be a little late, you won't mind waiting for me, will you?"

Shmuel mumbled, "Thank you." For ten minutes he stood at the window, trying to control his excitement. He took the inhaler out of his pocket and took two deep breaths. Then he sat down on the chair facing the window and looked out into the courtyard, which was glistening in the pale sunlight. He wondered what he would talk to Atalia about that evening. What did he know about her, in fact? That she was a widow, aged about forty-five, the daughter of Shealtiel Abravanel, who had tried to challenge Ben-Gurion just before the War of Independence and been removed from office, and now here she was in this secluded old house with the cripple Gershom Wald, who had described her as his "mistress." But what was their relationship? Which of them now owned the house, inscribed on its iron gate RESIDENCE OF

JEHOIACHIN ABRAVANEL WHOM G-D PROTECT, TO SHEW THAT
THE LORD IS UPRIGHT? Was Atalia, just like him, simply a lodger
of Gershom Wald's? Or was Wald Atalia's lodger? And who was
Jehoiachin Abravanel? And what was the nature of the bond between the old cripple and this strong woman who invaded your
dreams at night? And who were his predecessors in this attic, and
why had they disappeared? And why had he been made to sign an
agreement to keep his work here a secret?

Shmuel made up his mind to investigate all of these questions,
one by one, and in due course to find a full answer to each of
them. In the meantime, he took a shower, powdered his face with
baby talc, put on clean clothes, and tried unsuccessfully to comb
his beard. Despite his efforts, it remained as tangled as ever.

"Leave it. There's no point," Shmuel whispered to himself.

20

Here and there, even in the Middle Ages, some Jewish voices were raised against the crudeness of the stories that derided Jesus. An example is Rabbi Gershom Hakohen in the introduction to his book *The Portion of the Lawgiver*, where he writes that the contemptuous tales about Jesus are "foolishness and vanity that a man of learning should be ashamed to let past his lips" (though his book, too, Shmuel noted, attempts to cast doubt on the reliability of the New Testament stories). Rabbi Judah Halevi, in his *Kuzari*, written in the twelfth century, puts into the mouth of a Christian scholar the story of Jesus' divine birth, the main account of his life, and the idea of the holy Trinity. The Christian expounds all these before the Khazar king, who is not persuaded and does not accept the Christian faith, because the whole story seems to him remote from plain reason. It should be observed that Judah Halevi cites the essence of the story of Jesus' life without distortion, without mockery, and even with a measure of persuasive power.

As for Maimonides, who also lived in the twelfth century, in his *Mishneh Torah* he described Jesus as a false prophet, yet he believed that Christianity represented a step forward in humanity's march from paganism to belief in the God of Israel. In his

Epistle to Yemen Maimonides states that Jesus' father was a gentile and his mother a Jewess, and that Jesus himself had no hand in all that his disciples said and did, or in all the tales with which they surrounded his person after his death. Maimonides even states that Jewish sages in Jesus' day may have played a part in his death.

Unlike those writers who attacked Jesus' memory from Muslim lands, Rabbi David Kimhi (also known as RaDaK) wrote in Christian Provence. In *The Book of the Covenant*, a work that is attributed to him, we catch an echo of certain theological polemics that divided the Christian world itself. Some Christian theologians maintained that Jesus was the incarnation of God in flesh and blood, while others believed that he was entirely spirit and not flesh at all, which was why, when he was in his mother's womb, he neither ate nor drank. Kimhi makes fun of the latter claim and elaborates on the paradox of a fetus that is not flesh and blood inhabiting the body of a woman of flesh and blood. Jesus "came forth from the known place, as small as other babes, and excreted and urinated like other babes, and performed no wonder until he went down with his father and mother into Egypt, and there he learnt much wisdom [i.e., sorcery], and when he went up to the pure Land of Israel he performed the miracles described in your scriptures, all by virtue of the wisdom he learnt in Egypt," Kimhi writes in his *Book of the Covenant*. And he adds that if Jesus had not been flesh and blood, he could not have died on the cross.

It's a curious fact, Shmuel wrote in a note to himself on a loose piece of paper, that however much these Jews engage with the supernatural stories surrounding Jesus' parentage and birth, his life and his death, they studiously avoid any confrontation with the spiritual or moral content of his gospel. It is as if they are content to refute the miracles and contradict the wonders, and as if by this means the gospel itself will disappear without trace. And it is also strange that in all these writings there is no mention of Judas Iscariot. And yet, had it not been for Judas, there might not have been a crucifixion, and had there been no crucifixion, there would have been no Christianity.

21

THE EVENING AIR was cold and dry, and the narrow streets were empty, shrouded with a fine mist that thickened a little around the streetlamps. Here and there, a cat crossed their path, hurrying between two patches of shadow. Atalia was wrapped in a dark overcoat which left only the delicate outline of her head showing, while Shmuel wore his student duffel coat and the *shapka* which covered his head and shaded his forehead. Only his bushy beard projected forward wildly. He found it difficult to restrain his mad gallop to match Atalia's measured step. From time to time he pressed ahead, and then, ashamed of his haste, stopped for a moment to wait for her.

"Why are you running?" she asked.

Shmuel hastened to apologize:

"I'm sorry. I'm used to walking alone, and when I'm on my own I always hurry."

"Hurry where?"

"I don't know. No idea. Chasing my own tail."

Atalia slipped her arm through his and said:

"You're not chasing anyone this evening. And no one is chasing you. This evening you're walking with me. And you'll walk at my pace."

Shmuel felt that he ought to interest or amuse her, but the sight of the empty lane, with empty clotheslines and empty balconies floating above it and a solitary streetlamp casting a murky light, filled him with heaviness and he found no words. He pressed the arm that she had threaded through his against his ribs, as if promising her that all options were still open. He knew now that her power over him was complete and that she could make him do almost anything she asked. But he did not know how to begin the conversation he had been conducting with her in his mind for weeks now. When she said to him that this evening he must walk at her pace, it occurred to him that it would be better for him to wait until she saw fit to open a conversation. Atalia said nothing, except when she broke her silence to point out a night bird flying right overhead, or to warn him about a heap of junk on the pavement that in his haste he almost tripped over.

Meanwhile, they had crossed Ussishkin Street and passed the square in front of the forlorn Cultural Center and were making their way toward the center of town. Now and again they passed muffled pedestrians, couples walking arm in arm, and once a pair of old women moving so slowly they seemed to be frozen. The cold was dry and biting, and Shmuel turned his head and tried to inhale the mist of Atalia's breath, but he was afraid to get too close because he was not sure about his own breath. He suddenly felt a pleasant shiver down his spine as they walked arm in arm. It had been a long time since a woman had touched him. It had been a long time since any living being had touched him. The walls of Jerusalem stone reflected the lights of the cars and radiated a chilly pallor. Atalia said:

"And you so much want to ask me questions. You're so full of questions. Look at yourself, you're like a walking question mark. All right, then. Stop torturing yourself. Ask away. I'm granting you three questions."

"What film are we going to see?" Shmuel asked. And, unable to stop himself, he added: "Wald says you're a widow?"

Atalia replied in measured tones, almost gently:

"I was married for a year and a half to Micha, who was Gershom Wald's only son. Then Micha was killed in the war. Micha was killed in the war, and we were left on our own. Wald is my ex-father-in-law. I was once his daughter-in-law. Now you and I are going to see a French film, a thriller with Jean Gabin at the Orion Cinema. Anything else?"

"Yes," said Shmuel. But he did not continue. He quickly withdrew his arm from her clasp and put it around her shoulder, two layers of overcoats separating them. She let him do this, but she did not return his embrace, nor did she lean against him. His heart went out to her, but the words stuck in his throat.

It was cold in the Orion Cinema, and they both kept their coats on. The theater was half empty: this was the third week the film had been showing. Before the film there was a newsreel in which the brisk, bouncy figure of David Ben-Gurion could be seen climbing onto a tank, dressed in plain khaki. Then there was a report about a poor suburb of Tel Aviv whose houses had been flooded in the winter storms. Finally there was the ceremony of choosing the Queen of the Carmel, and Shmuel again put his coat-covered arm around the shoulder of Atalia's coat. She did not react. When the previews of "Coming Soon" and "Next Week" were over, she shifted her position and, as if incidentally, removed his arm. Jean Gabin was pursued by his enemies until it seemed there was no hope, but he never for a moment lost his *sang-froid* or his self-control. His ironic, skeptical toughness, his imperturbable tenacity, made Shmuel feel so jealous that he turned to Atalia and asked in a whisper if she wished for a man like Jean Gabin. She replied that she didn't make any wishes for herself. What was the point? Most men seemed to her to be childishly fixated on a constant stream of successes and triumphs, without which they turned sour, and withered. Shmuel fell silent, in despair at the realization that the woman sitting next to him was beyond his reach. His thoughts wandered, and he stopped following the action, and yet he noticed from time to time that Jean Gabin related to women, and particularly the heroine, with a hint of paternal irony not devoid of warmth. Shmuel longed to acquire that sort of irony himself, but he knew that it was neither in his character nor within his power. In the darkness his eyes filled with tears of pity, for himself, for Atalia, for Jean Gabin, for childish men, for the very existence of two different sexes. He recalled what Yardena had told him when she left and decided to marry Nesher Sharshevsky, her obedient hydrologist: "Either you're like an excited puppy, rushing around noisily—even when you're sitting on a chair you're somehow chasing your own tail —or else you're the opposite, lying on your bed for days on end like an unaired quilt."

She was right, he thought.

After the film Atalia took him to an inexpensive restaurant, a little Middle Eastern place with few customers. The tables were covered with oilcloth. The walls were adorned with photographs of Herzl leaning on the railing of the balcony in Basel, of President Ben-Zvi, and of David Ben-Gurion. There was also an imaginative and fanciful drawing of Solomon's Temple, looking like the Monte Carlo Casino which Shmuel had seen once on a picture postcard. The glass of the photographs was dotted with fly droppings. The reflections of the yellow light of the electric lamp on the counter capered and flickered on Herzl's black beard. Three large fans were suspended from the ceiling; one of them was covered in cobwebs. Shmuel took out his inhaler because he was suddenly out of breath. After two or three puffs he felt better. Instead of her big wooden earrings Atalia was wearing delicate silver stalactites. They chatted for a while about French cinema versus American cinema, and about the nights in Jerusalem compared to those in Tel Aviv. Abruptly Shmuel said:

"On the way to the cinema, you granted me three questions and I wasted them. Will you grant me one more?"

"No," said Atalia, "your quota of questions for today has been used up. Now it's my turn. Tell me, is it true that you were a very spoiled child?"

And at once she added:

"You don't have to answer. Your reply would be redundant."

22

BUT SHMUEL STARTED TELLING her about his childhood. At first he was hesitant, afraid of boring her, but then he spoke excitedly, breathlessly, piling sentence on sentence, interrupting himself and beginning all over again, only to interrupt himself again and start from a new angle. He was born and grew up in Haifa, in Hadar Hacarmel, or to be more precise, he was born in Kiryat Motzkin, but when he was two years old his family moved to a rented flat in Hadar, or rather, they were forced to move because the shack they had lived in in Kiryat Motzkin burned down. It went up in flames at two o'clock in the morning because of a paraffin lamp that fell over. That fire was actually his earliest memory, though it was impossible to tell how much was authentic recall and how much a memory of a memory—that is, a vague, blurred memory reinforced and strengthened by stories his parents and his sister had told him over the years. Maybe he ought to begin at the beginning. His father had built that shack with his own hands when he emigrated from Latvia in 1932. He came from Riga, where he had studied cartography. "My father was about twenty-two when he arrived with his father, Grandpa Antek, who was already forty-five—despite which the British ac-

cepted him for the Palestine Police Force because he was an expert forger. But how did we get on to Grandpa Antek, we were
talking about the burning of the shack? That's what always happens to me. No sooner do I start talking about something than
other stories come and take over my story, then those stories are
submerged by earlier things, each subject edging in to clarify
the previous one, until everything gets foggy. Why don't we talk
about you for a bit?"

"You were spoiled," Atalia said.

His parents had not spoiled him at all when he was a child;
perhaps they had merely been astonished by him. But Shmuel did
not contradict her. He folded a paper napkin along its diagonal
once, twice, and then a third time, made two precise ears, folded,
pulled, released, and again a little boat appeared, which he floated
across the table until it anchored next to Atalia's fork. She took a
toothpick from an ornate holder that stood in the center of the
table and put it through the middle of the sail to serve as a mast,
then she sailed the improved boat back across the table until it
touched Shmuel's hand so lightly he hardly felt it. Meanwhile
the waiter appeared, a slightly stooped young man with a thick
mustache and eyebrows that met above the bridge of his nose.
Without being asked, he placed before them pitas, tahini, hum-
mus, olives, pickles, vine leaves stuffed with meat, and a finely
chopped salad glistening with olive oil. Atalia ordered a chicken
kebab. Shmuel hesitated for a moment, then ordered the same.
When Shmuel asked if she would like some wine, she responded
with a derisive smile: in those days it was not usual to order wine
in Middle Eastern restaurants in Jerusalem. She asked for some
cold water. Shmuel said, "I'll have the same," and made a joke
about their shared tastes. The joke fell flat, and he tried to re-
phrase it, until Atalia smiled a smile that began at the corners of
her eyes and gradually spread to the edges of her lips, and told

him not to make an effort, there was no need, she was amused enough as it was.

After they moved to Hadar Hacarmel, his father started work in the government Land Survey Department. A few years later, he opened a private office for mapping and aerial photography in partnership with a thin Hungarian named László Vermes. The flat in Hadar was small: two cramped rooms and a kitchen, whose ceiling was always sooty from the paraffin wick stove and the Primus pressure stove. When his sister reached the age of twelve, they moved Shmuel out of the bedroom he had previously shared with her and put his bed in the passage. There he lay for hours on end, staring at the cobwebs above the heavy wardrobe. He could not invite friends there because the passage was dark and because in fact he hardly had any friends. Even now, he added, smiling through his bushy beard, he hardly had any friends, apart from the girlfriend who had left him to marry a successful hydrologist named Nesher Sharshevsky, and the six members of the Socialist Renewal Group, which had split into two factions, a majority and a minority faction. After the split there was no point, particularly since the two girls in the group had chosen to join the majority faction.

He saw Atalia's hand resting on the table across from him, and as in a dream he extended his fingers toward it. Halfway across, he changed his mind. She was many years older than he, and he felt shy in her presence and afraid of making her laugh at him. It struck him that Atalia was old enough to be his mother. Or almost. He stopped talking, as if he had suddenly realized that he had overstepped the mark. His mother had touched him only rarely when he was little. Most of the time she had paid no attention to what he was saying; her thoughts were elsewhere.

"Now you're having trouble deciding how to continue," Atalia said. "Don't try so hard. And there's no need for you to talk all the time. I'm not going to run away this evening if you pause for a bit. In fact, I rather enjoy being with you, because you're not a predator. Do you want some coffee?"

Shmuel began to explain that he never drank coffee in the evening because it stopped him getting to sleep, but he changed his mind in midsentence and said, Yes, why not, if she wanted a coffee, he would have one too. His older sister, Miri, who was studying medicine in Italy, had brainwashed him into believing that one should not drink coffee in the evening—or in the morning either, for that matter. When he was little she used to boss him around; she always knew what was right and what was wrong. She even knew better than their father. In any argument she was always right. "But how did we get on to Miri? Yes. Let's have coffee, and I'll have a little glass of arak. Would you like some too?"

"Let's have coffee," Atalia said, "and leave the arak for another time, if you don't mind."

Shmuel did not insist. Atalia paid the bill while he was fumbling in his pocket. On their way home a cat darted across the narrow street and disappeared into a garden. The streetlamps were ringed with murky mist. Shmuel said that he sometimes rambled on instead of saying what he meant to say. Atalia did not reply, and he felt emboldened to put his arm around her shoulder and draw it toward his. Since they had both put their winter coats back on, this touch was almost no touch. Atalia did not remove his arm but walked a little more slowly. Shmuel looked for something else to say, but could think of nothing. His eyes searched her face, trying to decipher it, but all he could see in the light of the streetlamp was a fine profile which seemed to him to be sunk in silent sadness. Finally he said:

"Look how empty it is here. Jerusalem on a winter night is truly a deserted city."

"That's enough," Atalia said. "Don't keep trying to find things to say to me. We can walk along together without talking. I can almost hear you even when you aren't talking. Though that doesn't happen too often."

And when they reached the house she said:

"That was a nice evening. Thank you. Good night. The film was not bad."

23

G ERSHOM WALD SAID WITH A CHUCKLE:

"In the old days, yeshiva students used to ask a bridegroom the morning after the wedding, "*Motse* or *matsa?*" If he said *motse*, they commiserated with him, but if he said *matsa*, they shared his happiness."

"I don't get it," Shmuel said.

Gershom Wald explained:

"The two words allude to two biblical verses: 'I find (*motse*) more bitter than death the woman,' and 'Whoso findeth (*matsa*) a wife findeth a good thing.' How about you—are you *motse* or *matsa?*"

"I'm still looking," Shmuel said.

Wald looked at him with his chin inclined to one side, as if hearing words that had not been spoken, and said:

"Listen. For your own sake. If possible, don't fall in love with Atalia. There's no point. Or am I already too late?"

"Why are you so concerned about me?" Shmuel asked.

"Maybe it's because there's something rather touching about you. You're like a caveman with a soul that's exposed, like a wristwatch with the glass removed. Pour us both some tea, won't you? Then would you kindly set the record player going and we shall listen to a Mendelssohn quartet. Have you ever noticed that every now and then a bittersweet strain creeps into Mendelssohn's music, a heartrending echo of an old Jewish melody?"

Shmuel pondered Gershom Wald's words for a while. He did not hasten to answer. In the batch of records he had brought here with him there was nothing by Mendelssohn. He had a few pieces by Bach, three or four other recordings of baroque music, Mozart's Requiem, Fauré's Requiem, seven or eight jazz records and popular French chansons, and a disc of revolutionary songs from the time of the Spanish Civil War.

"Mendelssohn," he said. "Yes. Too emotional for my taste."

Gershom Wald smiled.

"But you are such an emotional young man."

Shmuel did not respond, but stood up and went to the kitchen to warm the old man's porridge. He switched on the electric ring, put the saucepan of porridge on it, stirred, waited for three or four minutes, dipped the tip of the spoon in the porridge and tasted it, added a spoonful of sugar, stirred again, sprinkled some ground cinnamon on top, switched off the hotplate, spooned the porridge into a bowl, and carried it into the library. Here he spread a tea towel on the desk in front of the old man, served him the porridge, and waited. Mr. Wald ate unenthusiastically, and while he ate they both listened to the news. The commander of the French paratroopers in Algiers, a general by the name of Jacques Massu, had suddenly been recalled to Paris. There were rumors in the French capital that General de Gaulle was about to make a startling announcement about the future of Algeria. General Massu had told journalists at the airport that it was possible the army had made a mistake in deciding to put their faith in de Gaulle after the right-wing coup in Algeria a couple of years earlier.

"Anyone with eyes to see," Gershom Wald said, "could have predicted how all this would end. 'The rope has followed the bucket.'"

"Thousands more people will die," said Shmuel.

The old man did not reply. He stared at Shmuel, his left eye screwed up, his right one wide open, as if he had just noticed something new in his appearance.

Shmuel was struck by the fact that in this entire library, with its numerous shelves and hundreds of books, there was not a single photograph of Micha, Gershom Wald's dead son, his only son, who had been Atalia's husband. Had Atalia chosen him because he resembled his father in some way? Had Atalia and her husband lived together here, in her room, before he was killed? There must have been a mother, too. Both Micha and Atalia must have had mothers. Shmuel felt bold enough to ask:

"Your son. Micha?"

The old man shrank in his chair. His ugly hands, which had been resting on the desk, were now clasped in his lap, his face turned gray, and he closed his eyes.

"Do you mind if I ask when he was killed? And how?"

Wald did not reply. His eyes remained closed, as if he had to make a huge effort to remember, as if the reply demanded immense mental concentration. There was an empty tea glass on the desk in front of him, and he picked it up in his strong fingers and moved it about, but after a short while he changed his mind and returned it to its original spot. His voice when he spoke was dry and flat.

"On the night of the April 2, '48. In the fighting on the road to Jerusalem."

Then he fell silent, and said nothing more for a long time. Suddenly he shuddered, his shoulders shook, and this time his voice was low, almost a whisper.

"Now you must feed the fish. It's time. Then leave me. Please go to your room."

Shmuel took the bowl of porridge, which the old man had barely tasted, and the tea towel out to the kitchen, apologized for asking the question, said good night, stopped in the kitchen to eat his own portion of porridge, almost cold now, washed the dishes, and climbed up to the attic. Here he removed his shoes and sat for a while on his bed, his back resting against the wall, asking himself why he should not pack his few belongings tomorrow and go somewhere completely different. Maybe he could get a job as a night watchman in the Ramon Hills in the Negev, where a new desert town was being built. This house at the bottom of Rabbi Elbaz Lane now seemed to him like a prison in which he was gathering moss day by day. The old cripple with his witticisms and allusions and his solitary sorrow and the woman who was twice his age seemed to him tonight a pair of jailers who kept him here as if by bonds of enchantment, but he had the power to free himself from them simply by getting up and tearing his way through the invisible web in which they had ensnared him. Did he see in them a belated substitute for his parents? Yet he had moved to Jerusalem deliberately to get away from his parents once and for all, and it was weeks since he had exchanged a single word with anyone his own age. And he had not slept with a woman.

He stood up, undressed, and showered, but instead of getting into bed, he sat for another half hour on the cushion-strewn windowsill, wrapped in his quilt, staring into the stone-paved courtyard. The yard was frozen and desolate. Not so much as a cat stirred. Only the meager light of the streetlamp lit the iron lid of the cistern and the pots of geraniums. Shmuel told himself that it was time to sleep, and ten minutes later he got into bed in his underwear, but sleep did not come. Instead, he saw scenes from his childhood, which merged with thoughts about Yardena and Atalia. Both women made him feel anger and sadness, and a powerful throb of desire. He turned from side to side but could not sleep.

24

Sнмuel received a letter from his parents. Rainwater
had seeped into Gershom Wald and Atalia Abravanel's mailbox,
and some lines of the letter were smudged. His father wrote:

Dear Shmuel,

I am sitting here mourning for your abandoned university
studies. What a terrible waste of effort and talent! In the early
years of your studies you brought us high marks and even a
promise (though not a definitive one) from Professor Eisenschloss, who once said to you that if you persevered in your
work and if you managed to make some new discoveries, there
was a possibility that after you finished your MA you might
be hired as a teaching assistant—that is to say, a first step toward an academic career. And now, with a wave of the hand,
you have thrown away this chance. I know, my dear Shmuel,
that it is all my fault. Had it not been for the failure of my
firm (which was due to the dishonesty of my partner but also
in small measure to my own stupidity and blindness), I would
be continuing to pay for your studies and your maintenance,
and I would do so as generously as I did from the moment you
entered the university, just as I supported your sister's studies

in Italy. But is there any possibility that you could combine your present work with continuing your studies? Is there no way out . . . [*Here came two or three lines that were illegible because of the damp.*] . . . studies? Is there no way you can pay for your studies and your maintenance out of your wages? Miri is continuing her medical studies in Italy despite everything: she has not stopped studying even though we have been forced to stop supporting her. She is working in two jobs now, as an assistant in a pharmacy in the evenings and as a telegraphist in the central post office at night. She makes do, she wrote to us, with four or five hours of sleep, but she has not given up studying. She is clinging on tooth and nail. Could you not follow Miri's example? You wrote to us that you are working five or six hours a day. You did not tell us how much you earn, but you did say that your board and lodging are covered by your employers. Maybe if you made an effort you could do a few more hours of work in another job, and then you will be in a position to finance the rest of your studies. It will not be easy for you, but since when has a stubborn ox like you recoiled from hardships? After all, you are a socialist ideologically, a proletarian, a working man! (By the way, you have not told us what the relationship is between Mr. Wald and Miss Abravanel. Are they a married couple? Or father and daughter? Everything you do is wrapped in mystery, as though you were working in a secret security installation.) Your only letter to date was very short on details. You only said that you sit and chat in the afternoons and evenings with the elderly invalid and sometimes read to him. This work seems to me, if you don't mind my saying so, rather easy and not especially tiring. It would not be difficult for you in Jerusalem to find yourself some more paid work, and with the income . . . [*Here again a few lines were illegible because the ink had run.*] Let me add here with all due caution: it is possible that in a few months we shall also be able to contribute some modest sums. Although far from the extent of the support we gave you before the bankruptcy, yet it will be better than nothing. I beg you, my dear Shmuel, I even implore you: you have only missed a few weeks of the university year. You can, with an effort that you are definitely capable of, make up what you have missed and return to studying at full speed. The topic you have chosen for your master's thesis, "Jewish Views of Jesus," is remote from my own interests, and even seems rather strange to me. In the city where I was born, Riga, we Jews were in the habit of averting our gaze every time we passed a crucifix. You wrote to me once that in your view Jesus was our own flesh and blood. It is extremely difficult for me to accept this: how many evil decrees, how much persecution, how much suffering, how much innocent blood was shed by those who hated us in the name of That Man! And you, Shmuel, suddenly get up and cross the lines and take a stand for some reason on the other side of the barricades, on the side of That Man. But I respect your choice, even though I cannot understand it. Just as I respect your voluntary activity in some socialist group, even though I am far removed from socialism myself and consider it as a cruel attempt to impose equality on the human race. It seems to me that equality runs counter to human nature, because of the simple fact that human beings are not born equal but different from one another and actually quite alien from one another. You and I, for instance, were not born equal. You are a young man blessed with many talents, whereas I am a simple man. Think of the difference between you and your sister: she is quiet and self-contained, whereas you are boisterous and loud. But who am I to argue with you about politics etc.? It's not from me that you inherited your enthusiasm and dedication. You will do as you please. You always have done. Please, my dear Shmuel, write to me soon to say that you are seeking or have found a second job so that you

can go back to studying. Studying is what you are truly destined for. You must not betray it. I know full well that it is not
easy to work, to keep yourself and to finance your studies all at
the same time. But if our Miri can do it, so can you. You have
stubbornness enough and to spare, a trait you have apparently
inherited from me, not from your mother. I shall sign off here,
with much love and deep worry,

Your father

P.S.: Please write to us more often and tell us more about your
daily life in the house where you are living and working now.

Shmuel's mother had added below:

My Mooly, I miss you so much. It's been months since you
last came to see us in Haifa and you hardly ever write. Why
is that? What have we done wrong? . . . [*Here again a few lines
were unreadable because of the damp.*] Your father's failure nearly
broke his heart. He has suddenly become an old man. He
hardly talks to me. It was always hard for him to talk to me,
even before what happened. You should try to stand by him
now, at least by writing to him. Ever since you gave up studying he's been feeling rather let down. Miri has written too to
say that she hasn't had a letter or any sign of life from you for
many weeks. Is something the matter, heaven forbid? Tell us
the whole truth.

P.S.: I am sealing the envelope and putting in a hundred liras,
without your father's knowledge. It's not a large sum, I know,
but I haven't got more at the moment. I join your father in
asking you: please go back to university, otherwise you'll re-
gret it for the rest of your life.

Love, Mummy

25

I AM VERY FAR REMOVED from the many and various types of world reformer," Gershom Wald said, "though this man is actually not a world reformer but a great realist. He was the only one who noticed a tiny crack in history, and managed to get us through that crack at the right moment, while there was still time. Not on his own, definitely not. Had it not been for my son and his friends, we would all be dead."

"In the Sinai campaign," Shmuel said, "your Ben-Gurion tied Israel to the coattails of the colonial powers that were doomed to degeneration and decline, France and Britain, and by so doing he only deepened Arab hatred of Israel and finally convinced the Arabs that Israel is a foreign implant in the region, a tool in the hands of global imperialism."

"Even before the Sinai campaign," Wald replied, "your Arabs were not so enamored of Israel, and they even—"

Shmuel interrupted him:

"Why should they love us? Why do you think the Arabs are not entitled to resist strangers who come here suddenly as if from another planet and take away their land and their soil, fields, villages and towns, the graves of their ancestors, and their children's inheritance? We tell ourselves that we only came to this land 'to build and to be rebuilt,' 'to renew our days as of old,' 'to redeem our ancestral heritage,' et cetera, but you tell me if there is any other people in this world who would welcome with open arms an incursion of hundreds of thousands of strangers, and then millions of strangers, landing from far away with the weird claim that their holy scriptures, which they brought with them also from far away, promise this whole land to them and to them alone."

"Would you be kind enough to pour me another glass of tea? And please help yourself to a glass as well. Neither you nor I will budge Ben-Gurion from his beliefs, whether we drink tea or not. Shealtiel Abravanel, Atalia's father, tried in vain to persuade Ben-Gurion in '48 that it was still possible to reach an agreement with the Arabs about the departure of the British and the creation of a single joint condominium of Jews and Arabs, if we only agreed to renounce the idea of a Jewish state. Yes, indeed. That is why he was banished from the Zionist Executive Committee and the Council of the Jewish Agency, which was de facto the unofficial Jewish government at the end of the British Mandate. Maybe one of these days the spirit will descend upon Atalia and she will tell you the whole story. I myself, I admit with no sense of shame, stood in that conflict foursquare on the side of Ben-Gurion's ruthless realism and not on that of Abravanel's lofty views."

"Ben-Gurion," Shmuel said, on his way to the kitchen to set the kettle to boil, "may have been in his youth a workers' leader, a sort of tribune of the plebs, if you like, but today he heads a self-righteous, chauvinistic state and he never stops spouting hollow biblical phrases about renewing our days as of old and realizing the vision of the prophets."

And from the kitchen, while he brewed the tea, he raised his voice and added:

"If there is no peace, one day the Arabs will defeat us. It is only a question of time and patience. And the Arabs have endless time and boundless patience. They will not forget the disgrace of their defeat in '48 or the plot we hatched against them with Britain and France three years ago."

Gershom Wald drank the tea that Shmuel handed him while it was still very hot, almost boiling, whereas Shmuel waited patiently for his to cool a little.

"Once, a year or two ago," said Shmuel, "I read an article entitled 'The Limits of Power; or, The Eleventh Soldier.' I've forgotten the name of the author. But I can still remember what it said. When Stalin invaded Finland in the late thirties, the Finnish commander in chief, Marshal Mannerheim, went to see the president of Finland, Kallio, and tried to reassure him: every Finnish soldier can beat ten Russian *muzhiks*. We are ten times as good as they are, ten times as clever, and ten times as motivated to defend our homeland which is under attack. President Kallio pondered for a while, shrugged his shoulders, and said—perhaps to himself rather than to the marshal—'Well, who knows, maybe every one of our men is a match for ten Soviet peasants, that's all well and good, but what do we do if Stalin happens to send against us not ten but eleven?' And that, the article reasoned, is the unspoken quandary facing the State of Israel. For more than ten years now the Arabs have been beating their drums about wiping us out, but so far they have not invested even a tenth of their power in our destruction. In our War of Independence in 1948 fewer than 80,000 soldiers took part from all five Arab armies combined, compared to 120,000 conscripts out of a Jewish population of 600,000. What shall we do if someday the eleventh Arab soldier arrives? What shall we do if the Arabs send an army of half a million? Or a million? Or two million? Nasser is equipping himself right now with huge quantities of the best Soviet armaments and is talking openly about a second round of war. And what are we doing? We are drunk on victory. Drunk on our power. Drunk on biblical clichés."

"And what does Your Honor suggest?" Wald asked. "That we turn the other cheek?"

"Ben-Gurion was wrong to abandon the policy of nonalignment and tie Israel by bonds of serfdom and slavery to the Western powers, and not even to the strongest of them but to those on the way out—France and Britain. This morning's paper talked about dozens more killed and injured in Algiers. It turns out that the French army stationed there stoutly refuses to open fire on the rebellious French settlers. France is sinking into civil war while at the very same time Britain is shamefacedly folding up the remains of its empire. Ben-Gurion has embroiled us in an alliance with declining powers. Maybe instead of another glass of tea you'd like me to pour us both a thimbleful of brandy? In honor of Ben-Gurion? No? Or would you like your evening porridge now? Not yet? Tell me when you want it and I'll warm it up for you."

"Thank you," Gershom Wald said. "I like what you were saying about the eleventh soldier. If he suddenly turns up on the battlefield, we'll simply have to repulse him, too. Otherwise we shall not be here anymore."

Shmuel stood and began to pace up and down between the bookcases.

"Up to a certain point it's possible to understand a people that for thousands of years has known well the power of books, the power of prayers, the power of the commandments, the power of scholarship, the power of religious devotion, the power of trade, and the power of being an intermediary, but that only knew the power of power itself in the form of blows on its back. And now it finds itself holding a heavy cudgel. Tanks, cannons, jet planes. It's only natural that such a people gets drunk on power and tends to believe that it can do whatever it likes by the power of power. And what is it, in your opinion, that power cannot achieve?"

"How much power?"

"All the power in the world. Take the combined power of the Soviet Union and the United States and France and Britain. What can you not achieve with such power, by any manner or means?"

"I think that with such power you could conquer whatever you felt like. From sea to sea."

"That's what you think. That's what the Jews in Israel think, because they have no notion of the limits of power. The fact is that all the power in the world cannot transform someone who hates you into someone who likes you. It can turn a foe into a slave, but not into a friend. All the power in the world cannot transform a fanatic into an enlightened man. All the power in the world cannot transform someone thirsting for vengeance into a lover. And yet these are precisely the real existential challenges facing the State of Israel: how to turn a hater into a lover, a fanatic into a moderate, an avenger into a friend. Am I saying that we do not need military might? Heaven forbid! Such a foolish thought would never enter my head. I know as well as you that it is power, military power, that stands, at any given moment, even at this very moment while you and I are arguing here, between us and extinction. Power has the power to prevent our annihilation for the time being. On condition that we always remember, at every moment, that in a situation like ours power can only prevent. It can't settle anything and it can't solve anything. It can only stave off disaster for a while."

"So I lost my only son simply to delay a catastrophe that in your opinion there is no way to prevent?" Gershom Wald said.

Shmuel had the urge to get up and clasp the rough-hewn head of the man sitting opposite him to his breast with both arms, and perhaps mouth some words of comfort. But there is no comfort in this world. He chose to say nothing, so as not to cause more pain. Instead, he fed the goldfish. Then he went to the kitchen.

Rather than the usual porridge, Sarah de Toledo had brought a potato salad with mayonnaise and sliced vegetables. Gershom Wald ate in silence, as if he had exhausted his stock of quotations and allusions for this evening. He remained silent until nearly eleven o'clock, when Shmuel poured them both a little glass of brandy without waiting for the old man's agreement. Then he took his leave, ate the leftover potato salad, washed the dishes, and climbed up to the attic. The father stayed at his desk, jotting something down on a piece of paper, crumpling it up, tossing it into the wastepaper basket, then starting again. A deep silence now descended upon the house. Atalia had gone out. Or maybe she had not gone out. Maybe she was sitting in total silence in her room, where Shmuel had never set foot.

26

THE FOLLOWING MORNING at half past eleven, Shmuel put on his battered duffel coat, covered his unruly curls with the *shapka* (which looked like a kind of peaked coachman's cap), picked up the walking stick with its predatory fox-head handle, and went for a walk in Jerusalem. There was no rain, just a few gray tatters of clouds crossing the sky on their way from the sea to the desert. The morning light that touched the stone walls of Jerusalem was reflected back soft and sweet, honeyed light, the light that caresses Jerusalem on clear winter days between one rainstorm and the next.

Shmuel walked up Rabbi Elbaz Lane and turned onto Ussishkin Street, passed the Cultural Center, whose walls were faced in a smooth stone that looked like marble, and continued toward the town center. His head was thrust forward as if he were butting the air or forcing his way through obstacles, his body bent forward and his legs hurrying so as not to be left behind. His walk, as ever, looked more like a slow run. There was something amusing about this, as if he were hurrying to go someplace where people had been waiting for him for a long time but would not wait forever, and if he was late, it would be too late.

Yardena must be at work now, in the press-clipping agency

where she had worked since before her marriage. She would be sitting there, on the first floor of an old building on Rav Kook Street, in a dimly lit room, underlining in pencil the names of the clients of the agency wherever they appeared in the newspapers. Perhaps she had once or twice come across the name of her Nesher Sharshevsky, who was himself probably sitting at his desk in the Institute for Research on Seas and Lakes, hard at work on a report, his face as usual expressing calm contentment, like someone sucking a sweet. Only you are roaming the streets of Jerusalem, doing nothing. The days are slipping by, winter will pass, then summer will come, and then winter again, and you will slowly rot between memories of Yardena and fantasies of Atalia. At night Yardena sleeps in Nesher Sharshevsky's arms, and her warm, chestnutty smell permeates their double bed. Are you still in love with her? Or maybe you are not in love with her but with Atalia, a love that you do not admit to and that is totally unthinkable?

In his mind's eye he compared Yardena to Atalia with her long, soft hair falling over one shoulder of her embroidered dress. Her way of walking, which had something of an inner dance to it, her hips more awake than she was. An assertive woman, full of secrets, who relates to you with a mixture of sarcasm and detached curiosity, a woman who does not stop giving you orders, and who always looks at you with a faint mockery, blended perhaps with a few slivers of pity. You gather this pity into your heart. She might be thinking of you as no more than an abandoned puppy.

What does Atalia see in you from the heights of her condescending irony? She probably sees an ex-student, an ex-researcher, a wild, disheveled, muddled youth who is attracted to her but would never dare express his emotions, which are childlike sentiments, in words. Does your presence sometimes annoy her? Does it amuse her? Or maybe it does both?

On a rough concrete wall a large rat, perhaps a sewer rat, stood motionless. The creature fixed its little black eyes on Shmuel as though it were about to ask him a question. Or perhaps to put him to a test. Shmuel stopped and looked at the rat for a moment or two as if to say, Don't be afraid of me, my hands are empty and I've got nothing to hide. One of them, Shmuel understood, would have to give way now. Right away. And so he did indeed give way, and went on without a backward glance. After five paces he reconsidered, felt ashamed of himself, and turned back. But the creature had vanished and the wall was deserted.

At twenty past twelve Shmuel Ash entered the little restaurant on King George Street and sat down at his usual corner table, where almost every day he ate his lunch, which also served as his breakfast. Without inquiring what he wanted, the waiter, who was also the proprietor, a short, fat Hungarian with a red face and a forehead always covered with beads of sweat even in winter (Shmuel supposed he suffered from high blood pressure), brought him a deep bowl of hot, spicy goulash soup. Shmuel always ate goulash soup, accompanied by several slices of white bread, and he always rounded off his meal with fruit compote.

Once, the previous winter, he had sat here with Yardena. While they both ate their lunch, Shmuel had talked to her about the increasing isolationism of the leftist faction in the workers' party, MAPAM. Suddenly she had looked at him, startled, and grabbed his arm. She pulled him sharply to his feet, hurriedly paid the bill, held him with her fingernails as if she had just been seized by an attack of indecipherable rage, and dragged him to his room in Tel Arza. All along the way she did not utter a single word, and he, as though stunned, allowed himself to be dragged along behind her. As soon as they got up to his room, she pushed him by the shoulders, flat on his back in bed, and without a sound she lifted her dress and got on top of him; she rode him violently, subduing him as if taking revenge, and she did not let him go until she had come twice. He had tried to cover her mouth with his hand to silence her, so as not to alarm the landlady in the next room. Then she straightened her dress, drank two glasses of tap water, and left.

Why did she leave him? What did that Nesher Sharshevsky have that he didn't? What wrong had he done? What did she see in her dull hydrologist, whose square body resembled a packing case and who liked to talk in complicated, winding sentences about subjects that always bored everyone in the room? He would come out with sentences like "Tel Aviv is a much less ancient town than Jerusalem, but on the other hand it is more modern," "There's a great difference between old people and young people," or "That's the way it is: the majority decides and the minority simply has to abide by the majority view."

"An excited puppy" — that was what Yardena had called Shmuel the last time they had spoken. Though inwardly he had agreed with her, at the same time he had felt full of shame and humiliation.

He stood up, paid for his meal, and paused for a moment at the counter to glance at the headlines in the evening paper. The Israel Defense Forces were purging the southern sector of the Israeli-Syrian border. Nasser, the Egyptian president, was threatening again, while Ben-Gurion was warning. Why were Nasser's warnings always called threats, whereas Ben-Gurion's threats were called warnings?

Then he went out into the street, which was bathed in a pleasant winter light, a light of pine trees and stones. He was suddenly assailed by a strange, sharp feeling that anything was possible, that what was lost only seemed to be lost, but that in fact nothing was completely lost and what would happen depended only on his audacity. He decided to change there and then. To change his whole life from that moment on. Henceforth he would be calm and bold, a man who knew what he wanted and did everything in his power to achieve it, with no holding back and no hesitation.

27

A<small>TALIA FOUND SHMUEL SITTING</small> at the desk, bent over an old book he had borrowed from the National Library. She was wearing a light-colored skirt and a blue pullover that was too big for her and gave her a warm, homey look. Her face looked younger than her forty-five years; it was only her veined hands that betrayed her age. She sat down on the edge of his bed, leaned back against the wall, crossed her legs, straightened her skirt, and said, without apologizing for this sudden invasion of his territory:

"You're working. I'm disturbing you. What are you reading?"

"Yes. Please," Shmuel said. "Do disturb me. I really want you to. I'm tired of this work. In fact, I'm tired all the time. I'm even tired when I'm asleep. How about you? Are you free? Shall we go out for a little walk? It's a bright day outside, the sort of winter's day you only get in Jerusalem. Shall we go out?"

Ignoring the invitation, Atalia said:

"Are you still doing research on stories about Jesus?"

"Jesus and Judas. Jesus and the Jews," Shmuel said. "How Jews down the ages have seen Jesus."

"And why do you find that so interesting? Why not how they saw Muhammad? Or Buddha?"

"It's like this," Shmuel said. "I can easily understand why the

Jews rejected Christianity. But Jesus wasn't a Christian. He was born and died a Jew. It never crossed his mind to found a new religion. It was Paul, Saul of Tarsus, who invented Christianity. Jesus himself says explicitly, 'Think not that I am come to destroy the law.' If only the Jews had accepted him, the whole of history would have been different. There would never have been a Christian Church. And the whole of Europe might have adopted a milder, purer form of Judaism. And we would have been spared exile, persecutions, pogroms, the Inquisition, blood libels, and even the Holocaust."

"And why did the Jews refuse to accept him?"

"That is precisely the question I ask myself, Atalia, but I still haven't found an answer. He was, in today's terms, a kind of Reform Jew. Or rather, a fundamentalist Jew, not in the fanatical sense of 'fundamentalist,' but in the sense of a return to the pure roots. He longed to purify the Jewish faith of all sorts of self-satisfied cultic accretions that had attached themselves to it, all sorts of fatty protrusions that the priests had cultivated and that the Pharisees had burdened it with. It was only natural for the priests to see him as the enemy. I believe that Judas son of Simeon Iscariot was one of those priests. Or maybe he was just close to them. Maybe he was sent by the Jerusalem priests to join the community of those who believed in Jesus so as to spy on them and report their doings to Jerusalem. But he turned into a follower of Jesus and loved him so dearly that he became the most devoted of all his disciples and even served as the treasurer of the whole group. One day, if you like, I'll tell you what I think is the Gospel of Judas Iscariot. But I am amazed at the simple people, why they didn't accept Jesus in their masses, they who were groaning beneath the yoke of the rich, bloated priesthood in Jerusalem."

"I don't like the expression 'simple people.' There's no such thing as the simple people. There's a man and a woman, and another woman and another man, and each of them has reason and

feelings and inclinations and moral judgments of one sort or another. Though a man's moral judgment, if it exists at all, only exists in the brief moments when his urges are satisfied."

"When you came in I was studying what the Ramban writes
about Jesus. The Ramban, Rabbi Moses ben Nahman, whom the
Christians call Nahmanides, was one of the most learned Jews
who ever lived. And that was in the thirteenth century; he was
born in Gerona, in Spain, and died here in this country, in Acre.
He tells of a 'disputation' he was made to participate in by King
James I of Aragon, a public debate that lasted for four successive
days between the Ramban and an apostate Jew by the name of
Pablo Christiani, also known as Friar Paul. There was something
terrifying and blood-chilling about those public debates that the
Jews were forced to engage in during the Middle Ages. If the
Christian won, the Jews had to pay for their defeat with their
blood, because it had been proved that their scriptures lied. And
if the Jew won, the Jews still had to pay with their blood, for their
impudence. The Christian priest tried to prove by means of quotations from the Talmud—remember that he was an apostate Jew
—that the Talmud contains insults against Christianity as well as
clear hints that Christianity is the true faith and that Jesus really
was the Messiah, who came into our world and will return to
it one day. The Ramban claims in his writings that he won this
debate decisively, but in reality it appears that the disputation
was stopped with no decision reached. Maybe the Ramban was as
afraid of winning as he was of losing. Neither reason nor nature,
he argued in this disputation, which is known as the Barcelona
Disputation, can tolerate the story of the virgin birth, or that of
Jesus' death on the cross and his resurrection three days later. His
main reasoning was as follows: it says explicitly in the holy scriptures that with the coming of the Messiah bloodshed will cease in
the world, and that nation shall not lift up sword against nation,

neither shall they learn war anymore. These are the words of the prophet Isaiah. And yet, from the days of Jesus to the present, bloodshed has not ceased for a moment. Moreover, in the book of Psalms it says expressly that the Messiah 'shall have dominion also from sea to sea, and from the river unto the ends of the earth.' Now Jesus had no dominion, either in his lifetime or after his death. It was Rome that ruled the Land of Israel and the world, and even today (says the Ramban) the Muslims rule over more territory than the Christians. And the Christians themselves, the Ramban concludes, shed far more blood than all the other nations."

"All that sounds quite convincing to me," said Atalia. "I think maybe your Ramban did win the debate after all."

"No," Shmuel said, "these are not convincing arguments, because they don't contain a hint of an attempt to engage with the gospel itself, the gospel of Jesus, the gospel of universal love, and forgiveness, and grace, and compassion."

"Are you a Christian?"

"I'm an atheist. Three-and-a-half-year-old Yossi Siton, who was run over and killed while he was chasing his green ball yesterday not far from here, on the Gaza Road, is sufficient proof that there is no God. I don't believe for a moment that Jesus was God or the Son of God. But I love him. I love the words he used, such as 'If therefore the light that is in thee be darkness, how great is that darkness!,' or 'My soul is exceeding sorrowful, even unto death,' or 'Let the dead bury their dead,' or 'Ye are the salt of the earth: but if the salt have lost his savour, wherewith shall it be salted?' I have loved him ever since I first read his teachings in the New Testament, when I was fifteen years old. And I believe that Judas was the most loyal and devoted of all his disciples and that he never betrayed him, but, on the contrary, he meant to prove his greatness to the whole world. I'll explain to you one day, if you want to hear. Maybe we could go out again one evening, if you like, and sit down together in a quiet place where we can talk."

As he said this, he looked at her crossed knees in their nylon stockings and wondered whether the stockings were held up by garters or a suspender belt, and he shrank back in his chair so she would not notice he was stiffening beyond all hope.

"You're blushing under your Neanderthal beard again," Atalia said. "This evening you and I will go to the early show at the cinema. There's a neorealist Italian film. My treat."

Startled and excited, Shmuel murmured:

"Yes. Thank you."

Atalia came and stood behind him. She held his tousled head in her cool hands and pressed it for a moment against her breast. Then she turned and left the room without closing the door. Shmuel listened to the sound of her footsteps on the stairs until it stopped. A deep silence fell on the house. He drew the inhaler out of his pocket and took two breaths.

28

─

THAT EVENING HE ASKED Gershom Wald if he could leave
at half past seven just this once.

"We're going out, Atalia and I," he said, all aglow like a little
boy who has been kissed by the queen of the class.

"The honey will eat the bear. Well, you heartbroken thing.
Just be careful she doesn't singe your beard."

Later he waited for her impatiently in the kitchen. He did not
dare to knock on the door of her room. On the kitchen table's
oilcloth there were a few crumbs from her supper. Shmuel licked
his fingertip and picked them up one by one, then dropped them
into the sink and washed the sink and his finger. As if this would
prove to Atalia that he had been right. Right about what? He had
no answer to this question. He looked at an old print hanging on
the wall just above the table, a colorful poster for the Jewish National Fund showing a tough, muscular pioneer, his sleeves rolled
up with geometrical precision. The top button of his shirt was
undone, revealing a suntanned, hairy chest. He was holding the
handles of an iron plow drawn by a brown horse or mule striding toward the horizon where the sun was kissing the line of the
hilltops. Sunset or sunrise? The picture gave no clue, but Shmuel
imagined that the scene showed sunrise rather than sunset, as in

the song: 'To the mountains, to the mountains we are striding, /
Striding at the dawning of the day. / We have left all our yesterdays
behind us / And tomorrow is a long, long way away!' He pondered
the fact that after the sunrise would come a sunset, as always happens, and maybe the sunset was already here. Was Micha Wald
tough and suntanned? Did he look like the pioneer in the poster?
Did Ben-Gurion want us all to look like that pioneer?

More than once Shmuel had composed a fierce letter in his
mind to David Ben-Gurion, and once he even committed a draft
to writing. It was full of crossings-out. He explained to Ben-Gurion that it was a tragedy for the State of Israel that he had abandoned the socialism of his youth, and he went on to argue that
the policy of retaliatory raids was a fruitless and dangerous policy,
since violence begets violence, and vengeance begets vengeance.
Shmuel had destroyed this letter before he finished writing it.
Sometimes he conducted sharp arguments in his mind with the
prime minister, which resembled to some extent the arguments
he had had in the Socialist Renewal Group, except that in the
former he secretly hoped not only to be victorious and convince
Ben-Gurion, but also to win his admiration and even his affection.

Atalia appeared in a close-fitting orange winter dress. Her
eyes were delicately outlined in kohl. She had a fine silver chain
around her neck. On her lips there hovered not exactly a smile,
but rather something that might have been a secret promise of a
smile. She said in astonishment:

"You must have been waiting for me since this morning. If not
since yesterday evening."

At this moment she seemed painfully beautiful. He knew very
well that this woman was beyond his reach, and yet his whole
body felt strained as if holding her tight in his arms. She sat down
facing him at the kitchen table and said:

"No. We're not going to see a film this evening. The sky is

clear and there is a full moon. We're going to put our coats on and take a walk, to see what the moonlight does to the alleyways."

Shmuel agreed instantly. Atalia added:

"I don't know if I like Jerusalem or simply put up with it. But whenever I leave Jerusalem for more than two or three weeks, the city begins to appear in my dreams, and always bathed in moonlight."

Shmuel, in a sudden access of boldness, asked:

"What else do you dream about?"

Atalia answered without a smile:

"Good-looking young men."

"Like me?"

"You're not a young man, you're an old child. Tell me, you did remember to warm up Wald's porridge, didn't you?"

"Yes, and I sprinkled some sugar and cinnamon on it. He's already eaten it. Not all of it. There was some left over and I finished it. Now he's writing. I've no idea what. He's never told me what he writes and I haven't dared ask. Do you know, Atalia? Or can you guess what it is that keeps him so busy?"

"Abravanel. Micha. The war. He's been writing up some research for years now, or maybe a book, about Shealtiel Abravanel, and also a memoir about his son's life. Maybe he links the ostracism and banishment of Abravanel to his son's death. Maybe he thinks there is some connection between them."

"Connection? What connection?"

She did not reply. She rose, filled a glass with water from the tap, and drank it noisily like a thirsty peasant. Then she wiped her mouth with the back of a faintly wrinkled hand.

"Come on. Let's go. The moon will be up soon. I love to watch it rise from the hills and soar over the rooftops."

They went out into the dark yard, which was in the shadow of the trees, a shadow deepened by the row of cypresses behind the house. Shmuel could barely make out the iron lid of the cistern.

Atalia held his elbow and guided him along the path paved with dressed Jerusalem stone. Through the sleeve of his threadbare coat he could feel the warmth of her hand and each of her fingers, and he longed with all his being to lay his own hand on hers, which was now guiding him on the steps. But he was afraid of her sarcasm. Instead of touching her, he took the inhaler out of his pocket. After one deep breath he felt better and put the inhaler back in his pocket.

Rabbi Elbaz Lane was empty. A streetlamp from the time of the British Mandate, inlaid with little rectangular panels of glass, waved in the breeze on a cable strung across the lane. The lamp cast a ceaseless, restless movement of wave-like shadows onto the paving stones. The westerly breeze was light and silent, as if it had been sent to cool a glass of tea.

Shmuel said:

"Tell me what sort of man your father was."

Atalia replied in a soft voice, almost in a whisper:

"Let's not talk now. Let's walk without talking. Let's listen to the sounds of the night."

At the end of Rabbi Elbaz Lane the moon leapt above the tiled roofs, red and huge, like a demented sun determined to burst forth in the night, against every law of nature. Shmuel disliked this moon, because it had condemned him to silence. Atalia stopped, her hand still holding his elbow as if afraid he might stumble, and looked for a long time at the moon, or at the ring of brightness that surrounded it and poured down to whiten the walls of Jerusalem stone with a pallid, skeletal glow. Suddenly she said:

"I don't know why we think of the moon as white. It isn't white. It's all bloodshot."

Then they walked in silence along the narrow streets of the Nahlaot, Atalia leading and Shmuel following half a stride behind. She had let go of his sleeve, but from time to time she touched his shoulder gently to steer him to the left or right. A boy and girl passed them with their arms around each other, walking on up the street. The boy said:

"I don't believe it. It just can't be true."

The girl replied:

"Just wait. You'll see."

The boy said something they couldn't hear, but his voice sounded abject.

"How deep the silence is," Atalia said. "You can almost hear the stones breathing."

Shmuel opened his mouth to reply, but changed his mind, guessing correctly that she didn't want him to break the silence. So he said nothing and went on walking half a pace behind her. Suddenly his hand reached out and his fingers stealthily stroked the back of her neck and slid over the silver chain under her hair. His eyes filled with tears, because he guessed that nothing was possible between them. Atalia could not see his eyes brimming in the dark but she slowed her pace. What a fool you are, Shmuel said to himself, a fool and a coward. You could have pulled her body to you just now, put your arms around her shoulders and kissed her lips. But some inner voice warned him: No, don't try it, you'll only make a fool of yourself.

They wandered the streets for forty or fifty minutes. They crossed Agrippa Street and walked the length of Mahane Yehuda Market, which was deserted and shuttered, with dizzying smells of fruit and rubbish and overripe vegetables and offal and spices and faint decay coming from the darkened stalls. They emerged onto the Jaffa Road at the square opposite the sundial that had been placed on top of one of the buildings in the days of Ottoman rule. Atalia lingered, facing the sundial for a short while, then suddenly answered the question Shmuel had asked her earlier about her father:

"He didn't belong in our time. He may have come too late.

He may have been ahead of his time. He belonged in a different time."

Then she turned, with Shmuel behind her turning in her footsteps, to head for home, this time by different back alleys. They hardly exchanged a word all the way, apart from "Look out, there's a step" or "That washing hanging across the road is dripping straight on our heads." Atalia wanted this silence, and Shmuel did not dare contravene her wishes, though he was seething with excitement. Meanwhile, the moon had lost its bloody tinge; it had climbed up above the wall of the Bezalel Museum and was illuminating the whole city with a ghostly light. When they got home, Atalia took off her overcoat and helped Shmuel to free himself from his coat, as he had caught his arm in the torn lining.

"Thank you for this evening," Atalia said. "I enjoyed it. It's nice to be with you sometimes, especially when you don't talk. No, I don't want to eat anything now, thanks. You can make yourself something, if you like, from whatever you find in the refrigerator, and you can talk to yourself at the same time, as usual. You're full of words I didn't let you say. I'm off to my room. Good night. Don't worry, we didn't waste the evening. And don't forget to turn off the light on the steps when you go up."

With that, she turned and left on her flat-heeled shoes. Her orange dress shone in the doorway for a moment, then faded from view. A faint scent of violets hung in the air, and Shmuel inhaled it deeply. His heart, which the doctors had discovered to be enlarged ever since he was a child, beat hard, and he pleaded with it to calm down.

He decided therefore to eat two slices of bread and butter and cheese, to open a jar of yogurt, and perhaps fry himself an egg. But then he lost his appetite, which was replaced by a vague sadness. He went to his room, lay down in his underwear, and stared at the moon, which was in the center of the window. After twenty minutes he changed his mind, went back downstairs, opened a can of sweet corn and one of corned beef, and ate them both while standing in front of the open refrigerator. His appetite had returned.

29

HE THOUGHT ABOUT HIS PARENTS' little flat in a side street in Hadar, in Haifa, the one his family had moved to after the shack in Kiryat Motzkin burned down. The larger of its two rooms was used as living room, dining room, and also his parents' bedroom, while his sister Miri slept in the other. His own bed in the passage stood between the door to the tiny kitchen and the door to the toilet. At the head of his bed was a box painted brown that served as a clothes chest, a desk where he did his homework, and a bedside table. At eleven years old Shmuel was a thin, slightly stooped child, with big staring eyes, matchstick legs, and knees that were always scratched. It was years later, when he finished his military service, that he grew his tousled mane of hair and the caveman beard that hid his long, narrow face. He disliked the mane, the beard, and the childish face underneath, but he felt that the wild beard concealed something a man should be ashamed of.

As a child he had three or four friends, all of them from among the weakest pupils in his class. One of them was an immigrant from Romania, and another suffered from a slight stammer. Shmuel had a sizable stamp collection, and he loved to show it to his friends and to lecture them about the value and special features of rare stamps and about the various countries. He was a knowledgeable and talkative child, but he was almost incapable of listening when others were talking, and would lose interest after three or four sentences. He was especially proud of stamps from countries that had ceased to exist, such as Ubangi-Shari, Austria-Hungary, or Bohemia and Moravia. He could lecture his friends interminably about the wars and revolutions that had wiped these states off the map, those that had first been conquered by the Nazis and later by Stalin, and those that had become provinces of the new countries that arose in Europe following World War I, such as Yugoslavia and Czechoslovakia. The names of faraway countries like Trinidad and Tobago or Kenya, Uganda, and Tanganyika aroused some vague longing in him. In his imagination he would sail off to those remote regions and take part in the wars of daring guerrilla movements fighting for freedom from the foreign conqueror. He lectured his friends with enthusiasm and ardor, making up whatever he did not know. He read whatever he could get hold of: adventure stories, travel stories, detective stories, horror stories, and also love stories, which he didn't understand but which stirred a secret pleasure in him. Moreover, when he was twelve he decided to read the entire *Hebrew Encyclopedia*, volume by volume and entry by entry, in order, because everything interested him and even the things he could not understand fired his imagination. But when he was nearly halfway through the letter *alef*, he grew tired and gave up.

Once he went with his friend Menahem, a boy whose family had come from Transylvania, on an expedition in one of the overgrown wadis that ran down the western slope of Mount Carmel. They put on boots and hats, and each carried a stick, a water bottle, and a rucksack containing blankets to make a tent, and brought pitas, hard-boiled eggs, and potatoes to roast over a fire. They set off at half past five, just before sunrise, crossed the neighborhood, went down into the wadi, and advanced along the winding slope until almost eleven o'clock, counting birds they saw that neither of them knew the name of. Apart from the ravens, that is, which wheeled with guttural shrieks among the crags. Shmuel released some wild cries into the wadi and waited for the echo. At home he was never allowed to raise his voice.

By eleven the sun was hot and beat down on their faces, and both of them were red and dripping with salty sweat. Shmuel pointed to a level area between two oak trees and suggested they camp there and rest, then put up a tent, light a fire, and roast the potatoes. He knew from books about tall oak trees in Europe, though these oaks on the slopes of Mount Carmel were not trees at all but more like tangled bushes which gave hardly any shade. For a long while they both struggled with tent pegs and blankets, trying to erect a tent, but the poles refused to stick in the ground, even though they both used a stone as a hammer, taking turns, one holding the pole and the other hitting it with the stone. Shmuel bent down to pick up a bigger stone and a piercing scream burst from his chest. A scorpion had stung him on the back of his hand, at the base of the middle finger. The pain was sharp and burning, and so was the panic. And because they did not understand at first what had happened, Shmuel thought that perhaps a sliver of broken glass had penetrated deep in his flesh. Menahem took the hand, which was swelling, and tried to find and extract the splinter or piece of glass. Then he poured water from his water bottle on the sting, but the pain did not diminish, in fact it got worse, and Shmuel writhed and groaned, so Menahem suggested he sit down on a blanket while he went to get help. Suddenly Shmuel noticed a yellow scorpion crawling slowly among the dead leaves, perhaps the scorpion that had stung him, or another one. He began to tremble all over: he was certain he was going to die. A wave of terror and despair swept through him and sent him running quickly down the wadi, holding his burning hand with the other, stumbling as he ran, his feet catching on stones and dry branches. Once or twice he fell flat on his face, but he got up and went on running as fast as he could, panting wildly, while his friend Menahem ran after him but could not catch up with him because the fear and pain gave Shmuel wings.

Menahem, because he did not know what to do, started shouting for help in a weak, frightened voice, as though it was he who had been stung, and so the two of them ran on down the rocky slope, Menahem shouting as he ran and Shmuel running ahead and increasing the distance between them, no longer shouting but trembling all over.

Eventually they reached a new road that they didn't know, and they stopped, panting and terrified. After a few minutes a woman in a car stopped and took them to the hospital, where they were separated. Shmuel was given an injection and Menahem was given a glass of cold water. Shmuel fainted when he had the injection, and when he came to, he saw his mother and father leaning over him, their faces almost touching, as if at long last some transient truce had been agreed between them. He was proud of himself for having brought about this peace.

They both looked weak and confused. They kept looking at him in a frightened way, as if they were dependent on him now, and as if he had to take care of them. His hand was bandaged and the pain had subsided, to be replaced by a sort of pleasant pride that welled up inside him. "It's nothing," he murmured, "only a scorpion sting, it doesn't kill you." When these last words left his lips, he felt a flutter of disappointment, because in his mind's eye he saw his parents mourning for him and bitterly regretting all the wrongs they had done him since he was small. After a few hours the duty doctor discharged him and told him to rest at home, to eat little but to drink lots of fluids. His parents rang for a taxi. They dropped Menahem off on their way home.

At home they put Shmuel in his sister's bed, and banished Miri to Shmuel's corner in the passage, between the kitchen and the toilet. For two days they fed him on hot chicken soup, chicken livers with potato purée and boiled carrots, and vanilla-flavored custard. After two days they said to him:

"That's enough of being coddled. Tonight you're going back to your own bed, and tomorrow, back to school." Then came the rebukes and reprimands. His friend Menahem came to visit, all guilty, humble, and meek, as though it was he who had stung Shmuel. He even brought him a present, a rare, valuable stamp that Shmuel had coveted for a long time, a Nazi stamp with a swastika and a picture of Hitler. After a few days the swelling went down, but Shmuel never forgot the warm delight he had experienced along with the fear of death, and the secret sweetness at the sight of his parents and sister grieving over his fresh grave and feeling sorry for all the times they had wronged him since he was born. He also remembered the two prettiest girls in his class, Tamar and Ronit, standing before his tombstone, hugging each other tearfully. And he remembered the touch of his sister Miri's hand on his forehead and his hair. She was bending over and stroking him as he lay on her bed in her room, as she had never stroked him before or since. In his family they hardly ever touched one another. He sometimes received a burning slap in the face from his father, and on rare occasions his mother laid her cool fingers on his forehead for a moment. Maybe she was just checking to see if he had a fever. He never saw his parents touch each other, not even to brush a crumb off a sweater, but throughout his childhood years he felt that his mother nursed a private sense of being insulted, while his father suppressed a lasting resentment. His parents barely spoke to one another, and if they did, it was only about practical arrangements. A plumber. Forms. Shopping. Whenever his father spoke to his mother, his mouth twisted downward as if he had a toothache. What the reasons were for his mother's umbrage and his father's resentment he neither knew nor cared. From his earliest memories, when he was two or three, his parents were already distant from each other. Though they hardly ever quarreled in his presence, sometimes he saw his mother with red eyes. Now and then his father went out on the balcony to smoke a cigarette and stayed there alone for fifteen or twenty minutes, and when he came back inside, he sat down in his armchair and hid behind the newspaper. His parents were polite, reserved people who didn't believe in raising their voices. Throughout his childhood and his teens Shmuel was ashamed of them and was always angry at them, without knowing what he was angry about or why. Was it for their weakness? Their perpetual humiliation, the humiliation of immigrants who went out of their way to win the favor of strangers? For the warmth they did not lavish on him, because it was not in them? For the suppressed hostility that prevailed between them almost all of the time? For their miserliness? And yet they always took care of anything he needed: despite their parsimony, he was never short of clothes or books, an album or catalog for his stamp collection, a bicycle for his bar mitzvah; they even paid for him to study at the university, until they went bankrupt. Despite which he was unable to love his mother or his father. He loathed the mixture of submissiveness and bitterness they showed at all times. The depressing, low-ceilinged passageway they made him sleep in for the whole of his childhood and adolescence. His father's meekness, the way he was constantly reciting the slogans of the ruling party, and his mother's cowed silence. Throughout his childhood, he invented totally different parents for himself, strong, warm-hearted, devoted parents, maybe professors from the Technion, well-to-do scholars from the Upper Carmel, witty parents who radiated affection and charm, people capable of inspiring respect, love, and awe in himself and others. He never mentioned this to anyone, not even his sister. When he was little she used to call him an adopted child, a foundling, and she used to say, "We found you in the forests of Mount Carmel." Her father would sometimes correct her: "What are you talking about? We didn't find him in the forests of Mount Carmel, we found him in an alleyway near the port." His mother would say meekly, "It wasn't like that at all—the fact is that none of the four of us found the others on purpose." Shmuel was always angry at himself for being angry with them, and always blamed himself for his disloyalty. As if for all those years he was an enemy agent planted in the midst of his family.

As for Miri, she was a pretty girl with chestnut hair who always held herself upright. By the time she reached the age of fourteen or fifteen she was surrounded by a pack of giggling girls and tall boys, some of whom were two or three years older than she, and one of them was an officer in the commandos.

Shmuel carried the scorpion sting with him as one of the few sweet memories of his childhood. For all those years he had been enclosed by the walls of the gloomy passage he slept in, walls sooty from the paraffin heater that was lit during power cuts, and by the low, damp-infested ceiling. For a space of two or three days it was as if a crack had opened in one of the walls and through it something had emerged that Shmuel had never ceased to long for when he was growing up, and even now that he was an adult, when he remembered the scorpion sting he was filled with a vague urge to forgive the whole world and to love everyone who crossed his path.

30

O NE TUESDAY, DURING A BREAK between two rain showers, Shmuel got up early, at nine o'clock, thrust his tousled head
under the tap, and let the stream of cold water banish the rem-
nants of his slumber. Then he dressed and went down to the
kitchen, ate a slice of bread and cheese, and drank two glasses
of thick Turkish coffee. It was not yet ten when he walked to the
bus stop on Keren Hakayemet Street and took the bus to the
National Library at Givat Ram. This time he left the stick with
the sharp-toothed fox handle behind. A diminutive, bespectacled
woman, whose face radiated goodwill and kindliness but who
had a slight mustache, directed him to the reading room of the
Newspaper Department. Here he requested and was given nine
monthly volumes of the daily newspaper *Davar*, from June 1947
to February 1948. He settled in his seat, laid some sheets of paper
he had brought with him on the table in front of him, along with
a pen that he had taken from Gershom Wald's desk, and started
to work his way patiently through the binders, issue by issue and
page by page.

The only other reader in the room was an older, angular
man with a goatee, protruding ears, and gold-framed pince-nez.
Shmuel noticed that he was almost completely devoid of eye-

brows. The man was turning the pages of a thick-bellied weekly
that Shmuel could not see the title of, but he noticed that it was
an old foreign magazine and also noticed that the man was feverishly taking notes on pieces of paper while chewing his lower lip.

After half an hour Shmuel finally found a small item relating to Shealtiel Abravanel, a member of the Zionist Executive
Committee and the Council of the Jewish Agency. It was a modest paragraph tucked away in the middle pages of *Davar*, and it
reported that on June 18, 1947, Abravanel requested permission
to give evidence to the United Nations' special commission ex-
amining the question of the future of Palestine. Abravanel had
asked to be allowed to submit a minority view, or rather, an individual view, to the commission concerning the conflict between
Jews and Arabs. To suggest an original and peaceable solution.
The Council of the Jewish Agency had turned down his request,
arguing that the Jewish Agency and the Zionist Executive Committee should speak with a single voice to the UN commission
rather than present several discordant views. The *Davar* report
added that Abravanel had deliberated whether to appear before
the commission despite the Jewish Agency's ruling, but had decided to accept the majority's authority, perhaps because of hints
that if he did presume to appear before the commission in his individual capacity, he would no longer have a place in the central
institutions of the Jewish community in Palestine.

Shmuel Ash copied this item on a sheet of paper, which he
folded and tucked in his shirt pocket. Then he perused the issues
for September and October, paused to read the details of the rec-
ommendation of the UN commission that Palestine should be
partitioned into two states, one Jewish and the other Arab, then
pressed on in search of other references to the story of Shealtiel
Abravanel, but he could discover no mention of a public debate
and no appeal by Abravanel to Jewish or Arab public opinion.

After three hours or so he felt hungry, but decided that as long as the man with the goatee was sitting and working at the table opposite him he would not abandon his researches. He held firm to this decision for twenty minutes, then gave up and went to the cafeteria in the nearby Kaplun Building, where he used to slake his hunger when he was a student. He very much hoped he would not run into any of his former friends. If they started asking him questions, what would he tell them?

It was already half past one. He asked for a cheese sandwich, a yogurt, and a cup of coffee. Then, because he still felt peckish, he ordered another sandwich and another yogurt and another coffee, and this time he also bought a piece of cake to go with his coffee. When he had finished, he struggled with sleepiness. His body relaxed in the chair and his eyelids fluttered and closed. He sat for a quarter of an hour in a corner of the cafeteria, his bearded chin drooping on his chest; then he mustered the last of his willpower and returned to the reading room and sat down at his table. The man with no eyebrows and a goatee and gold-framed pince-nez was still taking feverish notes on little slips of paper. As he went past, Shmuel noticed that the title of the weekly magazine the man was reading was in Cyrillic characters, and that the notes he was taking seemed to be in Russian. He did not linger, but requested the volumes of *Davar* that he hadn't looked at yet, returned to his table, and continued to scan the newspaper page by page.

As he got closer to the resolution of the UN General Assembly, on November 29, 1947, he almost forgot what he had come for and greedily devoured one issue after another, one article after another, as though the result of the fateful vote in the Assembly were still in the balance and each wavering vote could still tip the outcome one way or the other. He thought about Wald's view of Ben-Gurion's historic greatness and found pros and cons. At half past four he remembered his duties, returned the bound volumes of *Davar* to the librarian, gathered up his papers, forgot the pen, and ran, puffing and panting, to the bus stop, so as to report for duty at Gershom Wald's by five o'clock. As he was running to the bus stop he had an asthma attack, so he stopped running, pulled out the inhaler, and took a couple of deep breaths. He reached the stop less than a minute after the bus had left, and had to wait for the next one.

From the bus, he ran home with the last of his strength.

He reached the house with the stone-paved courtyard on Rabbi Elbaz Lane at twenty past five, sweaty and panting, and found Gershom Wald deep in one of the witty, sarcastic conversations he often had with his friends. Shmuel waited till the end of the conversation, and apologized for being late.

"As you know," the invalid said, "I don't run away. As it is written in our holy scriptures, 'Blessed are they that dwell in thy house.' Yes. And you, if I may inquire, have you been pursuing one of the roes and the hinds of the field? To judge by your expression, it would appear that the roe succeeded in eluding you."

"A glass of tea?" Shmuel asked. "A slice of cake, perhaps?"

"Sit down, young man. It is the bear's nature to walk slowly, and you have been running, just to please me. There was no reason for you to run. As the prophet Amos says in Bialik's poem, 'From my cattle I learned to walk slow.' I am pleased with you even when you are late. Dreamers are always late. And yet, as another poet says, 'Dreams do not speak in vain.'"

Then the old man spoke for a long time on the telephone again with one of his interlocutors, quoting, joking, needling, then quoting again. When the conversation had ended, he turned back to Shmuel and asked about his teachers at the university. They chatted for a quarter of an hour about a professor who had fallen in love with a young student whose parents were friends of the professor's. Wald loved gossip, and Shmuel was not averse to it either. Then Shmuel asked abruptly:

"Shealtiel Abravanel. Atalia's father. Your son's father-in-law. What can you tell me about him?"

Wald sank in thought. He stroked his cheek, then stared at his hand as if the answer to Shmuel's question were written on it. Finally he said:

"He, too, was a dreamer. He may not have studied Jesus or Jewish views of Jesus, but in his own way he also believed, like Jesus, in universal love, the love of all those created in the divine image for all others created in that image. Ask, and it shall be given you; seek, and ye shall find; knock, and it shall be opened unto you. For every one that asketh, receiveth; and he that seeketh, findeth; and to him that knocketh, it shall be opened; and so on. I, my dear, do not believe in the love of all for all. Love is a limited commodity. A man can love five men and women, maybe ten, sometimes fifteen. And even that, only rarely. But if a man comes to me and declares that he loves all the undeveloped countries, or that he loves Latin America, or that he loves the female sex —that is not love, it is rhetoric. Lip service. A slogan. We were not born to love more than a handful of people. Love is intimate, strange and full of contradictions. Sometimes we love someone out of self-love, out of egoism, out of fancy, out of physical desire, out of a wish to rule over the beloved and enslave him, or the opposite, out of some urge to be enslaved by the object of our love. In fact, love is very much like hatred: love and hatred are much closer than most people imagine. For instance, whether you love or hate someone, in either case you are always anxious to know where they are, whom they are with, how they are, if they are happy, what they are up to, what they are thinking, what they are afraid of. The heart is deceitful above all things, and desperately wicked: who can know it? Thus spake the prophet Jeremiah. Thomas Mann writes somewhere that hatred is simply love with a minus sign placed before it. Jealousy is the proof that love is like hatred, because in jealousy, love and hatred are mixed together. In the Song of Songs, in the selfsame verse, we are told that love is strong as death, jealousy is cruel as the grave. Atalia's father dreamed that Jews and Arabs were bound to love one another, if only the misunderstandings between them were removed. But he was mistaken. There is not and never has been any misunderstanding between Jews and Arabs. On the contrary. For several decades they have shared a complete and total understanding: the local Arabs cling to this land because it is their only land, and they have no other, and we cling to this land for the very same reason. They know that we can never give it up, and we know that they will never give it up. The mutual understanding is perfectly clear. There is no misunderstanding between us and there never has been. Atalia's father was one of those people who believe that every conflict is merely a misunderstanding: a spot of family counseling, a handful of group therapy, a drop or two of goodwill, and at once we shall all be brothers in heart and soul and the conflict will disappear. He was one of those people convinced that all that is required to resolve a conflict is for both parties to get to know each other, and immediately they will start to like each other. All we have to do is drink a glass of strong sweet coffee together and converse in a friendly fashion, and all at once the sun will rise and the foes will fall on each other's necks in tears, as in a Dostoyevsky novel. Whereas I say to you, my dear, that if two men love the same woman, or two peoples claim the same land, they can drink rivers of coffee together and those rivers will not quench their hatred, neither can the floods drown it. And I say this also to you, notwithstanding all that I have said so far: blessed are the dreamers, and cursed be the man who opens their eyes. True, the dreamers cannot save us, neither they nor their disciples, but without dreams and without dreamers the curse that lies upon us would be seven times heavier. Thanks to the dreamers, maybe we who are awake are a little less ossified and desperate than we would be without them. Now, please be kind enough to fetch me a glass of water, and don't forget to feed the fish in the aquarium. It would be interesting to know what exactly a fish sees when it looks through the glass at the room, the bookcases, the square of light at the window. Your Jesus was also a great dreamer, perhaps the greatest dreamer who ever lived. But his disciples were not dreamers. They were hungry for power, and in the end, like all those who hunger for power, they became shedders of blood. Please don't trouble to reply. I know what you are going to say, and I can recite the words of your reply from beginning to end and vice versa. Yes. We have spoken enough for today, and now I want to read Gogol quietly. I reread Gogol every two or three years. He knew almost everything there is to know about our nature. And he fell about laughing. But don't you read him. No, you should read Tolstoy. He suits you much better. Bring me the cushion from the sofa. Yes, that one. Thank you. Please place it behind my back. Thank you. There is no one like Tolstoy for dreamers."

The following morning Shmuel Ash managed to wake at nine again, and by half past ten he was in the reading room of the Newspaper Department, and had found the issue of *Davar* dated November 30, 1947. A bold headline proclaimed HEBREW STATE WILL SOON ARISE above the news that UN ASSEMBLY DECIDES BY 2/3 MAJORITY TO ESTABLISH FREE JEWISH STATE IN PALESTINE. Below this headline was written: "Palestine will be partitioned into two independent states, one Jewish and one Arab, linked by economic ties and a joint currency. Jerusalem and Bethlehem will be under international jurisdiction." Under this announcement came the details of the General Assembly vote, with a list of the states for and against and abstaining. As Shmuel read this report he felt a powerful emotion and his eyes filled, as if the events described in the paper had just occurred. He noticed that the man from yesterday, with no eyebrows, a goatee, and pince-nez, was eyeing him curiously. But when their eyes met, the stranger hurriedly looked down at his papers, and Shmuel, too, lowered his gaze.

When he had satisfied his hunger with three cheese sandwiches, a yogurt, and two cups of coffee in the cafeteria in the Kaplun Building, he returned to the reading room to find, in addition to Goatee, a young woman wearing a sarafan, with her hair done up in a coiled plait and looking like a pioneer from a kibbutz. She might have been a student or a young teacher. She looked vaguely familiar. He went across to her and, leaning over, asked in a whisper if she needed any help. The teacher gave a faint smile and whispered, "Thank you, I'm fine."

Shmuel apologized, in a whisper, for disturbing her, and returned to his table and the volumes of *Davar* from December 1947 and January 1948. Half an hour or so before his time ran out and he had to rush back to his post at Wald's, he came across another item relating to Shealtiel Abravanel. Like its predecessor, it was tucked away in the middle pages of the paper, on page 3, under a piece about a call by the Haganah militia to all owners of trucks and vans to register them at the offices of the National Guard. The date of the paper was December 21, 1947. The report stated that Comrade Shealtiel Abravanel had resigned the previous day from his positions on the Zionist Executive Committee and the Council of the Jewish Agency following differences of opinion with his colleagues in both bodies. It was also reported that Abravanel himself had declined to answer the *Davar* correspondent's question about the reasons for his resignation. A brief statement issued on his behalf merely stated that in Comrade Abravanel's view, the line adopted by Comrade David Ben-Gurion and others would inevitably lead to a bloody war between the two peoples living in this land, whose outcome was far from clear and which could be seen as a reckless gamble with the very life or death of the six hundred thousand Jews of Palestine. In Abravanel's opinion, the statement continued, the way was still open to a historic compromise between the two peoples inhabiting the land. The correspondent added that Shealtiel Abravanel, a well-known lawyer and an Arabist, had served on both bodies for close to nine years.

At half past three the man with the goatee rose, closed the volume he had been reading, gathered up his pile of Cyrillic notes, and left. Shmuel continued for a while to leaf through the issues of *Davar*, but he was really waiting for the young woman to leave so he could follow her out and possibly engage her in conversation. But as four o'clock arrived, and then a quarter past four, and the woman was still poring over her papers, Shmuel remembered his obligations and hurried on his way.

31

ONE MORNING, when the two of them were in the kitchen and Shmuel had poured coffee for Atalia and himself into two glasses, and sweetened and stirred it, he felt uncharacteristically bold and asked her:

"What do you do?"

"Right now I'm drinking coffee with a muddled young man."

"No, I mean what do you do in general?"

"I work."

"In an office? As a teacher?"

"I work in a private investigation agency. But it seems now that our roles are reversed, and you're investigating me."

Shmuel ignored the sarcasm. He was on fire with curiosity.

"And what do you investigate?"

"Infidelity, for instance. Adultery. Grounds for divorce proceedings."

"Like in a detective story? You trail people, with your collar turned up, wearing dark glasses — men who keep mistresses, married women who have lovers?"

"That too."

"And what else?"

"Mostly the actual financial situation of potential business partners. Or the sources of income of investors. Or the owner-ship of property whose landlords cannot be reached or live far away. Are you, by any chance, interested in discovering some-thing about someone?"

"Yes. You."

"Perhaps you should approach a rival agency and pay them to follow me."

"And what will they discover? Infidelity? Adultery? Hidden property?"

"You're living here like a recluse but your imagination seems to be running wild."

"Do you want to censor my imagination?"

"Not censor, no. But I wouldn't mind taking a peep. You're something of an orphan, even though your parents are still alive. There's an air of despair about you sometimes. And that's not what our Wald needs. He needs a witty, amusing conversation partner who will constantly disagree with him."

"Who are the people he argues with on the phone?"

"Two old acquaintances from before the Flood. Eccentrics like him. Stubborn. Opinionated. Extinct volcanoes. Retired people who sit at home all day honing arguments. People a bit like him. Only they are even lonelier than he is, because they can't afford to keep a Shmuel Ash to amuse them for a few hours every day. Though, in fact, you're not that amusing. Or maybe you're amus-ing precisely when you don't mean to be."

Shmuel looked down and examined his fingers, which were spread out in front of him on the kitchen table. They struck him as ugly, short and fat. Then he raised his eyes to Atalia and re-minded her shyly that she had twice agreed to go out with him for an evening. And both times it was she who had taken the ini-tiative.

"It's a well-known fact," Atalia said, "that women are some-times attracted to lost boys."

Then she smiled but did not look amused.

"There were three or four lodgers before you who kept Wald company and lived in your attic. They were all a bit eccentric and all loners. This job seems to attract young men who have lost their way. All of them tried more or less to flirt with me, even though they were twenty or twenty-five years younger. Like you. Loneliness causes all sorts of strange effects. Or maybe you all bring the strangeness with you."

"And how about you?" Shmuel asked, his eyes still fixed on his ugly hands. "What does loneliness do to you?"

"Me? You've been staring at me for several weeks now and you still don't know me. There seems to be something that interests or attracts you, but that something definitely isn't me. The world is full of men who are attracted to women but aren't really interested in them. Weak women sometimes give in to men like that. As it happens, I don't need a man. I live alone. I work, I read books, and I listen to music. Sometimes I have a visitor in the evening. Sometimes on another evening I have a different visitor. They come and they go. I'm self-sufficient. Otherwise I would be like Wald, and hire some unemployed young man to entertain me for six hours a day."

"And when you're alone in your room?"

"I live there. That's enough for me."

"In that case, why did you suggest not once but twice that we go out together?"

"Okay," said Atalia, standing up and taking the two empty coffee glasses to the sink, washing them, and setting them upside down on the drainer. "Maybe we'll go out together this evening. Not this evening. Tonight. Or rather, in the early hours of the morning. I'll give you a present—a little nighttime adventure. Can you hide?"

"No," said Shmuel sheepishly. "Not at all."

"We can watch the moon over Mount Zion, facing the walls of

the Old City," Atalia said, leaning against the kitchen doorpost, left hip slightly raised and five fingers resting on it. A faint scent of violets came from her, along with a hint of shampoo.

"The moon isn't full tonight," Shmuel said.

"So we'll watch a defective moon. Almost everything in the world is defective. Be ready in the kitchen at three a.m. If you can get up that early. We'll climb Mount Zion and watch the sunrise together over the Mountains of Moab. Provided it's not cloudy. I've got a couple, both well educated, both quite well known in Jerusalem, both married but not to each other, and they plan to meet tonight to watch the sunrise from the top of Mount Zion. Don't ask how I know. I need to photograph them together at sunrise without them noticing me. If we're lucky, we'll catch them embracing. You'll be my cover."

From the passage, when Shmuel could no longer see her, she added:

"And dress warmly. These winter nights are cold."

Shmuel sat in the kitchen for another twenty minutes, staring at his fingertips. He made up his mind to cut his fingernails today, and trim his nose hair, and take a shower this evening, though he had showered that morning. He must not forget to put a new inhaler in his pocket; the present one was almost empty. He thought about the fact that he had intended to ask Atalia about her father and perhaps also about her husband, but for some reason he had felt that such questions would make her angry and distance her from him. Distance her? he said to himself. Distance her how? Distance her where? As if we were ever close. She said herself that she's only taking me on this nocturnal excursion as her cover. She's bound to feel uncomfortable wandering alone around Mount Zion before sunrise. And I'm not even sure. Does she like me? A little bit? Or is she just sorry for me? Is she treating me exactly the same way she treated the three or four previous lodgers? Or maybe she's just playing with me, like the child she never had. And all of a sudden, in an instant, all these questions lost their meaning, and instead a wave of joy swept through him and filled his chest and made the blood rush in his veins. For the first time in several months, the sharp pain caused by Yardena's leaving him and marrying Nesher Sharshevsky felt duller and weaker, and he felt calm, resilient, even virile. He said aloud to himself:

"Yes. At three a.m."

He left the kitchen, passed Atalia's closed door, climbed up to his attic, and stood for a while at the window. Then he dusted his beard and forehead with talcum powder, put on his duffel coat, picked up the stick with its predatory fox's head, and went out to eat goulash soup at the Hungarian restaurant on King George Street. But as he was eating the soup, dipping pieces of white bread in it, he was struck by panic—he could not remember whether Atalia had told him to wait for her at three a.m. in his room, or in the kitchen, or in the passage, or maybe she had told him to knock on her door at three? Worse still, he did not know if they were supposed to leave the house at three or to be at Mount Zion by three, to watch the defective moon, to wait for sunrise, and to trail the pair of clandestine lovers.

32

THAT NIGHT, after he had given Gershom Wald his porridge and had waited for him to finish eating it, then had eaten the leftover porridge himself, returned to the kitchen and washed the spoon and bowl, fed the goldfish, barred the library shutters, and gone up to his room, Shmuel did not get into bed. He had no alarm clock, and he knew that if he fell asleep there was no chance he would wake up in time for his nocturnal tryst. So he decided to stay awake, and to go down at half past two to wait for Atalia in the kitchen. He switched on his desk lamp, lit the paraffin heater, and waited for the flame to settle and for a blue-violet flower to appear in the concave metal panel at the back. Then he sat down at his desk and stared for a while at the darkness outside. The screaming of cats in heat in one of the neighboring yards pierced the stillness of the night. The night was clear, but the outlines of the tall cypresses hid the starry sky and the defective moon. Shmuel opened a book, then another, leafed through them, looked at his notes, and crossed out an entire paragraph from two days earlier because it seemed too literary. Then he started to write, and because his fountain pen was out of ink, he scrounged around in the drawer and found an old pen that had probably belonged to one of the previous lodgers. It was a splendid, rather heavy pen, with a gold stripe running its full length. It felt warm and pleasant in his fingers. Shmuel stroked the pen, thrust it into his curly mane and scratched himself with it, then began to write:

Rabbi Judah Arieh de Modena, who lived in Venice from the late sixteenth almost to the middle of the seventeenth century, was born into a wealthy family of bankers and merchants. He studied Judaism with various teachers, but also studied secular subjects. As he himself put it: "I also learned to play music, to sing, to dance, and a little Latin." He displayed an interest in theater and music, and wrote some comedies and put on performances and concerts. Not only Jews but Christians, too, flocked to hear him preach, including ordinary people, nobles, and religious dignitaries. The tragedy of Rabbi Judah Arieh de Modena's life was his addiction to games of chance, which ruined him and drove him to penury. His last years were spent in poverty and sickness.

He often debated with Christian scholars and priests, and at the end of his life he composed a work of systematic polemics against Christianity, under the title *Shield and Sword* (a "shield" against Christian attacks on Jews, and a "sword" in the hands of the Jews to prove the folly of the Christian faith). This work differed from all his previous writings in that it contained no apologetic undertone nor any abuse or invective against Christianity, but a consistent claim to make use of pure reason to substantiate the truth of the Jewish faith and to expose the inner contradictions in the Christian faith. To this end he read the New Testament in a way that today, so Shmuel wrote in his notebook, would be called critical. Rabbi Judah Arieh died having completed only five of the nine chapters he had intended to include in his *Shield and Sword*. Rabbi Judah Arieh saw Jesus as a Pharisaic Jew in every respect, a Pharisee who disagreed with his masters only in some marginal matters of religious law, but who did not rebel against the central tenets of the Jewish faith. It never occurred to Jesus, Rabbi Judah Arieh stressed, to represent himself as divine. Nowhere in the New Testament does he claim divine status. "In the entire Gospel you will not find him ever saying of himself that he was God but only . . . a man, and less than any other man: 'But I am a worm, and no man; a reproach of men, and despised of the people.'" On the contrary, in tens of places in the Gospels he calls himself a man. Moreover, "when he washed Peter's feet (John 13:4f.) he said of himself, 'The Son of man came not to be ministered unto, but to minister.'" And so Jesus explicitly calls himself a son of man.

Rabbi Judah Arieh also writes—and Shmuel copied the words with increasing wakefulness and joy, all his tiredness having left him, his mind overflowing to the point that he almost forgot the nocturnal tryst awaiting him: "Know that at that time among the Jews there were several sects, all of them acknowledging the law of Moses but divided over its interpretation and its commandments. There were the Pharisees and the scribes, that is our sages from whom issued the Mishnah, and besides them the Sadducees and the Boethusians, the Essenes and some more in addition . . . and out of all these the Nazarene chose . . . and followed the sect of the Pharisees, our Rabbis . . . and this is seen clearly in the Gospel when he says to his disciples: 'The scribes and the Pharisees sit in Moses' seat: all therefore whatsoever they bid you observe, that observe and do; but do not ye after their works' (Matthew 23:2–3). We find that Jesus acknowledges not only the written law but [also] the oral law: 'Think not that I come to destroy the law, but to fulfill [the law]' (Matthew 5:17). And he also says: 'Till heaven and earth pass, one jot or tittle shall in no wise pass from the law' (Matthew 5:18)." And, in what follows, Rabbi Judah Arieh de Modena explains how and why "by stratagems" Jesus described himself on certain occasions as the Son of God, for didactic purposes, so that the masses would follow him, and not because he saw himself as the offspring of God. All the rest, in the words of Rabbi Judah Arieh, is merely "vague inventions which those who were drawn to him introduced sometime after his death, things which [could] not occur and still do not occur to any simple, unbiased human mind in the world."

Beneath these words, half an hour or so after midnight, in a state of great excitement, Shmuel Ash wrote in his notebook:

Judas Iscariot was the founder of the Christian religion. He was a well-to-do man from Judea, unlike the other disciples, who were simple fishermen and tillers of the soil from remote villages in Galilee. The priests in Jerusalem had heard strange rumors about some eccentric wonderworker from Galilee who was attracting a following here and there in godforsaken villages and towns on the shores of the Sea of Galilee by means of all kinds of rustic miracles, just like dozens of other self-professed prophets, seers, and wonderworkers, most of whom were charlatans or madmen or both. This Galilean, however, was attracting a few more followers than the others, and his fame was spreading. Therefore the priests in Jerusalem decided to select Judas Iscariot—Judah of Kerioth, a well-to-do, sober, intelligent man, learned in the written and the oral law, and close to the Pharisees and the priests—and send him to infiltrate the group of believers who followed the young Galilean from village to village, to pretend to be one of them, and to report to the priests in Jerusalem on the character of the eccentric and on whether he presented any particular danger. After all, the visionary from Galilee worked all his provincial miracles in remote places, before an audience of ignorant villagers, who were ready to believe in all sorts of magicians, wizards, and tricksters. So Judas Iscariot dressed himself in shabby, threadbare clothes, went to Galilee, sought out and found Jesus and his band, and attached himself to them. He quickly succeeded in winning the affection of the members of the sect, the motley company of ragamuffins who followed the prophet from village to village. Judas also gained the affection of Jesus himself. By means of his sharp mind, and by pretending to be a fervent believer, he swiftly became one of Jesus' close companions, his confidant, one of the inner circle of his followers, the treasurer for this band of paupers, the twelfth apostle, the only one among them who was not a Galilean, and who was not a poor peasant or fisherman.

At this point, however, the story takes a surprising turn. The man who had been sent by the priests in Jerusalem, to spy on the Galilean visionary and his adherents and to unmask them, turned into a fervent believer. Jesus' humanity, the warm, infectious love that he radiated all around him, that mixture of simplicity, humility, endearing humor, and intimacy with everyone—together with the moral insight, the elevated vision, the poignant beauty of his parables, and the charm of his glorious gospel—converted the rational, sober skeptic from the town of Kerioth into a follower committed with all his being to the savior and his teaching. Judas Iscariot became the outstanding and devoted disciple of the man from Nazareth. Did this happen overnight, or was it the result of a long process of rebirth? We cannot know the answer, Shmuel wrote, and the question has no particular importance. Judah of Kerioth became Judas the Christian. The most enthusiastic of all the apostles. More than that: he was the first man who believed with total faith in Jesus' divinity. He believed that Jesus was all-powerful. He believed that very soon the eyes of all men, from sea to sea, would be opened, that they would see the light, and that redemption would come to the world. But for this to happen, Judas thought, being a man of the world and understanding a great deal about public relations, it was necessary for Jesus to leave Galilee and go to Jerusalem. He had to perform in Jerusalem, in the presence of the whole nation and before the entire world, a miracle such as had never been seen since the day God created heaven and earth. Jesus, who had walked on the water of the Sea of Galilee; Jesus, who had brought the dead girl and Lazarus back from the dead; Jesus, who had turned water into wine and driven out demons and healed the sick by the touch of his hand or even by the touch of the hem of his garment, had to be crucified in the sight of all Jerusalem. And in the sight of all Jerusalem he would drag himself down from the cross and stand whole and healthy at the foot of the cross. The whole world— priests and simple people, Romans, Idumeans, and Hellenizers, Pharisees, Sadducees, and Essenes, Samaritans, rich and poor, hundreds of thousands of pilgrims who had come to Jerusalem from all over the land and from the neighboring countries for the feast of Passover—would fall to their knees to dust themselves with the dust of his feet. And so the Kingdom of Heaven would begin. In Jerusalem. In the sight of the people and the world. And moreover, on the Friday before the Passover, the greatest of all the gatherings of the Jewish people, Shmuel wrote in his notebook.

But Jesus hesitated about accepting Judas' advice and going to Jerusalem. Deep down in his child's heart a worm of doubt had been gnawing: Am I the man? Am I really the man? Maybe I am not up to the task. What if the voices are leading me astray? And what if my Father in heaven is only testing me? Playing with me? Using me for some purpose whose secret is hidden from me? Suppose what he had managed to do here he was unable to do in Jerusalem, so down-to-earth, so secular, so assimilated, so Hellenized, Jerusalem of little faith, which had already seen and heard everything and was not impressed by anything? Perhaps Jesus himself was waiting for some sign from above, some revelation or illumination, some divine answer to his doubts: Am I the man?

Judas was relentless: You are the man. You are the Savior. You are the Son of God. You are God. You are destined to save all men. Heaven has laid this charge upon you, to go to Jerusalem and to work your wonders there. You will perform the greatest miracle of all in Jerusalem, you will come down from the cross safe and sound, and the whole of Jerusalem will fall at your feet. Rome itself will fall at your feet. The day of your crucifixion will be the day of the redemption of the world. This is the last trial to which your Father in heaven is subjecting you, and you will endure it because you are our Savior. After this trial the age of the redemption of mankind will commence. On that day the Kingdom of Heaven will begin.

After many tribulations Jesus went up to Jerusalem with his disciples. But there he was again beset by doubts. And not only by doubts but by the fear of death pure and simple, like any mortal man. Human, all too human fear of death filled his heart. "And he was affrighted in his spirit," "And the pangs of death came upon him," "Then he began to curse and to swear, saying, 'My soul is exceeding sorrowful unto death.'"

"If thou be willing," Jesus prayed to God in Jerusalem at the time of the Last Supper, "remove this cup from me." But Judas strengthened and encouraged his spirit: would he who walked on water and turned water into wine and healed lepers and drove out demons and raised the dead be unable to come down from the cross and so make the whole world believe in his divinity? And because Jesus continued to fear and to doubt, Judas Iscariot took it upon himself to manage the crucifixion. It was not an easy thing to do. The Romans took no interest in Jesus, because the land was full of prophets and wonderworkers and crazy dreamers like him. It was not easy for Judas to persuade his priestly colleagues to bring Jesus to trial: they did not consider him any more dangerous than dozens of his doubles in Galilee and other out-of-the-way regions. Judas Iscariot had to pull strings, to exploit his connections among the Pharisees and the priests, to win over hearts and minds, perhaps to pay some bribes, to arrange for Jesus to be crucified between two petty criminals on the eve of the sacred festival. As for the thirty pieces of silver, they were invented by Jew-haters in later generations. Or maybe Judas himself invented them so as to complete the story. For what did a well-to-do estate owner from the town of Kerioth need with thirty pieces of silver? In those days thirty pieces of silver was no more than the price of a single slave of medium quality. And who would have paid so much as three pieces of silver for the betrayal of a man whom everyone knew? A man who never tried for a single moment to hide, or to conceal his identity?

Judas Iscariot was therefore the author, the impresario, the stage manager, and the director of the spectacle of the crucifixion. In this his detractors and calumniators down the ages were right, perhaps more right than they imagined. Even when Jesus was dying in terrible torment on the cross, hanging hour after hour in the blazing sun, the blood flowing from all his wounds, and the flies swarming on them, even when they fed him vinegar, Judas' faith did not waver for an instant: it was surely coming. The crucified God would arise and shake himself free of the nails and descend from the cross and say to all the people falling on their faces in astonishment: love one another.

And what of Jesus himself? Even in the moments when he was dying on the cross? At the ninth hour, when the crowd was mocking him with cries of "Save thyself if thou canst and come down from the cross," the doubt still nagged: Am I really the man? And yet he may still have tried in his last moments to hold on to Judas' promise. With the last of his strength he pulled on his hands, which were fixed with nails to the cross, and he pulled on his nailed feet, suffering torments as he pulled, crying out with pain, calling out to his Father in heaven as he pulled, and he died with the words of the psalm on his lips, "*Eli, Eli, lama sabachthani?*" —that is, "My God, my God, why hast thou forsaken me?" Such words could only have come from the lips of a dying man who had believed, or who half believed, that God would indeed help him to pull out the nails, to work the miracle, and to descend whole from the cross. And with these words he died from loss of blood like a man, like flesh and blood.

And Judas, the meaning and purpose of whose life were shattered before his horrified eyes; Judas, who realized that he had brought about with his own hands the death of the man he loved and adored, went away and hanged himself. So died, Shmuel wrote in his notebook, the first Christian. The last Christian. The only Christian.

33

SHMUEL SHOOK HIMSELF and glanced at his watch. Did Atalia say that he should be in the kitchen at three a.m.? Or knock at her door? Or maybe she meant that by three they should be on their way together to Mount Zion? It was twenty past three, and he frantically powdered his forehead, face, and beard with baby talc, quickly struggled into his shabby student coat, put his *shapka* on his head, wrapped a prickly old woolen scarf around his neck, decided against the stick with the fox-head handle, and rushed down the stairs without stopping to close his door behind him.

When he reached the bottom of the stairs, he heard Gershom Wald's voice calling to him. He had almost forgotten that the old man was awake at night, sitting up in his library.

"Young man, step in here for a moment. Just for a moment."

Atalia came out of her room wearing a winter overcoat and a black knitted scarf over her head which made her look like a middle-aged widow. Shmuel caressed with his eyes the deeply etched furrow that descended from her nose to the center of her upper lip. In his dreams he would gently caress this furrow with his tongue.

"Go to him. But don't stay. We're late."

Wald was not sitting at his desk; he was lying on his wicker couch, his legs covered with the plaid rug. He was twisted, hunchbacked, his face ugly but striking, his chin jutting, his Einstein mustache covering a hint of an ironic smile half hovering on his lips, his glossy silver hair down to his shoulders. He was holding an open book with both hands and had another book lying face-down on his knees. At the sight of Shmuel in the doorway Gershom Wald said:

"By night on my bed I sought her whom my soul loveth."

And he added:

"Listen. Don't fall in love with her."

And then he said:

"It's too late."

And he also said:

"Go. She's waiting for you. I'm going to lose you too."

It was after half past three when Shmuel and Atalia walked into the outer darkness. The sky was cloudless. Large stars sparkled in it, ringed with a halo of milky mist, looking just like van Gogh's stars. The paving stones in the yard were damp from the rain that had fallen in the early evening. The black cypresses waved to and fro in silent devotion in the breeze blowing from the west, from the ruins of the Arab village of Sheikh Badr. The air was clear and cold; its sharpness seared the lungs and cast a lucid wakefulness over Shmuel.

He tried, as usual, to walk half a step behind Atalia so as to be able to watch her movement from the back. But she threaded her arm through his and hurried him on:

"Could you walk a little faster? You're always rushing, and just when we need to hurry you choose to dawdle. Like a sleepwalker. Can't you do anything briskly?"

"Yes. No. Sometimes," Shmuel said.

And then he added:

"At one time I used to wander around the streets on my own at this time of night. Not long ago. When Yardena left me and went—"

"I know. Nesher Sharshevsky. The expert on rainwater capture."

She did not say this mockingly but sadly, almost sympathetically. Shmuel squeezed her arm as a sign of gratitude.

There was no one in the streets. Here and there, a hungry cat ran across their path. Here and there, they saw dustbins that had been overturned by the wind, their contents scattered on the pavement. Jerusalem stood silent and attentive in the darkness of the small hours. As if at any moment something might happen. As if the buildings wrapped in shadow, the pine trees rustling in the gardens, the damp, low stone walls, the rows of parked cars, were all awake, standing and waiting. Within the deep silence some strange restlessness was seething. The city was only pretending to sleep; in reality it was fully alert, suppressing an inner trembling.

"The couple we are going to trail?" Shmuel began.

"Don't talk now."

Shmuel stopped talking at once. They crossed Keren Hakayemet Street, passed the semicircular Jewish Agency building, went a little way down the slope of King George Street, turned into George Washington Street, passed behind the YMCA building, and crossed again toward the King David Hotel, where a tall uniformed doorman stood outside the revolving door stamping his feet to keep warm. From there they walked downhill toward the Montefiore Windmill and the buildings of Mishkenot Sha'ananim. As they went down the flight of steps in Yemin Moshe they were joined by a stray mongrel that sniffed at the hem of Atalia's dress and let out a whimper. Shmuel paused for a moment, bent down, and quickly stroked the dog twice. It licked his hand and gave another low whimper, submissive and imploring. It started to follow them, with lowered head, wagging its tail and pleading for another demonstration of affection.

In the late fifties and early sixties, Yemin Moshe was still a slum with rows of stone houses, some with tiled roofs, others with flat roofs. In the little courtyards there were rainwater cisterns from the Ottoman era, each with an iron cover. Here and there in rusty tins grew geraniums, edible greens, and culinary herbs. All the houses stood dark and shuttered. No light shone in any of the barred windows. Only a pale streetlamp shed flakes of meager yellow light on the steps. Apart from the dog that had joined them and walked some way behind with its tail tucked between its legs, there was not a living soul to be seen. Shmuel and Atalia went down to the main road that wound its way along the Valley of Hinnom, and Shmuel whispered:

"This is Gehenna. We're in hell!"

"We're used to that, aren't we?" Atalia replied.

They walked along the rusty barbed wire that blocked the continuation of the road at the foot of the walls of the Old City and that marked the border of the mine-strewn no man's land that divided Israeli from Jordanian Jerusalem. Now they began to climb the winding path that snaked its way up to the summit of Mount Zion. The mount itself was a sort of finger of Israeli territory surrounded on three sides by Jordanian territory. Here the dog stopped, barked forlornly, beat the pavement with its front paws, decided that it was doomed to failure, then turned back with flattened ears, its mouth open in a soundless wail, belly almost scraping the ground. The cold penetrated Shmuel's duffel coat and dug sharp talons into his back and shoulders. He was shivering. Atalia, in her sensible shoes, was striding briskly ahead, and he was being dragged along on the narrow path, trying hard not to lag behind. But Atalia was more energetic than he and a widening gap opened between them, so that Shmuel was terrified of losing her, of losing his way in these forsaken places that abutted no man's land, exposed to the enemy gun posts. A solitary cricket sawed away in the darkness, and a chorus of frogs answered it from a pool amid the clefts of the rock. A night bird disturbed from its roost, perhaps a barn owl, suddenly passed low over their heads, beat its wings three or four times, and vanished. The dark shadow of the walls of the Old City stretched menacingly on their left all along the way. From the deserted Hinnom Valley burst a long, heartrending jackal's howl, answered immediately from all sides by a chorus of jackals whose voices rent the silence of the night. Dogs started to bark, and other dogs replied from far away, from the direction of Abu Tor. Shmuel was about to say something but thought better of it. Tiredness descended on him and he was short of breath from the winding climb. He feared an impending attack of asthma. The coarse woolen scarf pricked his neck. But the attack did not materialize.

When they reached the summit, at the entrance to the structure known as David's Tomb—there was an ancient coffin there, draped in a pall, where the faithful believed the bones of King David lay—a reservist stood before them, a man in his mid-forties, heavyset and short, wearing a coarse military greatcoat with its collar turned up and a stocking cap rolled down to protect his ears from the cold. The soldier stood with his legs apart, leaning on an old Czech rifle. He was smoking the dog end of a cigarette, and when he saw Shmuel and Atalia he spoke without removing it:

"Closed. No entry."

"Why?" Atalia laughed. The soldier raised the cap slightly from one ear and replied:

"Closed by order, lady. No entry."

"But we had no intention of going inside," Atalia said, pulling Shmuel by the arm.

Shmuel lingered and asked the soldier:

"When does your watch finish?"

"Another half hour," the soldier said, the cigarette almost burning his lips. And he added inconsequentially:

"Nobody understands anything."

Atalia turned and, without a word, took a few steps forward, to the iron railing that looked eastward from the summit of the mount toward no man's land. Shmuel lingered by the soldier as the fire touched his lips. The man spat the cigarette butt in a wide arc—a firefly soared to the height of his head, curved, fell to the ground, and went on glowing, refusing to die. Shmuel turned away and followed Atalia. She inspected the place as though sniffing the air, moved away to a corner of the structure, and hid among the deep shadows under the stone arch that concealed the starry sky and the swath of fine mist now enfolding the whole mount. Shmuel came and stood close to her, hesitated for a moment, then placed his arm around her shoulders. She did not push him away. Finally she broke her silence.

"We've got between half an hour and an hour," she said.

Then she whispered:

"Now, if you really must, you can talk. But only in a whisper."

"You see. Atalia. It's like this."

"Like what?"

"You and I have been living under the same roof for more than two months, nearly."

"What are you trying to tell me?"

"And we've been out together twice. Three times, if you count tonight."

"What are you trying to tell me?"

"I'm not trying to tell you anything. I'm asking."

"The answer is: not yet. Perhaps with time. Perhaps never."

And she added:

"Sometimes you're quite touching, sometimes you're a bore."

Close to six o'clock, the first glow appeared over the Mountains of Moab to the east. The outlines of the mountains became clearer, the sky paled, and the stars began to fade. The couple were probably not coming to watch the sunrise. Or perhaps there never was a couple. Perhaps Atalia had invented them. The middle-aged soldier who had been standing smoking at the entrance to King David's Tomb had vanished. No doubt he had finished his watch, smoked a last cigarette, and gone off to sleep fully dressed in his greatcoat and woolen cap in a basement somewhere. A piercing cold easterly wind blew, stopped, then blew again. Atalia let Shmuel wait with her for a few more minutes. Then she told him to go home.

"What about you?"

"I'm staying here for a bit. After that, I'm going to work," she said. Then she took his freezing fingers in her hand, put two of them into her mouth, and kept them there for a short while. Suddenly she said:

"We'll see." With that, she parted from him.

It was half past seven when Shmuel arrived, hungry, thirsty, and frozen, at the house on Rabbi Elbaz Lane. He made for the kitchen and ate four thick slices of bread spread with cream cheese, drank two glasses of hot tea, went up to his room, poured himself a little vodka, drained the glass in one, undressed, fell asleep, and slept till midday. Then he got up, showered, and went to his Hungarian restaurant. This time he took the splendid walking stick with the carved fox's head showing its predatory teeth as if to threaten all of Jerusalem.

At the Hungarian restaurant he found that his usual table was taken. A middle-aged couple, both wearing glasses and overcoats, were sitting eating, not goulash soup but sausages, fried eggs, and potatoes. A glass of red wine stood before each of them, and Shmuel had the impression that they were in a good mood. What was the matter? What had happened? Why were they so cheerful? Had little Yossi Siton, who had been run over chasing his ball on the Gaza Road a few days earlier, suddenly come back to life?

He hesitated for a moment or two in the doorway, wondering whether to leave, but his hunger got the better of him and he sat down at another table, as far as possible from the intrusive couple. The proprietor of the restaurant, its only waiter, was wearing a white apron which was none too clean, and was badly shaved. He came up to Shmuel after ten minutes or so and, without comment, placed before him on the table the goulash soup with several slices of white bread. For dessert he brought a bowl of apple compote. And since Shmuel had not slept all night, he remained slumped where he was at the end of the meal for half an hour, dozing. The sight of the sunrise from the top of Mount Zion seemed like a dream to him now. In fact, not only the sight of the sunrise but all the previous weeks seemed to him like a dream where you dream that you are awake, then wake up and find that you were right.

34

My dear brother,

This evening there was a light fall of snow here in Rome, but it melted before it could reach the pavements and statues. Pity. I've still never seen Rome under the snow. Not that I wander round the city. I've been here for three and a half years and I've still seen nothing. All day long I study or spend time at the lab, in the evenings I work as an assistant at a pharmacy, and at night—four hours at the telegraph office. The money I get from these two jobs is scarcely enough to pay for my course fees, the room I share with a neurotic student from Belgium, and a simple meal twice a day, of bread, milk, vegetables, spaghetti or rice, and a cup of black coffee.

I know your life hasn't been easy since our dad lost his case against that scoundrel and the firm went into liquidation. I know this even though you hardly ever write to me. In the past couple of months you've sent me just two short letters —all you said was that you've given up studying at university and that you've found employment and lodgings in an old Jerusalem house. You also wrote me a couple of lines about Yardena's marriage. The word "loneliness" never appears in your letters, but every word you write has a smell of loneliness about it. Even as a child you were always a child apart: immersed in your stamp collection or spending hours up on the roof, sitting and dreaming. For years I've been trying to talk to you about yourself, but you always change the subject and talk about Ben-Gurion or the Crusades. No, you don't talk: you lecture. I was hoping that Yardena would get you to come out of your shell. But the shell is part of you.

I imagine your life in the basement of some dark, dilapidated Jerusalem house, with your cripple, who's probably a sickly, capricious fusspot, a confused old man who sends you off all day long on all sorts of errands, to buy stamps or a newspaper or tobacco for his pipe, and you wait on him most of the day (from morning till evening? Or at night too?), and he or his family pay you a pittance because they've been good enough to let you live in their house. I hope at least you're warm enough in the Jerusalem winter?

Until a few weeks ago I was hoping you would marry Yardena, though to be perfectly honest I found her rather frightening. Once, two years ago, when Dad could still afford to pay for me to come home for a holiday, I came to visit you in Jerusalem—remember?—and it was there, in your room in Tel Arza, that I met her. She seemed to me as different from you as two people can be. Not necessarily in a bad way. You are as you are, and she was as she is: vivacious, loud, and almost childlike. You would sit there studying and she would sit opposite you, playing on a mouth organ that she actually had no idea how to play. You, as usual, were tired by nine o'clock and wanted to go to bed, and she would drag you, practically by force, to go out into town, to the cinema, to cafés, to visit friends. Despite everything I thought you suited each other quite well. I thought she might gradually draw another Mooly out of you, someone less inhibited, more lively, even hedonistic. Perhaps.

Why did you two split up? What do you mean, "She decided to go back to her previous boyfriend and marry him"? What happened? Did you quarrel? Did you cheat on her? Did Yardena want the two of you to live together and you refused? Did she want to marry you? Or maybe you wanted to break it off and go back to your perpetual loneliness? Did she drop out of university too? Actually, what do I care what she did? What I care about is that you went back to your desert island. And if you have decided to ruin your academic career with your own hands, just when you were close to getting your MA, with distinction, and had already started working toward your doctorate—you could have gone back to Haifa, for instance, you could have found a suitable job, been near our parents, made new friends or revived old friendships. As Yardena did.

I remember, Mooly, when you were eleven and I was sixteen, how we once went on our own to spend a day in Tel Aviv. Mum gave me some money and said, Enjoy yourselves. At that time Dad had a decent income from the firm. He encouraged us too: Go, he said. Compared to Tel Aviv, our Haifa is just a sleepy village. You can get the last bus back tonight. Or don't come back. Stay the night in Tel Aviv with your Auntie Edith. I'll phone her. She'll be happy to put you up.

I remember you following me onto the bus from Hadar to the station, in khaki shorts, with your usual pocketknife hanging from your belt, wearing sandals and a khaki hat that Mum made you wear because of the sun. I remember your short shadow falling on the walls, because you always walked close to the wall. Such a pale, silent, withdrawn child. When I asked you if you preferred to go to Tel Aviv by bus or by train, you said, What difference does it make? And then you said, Whatever you like. You were deep in your thoughts. Not thoughts, apparently, but one stubborn thought that you didn't want to share with me. You didn't want to share it with anyone.

I remember saying to you on the way (in the end we took the train) that you ought to be more enthusiastic: a day out in Tel Aviv, we had loads of money, we were rich, there were a thousand things we could do, what did you prefer? The zoo? The seaside? A boat trip on the River Yarkon? A visit to the port? To every suggestion I made, you replied, Yes. Lovely. When I pressed you to decide, at least to decide what we should do first, you said to me, It doesn't matter. And suddenly you started lecturing me about the system of reserve duty in the Swiss army, a system that we had copied.

That sadness of yours. Even though at times you could talk and talk, tirelessly, make whole speeches, give lectures, with a sort of passionate joyfulness, but always lectures and speeches. Never a conversation. You never listened.

I'm different from you. I always have two or three girl-friends. In Haifa I had a boyfriend. And after him I had an-other one. Aharon. You remember him. The scout leader. And here in Rome I've got someone too. A boy who was born and raised in Milan, a literary translator from Spanish to Italian, Emilio, he's not a boy actually but a divorced man of thirty-eight, so he's seven or eight years older than me. He's got a ten-year-old daughter, Sofia, but we call her Sonia, who is closer to me now than she is to her own mother. Her mother lives in Bologna and doesn't have much of a relationship with her. Sonia calls me Mari instead of Miri. Only Emilio insists on calling me by my proper name, Miri. Cara Miri. He strokes my neck with one hand and Sonia's with the other. As though making a link between us.

We only manage to meet on weekends because I have to study, and as I told you, I work at two jobs. Emilio works from home whenever it suits him, mostly early in the morning. He would be happy for us to see each other every day, and Sonia would love it if I went to live with them. But they live on the other side of Rome, a long way from the university, and a long way from the pharmacy and the telegraph office. And I am so busy with my classes and at the lab and with my two jobs. I only go to Emilio's on Saturday evening, and I stay with him and little Sonia until Sunday evening. On Sundays I always get up at four o'clock in the morning and cook for the two of them for the whole week. Then the three of us go out to the park near his house or for a short boat trip on the river or, when the weather is good enough, we take a bus out of town and have a picnic in a pine forest, in the shade of some ancient ruin.

On Sunday evening Emilio and Sonia accompany me to my evening job at the pharmacy and we say goodbye to each other with a long hug. During the week we talk on the phone almost every evening. I haven't got a phone in my room, but the pharmacist allows me to use his phone.

Emilio knows that I don't have any money and that I work beyond my strength. He also knows why the parents stopped paying for me to study. He knows well that I have to live from hand to mouth. And though he doesn't earn much from translating, he's offered several times to help me with a small financial contribution. I refused and refused again and got a little annoyed with him. Why I said no I don't understand. Why I was annoyed I understand even less. He was offended that I refused, apparently, but he didn't express it in words. Just like you. I love his generosity. I always think that generosity is the most attractive quality in a man, the most manly quality. And how about you, Mooly, couldn't you get some translating work instead, like Emilio, or give private lessons? Mum, Dad, and I are all bitterly disappointed that you've dropped out of university. I've always imagined you as a student, an academic, a researcher, a scholar, a lecturer, maybe someday a famous professor. Why did you give all that up? What made you suddenly turn your back on it? Was it really just because of Dad's bankruptcy?

If only I had some money, I'd take a short break right now and come to Israel for two or three weeks, come and see you in Jerusalem, drag you out of that grave you've dug for yourself, shake you with all my strength, find you a job, and force you to go back to university. After all, you've only missed one semester. There's still time to catch up. On that trip to Tel Aviv, when you were eleven and I was sixteen, we wandered the streets all day, past shop windows that we barely looked at, dripping with sweat from the heat and humidity, drank soda pop twice, ate ice cream twice, went to the cinema in the middle of a black-and-white French film, and returned to Haifa long before the last bus. We didn't stay with Auntie Edith. I remember asking you what you really wanted, Mooly, and you said you wanted to know what the point was. That was our only conversation that day. We may have talked about other things, like the soda pop and the ice cream, for instance, but I can only remember that sentence of yours: I want to discover what the point is. Maybe the time has finally come, Mooly, for you to stop looking for the truth which doesn't exist and start living your life.

Is there something inside you that wants to be punished? But what exactly are you punishing yourself for? Write to me. Don't just write five or six lines: "I'm fine everything's fine it's winter in Jerusalem I'm doing easy work for a few hours a day and I spend the rest of the time reading and wandering around the town." That's more or less all you said to me in your last letter. Write me a real letter. Write to me soon.

Miri

35

Oɴ ᴛʜᴇ ᴍᴏʀɴɪɴɢ of a spring-like winter's day in Jerusalem, a day drenched in blue and soaked in smells of pine resin and damp earth, a day wrapped in birdsong, Shmuel Ash got up early, soon after nine o'clock, showered, sprinkled baby talc on his beard and forehead, went down to the kitchen to drink some coffee and eat four slices of bread with strawberry jam, put on his coat, left behind his cap and the stick with the fox-head handle, and took two buses to the State Archives. He climbed the steps impatiently, at an angle, his disheveled, overgrown head thrust energetically forward, preceding his trunk and legs, hurried across the entrance hall, and looked for signs of life. At the information desk he found a young, fair-haired woman, wearing bold red lipstick and with her blouse generously unbuttoned. She looked up at him, recoiled a little at his caveman appearance, and inquired how she might help him. Shmuel, panting from the exertion of running up the steps, began by reminding her that today was definitely the loveliest day of the year. Then he said that it was a sin to sit in an office on a day like this. One should get out of town, go to the hills, the valleys, the woods. When she said he was right, he suggested shyly that they should go out together. Right away. Then he asked whether, and if so where, he could sit for a few hours and look through the minutes of the Zionist Executive Committee and the Council of the Jewish Agency from the middle of 1947 to the end of the winter of 1948.

Since she thought he looked thirsty, the receptionist asked if he would like a glass of water. Shmuel thanked her and said "Yes," then changed his mind and said "No, thank you. It's a pity to waste the time." She gave him a surprised, kindhearted smile and said:

"Here we never hurry. Here time stands still."

Then she sent him to Mr. Sheindelevich's office in the basement.

Mr. Sheindelevich, a small, vigorous man with a tanned, freckled bald head fringed with an amphitheater of shiny white hair, was sitting at his desk in front of a cumbersome, ancient typewriter, typing slowly with one finger, seeming to weigh each letter separately. The room was windowless, underground, lit by the feeble light cast by two bare bulbs. The man's shadow, like Shmuel's, fell on two different walls. On Shmuel's wall hung photographs of Herzl, Chaim Weizmann, and David Ben-Gurion, while on the wall behind Mr. Sheindelevich hung a large colored map of the State of Israel, on which the 1949 armistice lines were shown with a thick green line that bisected the city of Jerusalem.

Shmuel repeated his request. Mr. Sheindelevich looked at him for a long moment and then a tolerant, paternal smile slowly spread across his face, as if he were amazed at the strange request but was suppressing his amazement, and pardoned the ignorance of the person making it. He cleared his throat, paused, typed another two slow letters on his antique typewriter, looked up at Shmuel, and replied with a question:

"Are you a researcher, sir?"

"Yes. No. In fact, yes. I'm interested in the discussions that preceded the decision to set up the state."

"And for whom are you conducting this research?"

Shmuel, who had not expected this question, was confused for a moment and then replied hesitantly:

"For myself."

And he added with a surge of courage:

"Surely every citizen should have the right to look at the documents and study the history of the state?"

"And which minutes do you wish to look at, sir?"

"The Zionist Executive Committee. The Council of the Jewish Agency. From the middle of 1947 to the spring of 1948."

And he added without being asked:

"I am interested in the fundamental argument that preceded the decision to set up the state. If, indeed, there was such an argument."

Mr. Sheindelevich leaned forward, stunned, as if he had been asked to reveal his intimate bedroom habits:

"But that's not possible, sir. It is totally impossible."

"And why?" Shmuel asked gently.

"You have formulated two different requests at once, and you would receive two answers at once."

A Middle Eastern woman in her fifties, in a long black dress, a thin woman with drooping shoulders, silently entered the room bearing a tray with steaming glasses of tea. She set a glass before Mr. Sheindelevich. He thanked her politely and asked his guest:

"Will you have a glass of tea, at least? So as not to leave here entirely empty-handed."

"Thank you," Shmuel said.

"Yes thank you? No thank you?"

"No thank you. Not this time."

The woman picked up her tray, apologized, and left the room. Mr. Sheindelevich took up where he had left off, in a soft voice, as though sharing a secret:

"The records of the Zionist Executive Committee are not

here, sir. They are in the Zionist Archives. But you will find nothing there except transcripts of speeches, because their meetings were open to the public. As for the minutes of the Council of the Jewish Agency, the minutes of the secret discussions, that material is strictly classified. And it will remain strictly classified for another forty years, in accordance with the Archives Law and the State Secrets Order. If you so wish," the man added without a smile, " you are hereby invited to come and see me forty years from now; maybe by that time you will have changed your mind and will drink a glass of tea with me. I hope Comrade Fortuna's tea will not have cooled by then."

He stood up, extended his hand, and added in a sad voice that barely concealed a certain cheerfulness and faint glee at the other's misfortune:

"I am so sorry you troubled yourself to come here. I could have just as well refused you on the telephone. Please, make a note of our telephone number so that you can ring us in forty years' time and spare yourself a fruitless journey."

Shmuel shook the hand that was offered him and turned to go. As he reached the door, he was arrested by Mr. Sheindelevich's soft voice:

"What is it that you wish to know, precisely? After all, they all wanted as one man to set up a state, and they all knew as one man that we would have to defend ourselves by force."

"Even Shealtiel Abravanel?"

"But he," the man said, and stopped. He typed another single letter and concluded dryly:

"He was a traitor."

36

AT TEN O'CLOCK one morning, in the kitchen, Atalia said:

"He's been ill since the middle of the night. I've been nursing him most of the night. I've got to go out now, and you will have to go to his bedroom shortly. You've never been there. You'll have to change his pajamas every few hours because he's drenched with sweat. You must give him tea with honey and lemon from a teaspoon. You can add a little brandy. If he can't get out of bed, you have to slip a bedpan under him, then empty it in the toilet and wash it. This time you'll have to touch his body. He's an old man and you may find this uncomfortable or unpleasant. We brought you here to talk to him, and to look after him if necessary, not to be comfortable. And remember to wash your hands and change the damp flannel on his forehead. And on no account allow him to talk and talk today. On the contrary. You do the talking. Lecture him. Recite. His throat is inflamed."

It was a bad winter flu. The old man's temperature was high, his throat was on fire, his eyes were runny, his lungs full of fluid, and from time to time he had a fit of dry coughing. His ears, which Atalia had plugged with cotton wool, hurt, particularly the left one. At first he tried to joke: "The Eskimos are right, of course, to abandon their old folk in the snow." Then, citing various biblical and Talmudic verses, he referred to himself as a broken implement, a shattered vessel, a man of sorrows, acquainted with grief. When his temperature reached close to 104 degrees, the humor left him. He sank into melancholy, switched off his gaze, and wrapped himself in gloomy silence.

The doctor came and left. He listened to the patient's bare back and chest, injected him with penicillin, and told him to lie in bed with the upper part of his body supported by several pillows so that he would not develop pneumonia. He prescribed APC tablets to be taken several times a day, as well as cough syrup and eardrops, and told him to drink a lot of hot tea with honey and lemon, and yes, certainly, you could add a little brandy. And he instructed Shmuel to keep the bedroom warm.

"In the case of a man who is not so young, a man whose health is not fantastic even when he seems well, we must beware of complications," said the doctor with a slight stammer. He came originally from a small town near Frankfurt, and he had a small, square paunch, a triangle of white handkerchief showing from the breast pocket of his jacket, two pairs of glasses, both hanging from cords, and tiny hands as delicate as a little girl's.

So it came about that Shmuel Ash was allowed into Mr. Wald's bedroom. He had been living in the attic for more than two months and had not yet entered his employer's bedroom, or that of Atalia, or the other bedroom, whose door was always locked, farther along the passage opposite the door to the library. Shmuel imagined that this room had belonged to the late Shealtiel Abravanel. Up to now these three rooms had been out of bounds. Shmuel had access only to the library, which was his workplace, the kitchen, which he shared with Atalia, and his attic. The house on Rabbi Elbaz Lane was carefully compartmentalized.

This morning, for the first time, because Mr. Wald was ill, Shmuel was permitted to penetrate the old man's private room, to sit for a few hours by his bedside and read him a few chapters from the book of Jeremiah until he dozed off. From time to time, he woke and broke into a wet fit of coughing. Shmuel supported his back and fed him hot tea with honey and lemon, laced with brandy, from a teaspoon. It was the first time he had touched Mr. Wald. At first he had to force himself to touch the old man, because he guessed that the crooked, gnarled body would repel or disgust him. But when he made himself touch him, he discovered, to his surprise, that the bulky body was warm and very solid to the touch, as though, despite or because of his disability, he had strong back muscles and tough shoulder bones. Shmuel enjoyed this warmth and hardness so much that when he changed the old man's pajama top he rested his hands on the bare shoulders, and he may have let his fingertips linger on the rough skin a little longer than he should have.

When the old man dozed off, Shmuel got up and wandered around the room. The bedroom was rather small, much smaller than the library but bigger than Shmuel's attic. Here, as in the library, there were close-packed bookshelves which covered two of the walls and stretched from floor to ceiling. While the books in the library were scholarly tomes in Hebrew and Arabic and three or four other languages, about social studies, Jewish studies, the Middle East, history, mathematics, philosophy, as well as some books on mysticism and astronomy, here in the bedroom the shelves were packed with novels and poetry, mostly in German, Polish, and English, mainly from the eighteenth, nineteenth, and early twentieth century, ranging from *Michael Kohlhaas* to *Ulysses*; from Heine to Hermann Hesse and Hermann Broch; from Cervantes in German to Kierkegaard, Musil, and Kafka, also in German; from Adam Mickiewicz and Julian Tuwim to Marcel Proust.

Besides the bookcases and Gershom Wald's narrow bed, the room held a heavy, old-fashioned wardrobe, a bedside table, and a small round table covered by a cloth, with a vase of purple everlasting flowers on it. On either side of the table stood two identical chairs, their legs carved in the shape of plants. On the seat of each chair was an embroidered cushion with light brown tassels. The chairs contrasted with the simple, clean lines of the book-cases, the round table, and the bedside table. Beside the table stood a standard lamp with a brown shade, which shed a warm, soft light over the whole room. On the wall between the book-cases hung an old clock, made of walnut apparently, with a heavy pendulum of shiny brass that moved back and forth in a slow, dull rhythm, as if it had had enough. And in a corner of the room a paraffin heater burned all through the day and evening with a quiet flame that resembled a single blue eye.

At the head of the bed a pair of wooden crutches leaned against a chest of drawers. With the help of these crutches, the invalid moved from room to room or from his bedroom to the adjacent toilet, though in the library he always insisted on moving from the desk to the wicker couch and back without crutches, using the muscular strength of his shoulders and arms.

On the only empty wall, opposite the bed, facing the man who lay in it, Shmuel saw a small photograph in a plain wooden frame. This was the first thing he had seen on entering the room, but something had made him quickly look away. Again and again his eyes avoided the photograph, which aroused in him conflicting feelings of dread, shame, and envy. It showed a thin, fair-haired, somewhat fragile-looking young man with a long, introspective face and a shy look, as if he were deliberately avoiding the lens of the camera. As if his gaze were turned inward. One of his eye-brows was raised, skeptically, and this was the only feature that father and son shared. He had a high brow, and the fair hair that framed his face had not been cut for a long time and looked as if the photograph had been taken out of doors with a strong head-wind blowing. He was wearing a creased khaki shirt, which, con-trary to the fashion of the time, was buttoned up to the neck.

Gershom Wald sat up in bed facing his son's photograph, his

back resting on a pile of pillows. He was wearing brown flannel pajamas with lighter stripes, which Shmuel had changed for him earlier, and a gray scarf around his neck. His silvery mane spread out on the top pillow. When he noticed Shmuel looking at the photo on the wall, he said quietly:

"Micha."

"I'm sorry," Shmuel murmured. And at once he corrected himself:

"I'm very sorry." His eyes filled with tears. He turned away so the old man would not see.

Gershom Wald closed his eyes and said in a hoarse voice:

"The father of the grandchild I never had. And he had lost a parent when he was a child. He grew up with me without a mother. He was only six when his mother died. I brought him up on my own. I took him myself and led him to Mount Moriah."

He was silent for a moment, then he said with his lips, not with his voice:

"On April 2, '48. In the battle for Bab el-Wad, on the Tel Aviv-to-Jerusalem road."

His face suddenly twisted and he added in a whisper:

"He was a lot like his mother, he wasn't like me. From the time he was ten he was also my best friend. I never had a closer friend. He and I could talk for hours, or not talk for hours. There was hardly any difference. And sometimes he tried to explain things to me, higher mathematics, formal logic, which were beyond me. Sometimes he would laugh at me, old scripture and history teacher that I am, and call me a dinosaur."

Again Shmuel murmured:

"I share your pain."

And he corrected himself again:

"No. It's impossible to share pain. There's no such thing."

Gershom Wald fell silent. Shmuel poured him some hot tea with lemon and honey from the thermos on the table, laced it with a little brandy, supported the old man's back, and put the glass to his mouth while pushing an APC tablet between his lips. Gershom Wald took two or three sips, swallowed the tablet, and brushed Shmuel's hand and the glass away.

"When he was nine, because of an illness, they took out one of his kidneys. At the end of '47 he went and lied to the recruitment board. In the days of tumult and anarchy on the eve of that war it wasn't difficult to lie to the recruitment board. They were happy to be lied to. Atalia told him not to go. She forbade him to go. She made fun of him and said he was like a child running into the playground to play cowboys and Indians. She said he was ridiculous. She always considered the entire male sex ridiculous. She thought all men were eternal adolescents. Shealtiel also tried to make him swear not to go. Shealtiel said over and over again that this war was all Ben-Gurion's lunacy, the lunacy of the whole nation. In fact, the lunacy of two nations. In his view, the youth on both sides ought to drop their weapons and refuse to fight. He used to go at least twice a week to converse with his Arab friends. Even after the bloodshed began, in the autumn of '47, with roadblocks and sniper fire, he did not give up going to see his friends. The neighbors called him an Arab-lover. They called him Haj Amin, the Grand Mufti. And some people called him a traitor, because he justified, to some extent, the Arab opposition to Zionism and because he fraternized with Arabs. And yet he always insisted on calling himself a Zionist and even claimed he belonged to the small handful of true Zionists who were not intoxicated with nationalism. He described himself as the last disciple of that Zionist visionary Ahad Ha'am. He had known Arabic since his childhood, and he loved to sit surrounded by Arabs in the coffeehouses of the Old City and talk for hours on end. He had close friends among the Muslim and the Christian Arabs. He pointed to a different way. He had a different idea altogether. I argued with him. I stuck to my view that this war was sacred, a war of which it is written, 'Let the bridegroom go forth of his chamber,' et cetera. My child, Micha, my only son, Micha, might perhaps not have gone to this war had it not been for his father's talk of a sacred war: I had brought him up from an early age on tales of the heroic defenders of Tel Hai and Orde Wingate's Special Night Squads and the brave guards of the Jewish villages and the need for the courageous ancient Hebrew warriors to come back to life. I programmed him. Not just me. All of us. His nursery school teachers. His schoolteachers. His friends. Girls. In those years we all used to recite passionately the words of Hannah Senesh: 'Then a voice called and I followed.' A voice called him and he got up and went. I too was speaking with that voice. The whole country sounded that voice. 'No nation ever retreats when its back is to the wall.' 'This battle is for life or death.' He is gone and I am still here. No. I'm not still here. Micha is gone and I am also gone. Look at me: the man sitting opposite you is not alive. A dead chatterbox is sitting opposite you, chattering."

The old man began coughing again. He gurgled, nearly suffocated on his sputum, his distorted body twisted on the bed, and he started to bang his head against the wall. Shmuel hurried to stop him. He slapped his back a few times and tried to feed him a few more drops of tea. The old man choked, and spat into a crumpled handkerchief. After a while Shmuel realized that behind the cover of his coughing and hawking the man was sobbing, in a gasping, strangled voice. Then he wiped his eyes angrily with the handkerchief he had just spat into and scolded himself in a whisper.

"You must forgive me, Shmuel."

It was the first time since Shmuel Ash arrived in this house, a couple of months earlier, that the old man had addressed him by his name, and also the first time he had apologized to him.

Shmuel said gently:

"Rest. Don't talk. It isn't good for you to get excited."

The old man stopped beating his head against the wall and merely wept feebly, with frequent, shallow sobs that sounded like hiccups. Shmuel looked at him and realized how dear to him that rough-hewn face, whose sculptor seemed to have given up half-way, with its sharp jutting chin and unkempt white mustache, had become. He found the old man's ugliness fascinating, captivating, so fierce that it almost approached beauty. He was smitten with a powerful urge to comfort him. Not to distract him from his pain —there was no possible way of doing that—but to assume, to suck into himself, something of that pain. The old man's broad, rough hand lay on the quilt, and Shmuel delicately, hesitantly put his own hand on top of it. Gershom Wald's fingers were large and they clasped Shmuel's cold hand in a warm embrace. The old man's hand enfolded the young man's fingers for two or three minutes. At the end of the silence, Wald said:

"I know that people usually say about those killed in the fighting in '48 that their death was not in vain. I always said that myself. Everybody said it. Yes. How could I not have said it? The poet Alterman wrote, 'Maybe once in a thousand years our death has a meaning.' But it's harder and harder for me to repeat these words. Shealtiel's ghost makes them stick in my throat. Shealtiel used to say that in his opinion everyone who has ever died, not only in wartime but in an accident or from an illness or even in ripe old age, has died completely in vain."

From the mountains and valleys of the wrinkles on the twisted face, from under the thick white eyebrows, small, piercing blue eyes fixed on Shmuel. And below the bushy mustache the upper lip trembled. Gershom Wald's face suddenly screwed up as though in pain, but in the midst of the pain a sort of smile spread, which was not a smile.

"Listen, boy. It's possible that despite myself I'm starting to grow quite fond of you. Sometimes you seem like a tortoise that's lost its shell."

Toward evening Shmuel went out in the windswept rain to the pharmacy on the corner of Keren Hakayemet and Ibn Ezra Streets and bought Gershom Wald an electric humidifier to ease his breathing. He bought himself a new pocket inhaler. On the way back, he also bought a can of paraffin for the heater and a new bottle of cheap brandy called Cognac Médicinal.

When he got back to Gershom Wald's room, he found the old man lying curled up, wrapped in the quilt, which he had pulled up almost to his nostrils. He seemed to be breathing more easily. Shmuel prepared the humidifier and plugged it in. It hummed quietly and filled the room with mist. Suddenly the old man said:

"Listen to me, Shmuel. Be careful. Don't fall in love with her. You're not strong enough for that."

Then he added:

"There were three or four lads here before you, to keep me company. Most of them fell in love, and apparently she may have pitied one or two of them for a night or two. Then she sent them packing. In the end they all left here brokenhearted. But it was not her fault. Truly not. You cannot blame her. She has a kind of cool warmth, some kind of aloofness that attracts you to her like a moth to a flame. Sometimes I'm sorry for you. You're still a bit of a child."

37

ATALIA ENTERED THE ROOM without knocking. Shmuel
could not tell whether she had heard the old man's last words.
She brought with her the porridge that the neighbor had made.
She sat down on the old man's bed, plumped up the pillows under his head, asked Shmuel to support his back, and fed him five
or six spoonfuls. So the three of them sat there for a few minutes
with their heads so close they were almost touching. As though
they were all bending over to peer at some rare object. Shmuel
saw from close up the unusually deep furrow that extended from
her nostrils to her upper lip. He felt a powerful urge to trace
the line of this furrow gently with his finger. Then the old man
pursed his lips like an obstinate child and refused to eat any more.
She did not press him, but handed the bowl and spoon to Shmuel
and said:

"Take this to the kitchen. And then wait for me in the library."

He went to the kitchen, finished the rest of the porridge standing up, took a pot of yogurt from the refrigerator and ate it, then
ate a handful of olives and peeled and ate an orange, washed the
bowl and the jar and the spoon, dried all three, and put them
away in the drawer and the cupboard. There was a warmth in his

whole body now of the kind he had not felt since Yardena left
him.

Atalia was waiting for him in the library. Stretched out on the
couch, she motioned to Shmuel to sit behind the desk, on Mr.
Wald's high-backed, padded chair. He gazed at her with his sad,
shy almond eyes. She was wearing dark red woolen slacks and
a green pullover that matched her greenish-brown eyes. Brown
with a fleck of green. She lay relaxed, her knees together, hands
resting on the couch on either side of her hips, not exactly slim
but with a long, slim neck.

"You were talking about Micha," she said, not as though asking
a question but as though making a declaration. "You and Wald
were talking about him."

"Yes," Shmuel admitted. "I'm sorry. It was my fault. I asked
about the face in the picture and that's how I caused him pain. Or
perhaps I didn't ask. Perhaps he started talking to me about his
son."

"Don't be sorry. It doesn't matter. He talks and talks for days,
weeks, months on end, preaches, argues, and in fact he never says
anything. If this time you managed somehow to make him say
something at last . . ."

She did not finish her sentence. Shmuel, suddenly brave, said:
"You don't say much either, Atalia."

He went on to ask if he could ask a question.

Atalia nodded.

Shmuel asked how old Micha was when he died. She hesitated,
as if uncertain of the correct reply to the question, or perhaps the
question was too personal. After a short silence, she said that he
was thirty-seven. Then she fell silent again. Shmuel did not speak
either. Then she spoke quietly, almost to herself:

"He was a mathematician. He had published articles in jour-
nals about mathematical logic. He was set to become the young-
est professor in the history of the Hebrew University. Until he

was infected with the madness that always rages here, and dashed off excitedly one day to be slaughtered. Just like the rest of the herd."

Shmuel sat on Gershom Wald's chair and placed his hands on the desk in front of him. The fingers were too short: they all seemed to be lacking one knuckle. He was suddenly short of breath, but he mastered himself and did not reach for the inhaler in his pocket. Atalia eyed him slantwise from the couch, from bottom to top, and seemed to spit her words:

"You wanted a state. You wanted independence. Flags and uniforms and banknotes and drums and trumpets. You shed rivers of innocent blood. You sacrificed an entire generation. You drove hundreds of thousands of Arabs out of their homes. You sent shiploads of Holocaust survivors straight from the quayside to the battlefield. All so that there would be a Jewish state here. And look what you've got."

Shmuel was alarmed. After a moment he stammered politely:

"I'm afraid I don't entirely agree with you."

"Of course you don't agree. Why should you? You're one of them. You may be a revolutionary, a socialist, a rebel, but you're still one of them. Even Micha changed overnight into one of them. By the way, excuse me for asking, but how exactly did it happen that you weren't killed?"

"I was too young for that war. I was only thirteen."

Atalia did not let go:

"How come you weren't killed afterward? In the reprisal actions? Or in the Sinai campaign? Or in a raid? Or some special operation across the border? Or even in a training accident?"

Shmuel blushed. He hesitated for a moment, then he said:

"I was a noncombatant. I have asthma, and also an enlarged heart."

His eyes filled with tears, which he made an effort to conceal from Atalia, because he was ashamed of them.

"Micha only had one kidney. His left kidney was removed when he was nine at the Hadassah Hospital in the Street of the Prophets. He was an invalid like his father. He forged a medical certificate, and he also forged his father's signature. He cheated them and they were only too happy to be cheated. Everyone was being cheated. Even the cheats were being cheated. Wald, too. A whole herd of cheated people."

Shmuel said sheepishly:

"Don't you believe that in 1948 we fought because we had no alternative? That we had our backs to the wall?"

"No, you didn't have your backs to the wall. You *were* the wall."

"Are you trying to tell me that your father seriously believed that we had so much as a shadow of a chance to survive here by peaceful means? That it was possible to persuade the Arabs to agree to share the land? That it is possible to obtain a homeland by means of fine words? And do you believe that too? At that time, the entire progressive world supported the creation of a state for the Jewish people. Even the communist bloc supplied us with arms."

"Abravanel was never impressed by nationalism. At all. Anywhere. He was totally unimpressed by a world divided into hundreds of nation-states, like rows and rows of separate cages in a zoo. He didn't know Yiddish—he spoke Hebrew and Arabic, he spoke Ladino, English, French, Turkish, and Greek—but to all the states in the world he applied a Yiddish expression: *goyim naches*. Gentiles' delight. Statehood seemed to him a childish and outdated concept."

"So he was a naïve man? A dreamer?"

"It was Ben-Gurion who was the dreamer, not Abravanel. Ben-Gurion and the herd who followed him like the Pied Piper of Hamelin. To the slaughter. To violent expulsion. To eternal hatred between the two communities."

Shmuel shifted uncomfortably in Mr. Wald's upholstered chair. What Atalia had said seemed wild, menacing, almost hair-raising. The well-known replies, Wald's replies, were on the tip of his tongue, yet he could find no words. The thought that all nation-states were like cages at the zoo made him want to hurl in Atalia's and her father's face that if people treated each other like wild beasts, it might indeed be necessary to keep them in separate cages. But he reminded himself that Atalia was a war widow, and decided to say nothing. What he desired far more than to defeat her in an argument was to hold her, even for a moment, in his arms. He tried to imagine in his mind's eye her father struggling to block the waterfall of history single-handed. How could someone who did not believe in a Jewish state possibly have called himself a Zionist, and even sat for several years on the Zionist Executive Committee and the Council of the Jewish Agency? As if reading his mind, Atalia said, in a voice that blended contempt and sadness:

"He didn't reach this view overnight. The Arab revolt in 1936, Hitler, the underground movements, the killings, the retaliation operations of the Jewish underground, the hangings by the British, and especially his conversations with his Arab friends—all these brought him to the view that there was in fact room for the two communities and that it would be better for them to exist side by side, or one within the other, without the framework of a state. To exist as a mixed community, or as a conglomerate of two communities, with neither threatening the other's future. But you may be right. You may all be right. Perhaps he really was a naïve man. Perhaps it really was preferable for what you did here to happen—for tens of thousands to go to the slaughter and for hundreds of thousands to go into exile. The Jews here are actually a single big refugee camp, and so are the Arabs. And now the Arabs live day by day with the disaster of their defeat, and the

Jews live night by night with the dread of their vengeance. That way apparently you're all much better off. Both peoples are consumed by hatred and poison, and they both emerged from the war obsessed with vengeance and soaked in self-righteousness. Entire rivers of vengeance and self-righteousness. And as a consequence the whole land is covered with cemeteries and strewn with the ruins of hundreds of wretched villages.

"There are answers, Atalia. But I won't offer them. I'm afraid of hurting you."

"Nothing can hurt me anymore," Atalia said. "Except perhaps an armor-piercing shell."

And with that, she stood up, crossed the library with four sharp steps, and paused by the window.

"They slaughtered him," she said, not with sadness or hatred but with a fierceness that resembled euphoria. "They slit his throat. That's what. At the age of thirty-seven he was sent to accompany one of the convoys heading for Jerusalem, with a Sten gun and a few hand grenades. It was April 2, 1948. The road to Jerusalem wound through a deep valley, and Arab snipers shot at the convoys from the hills, on both sides of the road. Apparently it was nearly evening. The convoy commanders were afraid of getting stuck there on the narrow road through the wadi in the dark. Some of the fighters got out of their armored trucks and were told to dismantle a roadblock that the Arabs had made from rocks. Others, Micha among them, ran up the hillside with the intention of storming and destroying the snipers' positions with homemade hand grenades. Their attack was repulsed. As night fell they withdrew, dragging the injured and dead on their backs. But not all of them. As the convoy was approaching Jerusalem, someone realized that Micha was missing. Before dawn, a platoon went out to comb the slopes. His comrades, most of them ten or fifteen years his junior. They scoured the area all through the morning until they found him. He may have lain there dying all night. He may have called for help. He may have tried to crawl down toward the road on his stomach, bleeding. Or he may have been found by Arabs immediately after his comrades withdrew. They cut his throat, stripped the lower half of his body bare, cut off his penis, and put it in his mouth. We'll never know if they killed him before or after they castrated him. It's still an open question. They left it forever to my imagination. So that I'll never be short of something to think about at night. Night after night. They didn't tell me. They didn't tell me anything. Anything at all. I only discovered by accident: about a year after he died, one of his comrades was killed in a work accident in Galilee, and I was sent his diary to read. It was there, in the diary, that I discovered, written in fewer than a dozen words, how Micha was found among the rocks. And ever since then I can see only him. I see him all the time, with the bottom half of his body naked, his throat slit, and his severed penis thrust between his teeth. I see him every day. Every night. Every morning. When I close my eyes, I see him. When I open them again, I see him. And I went on living here, with the two grandfathers who would never be grandfathers. I went on looking after both of them. What else is there left for me to do? I can't love men. You've held the whole world in your hands for thousands of years and you've turned it into a horror show. A slaughterhouse. Perhaps I can just use you. Or sometimes even take pity on you and try to comfort you a little. What for? I don't know. Perhaps because you are so crippled."

Shmuel said nothing.

"Abravanel died a couple of years later. He died alone here, in the next room. He died hated and reviled by everyone. Even by himself. All his Arab friends were on the other side of the new borders. They had been expelled from their homes in Katamon, Abu Tor, Baka. He had no Jewish friends left. He was 'the

Traitor.' Between Micha's death and Abravanel's, Abravanel, Gershom Wald, and I lived here, just the three of us, with no one else. Like in a submarine. Me and the two grandfathers of the child I never had. Wald disagreed with Abravanel on everything, he disagreed with him fundamentally, but they didn't argue anymore. Ever. Micha's death had silenced them both. At one stroke all the arguments had gone. The words were choked. Silence reigned between them, and also between them and me. Wald must have suffered from this silence. He loves talking, and he needs to talk all the time. Abravanel, on the other hand, was comfortable with the silence. I looked after them both, and I worked for a few hours a day in a real estate office on Strauss Street. One evening shortly after the seven o'clock news, Abravanel was sitting in the kitchen, drinking coffee and reading the paper as usual. He sat there on his own in the kitchen every evening, drinking coffee and reading the paper. Suddenly his head fell and hit the coffee cup, overturning the cup. The right lens of his glasses shattered, as if a rifle bullet had hit him in the eye. The newspaper was soaked with coffee, which ran over the table, his chest, his knees, and onto the floor. And that's how I found him. Coffee, newspaper, smashed glasses, his face on the flowered oilcloth, as if he had dropped off to sleep at the kitchen table, though his forehead and hair were lying in a pool of coffee. I inherited some of Abravanel's ideas, but I didn't love him, except perhaps when I was a little girl. He was definitely an honest man, and a brave and original one, but he never wanted to be a father and he didn't know how, and in fact he was not much of a husband either. Once, when I was four, he forgot me in a shop in Ben Yehuda Market because he got into an argument with a priest, and to pursue the argument he went with him to the Jaffa Road and on as far as Abyssinia Street. Another time he was angry with my mother so he forbade her to leave the house for a fortnight, and to make sure she didn't, he hid her three pairs of shoes. Once he found her drinking a glass of wine in the kitchen and laughing out loud with a Greek friend of his. As a punishment he locked her in the attic. He was a solitary, self-centered, fanatical man. A walking exclamation mark. Having a family didn't suit him. Perhaps he was meant to be a recluse."

38

Jesus and all his apostles were Jews and the children of Jews. But in the Christian imagination the only one remembered as a Jew—and who represented the Jewish people—was Judas Iscariot. When the men sent by the priests and the Temple guard came to arrest Jesus, the other apostles were alarmed and feared for their lives and scattered in a panic in every direction, and only Judas remained there. He may have kissed Jesus to strengthen his resolve. He may have accompanied the jailers to the place where they took the teacher. Peter also went there, but before daybreak he had denied Jesus three times. Judas did not deny him. How ironic it is, Shmuel wrote in his notebook, that the first and last Christian, the only Christian who did not abandon Jesus for a moment and did not deny him, the only Christian who believed in Jesus' divinity to his final moment on the cross, the Christian who believed to the end that Jesus would indeed descend from the cross before all Jerusalem and all the world, the only Christian who died with Jesus and did not outlive him, the only one whose heart was truly broken by Jesus' death, is the one who has been considered, by hundreds of millions of people on five continents and over thousands of years, the archetypal, the most heinous and most despicable, Jew. As the incarnation of treachery, the incarnation of Judaism, the incarnation of the connection between Judaism and betrayal.

In modern times, Shmuel wrote in his notebook, the historian Heinrich Graetz wrote that Jesus is the only mortal of whom "one can say without exaggeration that he achieved more after his death than in his lifetime." Shmuel added in the margin in his hasty scrawl: Not true. Not only Jesus. Judas Iscariot also achieved much more after his death than in his lifetime.

Alone in his attic on a winter's night, with strong, steady rain falling on the sloping roof close to his head and gurgling in the gutters, the cypresses bowed by the westerly wind, a night bird uttering a single harsh screech, Shmuel sat bent over his papers, taking an occasional swig from the open bottle of cheap vodka that stood before him on the desk, and wrote in his notebook:

The Jews almost never spoke about Judas. Anywhere. Not a word. Even when they mocked the crucifixion, and the resurrection that took place, according to the Gospels, on the third day. Jews in every generation, including those who penned polemical writings against Christianity, were too afraid to touch Judas. Even those Jews who believed, like Graetz and Klausner, that Jesus was born and died a Jew and was close to the Essene sect, hated by the priests and sages because he associated with sinners, publicans, and harlots, they too passed over Judas in silence. Even those who held the view that Jesus was a charlatan, a cunning magician, the bastard child of a Roman soldier, all refrained from saying a word about Judas. They were ashamed of him. They disavowed him. Perhaps they were afraid to conjure up the memory of the man whose image had absorbed rivers of hatred and loathing in the course of eighty generations. Stir not up nor awaken.

Shmuel remembered well the image of Judas in several famous paintings of the Last Supper: a repulsive, twisted creature sitting shrunk like a reptile at the end of the table where all the other diners were handsome, dark-haired where they were blond, with twisted nose and large ears, with rotting yellow teeth, with a mean and greedy expression on his malicious face.

At Golgotha, on the Friday that was also the eve of Passover, the mob mocked the crucified one: "Save thyself and come down from the cross." And Judas too pleaded with him: "Come down, Rabbi. Come down now. The hour is late and the crowd is dispersing. Come down. Tarry no more."

Is there really, Shmuel wrote in his notebook, not a single believer who asked himself how it can be that a man who has sold his teacher for the paltry sum of thirty pieces of silver goes and hangs himself from sorrow immediately afterward? No other apostle died with Jesus of Nazareth. Judas was the only one who did not wish to go on living after the death of the Savior.

But Shmuel could not find in any text that he knew of the slightest attempt to defend that man, the man without whom there would have been no crucifixion, no Christianity, no Church, the man without whom the man from Nazareth would have been forgotten, just like dozens of other rough and ready Galilean wonderworkers and preachers.

It was after midnight when Shmuel powdered his beard, cheeks, forehead, and neck with baby talc, put on his old duffel coat and *shapka*, picked up the stick with the fox-head handle, and went down to the kitchen. He intended to spread a thick slice of bread with cream cheese for himself, as he was suddenly hungry, and to wander around the empty streets until he finally felt tired. Maybe in his heart of hearts he was hoping to bump into Atalia in the kitchen. Perhaps she too could not sleep? But the kitchen was empty and dark, and when Shmuel switched on the light, he caught sight of a plump brown cockroach scuttling under the refrigerator. Shmuel laughed. Why are you running away? I won't harm you. What have I got against you? What have you done to me? And in what way am I better than you?

He opened the refrigerator and found some vegetables, a bottle of milk, and a package of cheese. He helped himself to a large chunk of cheese with his fingers, placed it on a slice of bread, put that in his mouth, and chewed, paying no attention to the crumbs that clung to his beard. He deliberately scattered some crumbs on the floor, for the cockroach's breakfast. Then he shut the refrigerator and crossed the passage on tiptoe, because he knew that Gershom Wald, who was recuperating now, was sitting at his desk or lying on his couch in the library. On the way, he paused for a moment and listened at Atalia's closed door. Since he heard no sound, he left the house and stepped into the darkness, locking the front door behind him and testing the paving stones in the yard with his stick.

The rain had decreased to a fine drizzle. The wind had dropped. A deep silence held sway in the lane. The air was cold and crisp, cleansing his lungs and clearing his head of the cheap vodka fumes. All the windows and shutters were closed, no lights were on. The old-fashioned British Mandate streetlamp with its inlaid rectangles of glass gave little light but scattered a mass of nervous shadows that moved on the road and the walls. Shmuel advanced, with his head butting forward and his body dragged after, legs struggling not to be left behind, up Rabbi Elbaz Lane toward Ussishkin Street. Here he turned toward the Nahlaot, along a route similar to the one he had followed a few weeks before with Atalia. He remembered the silence that had hung between them on that walk, and he thought about the things she had told him now about Micha's death and about the death of her father, whom she never referred to as "my father" but always called him by his family name, Abravanel. He asked himself what he was doing spending all winter in this house full of the smell of death, between Abravanel's ghost and the old man who kept on talking like a broken mechanical toy and the unreachable woman who loathed the entire male sex. Even if on rare occasions her pity could be stirred. And he replied that he was shutting himself away. Just as he had decided he would do when Yardena had married Nesher Sharshevsky and he had given up studying. So far he had kept to his plan. But are you really shutting yourself away? Surely, even when you are sitting shut away in your attic room, your heart is downstairs, in the kitchen or on the threshold of Atalia's closed door.

A frozen, skinny alley cat, its belly hollow from hunger, its ribs protruding, tail tucked between its legs, stood shrinking between two dustbins, staring at Shmuel with glittering eyes, tense, ready to flee in an instant. Shmuel stopped, looked at the cat, and was suddenly filled with the compassion that sometimes took hold of him when he encountered someone whose luck had run out. This feeling hardly ever led to action. In his mind, he said to the cat: Just don't you run away from me too. We're rather alike, you and I, aren't we? We're both alone in the dark in this drizzle, wondering what happens next. We're both looking for some source of warmth, and while we're looking we recoil. He moved closer, his stick preceding him. The cat did not withdraw from its position between the dustbins, but bristled, arched its back, bared its teeth, and gave two hisses of quiet warning. The dim sound of a shot rang out in the darkness, followed by a short salvo of sharp shots, much closer, assailing the silence. Shmuel could not imagine which direction the sounds came from. Israeli Jerusalem was surrounded by Jordanian Jerusalem on three sides, and all along the border there were fortified firing positions, barbed-wire fences, concrete walls, and minefields. From time to time a Jordanian sniper hit a passerby, or random fire was exchanged by both sides.

After the shooting, the silence of a winter's night descended once more upon Jerusalem. Shmuel bent down in the roadway, stretched his hand out toward the cat, and tried to call it. To his astonishment, instead of running away the cat took three or four cautious steps toward him, sniffing the air, its whiskers quivering in the lamplight, eyes flashing with a devilish gleam, and tail erect. Its soft, lithe steps looked like a dance. Shmuel regretted coming empty-handed. He recalled the cheese in the fridge and was sorry not to have brought a few slices. He could have boiled an egg before coming out and fed it now to this starving alley cat.

"I haven't got anything. I'm sorry," he said softly. But the cat, unimpressed, moved closer to Shmuel as he bent down, and sniffed his outstretched fingers. Instead of leaving in disappointment, it chose to rub the side of its head against his outstretched fingertips, letting out a heartbreaking wail. Shmuel, astonished and excited, left his fingers extended so that the cat could go on rubbing itself against them. Then, taking courage, he laid his stick down on the asphalt and stroked the cat's head and back with his other hand, tickling it gently on the neck and under the ears. It was a gray-white cat, not very big, little more than a kitten, in fact, soft and warm and woolly to the touch. As Shmuel's hand stroked it, a low, steady purring sound broke from its throat.

After a minute, the cat rubbed itself twice against Shmuel's bent leg, let out another faint wail, then turned and walked off without a backward glance, disappearing between the dustbins with springy panther's steps.

Shmuel went on his way, crossed Mahane Yehuda, and passed through the area of Mekor Baruch, whose walls bore announcements by rabbis and synagogue functionaries, denunciations, curses, and bans: "We have suffered a great loss," "Touch not mine anointed," "It is forbidden to vote in the impure elections," "The Zionists are continuing the work of Hitler (may his name be blotted out!)."

His feet led him to the alley in the area of Yegia Kapayim, where his regular haunt was from the days of the Socialist Renewal Group, the proletarian café where the six members of the

Group used to sit around two tables pushed together, a table or two's distance from that gathering of craftsmen, plasterers, electricians, printer's apprentices, and plumbers with whom the members of the Group did not speak, though occasionally somebody asked one of them for a light.

When he reached the café, which was closed, its rusty iron shutter rolled down, Shmuel stood rooted to the spot, asking himself what on earth he was doing here. And he asked himself the question Atalia had asked him a few hours earlier:

How come you weren't killed?

He peered at his wristwatch. Ten past one. There was not a living soul to be seen in the entire area. Only in one window a feeble light glowed, and he pictured a young rabbinical student sitting there reciting psalms. He said to him in his heart: You and I are both searching for something that has no fixed measure. And for that reason we will not find it even if we search till morning and the next night and every night to come until the day of our death, and maybe after that.

On his way home, as he went up Zikhron Moshe Street, Shmuel thought about the death of Micha Wald, the brilliant mathematician who had been married to Atalia, and might have loved her, and she might have loved him, before she became so acidic. Even though his wife and his father-in-law were opposed to the war, even though they were opposed to the creation of the state, even though they were opposed with all their being to his enlisting for a fight they considered cursed, and even though he himself, like his father, had a disability, he still volunteered for the War of Independence. And he went on the assault that night, April 2, 1948, up a mountainside. Shmuel tried to visualize the injured man, not a youngster from the Palmach but a thirty-seven-year-old married man, not too fit, and perhaps, who knows, asthmatic like me, not adept at leaping about the mountains. His comrades withdrew back down the mountain, in the dark, to the convoy that was stuck on the road, unaware that he had been left behind. Was he afraid to call out in case the enemy fighters heard him? Did he lose consciousness? Or perhaps he tried with the last of his strength to crawl down the slope toward the road and the convoy? Or perhaps, on the contrary, he shouted and shouted with all the agony of his injuries, and that was how the Arab fighters found him in the dark. When they found him, did he try to talk to them? In their own language? Did he know Arabic like his father-in-law? Did he try to fight them? Did he plead for his life? He must have known, as everyone knew, that in that war, in the early months, both sides took hardly any prisoners. Did he realize, in a terrible, desperate panic, what they were going to do to him when they pulled his trousers down? Did the blood freeze in his veins? Shmuel started trembling and put one hand on his trousers, as if to protect his own penis, and hurried his steps, though the drizzle had stopped and there was just a biting cold with the smell of rotting leaves and damp earth in the Jerusalem air. How come you weren't killed?

Shortly before Davidka Square a police car with a flashing light screeched to a halt beside him, a window opened, and a nasal tenor voice with a distinct Romanian accent asked:

"Where you going, sir?"

"Home," Shmuel said, though he had not decided yet if his ramble had ended for the night. He had intended to walk the streets until his strength ran out.

"Identity card."

Shmuel moved the stick from hand to hand, undid his duffel coat with frozen fingers, felt in one pocket and then the other pocket of his shirt, and then in the back pocket of his trousers, and finally pulled out and handed to the Romanian policeman the cover of his identity card—identity cards consisted of a booklet with a cardboard cover. He continued to search and turned his pockets inside out until, in the depths of one of them, he found the body of the document. The policeman switched on a little light in the roof of his car, looked at the certificate, and handed the cover and the document back to Shmuel.

"Lost your way?"

"Why?" Shmuel asked.

"It says on your identity card that you live in Tel Arza."

"Yes. That is, no. I'm staying now, no, not staying, I'm working on Rabbi Elbaz Lane. In Sha'arei Hesed."

"Working? At this time of night?"

"The thing is," Shmuel said, "I work there, but I also sleep there at night. That is, the room is part of my pay. It doesn't matter. It's a bit hard to explain."

"Have you been drinking?"

"No. That is, yes. A little. The fact is that I had a few sips before I came out."

"And where exactly are you going, sir, if you don't mind my asking, on a freezing cold night like this?"

"Nowhere special. Just wandering around. Trying to clear my head."

But the policeman was getting bored. He said something to his colleague, who was at the wheel, and then said to Shmuel as he rolled up the window:

"It's not so healthy to wander around the streets alone at this time of night. A person could catch a sudden cold. Or meet a wolf."

And he added:

"Okay, just go straight home, and I mean straight home. This is not a time that decent people are out of doors. Make sure we don't see you again tonight."

It was a little after two o'clock when Shmuel Ash, frozen, soaked, and tired, returned home to Rabbi Elbaz Lane. He entered silently, on tiptoe, so the old man would not hear him.

Then he remembered that Wald was still unwell and would certainly be fast asleep in his bed facing the picture of his slain son. So he switched on the light in the kitchen, looked around for his cockroach, which had apparently retired for the night, ate a thick slice of bread and jam and some olives, and drank a glass of water, because he was too lazy to make himself tea, even though he was frozen and dying for something hot. Then he quietly climbed up to his attic, lit the heater, took off his duffel coat and his shoes, took three long swigs from the vodka bottle, undressed, and stood for a short while in front of the heater in his long johns. Suddenly he said to himself: It won't do you any good. And while he himself did not understand what these words meant, they soothed him a little and he got into bed and took two puffs from his inhaler—though he was not short of breath, he thought he could feel an attack coming on. Then he curled up under his quilt and fell asleep almost as soon as his head touched the pillow. He forgot to put out the light and the heater, and he forgot to put the cork back in the vodka bottle.

The following morning, he woke at eleven o'clock, dressed, picked up his stick, and went out, bleary and weary, to eat goulash soup and apple compote at his Hungarian restaurant on King George Street. The truth is he should have looked in on the invalid as soon as he got up, to ask if he needed anything. He ought to have washed him. Changed his sweat-soaked pajamas. Served him some tea and fed it to him on a teaspoon. Given him a pill and plumped up his pillows. But he went out without doing any of this, because he had been told when he first came here that the old man was always asleep in the morning. And besides, Atalia would surely have looked in to see how he was, or Bella, the cleaner, or the neighbor, Sarah de Toledo. Even so, you should have gone in to see if he needed you for anything. He might have been lying there awake, waiting for you. He might have been lying awake all night and found some new words he wanted to say to you. He might have needed to tell you something else about his son. How could you have forsaken him? Now, in the Hungarian restaurant, over a bowl of steaming goulash soup, Shmuel was sorry from the depths of his heart. But he said to himself: Too late.

39

Gershom wald recovered in the middle of February. Only an annoying dry cough lingered. Once more, at five o'clock in the afternoon he limped on his crutches from his bedroom to the library, where Shmuel sat with him until ten or eleven. He rarely mentioned his son. But whenever irony made him raise his left eyebrow, Shmuel recalled Micha and the horror of his lonely death. Gershom Wald and Shmuel listened to the news together. They discussed the first atom bomb exploded by France. They discussed the free movement of shipping in the Suez Canal, and Ben-Gurion's declaration that Nasser's threats were empty rhetoric. Then Shmuel would go up to his attic and the old man stayed where he was, with his books and papers, until five or six in the morning. Wald slept the whole morning in his bedroom, which Shmuel was now allowed to enter occasionally, to fetch a pair of glasses that had been forgotten by the bedside or to turn off the radio that had been left on.

Since the evening when Gershom Wald, on fire with a high temperature, had told Shmuel about his son's death, their relationship had changed: the old man's compulsive chatter seemed to have calmed. He still indulged, from time to time, in witticisms and wordplay, misquoting biblical verses, educating Shmuel with

high-flown lectures about the Uganda Question or the contrast
between old age and youth. Sometimes he spoke for half an hour
on the phone with one of his invisible interlocutors. Joking.
Quoting. Exchanging witticisms. But sometimes he stayed silent
for an hour or two. He sat in his leather-upholstered chair at his
desk or lay on his wicker couch, covered with the tartan blanket,
reading a book, his thick glasses slipping down his nose, his white
mustache quivering, little blue eyes scampering along the lines,
one eyebrow slightly raised, his lips moving as he read, his silvery mane lending a certain splendor to his fascinating ugliness.
Sometimes they exchanged pages from *Davar*. At nine o'clock
they listened to the news. Shmuel sat facing Gershom Wald on
the visitor's chair, reading Yizhar's *Days of Ziklag*, with which he
had been wrestling intermittently all winter, except when he was
reading the New Testament or consulting one of the books he
had brought with him from Tel Arza about Jewish views of Jesus. There was a book by Solomon Zeitlin, *Who Crucified Jesus?*,
which had appeared in Hebrew translation a little earlier, in 1958,
and also a book in English by Morris Goldstein, *Jesus in the Jewish
Tradition*, as well as some offprints of articles by his teacher, Professor Gustav Yomtov Eisenschloss. None of these books and articles mentioned Judas Iscariot except for some routine remarks
about his treachery and the fact that many simple Christians considered him the hated archetype of all Jews, in every country and
century.

A deep silence descended on the library. From outside, far
away, there could sometimes be heard, between rain showers, the
sounds of children playing. Occasionally the paraffin bubbled in
the tube inside the heater that stood in a corner and gave out a
pleasant warmth. The old man could again make his own way,
without crutches, from the desk to the wicker couch and back
again, relying on the strength of the muscles in his arms and back
alone. He never allowed Shmuel to assist him.

But on the days that followed a change took place: the old man allowed Shmuel to support his shoulders while he adjusted the cushions behind his back. When he lay down on the wicker couch Shmuel gently covered him with the tartan blanket. Every hour he gave him a glass of hot tea to which he still added some lemon and honey and a little brandy, though the flu had cleared up. He made himself some tea with honey as well. Once the total silence was broken by the voice of the old man, who looked up from his book and said, as if continuing a conversation with himself:

"They all thought he was crazy. People abused and reviled him, they called him a traitor, they called him an Arab-lover, they even spread a persistent rumor in Jerusalem that one of his grandfathers had been an Arab gardener from Bethlehem, but nobody took the trouble to argue with him. As though he were voicing some obsession and not an idea. As if his truth was not worth disputing."

"Are you talking about Atalia's father?" Shmuel asked.

"The very same. I also made it a rule not to debate with him. We were quite distant from one another. He used to read *Davar* every morning, and when he had finished he would come in here and leave it silently on my desk. We exchanged not a word apart from 'sorry,' 'thank you,' or 'would you mind kindly opening the window.' Once or twice he broke his silence and said to me that the founding fathers of Zionism deliberately exploited the age-old religious and messianic energies of the Jewish masses and enlisted these in the service of a political movement that was fundamentally secular, pragmatic, and modern. But one of these days, he said, this Frankenstein's monster will turn on its creator: the religious and messianic energies, the irrational energies that the founders of Zionism endeavored to harness to their secular, contemporary struggle, would burst forth and sweep away everything those founding fathers intended to achieve here. He resigned from the Zionist Executive Committee not because he had ceased to be a Zionist but because he believed that they had all deviated from the path, that they had been carried away with their eyes closed by Ben-Gurion's lunacy, that they had gone off the rails and become overnight followers of Jabotinsky, if not of Stern. And, in fact, he did not resign—he was thrown out. Both from the Zionist Executive Committee and from the Council of the Jewish Agency. They gave him twenty-four hours to decide whether to place a letter of resignation on Ben-Gurion's desk or to be expelled formally, in disgrace, from both bodies, by unanimous vote. He wrote a reasoned letter of resignation, but it was classified. No newspaper would publish it. Almost total silence surrounded his resignation. Yes. Perhaps they were expecting him to take his own life. Or convert to Islam. Or emigrate. I sent Atalia seven years ago to look for the letter, or a copy of it, in the Zionist Archives. She returned empty-handed. They did not say that it had been classified or lost, they brazenly insisted that no such letter had ever existed. It had sunk like lead in the mighty waters. Two years after the War of Independence he died here in this house. He died alone in the kitchen. He sat down one morning, as was his wont, to read the paper and suddenly he bent over the table as though to wipe some stain off the oilcloth and hit his head and died. When he died, he was possibly the most lonely and most hated man in Israel. His world was in ruins. His wife had left him many years earlier. The heart is so deceitful, above all things, and desperately wicked—who can know it?, to quote the prophet Jeremiah. Don't most of us sometimes wish in the darkest recesses of our hearts that we had a different father? After Shealtiel's death, Atalia searched his bedroom for any notes, articles, manuscripts. She scoured all the cupboards, turned out all the drawers, but found nothing. Not a single piece of paper apart from his will, in which he left her this house, some plots of land in Talpiyot, and his life savings, and urged her in strong words to let me go on living here for the rest of my days. He seems to have destroyed all his papers with his own hands. His personal archive. His invaluable correspondence with well-known Arabs in Jerusalem, Bethlehem, Ramallah, Beirut, Cairo, Damascus. No, he didn't burn it. He seems to have torn it all up into tiny pieces over several days and flushed it down the toilet. There is nothing left except the will, which Atalia has. She showed it to me once, years ago, and I remember its closing words: "All this has been written and sealed by me, being of sound mind, perhaps the only sound mind left here in Jerusalem." She found him in the kitchen with the newspaper spread out in front of him, his coffee spilled on the paper and his head pressed down on the table as though this stiff-necked man had finally decided to expose his neck to us all. You've asked me to try to describe him. Well. Descriptions are not my strong point. I could put it like this: he was a short, dark-skinned man with black-framed glasses, always elegantly turned out in a gray or navy blue suit, with a triangle of white handkerchief showing in his breast pocket. He had a small, neat black mustache and piercing black eyes and a fierce look that made us all lower our eyes. He always smelled of a well-known make of toilet water. I remember his hands, which were shapely and not like a man's hands but more like those of a beautiful woman. Despite our differences of opinion, which grew stronger, he was as dear to me as a brother. A lost brother, a doomed brother, a brother who has strayed from the path, but a brother nonetheless. It was he, after all, who took me in here, to live in this house, after our children's marriage, so that he would have someone to talk to. Perhaps he was afraid of being left alone in the company of the young couple. Perhaps he secretly hoped that when the time came we would raise the grandchildren together, all under one roof, like a Jerusalem family in bygone days. Like the fam-

ily he himself grew up in, in this house, the family of Jehoiachin
Abravanel. He did not know that Micha and Atalia were finding
it hard to have a baby."

Shmuel asked:

"You say that after the disaster you made it a rule not to debate with him. But why didn't you argue with him? After all, you
love arguing and you're good at it. You might have been able to
change his opinions. You might have been able to relieve his solitude. And yours."

"The distance was too great," said Gershom Wald, smiling
sadly under his mustache. "He was firm in his view that Zionism could not be achieved through confrontation with the Arabs,
whereas I had understood by the end of the forties that it could
not be achieved without some such confrontation."

"And how about Atalia? Is she closer to your views or her father's?"

"She is more extreme than he was. She told me once that the
very presence of the Jews in the Land of Israel is based on injus-
tice."

"In that case, why doesn't she leave?"

"I don't know," said Gershom Wald. "I have no answer to that
question. There was a certain distance between us even before he
died. And yet we are well suited to each other. Not so much like
father-in-law and daughter-in law as, say, a couple who have been
together for a long time and whose routine prevents the slightest friction. She looks after me and I leave her alone. Yes. The
main reason for your presence here is so that she will be relieved
of having to speak to me. You are paid, like your predecessors,
so that your presence will channel my desire to talk toward *you*.
But now even my desire to talk is abandoning me. Soon you will
start suffering from latent unemployment: one glass of tea after
another, one handful of pills after another, and prolonged silence
on both sides. As lead in the mighty waters. Will you tell me some

more now about Jewish views of Jesus? It's been a while since you've told me about the lies and slanders that generations upon generations of persecuted Jews invented so as to poke out a cowardly tongue behind the back of their own flesh and blood but whom their persecutors chose to see as the redeemer and savior."

Shmuel placed his fingers on Gershom Wald's brown, veiny hand, and left them there as he said:

"Thirty or so years ago, Aaron Abraham Kabak wrote a sort of novel about Jesus called *The Narrow Path*. It's tiresome, too sentimental. Jesus as described by Kabak is a delicate, vulnerable Jew who tries to bring love and compassion to the world. But the relationship between Jesus and his disciple Judas is described as a complicated one, of love and resentment, attraction and revulsion. Kabak's Judas is a pretty repulsive character. Kabak is as blind as the rest of them. He too failed to see that Judas was the most fervent of believers."

"The eyes," Gershom Wald said, "will never open. Almost everyone traverses their lifespan, from birth to death, with eyes closed. Even you and I, my dear Shmuel. With eyes closed. If we open our eyes for just a moment, a great and terrible cry will burst forth from us and we shall scream and never stop. And if we don't cry out day and night, that's a sign that our eyes are closed. Now will you kindly read your book and let's sit in silence. We have talked enough for this evening."

40

AT HALF PAST ELEVEN the next morning, before he went out to his usual Hungarian restaurant, Atalia knocked at his door. She was wearing a full-length black skirt, a tight red pullover that accentuated the curve of her breasts, and narrow high-heeled shoes. She had a white knitted scarf around her neck which went well with the sweater. Her blank, high-browed face, her warm brown-green eyes, her thin, arched eyebrows, the fascinating deep furrow from her nostrils to her upper lip, and the long dark hair flowing down over her shoulder all struck Shmuel as beautiful but inaccessible. The bitterness was concealed particularly in the corner of her pursed lips, which smiled only rarely. Her violet scent with its hint of starch and steam ironing entered Shmuel's ascetic room with her, and he inhaled it deep into his lungs. For a moment or two she stood tall in the doorway without coming into the room, looking at the bearded, armed images of the Cuban revolutionaries with which Shmuel had adorned the walls of his attic, as well as at the Pietà.

She had come to ask a favor. As part of her work for the investigation bureau, she had a meeting at three o'clock that afternoon, at Café Atara on Ben Yehuda Street, with a man who was somewhat unbalanced and was often drunk even in the afternoon. It had occurred to her that it might be better for her to turn up for the meeting accompanied by a man. They both smiled when she said the word "man."

Might Shmuel be free for half an hour, at three o'clock, to come and meet her and the poet Hiram Nehushtan at Café Atara? He would not have to join in the conversation, and in fact he would not have to do anything except be there and have a tea or a coffee. If he said no, if he was busy or not interested in taking part in the meeting, she would naturally understand and respect that. But he would surely not say no.

"Tell me something about Mr. Nehushtan," Shmuel asked. "If it's not top secret. Like everything about you."

"Hiram is a bit of a poet, not a well-known poet but somewhat esoteric. He was once a member of the Stern Gang. For the past ten years or so, since the state came into being, he has not found a place for himself. Like many people from the underground. He does all kinds of jobs: he's a tourist guide, a literary translator, he writes all kinds of booklets that he publishes himself. Two years ago he borrowed some money from a building contractor by the name of Ilya Schwarzbaum, who had been his friend in the underground, and now he is refusing to repay the loan and even claims that it never existed. Since the loan was made with no surety and no signed contract, on the basis of a friendly handshake between two comrades-in-arms, it won't be straightforward to get the money out of him. My bureau has been trying for several weeks now, in gentle and not so gentle terms, to get the poet-warrior to repay the money to Schwarzbaum. Today you and I are going to make another attempt."

"Why are you standing in the doorway?" Shmuel said. "Sit down." And he pointed to the only chair. He himself was sitting on the edge of his bed, still inhaling her subtle fragrance.

"If there's no contract and no other document, maybe the poet is right after all. Maybe there never was a loan and your contractor has invented it."

"There was a loan. Definitely," Atalia said. "We even have a witness. An accountant called Esther Levi, who was present in Café Atara when the contractor handed over the money in cash. Nehushtan has forgotten all about her, and I'm hoping to bring her to our meeting today. She's a bit eccentric too, but her eccentricity lies in the fact that she never forgets a thing. She remembers precisely, word for word, who said what and to whom ten years ago. It must be a terrible curse. Actually, you may find she and you have a common language. They said about her in the underground that she used to hide hand grenades in her bra."

"I hope she won't bring any hand grenades in her bra to the meeting today," Shmuel said. "Okay, then, three o'clock at Café Atara. I'll be there. Maybe your rich contractor will make me a small loan too."

Then he added:

"You already know. I'll always do whatever you ask of me."

"Why is that?"

To this question Shmuel found no answer. He felt that his eyes were about to fill with tears and turned away. Shmuel usually wept, either from sorrow for others or from self-pity. But this time he had no idea whom he was feeling sorry for. Suddenly emboldened, he said, his eyes still turned to the wall:

"I'd like to suggest that you and I could try to be friends. I mean ... not friends. The word 'friends' suggests something that's impossible between us. Pals."

At once, covered in shame and confusion, he hastened to correct himself:

"Not to be strangers. Not entirely strangers. After all, we've lived here all this winter, just the three of us under one roof. It would be nice if you and I—"

But he couldn't think how to finish this sentence. He blushed under his shaggy beard, lowered his eyes, and fell silent.

"Feelings," Atalia said. "Two of your predecessors who stayed here to keep the old man company were full of feelings. I'm getting rather tired of people with feelings. It seems to me that all feelings are unnecessary and end badly. Life could be so much simpler if feelings could be abolished. But I don't need to lecture you, Shmuel. Could you perhaps make do with the fact that I can more or less put up with you most of the time, and now and again a little more so."

It was the first time she had called him by his first name.

At half past two, after the goulash soup and apple compote in the Hungarian restaurant and following a short siesta, Shmuel Ash got up, dusted his beard, neck, and forehead with baby talc, changed his shirt and put on his worn ash-gray pullover, donned his duffel coat and his *shapka*, checked that he had his inhaler in his pocket, and set out to walk to Café Atara. When he stepped with all his weight on the improvised wooden step inside the front door, it seesawed up at one end and he almost lost his footing. He managed to recover his balance at the last moment, however, by leaning both arms against the wall.

The poet Hiram Nehushtan was a small thin man with sticky hair, long sideburns, a boxer's broken nose, and a high smooth brow with a single oily curl glued to it. Without getting up, he said:

"You've probably forgotten me, but I remember you very well. You're Shmuel Ash. You used to go to the meetings of the Socialist Renewal Group. I came to one of your meetings at Café Roth in Yegia Kapayim. There wasn't much renewal, and your socialism was half Bolshevik and half Cuban. I'm also a socialist and even a bit of a revolutionary, but unlike you lot I'm definitely a Hebrew socialist. Hebrew, not Jewish. I don't want to have anything to do with the Jews. The Jews are the walking dead. So what brings you here today? Are you on the bride's side or the groom's?"

He had a sour smell, and was missing an incisor.

"I'm a friend of Atalia Abravanel's," Shmuel stammered. "Well, not a friend. An acquaintance. A neighbor."

"I invited him," Atalia said. "I wanted us to have a witness. We'll wait another five minutes, and if Esther Levi doesn't turn up, we'll get down to business."

They were sitting on the upper, discreet floor of Café Atara, a kind of gallery, shrouded in mist. It was redolent of coffee and cakes and cigarette smoke mixed with the smell of wet woolen overcoats and winter body odors. The gallery was windowless, and the air was thick and smoky. At the neighboring tables sat various well-known Jerusalem figures. There was a middle-aged history lecturer, who did not recognize Shmuel despite the fact that he had attended one of his seminars the previous year. And there were two women, one an overweight Knesset member of the governing party and the other a journalist at *Davar*. They were drinking tea with milk and eating apple cake with cream.

"It's out of the question," the politician said. "You can't keep silent about something like that."

The journalist replied:

"But I'm not trying to justify them, not at all, don't get me wrong, there's no way I could justify them. Nevertheless, I feel sorry for them. People here have forgotten that there's room in the world for pity, as well as principles and ideals."

"You can't have pity at the expense of principles and ideals, Sylvia."

At a third table sat a well-known painter, no longer young, with a pockmarked face and bushy eyebrows, wearing a red silk scarf, reading a newspaper attached to a wooden stick, as was the custom in cafés in prewar Europe. A waiter in a white jacket was going around the tables, and at a sign from Atalia he hurried across to their table, a white napkin over his arm, bowed, and said in a Viennese accent:

"Good afternoon, ladies and gentlemen. What is your pleasure today? We have all sorts of lovely cakes. I particularly recommend the chocolate torte."

Atalia ordered strong black coffee for Shmuel and herself, while the poet, with a sigh that suggested he was making a special exception, through gritted teeth, ordered a tiny glass, really just a thimbleful, of brandy. But it must be real brandy, imported brandy, not the piss they make here. Then he lit a cigarette, took three or four deep puffs, stubbed it out in the ashtray, sniffed his fingertips, lit another, and said:

"I'd still like to know why we've met here today. To draw up a new manifesto? To sign another declaration? To organize a mass rally with six or seven participants?"

"You know why we're here," Atalia said. "Ilya Schwarzbaum."

The poet stared at her. He carefully stubbed out the cigarette of which he had smoked less than a third, took a new one from the pack without offering one to Atalia or Shmuel, blew streams of smoke out through his nostrils, and burst into gurgling, resentful laughter, so that the people sitting at the nearby tables turned and looked at him in surprise through the cloud of smoke.

"Firstly," he said, "I've never borrowed a cent from Ilya Schwarzbaum. And I never would. He's a loathsome individual. A miserable Jewish go-between for all sorts of building sites and depots. Secondly, as I've already told you at least twice, I'll repay him when I've got money. If I get money. And why should I have money? Whereas that Ilya has more money than he has hairs in his nose. Actually, the reason I came here today was to ask him, through you, for a small loan, five thousand liras, for three months. Tell him I'm willing to pay interest. Compound interest even."

"Let's go back to the previous loan," Atalia said. "We have a witness. Esther Levi. You don't remember her, but she was with you here in Café Atara two years ago when Ilya gave you the money in cash. Esther Levi will testify against you if we take you to court. And we will."

"Hey, you," the poet suddenly turned to Shmuel, "why are you sitting there saying nothing? It looks like you're going to be the second witness against me? Without two witnesses you haven't got a case. You're a socialist. Or maybe not anymore. Once you were a socialist, a follower of Fidel Castro. So please explain to me, where's the justice in this? How and why should a poor poet like me finance a filthy bloodsucker like Ilya Schwarzbaum?"

The waiter returned with a brandy for Hiram Nehushtan and a black coffee each for Atalia and Shmuel. He put a little milk jug down next to the coffee cups. Then he inquired politely if he could suggest an apple cake with whipped cream? Or the chocolate torte, also with whipped cream? Or some crumble?

Atalia refused all three suggestions politely, thanked the waiter, and said:

"Esther Levi hasn't turned up. But we'll definitely take her to the court hearing. She also told us that your parents left you a windowless one-room basement flat in an alley behind the Edison Theater. The place you call your den. You wouldn't want the court to take that flat away from you. Where would you go?"

Hiram Nehushtan balanced his lit cigarette on the edge of the ashtray, forgot it there, lit another one, and moaned:

"Where would I go? Where would I go? I'd go to hell. Anyway, I've been on the road to hell for ages. I've gone most of the way. I'm nearly there."

Suddenly he stood up and said:

"That's it. I've had enough. I'm leaving. This very minute. I don't want to sit with you anymore. I don't want to go on talking to you. You're cruel people. Cruelty, ladies and gentlemen, is the curse of mankind. We weren't driven out of Paradise because of that apple, to hell with the apple, who cares about one apple more or less. We weren't driven out because of any silly apple, we were driven out of Paradise because of cruelty. To this day we are driven from place to place only because of cruelty. Tell your revolting contractor he'll get his money back with compound interest, he'll get it back several times over, he'll get it back in sacks stuffed with coins and banknotes, he'll get it back in a shower of cash, only not from me. He'll get it back from the rich and not from someone who's got nothing. And by the way, I'm cruel too. I won't deny it. I'm a cruel man, a petty man, a man eager for respect, driven from place to place all these years. A totally redundant individual. But three thousand liras! Ilya Schwarzbaum! That reptile could easily give three thousand liras as a tip to some shoeshine boy. I haven't even got three liras to pay for this piss brandy. Anyway, I'm leaving, because a sensitive man shouldn't spend a minute more than necessary in the company of evil-minded people. As for you"—he turned toward Shmuel and laughed that wet, dishonest laugh of his—"you'd better watch out for her. If you happen to have fallen for her already, heaven help you. Yes, yes, I'm going. There's nothing for me here. Anyway, everyone's forgotten me. Why don't you all forget me too? Forget me once and for all. And that'll be that."

He turned and stumbled down the steps. Atalia and Shmuel, looking down from the gallery, could see him fumble among the coats on the coat stand at the entrance, eventually pull out of the heap a torn raincoat that looked as if it had once belonged to a British soldier, put it on, wave to the photograph of President Yitzhak Ben-Zvi, and stagger uncertainly into the cold, damp street.

41

After the poet left, Shmuel and Atalia remained facing each other with their empty coffee cups in front of them, talking about Mount Scopus and the university, which had been cut off from its buildings because of the war. Shmuel remembered that in less than an hour he had to be back on duty with Gershom Wald. He ought to tell Atalia. He ought to tell her now, without delay. But what should he tell her? He smiled absent-mindedly, his gaze fixed on her veiny hands on the table before her, her skin dappled with brown spots, as if the hands really were much older than she. He said softly:

"Maybe we could meet this evening? We could go to the cinema and then eat at your restaurant? Wald will surely agree to let me go a few hours before the end of my time with him."

"Tell me," Atalia said, "aren't there any girls your age left in Jerusalem?"

Shmuel protested. He too was quite an old young man, in fact. "So what?" he asked, and, after a moment's hesitation, added, "After all, we are both on our own."

"You wanted to be on your own. Isn't that why you came to us, to be on your own?"

"I came because my girlfriend left me and married her ex-boyfriend. I came because my father lost a lawsuit and declared bankruptcy and couldn't afford to pay for me to study anymore. And also because I'd been at a standstill with my thesis for several months. Although I still haven't stopped wondering how the world and the Jews would look if they hadn't rejected Jesus. I can't stop thinking about the man who betrayed Jesus to his enemies—for what, thirty pieces of silver? Tell me, does this seem logical to you? Thirty pieces of silver! A wealthy man like Judas, who apparently owned land in the town of Kerioth. Do you happen to know roughly how much thirty pieces of silver was worth at that time? Not much. The price of an average slave. Maybe you'd like to hear some of my thoughts about Jesus and the Jews. I could read you something from my drafts this evening."

She ignored his offer. She waved a hand to disperse the smoke that still hung between them. The waiter came over, and she paid for the coffee and the brandy and asked for a receipt. Shmuel had pulled his wallet out, but too late. She told him not to bother, to save his money, this small expense would be covered by the investigation bureau where she worked.

"I pay you so little for your work with us. A pittance. Tell me, do you get some enjoyment from the hours you spend with Wald? Maybe in the midst of his outpourings there's a minute or two that makes sense? You must forgive him. Since his son died he's got nothing left except words. And in fact you're fond of words yourself. The work you do for us suits you through and through."

Atalia folded the receipt and they both stood. They went down from the Café Atara gallery, found their coats on the rotating coat stand at the entrance, and Shmuel tried to help Atalia on with hers. But he was so clumsy that she pulled her coat away from him, put it on, buttoned it, and then turned to help Shmuel, who, instead of sliding his arm into the sleeve, had thrust it into the torn lining. As they stood at the entrance, while he was putting on his *shapka*, her finger touched his cheek lightly, quickly, as if brushing a crumb off his beard, and she said:

"Sometimes you're quite touching. Though I have no heart to touch."

At that moment Shmuel regretted that his face was covered by an unkempt beard.

They started walking toward Rabbi Elbaz Lane but stopped by a telephone kiosk, because Atalia wanted to make a phone call.

"I'll wait here," Shmuel said.

After five or six minutes, Atalia came out and bestowed on Shmuel one of her rare smiles, a faint smile that began at the corners of her eyes and only later reached the corners of her lips. She took his arm, squeezed it lightly, and said:

"Okay. I'll see you this evening. Not for a late-night ambush on Mount Zion this time, or for supper and a film, but at a place I'm sure you don't know. Fink's Bar. Have you heard of Fink's? All sorts of people get together there over a glass of vermouth or whiskey—journalists, foreign correspondents, theater people, consuls of various countries, lawyers, UNO army officers, men and women who are married but not to each other, sometimes young poets who come with their girlfriends to see and be seen. I have to sit there for an hour or two this evening, to watch an important man. Only to watch him. That's all. If you're so keen, you can talk to me, while I'm watching, about the Jews and Jesus and Judas. I promise to listen at least part of the time, even if my eyes are busy."

And she added:

"We'll be a couple. Because of your beard and your mane of hair, you look more or less ageless. People will take you for my companion. And in fact they'll be right: this evening you will be my companion."

"There's something I have to tell you," Shmuel said. "It's like this: several times I've dreamed of you at night. You and your father. Your father looked a bit like Albert Camus in a photo I saw once in a newspaper. In the dreams you are even more beyond my reach than in real life."

"Beyond your reach," Atalia said. "How banal."

"What I mean is . . . ," Shmuel said, but couldn't explain.

"Your predecessors in the attic also began to tell me their dreams. Then they left us, each one in turn. You'll leave us soon too. This monotonous life in a dark, aging house with a garrulous old man and an embittered woman for company doesn't suit a young man like you. You're so full of ideas. So full of brain waves. One day you may write a book, if you can get over your laziness. Soon you'll be off to search for signs of life elsewhere. Maybe to the university. Or maybe to Haifa, back to your mom and dad."

"They're building a new town in the Negev, on the edge of the Ramon Crater. Before I came to you, I was thinking of going there. I was hoping they might give me a job as a night watchman or a warehouseman. But no. I'm going to stay with you two till you throw me out. I'm not going anywhere. Anyway, I've got no willpower left. My willpower has faded, if you can say that."

"Why should you stay with us?"

Shmuel mustered all his courage and muttered:

"Don't you know, Atalia?"

"It'll end badly," Atalia said as they reached the front door and she turned the key in the lock. "Be careful of that step. Tread on it gently. Come to Fink's Bar at ten o'clock. You'll have to get there on your own. I'll be waiting for you. It's on Hahistadrut Street at the corner of King George Street, opposite the Tel Or cinema and the Cooperative Restaurant. Don't eat first. I'll treat you to a proper dinner tonight instead of your usual leftover scraps. Don't worry, the bureau will pick up the bill."

Shmuel inhaled the smell of the house, that smell of fresh laundry, of cleanness, of starch and ironing, mingled with a hint of the odor of old age. He went up to his room, threw his cap and coat on the bed, took a long piss, was so impatient that he flushed before he'd finished, coughed, flushed again, and cursed himself for the expression "beyond my reach," which he'd used earlier about Atalia. Then he went down to the library and found Gershom Wald sitting at the desk, with the crutches resting at an angle against his wicker couch. The old man was reading a book, scribbling notes on a piece of paper covered in crossings-out, his thick white mustache bristling like a brindled polecat, his snowy eyebrows thick and bushy, and his lips moving soundlessly. At that moment Shmuel felt close to the old man. As though he had known and loved him since childhood. But almost everything they talked about in their protracted conversations on these long winter evenings suddenly seemed to him to be very far from what they truly ought to be talking about.

42

—

"THEY CALLED HIM A TRAITOR," Wald said, "because he fraternized with Arabs. He went to see them in Katamon, Sheikh Jarrah, Ramallah, Bethlehem, and Beit Jallah. He often entertained them here in his home. All sorts of Arab journalists used to come here. Public figures. Union leaders. Teachers. They called him a traitor because in '47 and even in '48, at the height of the fighting in the War of Independence, he continued to argue that the decision to create a Jewish state was a tragic mistake. Yes. It would be better, he used to say, if instead of the crumbling British Mandate we had an international mandate or a temporary regime of American trusteeship. It was fairly certain, he said, that permission would be given for a hundred thousand Holocaust survivors from the DP camps scattered around Europe to come here—even the Americans would support such a one-off immigration—and the Jewish presence would grow from six hundred and fifty thousand to three-quarters of a million. That would resolve the urgent distress of the displaced European Jews. After that, it would be best to call a halt. We should let the Arabs gradually absorb the fact of our presence here, over ten or twenty years. In the meantime, things might calm down a little, on condition that we did not brandish the claim to a Jewish state. Arab opposition, Abravanel asserted, was mainly not directed against the existing Zionist enterprise, which consisted essentially of a handful of small towns and a few dozen villages along the coastal plain, but flowed from fear of the power buildup of the Jews and their far-reaching ambitions. In the course of long years of conversations with his Arab friends in Palestine and the neighboring countries, he had come to the conclusion that the Arabs were principally afraid of what they imagined as the superiority of the Jews in skills, technology, cunning, and motivation, which would eventually lead them to spread and to take control of the entire Arab region. What they feared, Abravanel claimed, was not so much the tiny Zionist embryo but the destructive giant contained within it."

"Some giant," Shmuel remarked softly. "That's a joke. After all, compared to them we are no more than a drop in the ocean."

"That's not how the Arabs see it, according to Abravanel. The Arabs do not believe for a moment in the Zionist rhetoric, that a handful of Jews came here to find a tiny refuge from their persecutors in Europe. There was once a prime minister of Iraq, Hamdi al-Pachachi, who declared in 1947 that when the number of Jews in Palestine reached one million, no one in Palestine would be able to resist them. When their number reached two million, no one in the whole Middle East could resist them. And if they reached three or four million, the whole Muslim world would be powerless to withstand them. It was these fears, Shealtiel Abravanel said—fear of the new crusaders, a superstitious belief in the satanic powers of the Jews, the Arab dread that the Jews would demolish the mosques on the Temple Mount and replace them with the Jewish Temple, and set up a Jewish empire from the Nile to the Euphrates—these were the source of the Arabs' fierce opposition to the gradually emerging reality of a Jewish entity extending from the coast to the foothills of the mountains. We still had the ability to soothe these Arab fears, Shealtiel

Abravanel believed, if we worked with patience, with goodwill, with tireless efforts to talk to the Arabs, by setting up joint trade unions, by opening up Jewish settlements to Arab residents, by opening our schools and our university to Arab students, and above all by abandoning the pretentious idea of setting up a separate state for Jews with a Jewish army, Jewish rule, and attributes of sovereignty that would belong to the Jews, and to the Jews alone."

"His thinking," Shmuel said sadly, "has something attractive, even moving, about it, but it's just too sweet-natured. I actually think that more than the Arabs feared the future power of the Jews, they were tempted by their present weakness. Shall we have a glass of tea now? And maybe a few biscuits? And soon you've got to take your cough syrup and two pills."

"They called him a traitor," Wald repeated, ignoring the offer of tea, "because the slim chance which opened up in the mid-thirties of setting up a state for Jews here, albeit in a tiny section of the country, dazzled most of us. Including myself. Abravanel, for his part, did not believe in any state. Not even a binational one. Or a state shared by Jews and Arabs. The very idea of a world divided into hundreds of states with border crossings, barbed-wire fences, passports, flags, armies, and separate currencies seemed to him like an archaic, primitive, murderous delusion, an anachronistic idea that would soon disappear. He would say to me: Why do you need to rush to set up another Lilliputian statelet here, with blood and fire, at the cost of perpetual war, when soon all states are going to vanish, to be replaced by various communities speaking different languages living side by side with each other, among each other, without the lethal toys of sovereignty, armies, border crossings, and all sorts of deadly weaponry."

"Did he try to win converts to his ideas? Among the leadership? In the press? In the wider public?"

"He tried. In little circles. Both among Arabs and among Jews.

At least twice a month he would travel to Ramallah and Beth-lehem, to Jaffa, Haifa, or Beirut. He took part in private meet-ings in Rehavia, in the salons of immigrant scholars from Ger-many. Yes. It would be better for us not to try to set up either an Arab state or a Jewish state, he argued: let us live here next to each other and among each other, Jews and Arabs, Christians and Muslims, Druze and Circassians, Greeks and Latins and Ar-menians, a group of neighboring communities not divided by any barriers. Maybe the Arab fear of what appeared to them as the ambitious Zionist scheme to Judaize the whole land would gradually be dispelled. In our schools the children would learn Arabic, and in their schools they would learn Hebrew. Or better still, he said, let's develop joint schools. Thirty years of British troublemaking based on the principle of divide and rule would finally come to an end. And in this way, not in a single day or a single year, the first shoots of trust and even personal friend-ship between Jews and Arabs might sprout. And, in fact, shoots like this existed under British rule, in Haifa, Jerusalem, Tiberias, Jaffa, and other places. Many Jews and Arabs were linked by ties of business and were often invited into each other's homes. Like Abravanel and his friends. Surely there is so much that these two peoples share: the Jews and the Arabs, in their different ways, have been the victims of Christian Europe through long histori-cal periods. The Arabs were humiliated by the colonial powers and suffered the ignominy of oppression and exploitation, while the Jews suffered generation upon generation of contempt, ban-ishment, persecution, exile, massacre, and finally genocide unpar-alleled in human history. Surely there is a deep historic basis for ties of sympathy and understanding between these two victims of Christian Europe, Shealtiel used to say."

"I like that," said Shmuel. "A little naïve. Overly optimistic. Totally contrary to what Stalin said about the national question. But attractive."

He stood up, switched on the light, and went from window to window closing the shutters, which creaked on their hinges. As he opened the windows to pull the shutters to, the library was flooded with cold, dry Jerusalem air that bit the throat and pinched the lungs. Shmuel felt for the inhaler in his pocket but put off using it. Gershom Wald continued:

"If the Jews persisted in setting up an independent Jewish state when the British Mandate came to an end, Abravanel warned, on that day a bloody war would break out between them and the whole Arab world, or perhaps the entire Muslim world. Half a million Jews against hundreds of millions of Muslims. That war, Abravanel predicted, the Jews could not win. Even if a miracle occurred and they managed to overcome the Arabs in one round, or two, three, or four, in the end Islam would get the upper hand. The war would continue for generations, because each Jewish victory would only deepen and redouble the Arab fear of the Jews' satanic abilities and their crusading ambitions. Shealtiel used to repeat these words, or something like them, to me here in this very room. Before it all happened. Even before I lost my son, my only son, in the Jerusalem hills on the night of April 2. He used to talk standing up, by the window, with his back to the darkness outside and his face turned not toward me but toward that painting by Rubin over there. He was very fond of the land-scape in the picture. He loved the mountains of Galilee and the slopes of the valleys and the Carmel. He loved Jerusalem and the desert and the little Arab villages on the coastal plain and in the foothills. He also loved the lawns in the kibbutzim and the Jewish settlements, with their casuarina trees and their red-tiled roofs. There was no contradiction.

"A few weeks after Micha and Atalia married, in 1946, Sheal-tiel turned up one evening at my little flat on the Gaza Road and invited me to come and live with them here in this house. There's plenty of room for all of us, he said. Why should you live on your own? I was a history teacher at the Rehavia Gymnasium. And, in fact, I was well on the way to retirement. At that time Micha and Atalia were living in your attic. This room was Shealtiel Abravanel's library. The only books I brought with me are the novels now in my bedroom. He used to pace back and forth in this room, from wall to wall, from the windows to the door, from the door to the bead curtain in the doorway to the kitchen, with short, quick steps, expounding his vision of a multiplicity of communities. He called the state—any state—a ravening dinosaur. Once he came back here very upset after a half hour face-to-face meeting with David Ben-Gurion and David Remez in Ben-Gurion's office in the Jewish Agency building, and he said to me—I can remember how his voice shook as he spoke—'That little man sometimes sounds like a hysterical woman! He has become a false messiah. Another Shabbetai Zevi. Or Jacob Frank. And he is going to embroil all of us—Jews, Arabs, and in fact the whole world—in catastrophic bloodshed which will have no end.' And he went on: 'Ben-Gurion may yet manage in his lifetime, and even quite soon, to be the king of the Jews. King for a day. A pauper king. The Paupers' Messiah. But future generations will curse him. He has already dragged his more cautious comrades after him. He has sown the seeds of nationalistic radicalism within them. The real tragedy of humankind,' Shealtiel used to say, 'is not that the persecuted and enslaved crave to be liberated and to hold their heads high. No. The worst thing is that the enslaved secretly dream of enslaving their enslavers. The persecuted yearn to be persecutors. The slaves dream of being masters. As in the book of Esther.'"

Gershom Wald stopped for a moment, then, shaking his head, he added:

"No. In no way. I did not believe in any of it. Not for a minute. I even made fun of him. It did not occur to me for a second that Ben-Gurion ever aspired to dominate the Arabs. Shealtiel lived in a Manichaean world. He had set up a sort of utopian paradise and portrayed the opposite as hell. Meanwhile, they had started calling him a traitor. They said he had sold himself to the Arabs for a lot of money. They said he was the bastard son of an Arab. Hebrew newspapers mockingly called him the Muezzin, or Sheikh Abravanel, or the Sword of Islam."

"How about you?" Shmuel asked, so overwhelmed that he forgot to feed the goldfish or to give the old man his evening pills. "Didn't you quarrel with him?"

"Me?" Gershom Wald sighed. "I was powerless. At one time I used to argue with him passionately. Until the night of April 2. That night all the arguments between us died once and for all. The disaster stifled our arguments. In any case, by that time his ideas did not have a chance in this country. We could all see plainly that the Arabs would not tolerate our presence here even if we abandoned the idea of setting up a Jewish state. It was as clear as day, even to the moderates among us, that the Arab position did not leave room for the tiniest shadow of compromise. And I was already a dead man."

"I was only thirteen at the time," Shmuel said. "I was in a youth movement. I believed like everyone else that we were the righteous few, while they, the Arabs, were the wicked many. I had no doubt that their aim was to wrest the strip of land under our feet away from us by force. The whole Arab world was unanimously resolved to destroy the Jews or drive us into the sea. Such were the cries of the muezzins from the minarets at midday on Fridays. Although, when I was little, Arab clients used to come to my father's small land surveyor's office in Haifa. Occasionally a landowner, an *effendi* wearing a red *tarboosh* and suspenders, and a suit with a gold chain that wound around his belly and ended at a gold watch hidden in a side pocket. These visitors would be received with liqueurs and sweetmeats, and my father and his partner would converse with them in a leisurely, comfortable manner in rounded, courteous English or French. They would praise the sea breeze at evening or the olive harvest. And sometimes they invited us, my mother and father, my sister and me, to eat cakes in their homes on Allenby Street. The servants brought tray after tray of coffee or strong Arab tea, peanuts, walnuts, almonds, halva, and baklava. They smoked a cigarette together, and then another, and agreed that all politics is totally unnecessary and brings only sorrow and harm to us all. That without politics, life could be peaceful and beautiful. Until one day Jewish buses began to be attacked in Haifa, Jewish fighters launched bloody retaliatory raids on villages around the bay, and inflamed Arab mobs butchered the Jewish workers in the refineries. Then more retaliatory raids followed, Jewish and Arab snipers took up positions on rooftops behind barriers of sandbags, and fortified checkpoints were set up at the crossings between Arab and Jewish neighborhoods. And in April '48, a month or so before the British left, tens of thousands of Haifa Arabs boarded a fleet of fishing boats and other vessels and fled en masse to Lebanon. On the last day, Jewish leaders were still distributing leaflets begging them to stay. However, in Lydda and many other places we did not beg them to stay but murdered them and drove them out. Even in Haifa these leaflets did not do much good: the Arabs there were in mortal panic. They were terrified of being massacred: a rumor had spread that the Jews meant to kill them all, just as they had killed the inhabitants of the Arab village of Deir Yassin, which used to be right here, on the other side of that hill, not far from this house. Overnight, Haifa was emptied of most of its Arab inhabitants. To this day, when I'm at home, I walk through Arab neighborhoods that are now full of recent Jewish immigrants, or wander in the early evening among alleyways where the few thousand Arabs who chose to stay in Haifa still live, and I wonder whether what happened really had to happen. My father, on the other hand, maintains to this day that there was no alternative. That the War of Independence in 1948 was a total war for life or death, us or them, a war that was not fought between two armies but between two entire populations, street against street, neighborhood against neighborhood, a window of one house against a window of the house opposite. In such wars, my father says, civil wars, entire populations are always uprooted. It's the same everywhere. The same thing happened between Greece and Turkey. Between India and Pakistan. Between Poland or Czechoslovakia and Germany. I used to listen to him, and I used to listen to my mother's view, that it was all the fault of the British, who promised the land twice over and enjoyed stirring up one people against the other. Atalia told me once that her father did not belong to his time. He may have come too late, or too soon. But he didn't belong to his own time. He and Ben-Gurion were both men with great dreams. I, on the other hand, sometimes see the cracks. You may have influenced me somewhat in the matter of the cracks. I have learned in our evening chats to have doubts. Maybe that's why I shall never be a real revolutionary, just a café revolutionary. I'm going to the kitchen now to warm up our porridge. Do you mind if I leave you a little early tonight, because Atalia has invited me to have dinner with her in some club or bar that I've never been to before."

Shmuel placed a checkered tea towel over Gershom Wald's shirt, tucked the corner under his collar, served him the warmed-up porridge on which he had sprinkled some sugar and cinnamon, and spread two thick slices of bread with margarine and cream cheese for himself. Atalia had told him not to eat anything before they met at Fink's, but hunger got the better of him.

Gershom Wald said, while he ate the porridge:

"I consider Ben-Gurion the greatest Jewish leader of all time. Greater than King David. Maybe one of the greatest statesmen in history. He is a clearheaded, sharp-sighted man who understood a long time ago that the Arabs will never accept our presence here of their own free will. They will never agree to share either territory or power with us. He realized long before his comrades that nothing is going to be offered us on a silver salver, that no amount of sweet-talking will induce the Arabs to like us, and he also saw that no external power will protect us when the Arabs set out to uproot us all from here. As early as the 1930s, after long talks with Arab leaders, including Shealtiel Abravanel's lovely and pleasant friends, Ben-Gurion arrived at the conclusion that whatever we did not achieve for ourselves would not be handed to us on a plate. Micha used to go for weapons training at night in the Tel Arza woods because he knew that too. We all knew. Only I didn't know that my son—I didn't imagine that my son—I didn't even want to think about it. He's not a boy anymore, I said to myself, he's thirty-seven years old and nearly a professor. Sometimes, in the weeks after the disaster, without his saying a word, I seemed to hear Shealtiel Abravanel asking me silently if I still believed that it was all worthwhile. The question that Shealtiel never asked wounded me over and over, as if he had stuck a knife in my throat. And after that we didn't speak to each other. Neither of us. We shut up. Everything faded away. Except for very occasional exchanges about repairing the roof or buying an electric refrigerator. Now, please leave the bowl with the spoon in the sink. Don't bother to wash them up and put them away. Then run off to chase after the hem of her dress. For my part, I don't expect any good from your pursuit of her. You were not meant for her and she was not meant for you. In fact, she was not meant for any man. She will be a woman on her own till her dying day. And after I die, she will be a woman alone in this empty house. No stranger will come. Or perhaps he will come, and be thrown out the next day, or after a while, leaving just as he came. You're going to be thrown out soon as well, and I'll lose you, too. Get a move on. Put on your best shirt and hurry on your way. Don't worry about me. I shall go on sitting here with my books and notebooks until the dawn watch, and then I shall get myself to bed under my own steam. Go, Shmuel. Go to her. You no longer have any choice."

43

B̲UT SHMUEL ASH DID NOT make it to his date with Atalia that evening. As he was about to dash out of the house, with
his *shapka* on his disheveled head, his duffel coat done up to the
neck, and one of his trouser buttons missing, he tripped on the
improvised step inside the front door. He didn't trip, in fact, but
stepped with all his weight on one end of the step, which made
it lift like a lever and hurled him backward. He turned over, his
back thumped against the wall, his head hit the other wall and
then the flagstones, and he finally landed on his back with his left
foot twisted under him. A sharp pain pierced his ankle. At first he
was more preoccupied by the pain in his head than by the pain
in his ankle. The cap was dislodged and rolled down the passage.
Shmuel lay sprawled on his back, and pushing his fingers under
his head, he could feel a pool of blood forming. He lay there for
a few minutes without moving and then, to his surprise, found
that he was laughing. Laughing and groaning at the same time.
Despite the pain, the fall made him laugh as if it had happened to
someone else, or as if he had pulled off a surprising, even amusing, prank. While he was trying unsuccessfully to stand up or at
least to get to his knees, Gershom Wald's crutches sounded in the
distance. The old man had heard the impact of the fall, limped

into the passage, and now took in at a glance the bent body, the blood that was flowing from the thicket of hair and forming a rivulet on the floor, the twisted ankle. He turned back, hurried on his crutches to his desk, and telephoned for an ambulance. Then he hobbled back down the passage and, leaning his weight on one crutch, bent over, took a handkerchief out of his pocket, pressed it to Shmuel's bleeding head, and said:

"This house does not bring you much luck. In fact, it brings none of us much luck."

Shmuel laughed.

"I'm going to need crutches now. If not a wheelchair. There will be four crutches here." But his laugh trailed off into a groan of pain.

In about twenty minutes an unshaven paramedic wearing a white gown arrived, accompanied by two agile, darker-skinned stretcher-bearers, both thin and as alike as a pair of twins, except that one had preternaturally long arms; both were bald, and the one with long arms, Shmuel noticed, had a fleshy wart on the left side of his head. The stretcher-bearers carried Shmuel to the ambulance. They barely spoke a word. The paramedic bent over and took Shmuel's pulse, then cut off a patch of his curls with a small pair of scissors, disinfected the bleeding wound on his head, and covered it with several layers of gauze and a sticking plaster. And since Shmuel had overturned the wooden step when he fell, the stretcher-bearers had to raise the stretcher at an angle as they climbed up from the passage to the area in front of the door. First they laid the foot of the stretcher on the higher surface, then the one with the wart climbed from the passage onto the flat surface in front of the door and dragged the foot of the stretcher over the threshold. Meanwhile, his colleague replaced the wooden step that had turned upside down and, taking hold of the two handles on either side of the injured man's head, he heaved the stretcher up and the two of them carried it out into the garden, through the broken gate, and into the flashing ambulance, which stood with its engine running and its rear doors open, facing the gate.

On the way, the paramedic wrapped Shmuel's head in a white bandage on which a bloodstain immediately spread. It was a few minutes before ten when they brought him to the emergency ward of Shaare Zedek Hospital on the Jaffa Road. They injected him with a painkiller and x-rayed his ankle. They found a hairline fracture, put his ankle in plaster, and left him in the orthopedic ward for further observation.

At seven o'clock the next morning, Atalia arrived, wearing a pale blue pullover, a dark blue skirt and a red scarf, with her big wooden earrings dangling from her ears, and a small silver brooch in the form of a shell, half concealed by the cascade of hair over her left shoulder. She stood in the doorway scanning the eight beds in the ward, four on each side, two of which were empty. When she caught sight of Shmuel she did not hurry over to him but stayed by the door for a moment, looking at him as if she had discovered some new aspect of his appearance. His eyes caressed her with a submissive gentleness that lightly touched her heart. Shmuel was lying covered with a sheet in the third bed on the left. The leg in plaster was exposed and raised. When she came over to him, he closed his eyes. Atalia leaned across, delicately straightened the sheet, and gently stroked his beard. She felt the bandage and ruffled his curls.

He opened his eyes. Cautiously he stroked the hand that was stroking him and was about to smile. But an expression spread on his face that reflected both the pain and the pleasure.

"Does it hurt a lot?"

"No. Hardly at all. Yes."

"Have they given you any painkillers?"

"Yes, they have."

"Didn't they help?"

"No. Hardly at all. A little."

"I'll go and speak to them. They'll give you something that'll help. Do you want a drink first? Some water?"

"Never mind."

"Yes or no?"

"Never mind. Thank you."

"They told me you've cracked your ankle joint."

"Did you wait for me last night?"

"Till nearly midnight. I thought you'd forgotten. No, I didn't. I thought you'd fallen asleep."

"I didn't fall asleep. I was running to see you, I was afraid I was late, and I fell over the step."

"Were you running because you were excited?"

"No. Perhaps. Yes."

Atalia laid a cool hand on Shmuel's bandaged forehead and brought her face so close to his that for an instant his nostrils caught the scent of violets and the toothpaste smell of her breath. Then she went off in search of a doctor or nurse who could give him something to relieve the pain. She felt responsible for his injury, though she could find no logical explanation for this feeling. Nevertheless, she decided to stay with him until he was sent home at lunchtime, after the doctors' rounds. A tall, thin nurse whose hair was gathered in a little coil at the back of her neck came and gave Shmuel a pill with a glass of water and told him that the physiotherapist would be there at ten o'clock to show him how to use crutches, after which he would probably be discharged. He recalled the hospital in Haifa where he was taken when he was little, after the scorpion bite. He remembered the touch of his mother's cold hand on his forehead. He put out a hand to feel, and found Atalia's hand; he held on to it and interlaced his fingers with hers.

"You're always running," Atalia said. "Why do you run all the time? If you hadn't been running, you wouldn't have fallen over in the passage."

Shmuel said:

"I was running to you, Atalia."

"There was no reason for you to run. The man I was supposed to watch at Fink's Bar never turned up. I sat there on my own till nearly midnight waiting for you. Two young men, one after the other, came over to my table, and one of them tried to interest me in some gossip about an actress, the other in a confidential snippet about the exploits of the secret services. But I sent them both packing. I told them that I was waiting for someone and preferred to wait on my own. I drank a gin and tonic, nibbled some peanuts and almonds, and went on waiting. Why I waited for you I don't know. Maybe because I was sure that you must have got lost."

Shmuel did not reply. He tightened his hold on her fingers and looked for something to say. Not finding anything, he drew the hand that was clasped in his to his lips and pressed them to her fingers, not in a kiss but a touch.

Just before ten, a short, plump lad appeared, with red cheeks that looked as if they had been flayed. He was wearing a crumpled white gown and a drab skullcap secured with a clip on his thinning hair. He got Shmuel out of bed, made him stand on one leg, and started to teach him how to use crutches. Perhaps because he had had so many opportunities to watch Gershom Wald, Shmuel had no difficulty in learning how to position the crutches under his armpits, take firm hold of the handgrips, and advance cautiously down the space between the rows of beds with the leg that was in plaster raised slightly off the ground. Atalia and the physiotherapist supported him on either side. Within a quarter of an hour he was able to leave the ward with the assistance of his two angels, walk on his crutches to the end of the corridor, and return nimbly back again. Then, after a short rest, he went on another expedition, this time under his own steam. Atalia stayed a couple of paces behind, ready to support him if necessary. Shmuel said:

"Look. I can walk on my own."

Then he said:

"It'll be a few weeks before I can go back to work."

Atalia replied:

"There's no problem. You'll be back at work this evening. The two of you can sit facing each other as usual. The old man will talk and you will naturally disagree with him about everything he says. I'll take care of the porridge and the tea and I'll feed the goldfish."

When they had returned to Rabbi Elbaz Lane in a taxi called by Atalia, she cut the left leg of his corduroy trousers and helped him put them on over the plaster. Then she laid him down in the library on Gershom Wald's wicker couch, gave him a glass of tea and a slice of bread and cheese, and went off to open the next room, to air it out and prepare it for Shmuel's stay. This was the ground-floor room that was always kept locked, the room where Shmuel had never set foot, her father's room. She made up a bed for him on the narrow sofa. He could not climb up to his attic room while his leg was in plaster. Shmuel had longed to penetrate this locked room almost from the day he arrived in the Abravanel house. He had been expecting a revelation. Or an inspiration. As if this were the sealed heart of the house. And now, thanks to his accident, the door had finally been opened for him. He wondered what dreams he would dream here this night.

44

He lay on his back on the sofa that had been Sheal-tiel Abravanel's bed, with his plaster-covered foot raised on three cushions and his pink toes peeping out from the bottom, open end of the cast. His bandaged head rested on two more cushions. He was wearing his corduroy trousers, which Atalia had cut so that he could get his leg in with the plaster cast, and a pajama top that belonged to Gershom Wald. He was sucking a sweet toffee, and an open book lay face-down on his chest—Yizhar's *Days of Ziklag*—which he didn't feel like reading. A faint smell of melted candle wax and dried flowers hung in the air. He found the unfamiliar smell pleasant, though he had no idea what it was. Shmuel inhaled the strange odor deep into his lungs and wondered if this was how rooms that had been shut up for many years always smelled, or whether it was the smell of candles that had burned here years earlier on long winter evenings, or a trace of the smell of the ostracized, hated man who had spent the last years of his life here in total solitude. A slanting beam of sunlight filtered through the slats of the shutters, and innumerable tiny specks of dust whirled in it, like so many brightly lit worlds in a shining Milky Way. Shmuel tried to fix his gaze on one of these shining specks, no different from all the rest, and to track its path.

After a moment he lost it. Shmuel enjoyed lying on this sofa in this room, and the pleasant feeling percolated through his limbs, bringing back memories of his solitary days of illness when he was a child in Haifa, in that house he disliked, in the dark passage where his bed stood, between damp-stained walls.

What did Shealtiel Abravanel do after he was ostracized? What did he do during the siege of Jewish Jerusalem, the shelling, the house-to-house fighting, the fall of the Jewish Quarter in the Old City, the shortage of water, the lines for flour, oil, paraffin, powdered milk, and powdered eggs? Did he write notes to himself? Memoirs? Prophecies? Did he try to draw his angry daughter close to him? Did he somehow try to maintain indirect ties with his friends in Arab Jerusalem, beyond the firing lines? Did he draw up a memo to send to the interim government? Did he feverishly follow the course of the fighting? Did he shut himself up here and think day and night about his mortal adversary David Ben-Gurion, who at that time was commanding the bloody fighting from his tiny office on a hill in Ramat Gan?

The color of the walls and the ceiling was white which had faded almost to gray. There was no ceiling light, only a wall light at the head of the sofa on which Shmuel was lying, and a lamp on Shealtiel Abravanel's desk. This desk, unlike Gershom Wald's, was completely clear. There was not a single book, booklet, newspaper, or piece of paper on it. No pen, pencil, or ruler; no cup filled with rubber bands or paper clips. Nothing. Only the desk lamp, shining at the top of a hunched metal tube and shaded by a hemisphere of metal. The desk was free of dust, and Shmuel wondered whether the woman who came to clean the house once a week entered this locked room, or whether it was Atalia who dusted the few pieces of furniture from time to time.

The ornate black writing desk had thin black legs and a high back with two sloping side panels set with drawers and all sorts of little pigeonholes and secret hiding places. Shmuel dimly recalled from his childhood in Haifa that in the homes of Arab acquaintances such desks were called "secretaires." This word suddenly aroused in him a longing for the homes of those wealthy Arab notables on Allenby Street, which he visited with his father and where he was served pomegranate juice and sickly-sweet pastries that stuck between his teeth, under his tongue, and along his palate.

Besides the secretaire and the sofa on which Atalia had made Shmuel lie with his leg raised, the room contained two high-backed black chairs, a locked, severe-looking wardrobe, and three bookshelves containing some thirty or forty old tomes, in French, Arabic, Hebrew, Greek, and English. From where he lay on the sofa, Shmuel had difficulty making out the writing on their spines, but he promised himself he would examine them all as soon as he had a chance. And also secretly peep into the drawers of the secretaire.

Two delicate sketches of landscapes in the Judean Desert, under glass in dark frames, hung on the wall above the sofa. One of them showed a dry, windswept hill against a background of distant mountains, while the other showed the mouth of a dark cave in a wadi where a few battered bushes grew. A large, outdated map of the eastern Mediterranean basin was pinned to the wall behind the secretaire. Above it was a title in French: *Pays du Levant et leurs environs.* Beneath this heading stretched Syria and Lebanon, Cyprus, Palestine, and Transjordan, Iraq, northern Egypt, and the northern part of Arabia. Across Palestine and Transjordan was written *Palestine*, and in brackets *Terre Sainte*, while Lebanon bore the legend *Grand Liban*. The British sphere of influence, including Cyprus, was shaded pink; the French sphere of influence was marked in pale blue. The Mediterranean and Red Seas were colored dark blue. Turkey was green, and Saudi Arabia was yellow.

The shutter on the only window was closed, and the window

itself was shut and covered by a pair of thick brown double curtains. Through the crack between the curtains and between the
slats of the shutters filtered the solitary beam of sunlight that fell
at an angle and along whose entire length the thousands of shimmering spots of dust danced. This sunbeam mesmerized Shmuel.
Despite the dull pain in his ankle and head, he felt surrounded
by a sweet tranquility, as if he had finally come home—not to his
parents' home, the dark passage where he had slept as a child, but
the home he had always longed for, the home where he had never
been, his own home, his real home. The home toward which he
had been going all his life. He had not felt such deep inner peace
since he first came to this house on Rabbi Elbaz Lane in search
of a job. As if from the outset he had secretly yearned, all these
weeks, to earn the right to lie someday as an invalid in this room,
on this sofa, by the light of the desk lamp and the wall light, facing the French map of the lands of the Levant and their environs,
and at the foot of the sunbeam in which the molecules of dust
glittered and whirled ceaselessly.

Atalia entered the room without a sound, leaned over him, and
adjusted the cushions supporting his back. She sat down beside
him on the edge of the sofa holding a bowl of thick, steaming
vegetable soup. Sarah de Toledo had made the soup as usual for
Mr. Wald, but this time Atalia had asked her to make an extra
portion. She spread a tea towel over Shmuel's beard and chest
and fed him with a spoon, even though he was startled and said
there was no need, that he could perfectly well feed himself. But
Atalia insisted:

"You'll get it all over your beard and your pajama top."

And she added:

"During the last months I fed him, too. Here in this room.
Not on the bed but at the desk. We sat close together on those
two chairs and I spread a tea towel over him and fed him spoonful
by spoonful. He loved thick, well-seasoned soups like this, bean

soup, lentil soup, pumpkin soup. No. He was definitely not an
invalid at the end of his life. He wasn't paralyzed or senile. Only
weak and apathetic and withdrawn. At first I used to bring him the
hot soup—he liked it to be almost boiling—and leave the bowl
on the desk, and I would come back after a quarter of an hour to
fetch the empty bowl. In the last months of his life he wouldn't
eat unless I stayed in the room with him and implored him to eat,
and told him a story while he ate. He loved all kinds of tales and
fables. After a while, my presence and the story weren't enough:
he would sit and listen to me, but he wouldn't touch his food. So
I started feeding him with a spoon. When he'd finished, I'd wipe
his mouth with the tea towel and sit with him for an hour or so,
telling him about some old trip to Galilee or about a book I was
reading. I've already told you that I didn't love him, except maybe
when I was a little girl, but toward the end, when he himself
turned into a child, a belated closeness developed between us. He
had always spoken with sharp logic, in short, measured sentences,
in a low, persuasive voice. Even in the course of a bitter argument
he never raised his voice; he couldn't, and wouldn't, listen to what
others were saying, and he never bothered to listen to my mother
or me. But in his last months he spoke very little. He may even
have finally begun to listen to others. He used to sit sometimes
with Wald in what had been his library until he vacated it and left
it to Wald, just as in fact he left the rest of the house to us, apart
from this one small room. They would sit together in the library,
Wald saying almost nothing and Abravanel sitting in silence, listening to what Wald hadn't said. He would twist a paper clip between his fingers and attempt to straighten it again. Or maybe he
wasn't listening. There was no way of telling if he was listening
or just staring. Nobody entered his room except Wald and me.
Ever. No visitors, no acquaintances, no workmen. Only Bella, the
cleaner, flitted silently from room to room once a week, like an
evil spirit. We were all a little afraid of her. Sarah de Toledo used

to bring over the soup with pieces of meat in it, and the porridge, and sometimes some fruit or vegetables. No one visited him. No neighbors knocked at the door. No one ever came to see us, apart from five or six people who came to offer condolences on the first evenings after Micha was killed; they sat in the library for a while, doing their best to reduce the silence. Those people disappeared after a few days. The front door closed behind them, and after that we were alone for years. Nobody wanted to be associated with a traitor. He himself didn't seek any company. Two or three times, a letter arrived from beyond the border, from Beirut or Ramallah, forwarded by some contact in Europe. He didn't bother to reply to the letters. Once, a well-known French journalist got in touch by telephone, a radical figure known for his sympathy for the Arab cause, requesting permission to visit, to exchange views and put some questions. He didn't receive an answer. I was about to write to him that Abravanel no longer gave interviews, but I was told to leave the message unanswered. He lived the last years of his life under self-imposed house arrest. He never went through the gate. Not to the shop, or to the newspaper stand, or for an afternoon walk in the field at the bottom of the lane. I thought he was punishing himself, but I was wrong: he wasn't punishing himself, he was punishing the world. He never spoke to me or to Wald about the establishment of the state, for example. Or about our winning the war. Or the expulsion of the Arabs. Or about the hundreds of thousands of Jews who had begun to arrive from Arab lands and from Europe. Or the bloodshed on the new borders. As if all these things were happening on another planet. Only once, one evening, he broke his silence to say to me and Wald, at the kitchen table: 'You'll see. All this will hold for a few years at best. Two or three generations at the outside. Not more.' And with that he shut up again. Gershom Wald looked as if he were about to burst, so eager was he to reply, but he thought better of it and chose to stay silent. In the mornings,

Abravanel used to sit on the sofa and read the paper for a quarter of an hour or so, then he would silently hand it to me to read and to pass on to Wald. Then he would walk up and down his room or in the garden by the water cistern for an hour or more. When he got tired, he would take a chair outside and rest in the shade of the fig tree, in the paved area. He would shift his chair as the sun moved around, chasing the shade. After his midday bowl of soup he lay down for an hour or two. When he got up, he would sit at the desk and write. Or read. Or read and write alternately, until it got dark. Then he would switch on the desk lamp and go on reading, taking notes on little bits of paper. But we didn't find any of them after he died. Not a single piece of paper. Not so much as a little note. I looked in every drawer, on every shelf in the cupboard, and between the pages of the books in the book-case. He didn't burn his papers: I didn't find any trace of burning anywhere in the house or the garden. No. He must have torn everything up into tiny bits and flushed them down the toilet day by day. Both he and Wald wrote and destroyed, then wrote and destroyed again. Do you do that too? No? Everybody writes in this house except me. Your predecessors in the attic also tried to write, apparently. There must be something in the walls or under the flagstones. I'm the only one who doesn't write anything, ex-cept for instructions to Bella. After his death I locked this room, and I kept it locked, and it was only yesterday that I decided to open it for you, because there's no way you'll be able to climb up to the attic for a while."

She got up from the edge of the sofa and covered Shmuel with a light blanket, then left the room, taking the empty soup bowl with her. As she left she said:

"If you need anything, just call me. I'll hear you from the kitchen or my room. This house may have thick walls, but my hearing is sharp."

Shmuel lay on his back, watching the illuminated band of dust until the angle of the light changed and the indoor Milky Way, radiating sparks of brightness, vanished. A cool, calm dimness filled the room. He closed his eyes.

When he opened them, it was dark. Atalia lit the desk lamp but not the wall light. The room was full of shadows. She sat him up with the help of the three cushions behind his back and laid a tray on his stomach bearing a slice of bread and cream cheese, a finely chopped salad, a hard-boiled egg, and some black olives. This time Shmuel ate with gusto, and again Atalia sat on the edge of the sofa watching him, as if she were counting the olives as he ate them. For an instant his almond eyes met her brown-green eyes and an innocent gratitude that she found quite touching shone from his look. This time she did not feed him. He wrapped himself up in his blanket because he was afraid she would notice his rising desire. When he had finished eating, she took the tray away and left the room without a word, and a few minutes later she returned carrying a basin of soapy water, a sponge, and a towel. Shmuel protested that there was no need, that he could get out of bed and walk to the bathroom on his crutches; he had already been to the toilet two or three times on his own. But Atalia, ignoring his protestations, stroked his forehead quickly with her cool hand, told him not to interfere, and with brisk movements removed the blanket, took off the pajama top Shmuel had borrowed from Mr. Wald, and proceeded without a moment's hesitation to strip the corduroy trousers off both legs, the good one and the one in a cast, then removed his underpants, so he was lying on his back on the sofa, naked and stunned, hiding his private parts with one hand. She set to work washing his body with circular movements, which he found very pleasant once the initial shock and embarrassment had passed. First she sponged his shoulders and his hairy chest, then she told him to sit up and washed his back and waist, then laid him flat again, firmly scrubbed his stomach, his thick pubic hair, and, pushing his hand aside without a

word and without batting an eyelid, encircled his semi-erect penis, moving on swiftly to scrub his crotch, and finally washed his
good leg and, one by one, the pink toes peeping out of the bottom
of the cast. When the washing was done, she dried him rapidly
all over, from his forehead to his toes, with a thick, rough towel,
which he enjoyed a lot, as if he were just a little boy wrapped in a
towel after his bath on a winter evening. He curled up and closed
his eyes in embarrassment: despite his desperate efforts, his penis now stood erect in the hairy bush at the base of his stomach.
Atalia picked up the basin, folded the towel, dropped the sponge
into the bowl of soapy water, put everything down on the floor,
and leaned over Shmuel, her lips brushing his forehead while her
hand touched his penis for a moment. It was a touch that barely
happened. Then she covered him with the blanket, switched off
the light, and left the room silently, closing the door behind her.

45

THREE OR FOUR TIMES the next day, Shmuel got up and hobbled to the toilet on his crutches, stopping in the kitchen on the way back to drink three glasses of water and eat a thick slice of bread and jam, then limped back to bed and promptly fell asleep again. The pains were dull but persistent. He could feel them vaguely even when he was asleep, as if his body were still angry with him. And yet his pains were also pleasant, and he somehow felt he deserved them, that they were justly earned. Half awake, he waited tensely for Atalia to come back again to feed and wash him. But Atalia did not come.

At five in the afternoon, he was woken by Gershom Wald, who entered the room noisily, with a push of the door, coughs, and a clatter of crutches, and sat down expansively on one of the high-backed black chairs, propping his crutches up against the secretaire next to Shmuel's, and joked about their change of roles: "You're the invalid now, and I have to entertain you and keep you company." His white hair shone in the light of the lamp and his Einstein mustache quivered as if it had a life of its own. He was large and twisted, and whatever his pose, he looked uncomfortable, as if the seat were too low or too high, forever trying to change his position, his strong, broad hands moving restlessly. He recounted at great length some story about a king who changed places with a wayfarer, then said jokingly that Shmuel's fall was nothing but a transparent ploy to gain Atalia's favor, but that her favor was always illusory. And he added that it was some years since his crutches had set foot here in Abravanel's secret den, which Atalia always kept closed and locked.

Shmuel's three predecessors, who had inhabited the attic room, had apparently, according to Gershom Wald, never set eyes on this room. Nor were they ever allowed into Atalia's room, though all three, in their different ways, had longed for her and never ceased to hope for a miracle. Then, in an instant, Gershom Wald's cheerful mood passed, the sarcastic sparkle in his eye gave way to a suppressed sadness, and he let Shmuel talk for a few minutes about the designation "traitor," which ought really to be seen as a badge of honor:

"Not long ago in France, de Gaulle was elected president by the votes of the supporters of French rule in Algeria, and now it transpires that his intention was to abandon French rule and grant full independence to the Arab majority. Those who previously enthusiastically supported him now call him a traitor and even threaten to make an attempt on his life. The prophet Jeremiah was considered a traitor both by the Jerusalem rabble and by the royal court. The Talmudic rabbis ostracized Elisha ben Abuya and called him *Aher*, 'the Other.' But at least they didn't delete his teachings and his memory from the book. Abraham Lincoln, the liberator of the slaves, was called a traitor by his opponents. The German officers who tried to assassinate Hitler were executed as traitors. Every so often in history, courageous people have appeared who were ahead of their time and were called traitors or eccentrics. Theodor Herzl was called a traitor just because he dared to entertain the thought of a Jewish state outside the Land of Israel when it became clear that Ottoman-ruled Palestine was closed to the Jewish people. Even David Ben-

Gurion, when he agreed twelve years ago to the partition of the
land into two states, one Jewish and the other Arab, was called a
traitor by many Jews here. My parents and my sister now accuse
me of betraying my family by giving up studying. Actually, they
may be more right than they think, because in fact I betrayed my
family long before I gave up studying. I've betrayed them since
I was a child, when I fantasized about having different parents.
Anyone willing to change," Shmuel said, "will always be considered a traitor by those who cannot change and are scared to death
of change and don't understand it and loathe change. Shealtiel
Abravanel had a beautiful dream, and because of his dream some
people called him a traitor."

Shmuel stopped talking. He suddenly thought of his paternal
grandfather, Grandpa Antek, the one who came from Latvia in
1932 and was accepted for the British CID because of his talent
for forgery. During World War II he supplied the British with
dozens of forged Nazi documents that they issued to their spies
and agents behind enemy lines. The real truth was that Grandpa
Antek joined the CID so as to pass classified information to one
of the Jewish underground groups and also forged quite a few
documents for the underground. Yet it was members of his own
underground group who murdered him in 1946, because they
suspected him of being a double agent collaborating with the
British. Shmuel's father had spent a long time working to purge
his father's name of the taint of treachery. Shmuel added in a
hushed voice, as though afraid that strangers might hear:

"After all, the kiss of Judas, the most famous kiss in history, was
surely not a traitor's kiss. The men sent by the priests from the
Temple to arrest Jesus at the end of the Last Supper didn't need
Judas to point out his teacher to them. Only a few days earlier, Jesus had stormed the gates of the Temple and furiously overturned
the moneychangers' tables in front of all the people. Further-
more, when they came to arrest him, he didn't try to escape but

stood up and willingly accompanied them. Judas' betrayal didn't happen when he kissed Jesus as the jailers arrived. His betrayal, if betrayal it was, occurred at the moment of Jesus' death on the cross. That was the moment when Judas lost his faith. And when he lost his faith, his life lost all meaning."

Gershom Wald leaned forward and said:

"In every language I know, and even in languages I don't know, the name Judas has become a synonym for betrayal. And perhaps also a synonym for Jew. Millions of simple Christians think that every single Jew is infected with the virus of treachery. When I was still a student in Vilna, fifty years ago, once in a second-class railway carriage I was sitting opposite two nuns in black habits with gleaming white cowls. One of them was older and more severe, with wide hips and a protruding belly, while her companion was young and sweet-looking, with a delicate face, and she glanced at me with clear blue eyes, all innocence, compassion, and purity. She looked like a picture of the Madonna in a village church, more like a girl than a woman. When I took a Hebrew newspaper out of my pocket, opened it, and started to read, the elder nun said to me, in formal Polish, in tones of astonishment and disappointment: 'But how can it be, sir, that you are reading a Jewish paper?' I replied at once that I was indeed Jewish and that I was planning soon to leave Poland and settle in Jerusalem. Her young companion looked at me with her innocent eyes, which were suddenly full of tears, and rebuked me in her bell-like voice: 'But He was so, so sweet, how could you have done that to Him?' I made a supreme effort not to respond that at the moment of the crucifixion I happened to have had a dental appointment. You ought to sit down and finish writing your thesis, and maybe publish a book someday, or rather, two books, one on Judas and one on Jewish views of Jesus. Maybe after that it will be the turn of Jewish views of Judas?"

Shmuel adjusted his position, carefully straightened the leg that was in plaster, took a cushion out from under his head and placed it between his knees, and said:

"In 1921, the writer Nathan Agmon, who sold better under the name of Nathan Bistritzky, published a dramatic tale, which is essentially a play, entitled *Jesus of Nazareth*. In Bistritzky's play Judas comes back on the evening of the Last Supper from the house of Caiaphas, the High Priest, where he has learned that the leading priests have decided that Jesus must die. Judas urges Jesus to join him, saying that they must flee from Jerusalem that very night. But Bistritzky's Jesus refuses to flee: his soul is weary, he says, and he wishes to die. He asks Judas to help him die by betraying him, by testifying that Jesus does indeed profess to be the Messiah, or the king of the Jews. On hearing this, Judas 'pulls away from him in terror,' 'withdraws his hands in horror,' and calls Jesus 'a snake . . . a snake disguised as a dove.' Jesus replies: 'So crush me then.' Judas brazenly reproaches him: 'Don't be so sanctimonious,' and pleads with his master not to impose the dreaded mission on him. Jesus stands his ground: 'I command you to hand me over, for I wish to die upon the cross.' Judas refuses. He turns away from Jesus with the intention of fleeing to his town. But some inner force, too strong for him, makes him retrace his steps at the last minute, kneel before his teacher, kiss his hands and his feet, and meekly accept the dreadful mission that has been imposed upon him. The traitor, in this version, is actually a faithful disciple: in handing Jesus over to his pursuers, all he is doing is submissively fulfilling the task his master has forced upon him."

Gershom Wald said with a snigger:

"If Pilate had ordered Judas to be crucified on Jesus' right side instead of the good robber, Judas would have been raised by the Christians to the rank of a saint. His crucified image would adorn tens of thousands of churches, millions of Christian babies would be baptized 'Judas,' popes would have adopted his name.

Nevertheless, I say to you, Judas or no Judas, Jew-hatred would not disappear. Or even diminish. With or without Judas, the Jew would continue to incarnate the role of the traitor in the eyes of the faithful. Generations of Christians would remind us how the crowd before the crucifixion shouted, 'Crucify him! Crucify him! His blood be on us, and on our children.' And I'm telling you, Shmuel, the row between us and the Muslim Arabs is only a small episode in history, a brief and fleeting moment. In fifty or a hundred or two hundred years no memory of it will remain, while what is between us and the Christians is a deep, dark affair that will go on for another hundred generations. So long as each Christian baby learns with its mother's milk that God-killers still tread the earth, or the offspring of God-killers, we shall know no rest. It seems you already know how to use your crutches. Soon you and I will be able to dance together on eight legs. So I'll expect you tomorrow afternoon, as usual, in the library. Now I shall telephone one of my beloved enemies, rake him over the coals, and tomorrow you will sit with me and lecture me about world reform, Fidel Castro and Jean-Paul Sartre, and the greatness of the communist revolution in China, and I, as is my wont, shall laugh, because in my view this world cannot be mended."

46

A ND ON ONE of the following days, which was a Saturday
with dark low clouds in the sky, when the house at the bottom of
Rabbi Elbaz Lane stood shrouded in shadows between the thick
walls of cypress trees, Shmuel Ash tried climbing up the spiral
staircase to his attic room at nine o'clock in the morning. He
propped his crutches at the foot of the stairs, took hold of the
railing with both hands, and endeavored to hop on one leg from
step to step, with the leg that was in plaster thrust out in front in
the air, with the knee bent, so as not to hit it on the next step up.
But after three steps he suffered an asthma attack. He gave up,
sat on the third step for a few minutes to rest, and hopped down
to the bottom of the stairs again. There he picked up his crutches
and limped back to his temporary quarters on the ground floor,
threw himself down on the sofa, and breathed in deeply from
the inhaler. He lay on his back for a quarter of an hour, mentally
arguing with Shealtiel Abravanel. Why did Shealtiel regard the
Jews as the single nation in the world who did not deserve a land
of their own, a homeland, self-determination, be it only in a small
part of their ancestral land, a tiny state, smaller than Belgium,
smaller even than Denmark, a state of which three-quarters was
barren desert? Had some sinister punishment been handed out

to the Jews to the end of time? "Because of our sins we were exiled from our land"? Because the Jews were God-killers? Did Abravanel himself believe that an eternal curse lay upon the Jews and the Jews alone?

And even if we suppose that Shealtiel Abravanel was right in his opinion that all nation-states were a disaster and a scourge, even if he was right in saying that the scourge of nationalism would soon disappear and all states would wither, surely at least until the vision of a stateless world finally became a reality, at least so long as every nation had bars on its windows and bolts and locks on its doors, was it not also right that the Jewish nation should have a small house with bolts and bars, just like all the others? And especially after a third of this nation was slaughtered a few years earlier, only because they did not have a house or a door with a lock or a piece of territory of their own? Or an army and weapons to defend themselves? When the day came that all the nations would finally rise up to demolish the walls dividing them, then definitely, by all means, we too would willingly demolish the walls we had built around us and happily join in the general festivities. Even if, out of neurotic caution, perhaps this time we would not necessarily be the first in the world to give up our bolts and bars. Perhaps this time, for a change, we would be the third in the world or the fourth in our region. Just to be on the safe side. And if we are to be like everyone else, Shmuel continued to argue with Atalia's father, was it not only fair to ask where in this world was the land of the Jews if not here in the Land of Israel, which was the only home they had ever had? A land that had enough space for the two nations who could live here side by side in friendship and cooperation? And maybe someday they would both live here under the banner of humanistic socialism, a shared economy, a federal constitution, and justice for all people.

It occurred to him to share this thought with Atalia, and so he got up and hobbled to the kitchen, calling her name two or three times. But she was not there or did not hear him calling, though she had assured him that her hearing was acute. As he limped toward the sink to get a glass of water, he bumped into a corner of the table and lost one of his crutches. He tottered and nearly fell, but at the last moment he managed to grab the side of the cupboard and steady himself, in doing so pulling down and smashing to the ground a jar of jam and another of pickled cucumbers. Their contents and splinters of glass scattered on the kitchen floor. With his left hand he clung to the edge of the counter, and he tried to bend down without his injured leg touching the floor and use his right hand to pick up the pieces and clean up the mess. But in bending down he lost his balance, the crutch he was leaning on slipped in the sticky pool of jam, and he fell on his side and rolled over on the floor, hitting his shoulder hard on the marble drainer by the sink as he fell.

It was morning. The old man was fast asleep, as he always was in the morning. It was Atalia who, at last, emerged from her room, wearing a blue flannel dressing gown, her hair freshly washed and steaming. She pulled him up into a sitting position, and while she felt his back and the rest of his body with both hands, Shmuel assured her that everything was fine and that this time he had not injured himself or broken any bones. After a moment, he changed his mind and complained of a pain in his neck. She bent down and raised him up on his good leg, put his arm around her shoulders, and helped him, leaning on her and hopping on one leg, back to his room, where she laid him down on her father's sofa. She said, without a question mark at the end of the sentence:

"What am I going to do with you."

And then she said:

"Perhaps we should take on another student to look after the two of you."

And as Shmuel, ashamed of himself, said nothing, she added:

"Look. You're all covered in jam."

She disappeared and came down three or four minutes later from the attic room carrying clean underwear and a long-sleeved T-shirt, a pair of baggy trousers, and his threadbare gray pullover. She took a pair of large scissors from a drawer in the desk and cut the left leg of the clean trousers along its full length, so that he could put it on over the plaster cast. Then she leaned over Shmuel and undressed him as she had done a few days earlier. When he attempted to cover his private parts with his hand, she pulled it away sharply, like an impatient doctor with a child, and said:

"Don't get in my way."

Shmuel shut his eyes tight, the way he used to when he was a small boy and his mother washed him in the bathtub and he was afraid of getting soap in his eyes. But this time Atalia had not brought a cloth soaked in soapy water and did not wash his body, but slowly caressed his hairy chest three or four times, slid a finger over his lips, and, leaning away from him for a moment, said: "Just don't say anything now. Nothing." She picked up a pillow from the bed and covered her father's photograph, which stood staring at them in the middle of the secretaire, then undid her blue flannel dressing gown and let it fall to her feet. Before Shmuel dared to open his eyes, he felt her warm body enfolding his, and her fingers, without any preliminaries, putting him inside her. And because Shmuel had not touched a woman for several months, it was all over almost before it had begun.

She stayed with him for a few minutes, her hands groping as if looking for something she had lost in his thick curls, his beard, and the hair on his chest. Then she removed her hand, picked up her dressing gown and wrapped herself in it from her neck to her ankles, and tied the belt tightly around her waist. She left the room and returned carrying a basin, sponge, and towel, briskly washed and dressed Shmuel, and covered him carefully with the blanket, tucking his feet and shoulders in. Finally, she turned and removed the pillow with which she had buried her father's picture. Shealtiel Abravanel looked thoughtful and calm. Without so much as a glance at the photo, she drew the curtains, turned out the light, and left, closing the door behind her.

Shmuel lay on his back with his eyes closed, stunned. Then he got up and found his crutches and hurried after her to the kitchen. He felt he ought to say something, to break the violent silence that Atalia had imposed on them, but he could find nothing to say. While the water boiled, Atalia went out and came back with a mop, a floor cloth, and a dustpan. She washed the kitchen floor and dried it meticulously. Then she washed her hands in cold water and made them both coffee. When she put the cups down in front of them on the kitchen table, she looked up at him blankly, as if he were a child of strangers who had been entrusted to her against her will, to be entirely her responsibility, and while she quite liked him, she had no idea what more she could do with him. Shmuel pulled her hand toward him, clasped the fingers, and drew them to his lips. He still couldn't find anything to say. He still didn't entirely believe that what had happened a few minutes earlier in Shealtiel Abravanel's room had really taken place. He was embarrassed and ashamed about his body's feverish haste and the fact that he had not managed or even had time to try to gratify her too. It had come and gone in an instant, and in an instant, too, she had pulled away from him and wrapped herself in her dressing gown. At that moment Shmuel longed to take her in his arms and make love to her again, now, here on the kitchen floor, or standing up, leaning against the marble counter, to demonstrate how eager he was to repay her at least something for the grace she had lavished on him in her father's room. Atalia said calmly:

"Just look at him."

And she added:

"There's a fantasy in which a woman decides to bestow his first sexual experience on a dazed young boy and harvests the full crop of his shy, enthusiastic gratitude. I read somewhere that if a woman grants a young man his first time, she goes straight to paradise. Not you, not you, I know you've had a girlfriend, or maybe several. And I'm not going to any paradise. I've no business there."

Shmuel said:

"Atalia."

And then he said:

"I can be whatever you like. A virgin boy. A monk. A knight. A ravenous savage. A poet."

Then, startled by what he had said, he corrected himself:

"Almost from my first day here, I—"

Atalia interrupted him:

"That's enough. Be quiet. Stop talking now."

She cleared the table and put the cups in the sink, then silently left the kitchen. The scent of violets trailing after her contained a hint of something new and intoxicating. Shmuel sat there for another quarter of an hour on his own, feverishly excited, beside himself. What you think happened, he said to himself, only happened in your imagination. You dreamed it. It didn't really happen.

Picking up his crutches and leaning on them, he made his way with special care back to Shealtiel Abravanel's room. There he stood on one leg for a while, staring at the map of the Levant. Then his glance rested on the fine, thoughtful face of the man with a mustache, who reminded him of Albert Camus. He went across to the window, opened the curtains and the shutters, and looked out to see if the rain had stopped. It had indeed stopped, but a powerful west wind was testing the panes of glass. Westward, there extended only forlorn windswept fields. Your time has come to get up and leave this place. You know that the biblical words "The place thereof shall know it no more" apply to all the dwellers in this house, both the living and the dead. And you know, too, how the time of your predecessors in the attic room ended. How are you better than they? How have you improved the world all the days of this winter?

Suddenly his heart ached for Atalia, for her orphaned state, her loneliness, the perpetual coldness that surrounded her, her beloved who was slaughtered like a lamb on the mountainside alone in the darkness of the night, the child she would never have, and for his own inability to revive, if only for a few weeks, a little of what had died and been buried in her.

At the end of the empty fields, the ruins of the destroyed Arab village of Sheikh Badr, on which for ten years now a gigantic festival hall was being erected, stood wet and crumbling in the gloom. The structure had been abandoned while it was still being built, then built a little more and abandoned for a long time. It was a gray, unfinished skeleton with partially constructed walls, wide staircases raked by the rain, and dark concrete joists with rusty iron reinforcements protruding from them like the fingers of the dead.

47

Aʟᴏɴᴇ ɪɴ ᴛʜᴇ ᴇᴍᴘᴛʏ tavern a short while before closing
time, a short while before the arrival of the Sabbath and the Passover festival. A glass of wine and a dish of lamb in a sauce are on
the table in front of him, but, though he has not eaten or drunk
since last night, he does not touch the meat or the wine or the
washed fruit that the pregnant servant girl has placed before him.
As soon as he set eyes on this poor, short, pockmarked girl, he
knew that she had no living soul, no friend or relation, in the
world, and that she must have been made pregnant one autumn
evening by some wayfarer, by someone staying in the tavern, or
perhaps by the innkeeper himself. In a few weeks, when the birth
pangs assailed her, she would be cast out from here into outer
darkness and no one in heaven or on earth could save her. She
would give birth in the dark and roll in her blood all alone in
some forsaken cavern, among bats and spiders, like a beast of
the field. Then she and her babe would grow hungry, and if she
did not manage to find employment as a serving girl in a tavern,
she would surely become a cheap wayside whore. The world was
devoid of mercy. Three hours ago in Jerusalem, grace and mercy
were murdered, and henceforth the world was empty. Not for
a moment did this thought silence in his ears the echo of the

screams that lasted for six hours and that even now in this empty tavern would not leave him. He could not stop catching, from far away beyond valleys and hills, the wailing and the tortured groans; he caught them in his skin, in the hair on his head, in his lungs and his entrails. As if the screams still continued and echoed there in the place of crucifixion and only he had arisen and fled from them outside the city, to this remote tavern.

He sat hunched on the wooden bench with his back to the wall, with his eyes closed, trembling all over, though the evening was warm and humid. The little dog that had attached itself to him on the way lay at his feet under the table. This skinny, mangy, light brown cur had an open wound on its flank, oozing pus; it was an abandoned dog schooled all its days to hunger, loneliness, and kicks from strangers' boots. For six hours the crucified man had not ceased to groan and sob. So long as his death throes continued, he wept, shouted, and screamed with pain, calling over and over again for his mother, calling for her repeatedly in a shrill, piercing voice, like the crying of a fatally wounded infant abandoned in a field alone, parched with thirst as the last of its blood seeped out under the beating sun. It was a desperate scream, rising and falling and rising again, freezing the heart, Mother, Mother, then a penetrating shriek, and again, Mother. Then another piercing wail, followed by a long, drawn-out howl, fainter and fainter, from the depths of his soul.

Only rarely did the other two crucified men cry out. Periodically, one of them uttered a low growling sound that seemed to come from deep in his gut. From time to time, they both groaned in agony through clenched teeth. Every half hour or so, the other one, on the left, gave a deep, sustained bellow, like that of a slaughtered animal. A black cloud of eager flies closed in on the three crucified men, clinging to their skin and feasting on the blood that oozed from the nail wounds.

Masses of black birds of prey huddled expectantly on the

branches of the nearby trees, some large, some small, some with
hooked beaks or bald necks or ruffled feathers. At odd moments,
one of them let out a shrill guttural shriek. Now and then, a fierce
squabble broke out and they pecked each other's flesh and clus-
ters of torn-out feathers flew about in the close, hot air.

In the noonday hours the sun poured down on the earth, on
the crucified men, and on the watching crowds, like molten lead.
The sky was low and dusty, a dirty color somewhere between
brown and gray. The place was packed with people, standing
shoulder to shoulder and hip to hip. The chatter was constant,
and sometimes voices were raised to shout to someone farther
off. Some pitied the crucified men, some pitied only one or two
of them while others gloated. The kin and friends of the dying
men were gathered in small groups, leaning on each other, holding each other, embracing, sobbing, still hoping for a miracle.
Here and there, vendors circulated among the crowd carrying
metal trays and crying their wares: cakes, drinks, dried figs, dates,
fruit juices. The curious pushed themselves eagerly to the front,
the better to witness the death pangs of the crucified, to hear their
screams, sighs, and groans, to see from close up the contorted
faces and the eyes that seemed to be popping out of their sockets,
the bleeding wounds, the blood-soaked rags. Some compared the
three victims at the top of their voices. Others, however, elbowed
their way to the back, because they had seen enough and wanted
to hurry home to prepare for the impending festival. Many spec-
tators had brought provisions with them and were eating and
drinking. Those who had managed to push their way to the front
were sitting comfortably on the ground, the hems of their gar-
ments gathered in, their legs folded, some leaning on their neighbors' shoulders, chatting, joking, nibbling their food, or betting
loudly among themselves which of the three would be the first to
give up the ghost. And there were four or five of the loud-voiced
people in the crowd who did not stop mocking and teasing the

figure in the middle, asking where his father was, why he didn't come to help him, and, more to the point, why he didn't save himself as he had saved so many other sufferers. Why did he not arise at last and descend from the cross?

The crowd had begun to disperse, disappointed or tired. Groups of watchers were slipping away, no longer expecting a pardon or a miracle or some surprising turn in the drama of the death throes of the three crucified men. Men and women were turning their backs on the row of crosses, descending slowly from the hill and beginning to wend their way home. The hour was getting late: the Sabbath and the festival would start at nightfall. The blazing heat was extinguishing curiosity and excitement. Everyone, the men dying on the three crosses, the onlookers, the Roman soldiers in their glinting brass helmets and body armor, and the Chief Priests' representatives, all were soaked in sticky sweat mixed with a cloud of dust raised by the feet of the crowd. This ash-colored dust filled the scorching air, made it hard to breathe, and turned the whole scene gray. Two short, stocky priests stood a few paces away from the mass of the crowd; now and again, one of them leaned over and whispered something to the other, who responded with lazy nods. One of them occasionally broke wind.

And standing directly at the foot of the central cross were four or five forlorn, veiled women supporting one another, shoulder leaning against shoulder, their arms hanging limply at their sides. From time to time, one of them raised an arm to put it around the shoulders of an older woman, stroked her cheek, and wiped her brow. The older woman stood rooted to the spot, as if struck dumb, never removing her gaze from the cross, her eyes dry. Only occasionally her hand strayed unconsciously and touched those places on her own body where the nails had been hammered into the crucified man. The younger woman wept ceaselessly, her weeping calm and even. She wept with open eyes, with a straight face, as if her face were unaware that her eyes were weeping. Her lips were slightly parted and her fingers clasped. Her wide eyes never left the crucified man. As if the last of his life depended on her gaze alone. As if his soul would depart were she to turn away for an instant.

The tall man standing there, a little apart from the crowd, suddenly felt himself being drawn toward those women, as if his feet carried him to them of their own accord. But he stopped and remained where he was on the edge of the crowd, leaning on the broken wooden beam of an old cross left over from an earlier crucifixion. The miracle, the man believed beyond all doubt, would take place now. At any moment. Now, right now, hallowed be thy name, thy kingdom come, thy kingdom that is not of this world.

Throughout those burning hours, while his blood oozed from his wounds and drained away, the man on the middle cross cried out for his mother. He may indeed have seen her with his fading eyes standing bereft at his feet in the group of veiled and mourning women, her eyes seeking his. Or perhaps his eyes were already closed and he was looking only inward, no longer able to see her, or the other women, or the crowd. Not once in the course of those six long hours did the crucified man call on his father. Again and again, he cried out, Mother, Mother. Only at the ninth hour, just as his soul was departing, he bethought himself and suddenly called to his father. But even in this last cry he did not call him Father, but murmured, My God, my God, why hast thou forsaken me? Judas knew that with these words both their lives were ended.

The other two who were crucified, on the right and the left of the dead man, continued to suffer on their crosses in the scorching sun for another hour or more. The nail wounds were swarming with a cloud of fat green flies. The man on the right cursed terribly and white foam bubbled and seethed around his dying lips. The man on the left let out another low, forlorn bellow of distress, fell silent, then bellowed again. Only the man in the middle had attained his just repose. His eyes were closed, his tortured head sunk on his chest, his thin body slack and feeble like that of a young boy.

The tall man did not wait for the three corpses to be lowered from the crosses and carried away. As soon as the soul of the last victim departed with a curse, he turned and left, went around the city wall, impervious to tiredness, heat, hunger, or thirst, empty of thoughts or longings, empty of all that he had been during all the days of his life. As he walked his feet felt light, as though a heavy burden had been lifted at last from his shoulders. A mangy, pale brown cur with bowed legs and pus oozing from a wound in its flank attached itself to him on the way and ran around him pleadingly. The man took a slice of cheese out of his satchel, bent down, and set it before the dog, which devoured it lustily, barked hoarsely twice, and ran on after the man. His feet led him to an old tavern on the road to his town, Kerioth. At the entrance to the tavern, the man stooped once more toward the dog. He patted its head twice and whispered, Run along now, dog, don't believe. The dog turned and went off with its head lowered and its tail between its legs, but a few moments later it was back again, entering the tavern almost on its belly and crawling under the man's table. There it lay without making a sound, carefully resting its head on its benefactor's dusty sandal.

I murdered him. He did not want to go to Jerusalem and I dragged him there. For weeks I tried to persuade him. He was beset with doubts and fears. Again and again he asked me and then asked the other disciples, Am I truly the man? The hesitations never left him. Again and again he sought a sign from above. Again and again he felt a searing need for one more sign. Just one last sign. And I, who was older than he, and calmer and more experienced in the ways of the world, I, on whose lips he would fix his eyes in his moments of doubt, I said to him repeatedly: You are the man. And you know you are the man. And we all know that you are the man. I told him morning and evening, and the next morning and the next evening, that it had to be Jerusalem, and only Jerusalem, and that we had to go to Jerusalem. I deliberately played down the worth of the miracles he worked in the countryside, the rumors of which became confused with rumors concerning all kinds of wonderworkers, of whom there were many wandering the villages of Galilee, healing the sick with a touch of their hand. These rumors echoed for a few weeks among the hills and then died away.

But he refused to go to Jerusalem. Next year, he would say, maybe next year. I almost had to drag him there by force for the Passover. Again and again he said to me that Jerusalem would turn him to mockery and derision, that Jerusalem "killeth the prophets," that death awaited him there. He trembled with fear at the thought of his death, he feared death like any human being, though in his heart of hearts he knew well . . . He knew what awaited him. And even so, he refused to accept what he had always known, and he prayed daily that he might be allowed to remain forever a mere Galilean healer traveling from village to village, awakening hearts by his gospel and his wonders.

I murdered him. I dragged him to Jerusalem against his will. True, he was the teacher and I was one of his disciples, but even so, he obeyed me. As those who hesitate and doubt are always attracted by the strong-mindedness of those who are convinced and have no doubts. He often obeyed me, though I always had some subtle, calculated way of making him feel that the decision had come from him, not from me. The others, his disciples, his followers, who hung on his every word, also did my bidding: I knew how to make them, too, feel that my opinion was merely a humble echo of their own. They entrusted the common purse to me, because I was the oldest, the most experienced in the ways of this world, the most skilled bargainer, the most firm-minded, and because they recognized that shrewd strangers would never manage to cheat me or catch me out. Wherever we encountered representatives of the authorities, it was I who did the talking. They were villagers from the shores of the Sea of Galilee, whereas I had come from Jerusalem. They were paupers, visionaries, and dreamers, whereas I had left behind houses, fields and vineyards, and an honored position among the priests of Kerioth. I represented Jerusalem that had come down to rebuke them and expose their deceptions, to denounce them as a bunch of rogues and charlatans, but lo and behold, like Balaam in the scriptures, I had ended up blessing them and joining them, wearing their ragged clothes and sharing their frugal fare, walking barefoot with bleeding feet like them, and believing just like them, and even more than they did, that the Savior had been revealed, and that this solitary, introspective youth, this shy, humble youth who heard voices, who hewed wonderful parables out of his pure soul, and from whom there flowed like clear spring water simple teachings that won every heart, teachings of love and compassion, of self-denial, joy, and faith, that this slim youth was indeed the only begotten Son of God, who had come to us at last to save the world, and here he was, now walking in our midst like one of us. But he was not one of us and never would be.

He always feared Jerusalem and recoiled from it—from the Temple, the Chief Priests, the Pharisees, the Sadducees, the sages, and the wealthy and powerful. It was the fear of a countryman, the dread of a shy young man, a gnawing apprehension lest they expose him there, lest he become an object of mockery and derision, lest the severe gaze of the sages and the mighty ones strip him naked. Had Jerusalem not already witnessed dozens upon dozens of country folk like him? It would eye him for a brief moment with a bored smile on its lips, then shrug its shoulders and turn its back.

And when we arrived in Jerusalem, I made the crucifixion happen for him almost single-handedly. I did not slack. I was stubborn and determined, imbued with a burning faith that we were standing on the very threshold of the Last Days. It occurred to no one in Jerusalem to crucify him. No one saw any reason to crucify him. On what account? Peasants intoxicated with God, bearing gospels and working wonders in the marketplace, poured into the city almost daily from the remoter regions of the land. In the eyes of the Chief Priests this lad from Galilee was merely another feeble-minded preacher dressed in rags. Whereas for the Romans he was simply a demented beggar, sick with God like all the Jews. Four times I went to the Chamber of Hewn Stone and stood before the High Priest and the Chief Priests and talked and talked until I managed to convince them that this prophet was different from all the others, that the whole of Galilee was under his spell, that I had seen him with my own eyes raising the dead and walking on the water and driving out demons and turning water into wine and stones into loaves and fishes. I also went to the Romans, to the commanders of the army and the police, to the advisers of the prefect. I spoke fluently and eloquently to them, and eventually I managed to plant in their minds the suspicion that this delicate man was actually the cause of the unrest, the source of inspiration of those who were about to rise up against Roman rule. At last I made them decide, without too much enthusiasm, to accept my advice. Not because they were really persuaded that the young man I was talking about was more dangerous than the rest, but only from indifference: what is one crucifixion more or less? I hammered every nail into his flesh. I shed every drop of blood that fell from his holy body. He knew from the outset the limits of his power, and I did not. I believed in him much more than he believed in himself. I pushed him to promise a new heaven and a new earth, a kingdom that is not of this world. To promise redemption. To promise eternal life. While all he wanted was to continue to walk the land, healing the sick, feeding the hungry, and sowing seeds of love and compassion in men's hearts. Nothing more.

I loved him with all my soul and I believed in him with perfect faith. It was not just the love of an elder brother for his better younger brother, not just the love of an older, more experienced man for a delicate youth, not just the love of a disciple for his greater but younger teacher, not even the love of a perfect believer for the worker of miracles and wonders. No. I loved him like God. I loved him much more than I loved God. In fact, since my youth I have not loved God at all. I recoiled from him: a jealous and vengeful god, visiting the iniquities of the fathers on the sons, a cruel, angry, bitter, vindictive, petty, blood-shedding god. Whereas the Son seemed to me loving, compassionate, forgiving, but also, when he wished, witty, sharp, warmhearted, and even funny. He usurped the place of God in my heart. He became my God. I believed that death could not touch him. I believed that this very day the greatest miracle of all would occur in Jerusalem. The final and ultimate miracle, after which there would be no more death in the world. After which there would be no need for any more miracles. The miracle after which the Kingdom of Heaven would come and love alone would rule the world.

I left, beneath the table for the dog to eat, the plate of meat that the pregnant, pockmarked serving girl had placed before me. I left the wine on the table. I rose and brought out from my pocket our common purse and thrust it with a gesture that was almost coarse into the girl's bosom without exchanging a word with her. As I walked out of the place, I saw that the sun had begun its descent. The harsh light was softening as though beset with doubts. The nearest hills looked empty and the road continued empty and dusty to the farthest horizon. His agonized, faint voice, the voice of an injured child abandoned to suffer and die in a field, Mother, Mother, did not cease to ring out in my ears

either when I sat in the tavern or when I left to pursue my journey. I longed for his kind smile and for his habit of relaxing in
the shade of a sycamore or a vine and talking to us as though he
himself were surprised by the words that came out of his mouth.

The road was lined on either side by olive groves and vineyards and by fig and pomegranate trees. On the horizon a light
mist was floating above the distant mountains. The orchards were
cool and shady. In one orchard I spied a rock-hewn wellhead with
a wooden roof above it. I was suddenly filled with a great love of
that well. I hoped that it would never cease to give its water to
all who thirst. I left the road for a moment, approached the well,
drank pure water from the bucket, then removed a length of rope
from the pulley and wound it around my forearm before continuing on my way.

Beyond the orchards and vineyards, on the gentle slopes, lay
green fields of wheat and barley as far as the eye could see. They
seemed vast and deserted. So much so that they made me feel a
little better. The piercing cry that had been echoing in my ears
all day faded. At that moment I received a simple illumination,
and I knew in my heart that all this—the mountains, the water,
the trees, the breeze, the earth, the evening twilight—would continue for generation upon generation without any change. The
words in our mouths come and go, but all this would not change
or fade but would last forever. And if ever any change did come,
it would be slight. I murdered him. I put him on the cross. I hammered the nails into his flesh. I shed his blood. A few days ago,
on our way to Jerusalem, as we walked down one of these hills,
he suddenly felt hungry. He stopped in front of a fig tree, one of
those which are covered in leaves long before the fruit ripens.
And we stopped with him. He felt with both hands among the
leaves, looking for a fig to eat, and when he did not find any, he
stood there and cursed the fig tree. Instantly all the leaves on

that tree withered and dropped. Only the trunk and branches remained, bare and dead.

Why did he curse it? What harm had it done him? There was no fault to be found in that tree. Surely no fig tree gives fruit or can give fruit before the Passover. If in his soul he desired to eat figs, what was there to prevent him from working one of his wonders and causing the fig tree to put forth her green figs at once, long before their time, just as he had turned stones into loaves and water into wine? Why did he curse the tree? How had the fig tree wronged him? How had he forgotten his own gospel and become full of cruelty and loathing? It was there, beneath that fig tree, at that instant, that my eyes should have been opened wide to see that, after all, he was no more than flesh and blood like the rest of us. Greater than us, more wonderful than us, immeasurably deeper than all of us, but flesh and blood. I should have taken hold of the hem of his garment, there and then, and turned him and all of us around: We are retracing our steps and returning to Galilee right now. We are not going to Jerusalem. You must not go to Jerusalem. They will kill you in Jerusalem. We belong in Galilee. We shall return there and wander from village to village, spending the night wherever we may. You will do your best to heal the suffering and spread your gospel of love and compassion, and we shall follow you until our time comes.

But I ignored the cursing of the fig tree. I insisted on taking him to Jerusalem. And now evening is falling and the Sabbath and the festival are beginning. Not for me. The world is empty. A last faint light is caressing the hilltops, and this light is no different from the evening light we saw yesterday and the day before. Even the breeze blowing from the sea is just like the breeze that blew over us last night. The whole world is empty. Perhaps it is not too late to turn back to the tavern, to return to the ugly, pockmarked, pregnant serving girl, take her under my wing, be a father to the child in her belly and remain with her and the child until my dying day. We could adopt the stray dog. But the tavern is locked and dark, and there is no living soul there. A first star has appeared in the darkening sky, and I whisper to it, Star, do not believe. Then, in a bend in the road, that fig tree is waiting for me. I stand and carefully examine each branch, one at a time. I find the right branch and tie the rope to it.

48

THEY OCCASIONALLY BUMPED INTO each other in the kitchen. She would make a cheese and parsley omelet and butter the bread, and put some vegetables, a dish, and a knife on the table for him to prepare a salad. He would chop the vegetables, and often he would splash tomato juice on his trousers or cut his finger. On one occasion, she stopped him sprinkling white sugar on the salad instead of salt. Shmuel sought some pretext, however flimsy, to remind her indirectly of what had happened. But Atalia could not be easily caught.

"You look nice this morning in that green dress. And the necklace. And the scarf."

"You should look at your shirt instead. You've skipped two buttons."

"I think you and I ought to talk."

"We are talking."

"And where could this conversation about necklaces and buttons lead us?"

"Where is it supposed to lead us? Just don't start lecturing. Keep your lectures for Wald. You and he can shower each other with lectures. Wait. Don't say anything. The old man has been coughing in his sleep all morning. And you with your crutches, you can't even make him an occasional cup of tea."

"I know. I'm just a burden. Tomorrow or the day after I'll set you free. I'll arrange for someone to come and collect my things."

Atalia laid two fluttering fingers on the back of his neck and said that there was no reason to be in a hurry. In another day or two his plaster cast would be replaced by an elastic bandage, and a few days after that he wouldn't need the crutches anymore. Or he might use just one crutch for a while.

"I can still remember almost word for word the ad you pinned up in the cafeteria in the Kaplun Building at the university a few months ago. The ad that brought me here. Why don't you put up the same notice again, and I'll vacate the attic for the next person?"

"The next one won't put sugar on the salad. We've got rather used to you."

"But I'll never get used to you, Atalia. And I'll never forget you."

"I've asked Sarah de Toledo to look in a couple of times every afternoon and evening over the next few days while your leg is in plaster. She will make you both tea, and she'll serve you the porridge between seven and eight o'clock. She's also agreed to wash the dishes and feed the goldfish. Before she leaves she will close the shutters. Of course you will forget us after two or three weeks. Everybody does. The city is full of girls. You'll find others. Younger ones. You're a tender-hearted, generous boy. Girls love these qualities because they are so rare in men. And, in the meantime, your only task is to sit and chat with Wald in the afternoons and evenings. Try not to agree with him about anything. Try to provoke arguments and disagreements to keep him awake and on his toes for at least a few hours a day. I'm struggling as hard as I can to make sure he doesn't fade away. I have to go out now. You sit quietly and finish eating. There's nowhere for you to hurry to. Look at you, sitting staring at me, feeling sorry for yourself. That's enough self-pity. There's little enough pity in the world. It's a shame to waste it."

At that, she stopped talking and shot him a sharp look, as if appraising him all over again. Suddenly she laughed and said:

"All sorts of women will love you, with your wild beard and your disheveled curls that are impossible to comb. Even with a garden rake. Always in a muddle and always touching and, in fact, also quite dear. You're not a predator. You never boast, you never throw your weight around, you're not too much in love with yourself. And another thing I like about you: everything is always written on your face. You're a child with no secrets. You're always running around between all sorts of loves, but really you don't run around at all—you simply wait with your eyes closed for love to come and find you and make a fuss over you without your having to wake up. I like all that. Jerusalem nowadays is full of young men with thick voices and thick arms who were all, without exception, war heroes in the Palmach or the trenches, and now they're at university, studying something or other, writing something or other, researching something or other, migrating from department to department, some of them are teaching. And if they're not at university, they're working for the government, they're involved in secret operations, going on hush-hush missions, and they're all dying to tell you, dying to tell any girl, in strict confidence, all sorts of top-secret state business they're engaged in, in a leading role. There are also those who pounce on you in the street as if they've just this minute come down from some hilltop trench. As if they haven't set eyes on or touched a woman for the last ten years. I like it that you're not like them: you're not entirely awake and you sometimes seem to be elsewhere. Leave the dishes in the sink. Sarah de Toledo is coming today and she'll tidy everything up."

At half past eleven that night, when he had been reading in

bed and his eyes were closing with tiredness, he started suddenly and covered his body hastily with the blanket as she came to him barefoot. He hadn't heard her open the door or close it behind her. By the feeble light of the streetlamp through the slats of the shutters, she went first to the desk and turned her father's photograph face-down. Then, without uttering a word, she removed the blanket and sat down on the bed next to him. She leaned over and ran her fingers through the hair on his chest and stroked his stomach and his thighs and held his penis in her hand. When he tried to whisper something, she covered his mouth with her other hand. Then she took both of his hands and laid one of them on each breast, and brought her lips to his forehead and fluttered her tongue on it and on his eyelids. Slowly and gently she led him step by step, as if he were half asleep. But this night she did not get up and abandon him as soon as he was slack, but stayed to guide him like a visitor in an unknown land, patiently holding his fingers in hers and familiarizing them with her body, until she taught him how to repay pleasure with pleasure. For a while, she lay next to him without moving, her breathing so slow and peaceful she seemed almost to have fallen asleep in his bed. But she whispered, "Don't fall asleep," and she got up again and rode his body, and this time she did things to him that he knew only from his dreams, and this time he also managed to give her body pleasure. It was one o'clock in the morning when she left him, after ruffling his curls and stroking his lips for a moment with one soft finger, whispering, "You are probably the only one out of all of them that I'm going to remember." Then she replaced her father's picture in an upright position on the desk. And she floated away in her nightdress, closing the door behind her without making a sound.

At half past eight the following morning she entered his room again. This time she was dressed in her black skirt and tight, red, high-necked pullover and a fine silver necklace. She helped him to dress, supported his shoulder as he hobbled to the toilet, waited behind the door while he finished and brushed his teeth and wet his beard and dusted it with baby talc. When he came out, she kissed him hurriedly and lightly on the mouth; she didn't say a word about what had taken place the previous night, but turned and went on her way, leaving behind a faint echo of violets. He stood there for a while, perhaps waiting for her to come back and give him some explanation. Perhaps he was regretting not kissing her at last in the dizzying furrow that descended from her nostrils to her upper lip. Finally he smiled, without realizing he was doing so. He limped to the library to wait for the old man. While he waited, he took down from a shelf the *Arabian Nights* in Yosef Yoel Rivlin's Hebrew translation and read it for a while. In his mind, he compared the book with the Song of Songs and the *Letters of Abelard and Heloise*, wondering if someday he would manage to write her a beautiful love letter. He pulled his inhaler out of his pocket, inhaled deeply, and held his breath, trapping the vapor in his lungs, then released it with a single long exhalation.

All that afternoon, Gershom Wald lay on his wicker couch, with his ugly hands spread out on the arms of the couch like a couple of worn tools, his bushy white mustache quivering in the light of the lamp as if the old man were whispering to himself. But when he spoke aloud, his voice contained its usual hint of mockery, as though to negate his own words, thoroughly and sarcastically, even as he spoke them:

"According to Joseph Klausner, Jesus of Nazareth was not a Christian at all, he was a thoroughgoing Jew. He was born a Jew and he died a Jew and it never occurred to him to found a new religion. The father of the Christian religion was Paul, Saul of Tarsus. Jesus only wanted to awaken hearts and to make the corrupted Jews—the Sadducees and the Pharisees on the one hand, and the publicans and prostitutes on the other—repent, to bring them back to the original pure springs of faith. You have been sitting in my house for the past several weeks and every day you have been telling me a story in installments, about how in almost every generation some professedly wise Jew has appeared and cast a stone at him. Mostly these 'stones' were contemptible and cowardly, with all sorts of gossip about his origins and the circumstances of his birth and petty objections to his healings and miracles. Maybe one day you will sit down and write for us about those miserable Jews and denounce their petty-mindedness. Maybe you will bring Judas into your story, because they poured pitcherfuls of filth on him as well as on Jesus. Even though without Judas there would have been no Church and no Christianity. I shall not say a word about your relations with her. Now she is showing you some kindness. Don't you believe it. Or do believe it. As you wish. Those who were here before you cast their eyes upon her and sometimes she gave way and maybe granted some of them two or three nights, then she sent them packing. Now your time has come. The fact is that each time I am astonished all over again: the way of a man with a maid and the way of a maid with a man are among the things that have 'no fixed measure.' But what does a man like me understand of the vagaries of a woman's heart? Sometimes I have the impression that—but no. Not a word. Better pass over it in silence."

After a couple of days, Atalia took Shmuel in a taxi to the out-patient clinic, where they x-rayed him and removed the plaster cast, replacing it with a tight elastic bandage. He tried to joke about his fall and even attempted a poor pun, but Atalia cut him short:

"Stop it. It's not funny."

Shmuel tried to tell her the story about Rothschild and the beggar, and then the one about Ben-Gurion meeting Stalin in the afterlife. She listened in silence. Twice she nodded. Then she put her cold fingers on his hand and said in her quietest voice:

"Shmuel. That will do."

Then she said:

"We've almost grown accustomed to you."

After a long silence, she added:

"If you are comfortable in that room, as far as I'm concerned you can stay there for a few more days. Until your foot is better. When you're ready, leave me a note on the kitchen table and I'll come and help you pack your belongings from upstairs and downstairs. Abravanel's room is only happy when it's empty, darkened, and locked. With his photograph talking to the walls day and night. Even when I was a child, I thought of that room as a dark monastic cell. Or a prison cell. Solitary confinement. I had no brothers or sisters. I'll tell you something that you don't have to listen to. But you are actually only here in our house to listen. You are paid to listen. When I was a little girl of ten, my mother left us and went to Alexandria to find a Greek businessman who was a frequent visitor of Abravanel's. He liked to recite poetry in five or six languages. Occasionally he stayed the night up in the attic room. I was always convinced that this Greek, who was not a young man, was only interested in Abravanel and was indifferent to my mother and me. It's true that he was a polite man: he always kissed her hand, sometimes he brought her a bottle of perfume, and Bakelite dolls for me with muslin dresses and a little button on their tummy. If you pressed the button they would cry. Or laugh. But he almost never stopped to talk to my mother or to me. He only spoke for hours to Abravanel. Sometimes the two of them argued in low voices. Sometimes they sat in this room smoking till late at night, reading poetry and speaking to each other in Greek. It was only when he went to the kitchen to request fresh coffee that the Greek man lingered for a few minutes and conversed in whispers with my mother in French. Sometimes he made her laugh aloud. She loved laughing, and I was amazed at her because in our home laughter was a rare visi-

tor. One evening I was standing at the kitchen door and I saw that
her hand was resting casually on his shoulder. In the winter he
used to bring a bottle of wine. One day, when Abravanel was in
Beirut and I was on a school trip, she got up early in the morning, packed an ancient suitcase, and went to Alexandria to look
for the Greek. He was not particularly good-looking, but his eyes
sometimes sparkled with good humor and wit. She left a letter
behind in the kitchen saying that she had no choice, that nobody
has any choice, we are all at the mercy of forces that make us do
what they want. There were all sorts of feelings in her letter that
I don't remember and don't want to remember. After she left,
Abravanel turned this room into his own penal colony. He would
summon me and sit me down by his desk, just to lecture me. He
never asked me a question. Not once. Ever. Not about how I
was doing at school, about my friends, where I had vanished to
yesterday, whether there was anything I needed, if I missed her,
how I'd slept the previous night, or whether it was tough growing up without a mother. Whenever I asked him for money, he
gave it to me at once without question. But he never brought me
with him when he went to meet people. He never took me to the
cinema or a café. He never told me a story. Never went shopping
with me. If I ever went into town on my own to buy a new dress,
he never noticed. If a girlfriend came to visit me, he would shut
himself in his room. If I was ill, he would call the doctor and ask
Sarah de Toledo to come and help around the house. Once I left
home without saying a word to him. I didn't leave a note. I stayed
with a girlfriend for five or six nights. When I returned, he asked
quietly, perhaps even without looking at me, 'What's the matter, I
didn't see you yesterday. Where did you get to?' And once, when
I reminded him that I would be fifteen the following Monday, he
turned away and searched for something on his bookshelves. He
stood like that for a few minutes, with his back to me, scrabbling
about on the shelves. Eventually he pulled out a book and gave

it to me as a present, an anthology of Middle Eastern poetry in translation, and he wrote on the flyleaf: 'To my dear Atalia, in the hope that this book will explain to you where we are living.' Then he sat me down on the sofa and he sat at his desk and gave me a long lecture about the golden age of Jewish-Muslim relations. All I said was 'Thank you.' I took the book, went to my room, and closed the door behind me. But why am I suddenly telling you old stories about Abravanel? In a few days you will leave us too. This room will be locked again and the shutters closed. It's right for this room to always be locked. It doesn't need anyone. I have the feeling you don't love your parents either. You're also a kind of private investigator. But now even you hardly ever ask me anything."

49

Within a few days, Shmuel was able to manage without the crutches and supported himself occasionally with the fox-head walking stick. He was able once again to make a glass of tea for Gershom Wald every hour or two, to feed the goldfish, to turn the light on when it got dark, and to go and wash the dishes in the kitchen. Ostensibly, everything was back to normal, but Shmuel knew in his heart that his days in this house were numbered.

Had she also brought his predecessors down from the attic room and opened her father's room for them for two or three nights before throwing them out? Had she also turned her father's photo face-down for them or smothered it under a pillow? He did not dare to ask, and Atalia did not say. But she sometimes looked at him with amused affection and smiled as if to say, Don't worry.

If they bumped into each other in the kitchen or the passage, she would ask how his leg was. He would reply that it was almost better. His injured leg, he understood, granted him a short respite, a few more days, a week at the outside. Not a word was said about the possibility of his returning to the attic, despite the fact that he was capable of hobbling upstairs if she told him that the time had come to vacate Shealtiel Abravanel's room. But she didn't.

Most of the morning he sat by himself at the kitchen table, biting into a slice of bread and jam, tracing simple lines on the blue flowers printed on the oilcloth. He did not know what these flowers were called. He suddenly regretted never having thought to bring her a bunch of flowers. Or some perfume. Or perhaps a scarf. Or a pair of delicate earrings. He could easily have surprised her once or twice. Bought her a book of poems. Complimented her on one of her dresses. Never again would he fold little paper boats for her and sail them across the breakfast table. Never again would he follow her at night through the labyrinthine alleyways of Jerusalem in pursuit of hungry cats.

One whole morning he sat at Shealtiel Abravanel's secretaire writing a long letter to Yardena and Nesher Sharshevsky. The idea was to tell them about what had happened to him here and possibly hint at what had taken place between him and Atalia. But halfway through, he realized there was no point. And he recalled his written agreement not to tell a soul about what occurred in this house. He tore the letter into little pieces and flushed them down the toilet, and decided instead to write to his sister and his parents. He was sitting wondering what he could say to them when he felt tired and limped to the kitchen in the hope of bumping into Atalia. She did not come. Maybe she had gone to work. Perhaps she was sitting alone in her room, reading or quietly listening to music. He spread two thick slices of black bread with cream cheese and chomped his way crudely through both, one after the other, washing them down with black coffee.

He went on sitting for a long time in the kitchen, picking up crumbs from the oilcloth one by one and pressing them into a squashed mass that he threw in the trash. He made up his mind not to bother taking down the posters on the walls of his attic room, the pictures of the leaders of the Cuban Revolution. He would leave them for the benefit of his successor. He would also leave the reproduction of the picture of the Pietà, because it suddenly struck him as too cloying, with its throngs of chubby little angels hovering in the air. As if the pain had been forgiven.

He still had no idea where he would go from here, but he felt that the opinions he had held since his youth were fading, just as the Socialist Renewal Group was becoming less important to him and his research on Jewish views of Jesus had become more and more involved, and he could not imagine how to finish it, because the old story of Jesus and the Jews had not yet ended and was not going to end soon. There was no end to that story. He knew now that everything was in vain and that there was no point and never had been any. He felt an urge to leave this cellar-like house and go to wide-open places, to the mountains or the desert, or perhaps to sail away to sea.

Early one evening he put on his student coat, buttoned it, turned up the collar, squashed his *shapka* on top of his curls which had grown wilder and longer than ever, took the stick with the fox-head handle, and limped out into the lane. The streetlamp from the period of British rule was on, and cast a little light and many patches of shadow. There was not a soul outside, but lamps shone feebly in the windows, and at the foot of the lane to the west the remains of the sunset were still dying, glimmering splashes of purple wine on a crimson backcloth. Shmuel walked around the lane, straining his eyes in the dim light to make out the names of the residents in the neighboring houses. Finally he managed to read on a little ceramic plaque the names of Sarah and Avram de Toledo, painted in black letters on a pale blue background. He hesitated for a while before knocking at the door. He knew Sarah de Toledo from her short visits, but he had never exchanged more than a few words of greeting with her. The husband, a short, broad, compact man with a square, anvil-like head, opened the door a crack and eyed with suspicion the stranger

who stood before him. Shmuel introduced himself and asked if
he could have a few words with Mrs. de Toledo, please.

Avram de Toledo did not reply. He closed the door and
seemed to be having a whispered conversation with someone in
the depths of the house. Then he opened the door a crack again
and asked if Shmuel would mind waiting a little longer. Then he
turned his head and had a discussion with someone whose voice
Shmuel could not hear. Finally he said:

"Come in. Mind the step."

And he added in a hoarse voice:

"Thirsty?"

Then he said:

"Sarah's just coming."

He sat Shmuel down in an armchair with two burgundy-col-
ored cushions, excused himself, and left the room, but Shmuel
had the impression that he was standing nearby, in the passage,
still keeping an eye on him from the shadows.

The room was lit by a dim ceiling light fixture with two yellow
bulbs. A third bulb was burned out. In addition to the chair he
was sitting in, there were two more old chairs in the room, which
did not match each other or his chair, a threadbare low couch,
a paraffin heater, a heavy wardrobe on curved legs, a black dining table, and a shelf attached by two strings to two nails in the
wall. On the shelf stood a row of ten or twenty religious books
with gold writing gleaming on their spines. The crude turquoise-
colored vase in the middle of the table was also decorated in gold,
and had two wide handles. In one corner of the room was a large,
rough, dark wooden chest which probably contained bedding or
clothes and objects for which there was no room in the wardrobe.
It was covered in a colorful embroidered cloth.

Some ten minutes passed before Sarah de Toledo came in,
wearing a loose housecoat, with a dark shawl covering her head
and shoulders, and slippers on her feet. She remained standing in

the shadow between the passage and the room, leaning with her back against the wall, and asked Shmuel if heaven forbid something bad had happened. Shmuel reassured her that everything was perfectly all right. He was sorry to disturb her at such an hour, but he would like to be allowed to put a question to her. Did she know the previous owner of the house, Mr. Abravanel, and what sort of man was he?

Sarah de Toledo did not speak. She nodded a few times, slowly, as if agreeing with herself, or as if lamenting some deed that was done and could not be undone.

"He loved Arabs," she said at last in a sad voice. "He did not love us. Maybe the Arabs paid him."

After another short silence she added:

"He did not love anyone. He did not love Arabs either. When all the Arabs fled, or when we helped them to flee, he stayed at home. He didn't go with them. He didn't love anyone. Will you stay? Would you like a glass of coffee?"

Shmuel declined with thanks, rose, and turned to leave. Sarah de Toledo said:

"I'll be there tomorrow lunchtime. How come hardly anyone ever comes to see Mr. Wald? How can that be? Hasn't he got any family? Friends? Pupils? He's such a good man. A clever man. So learned. His son died in the war, poor thing, his only son, and he's got no one left except for that girl who's not a girl anymore, Mr. Abravanel's daughter. She was the wife of the son, but only for one year. Maybe a year and a half. She's got nobody left either. You study college?"

Shmuel explained that he used to be a student, but that now, soon, he intended to start looking for a job. Before he left he said:

"Thank you. I'm sorry. Excuse me."

The short, compact man emerged quickly from the darkness of the passage and accompanied Shmuel to the front door.

"My wife wants to stop working at your place. She's not so

young anymore. And your house, I think, maybe it brings bad luck."

Shmuel stood under the streetlamp for another quarter of an hour. Waiting. For whom, he did not know. Meanwhile, he thought to himself that there was nothing so extraordinary about standing and waiting: most people live from day to day waiting without knowing who or what they are waiting for. With that thought, he hobbled back to the house, hastened to the library, and asked the old man if he needed anything: tea, or biscuits, or maybe he could peel him an orange.

Gershom Wald said:

"She has a small radio in her room. On evenings when she doesn't go out, she listens to music broadcasts. Or she jumps from station to station and listens to programs from Arabic stations. Her father taught her a little Arabic, but apparently she did not inherit his dreams about brotherhood between Jews and Arabs. All she inherited from him is his anger. His anger and resentment. Maybe she has other dreams. Maybe you know? In his last years, when he sat shut away in this house, he almost stopped talking about his vision of brotherhood between the two nations. Once he told me that when he was young he believed wholeheartedly, as we all did, that we Jews were setting up a homeland here without evicting anyone and without doing anything wrong. Yes. By the 1920s he had begun to have doubts, and in the 1930s he realized that the two nations were moving swiftly on trajectories that would inevitably lead them to a head-on collision, to a bloody war at the end of which only one of them would survive. The losers would not be able to remain here. But he did not quickly abandon his youthful views. For quite a few years he swallowed his doubts and continued to toe the line and to say more or less what everyone expected of a representative of the Jerusalem Sephardi aristocracy in the institutions of the Zionist movement. From time to time, he called for dialogue with the neighboring

nation. From time to time, he warned against the ways of violence. But his words received almost no attention. The others
accepted with indifference and even with a certain boredom the
fact that now and then Shealtiel Abravanel displayed a sensitivity,
a Sephardi sensitivity supposedly, to the complexities of the Arab
problem. In his thinking he was already moving away from all
his colleagues. He still believed that the Jews were right to aspire
to establish a homeland here, but he had reached the conclusion
that that home should be shared between Jews and Arabs. It was
only in the 1940s that he began to raise a distinctive voice sometimes in meetings of the Council of the Jewish Agency and the
Zionist Executive Committee. In 1947, when he expressed a solitary view against the United Nations partition plan and against
an independent Israel, some people began to call him a traitor.
They thought he had gone out of his mind. In the end, as you
know, they gave him twenty-four hours to decide between resignation and dismissal. After his resignation, he shut up completely.
He did not say a single word in public. He wrapped himself in
resentment like a shroud. He realized that no one was listening to
him. On the eve of the creation of the state and during the War
of Independence, in any case, there was no chance that anyone
would bother to listen to views like his. We all understood by
1947 that the impending war would be a war to the death and
that if we were defeated, not one of us would be left alive. On
April 2, Micha, my only son, was killed. My son, my only son, was
killed. Micha. For more than ten years now I've stayed awake all
night. Night after night, they come and slaughter him among the
rocks on that hillside in that pine forest. And after that the three
of us were shut up here in this coffin, after that we were shut
away. During the months of the Jordanian siege of Jerusalem the
thick stone walls protected us from bullets and shells. Atalia was
the only one who left the house occasionally to queue for the paraffin cart and the ice cart, and she also stood with our ration cards

in the long lines for food. After the war was over, he continued to shut himself away at home, he severed his last remaining links with the outside world, he stopped answering letters, he refused to go to the phone, he read the newspapers in his room all morning, and it was only to me and to his daughter that he expressed at unexpected moments his despair at the new state, which he considered to be given over to the worship of militarism, drunk on victory, and consumed by hollow chauvinistic euphoria. He thought Ben-Gurion was suffering from a messianic complex and considered his former friends runts and lackeys. He shut himself away in his room for hours on end, writing. What he wrote there I do not know. He left nothing behind other than the scent of disappointment and a sadness that fills the house to this day. It must be his ghost, refusing to leave these rooms. Soon you will leave too, and I shall be left alone with her. She will no doubt find me some other young eccentric who will consent to take your place. She always finds someone, she always turns his head, sometimes she gives in for a moment, and then she sends him packing. Visitors sometimes come to her at night and leave at night. I usually don't see them, but I hear them. They come and they go. Why? That I cannot say. Maybe she hasn't found what she's looking for yet. Or maybe she isn't looking for anything but just flitting from nectar to nectar like a hummingbird. Or the opposite: she is always mourning, even when she finds herself a partner for a night or two. Who knows? For thousands of years we have taught ourselves to believe that women are different from us, as different as can be, absolutely different. Perhaps we were exaggerating. What do you think? Soon you'll go on your way, and I shall miss you sometimes, especially at our times, when the light is fading and the evening gets into my bones. I live from one leave-taking to the next."

50

Aт тне beginning of march, the winter rains stopped. The air was still cold and dry, glassy, but in the mornings the sky brightened and a strong, luminous azure spread over the city and over the hills and valleys. The cypresses and the stone walls on Rabbi Elbaz Lane stood washed of dust and appeared lit from within by a sharp, precise light. As if they were created this very morning. The newspaper headlines told of a powerful earthquake in Agadir, in Morocco, in which thousands of people had died. Gershom Wald said: "Life is but a fleeting shadow. Even death is but a fleeting shadow. Only pain remains. It goes on and on. Always."

At the end of the lane wound the shallow wadi, where a few pools of rainwater still stood. Far away, beyond the wadi, empty fields and forsaken hillsides spread, on which here and there a solitary olive tree stubbornly grew. The olive trees seemed from a distance as though they had long ago left the vegetable kingdom and joined the realm of the inanimate. Now that the winter was over, the fields and hillsides were covered in a dark green carpet dappled in places with rain flowers: cyclamens, anemones, and poppies. In the distance could still be seen the ruins of the deserted Arab village of Sheikh Badr, and above the ruins, rising like a primeval dragon, the clumsy skeletal outlines of the gigantic half-built festival hall.

Sometimes, toward evening, low dark clouds lay upon the Jerusalem sky, as if winter had changed its mind and returned to rest upon the city, but by morning they dispersed and limpid azure once more spread over the minarets and domes, spires and high walls, winding alleys, iron gates and stone steps and water cisterns. The rains had departed from Jerusalem and only scattered puddles remained. The glazier, the peddler, and the rag-and-bone man went again from street to street announcing their arrival with hoarse cries. As if the three of them had been sent to warn the city of a plague or a fire. Geraniums blazed on window-sills and balcony railings. The trees were full of the shrill twittering of birds, as if they had received some sensational news they had to spread urgently all around the city.

One morning, Atalia entered without knocking on the door of her father's dark room. She brought Shmuel an old, faded khaki army kit bag, which she put down on his bed. Shmuel guessed that it had once belonged to Micha. Then he remembered that it was his own kit bag, the one in which he had brought his belongings and books here at the beginning of the winter. Atalia said:

"Your foot is nearly better."

She said this as a statement, not a question. She added:

"I've come to help you. You'll never manage to pack on your own."

Then she went up to the attic and back twice and brought down all his clothes and books, though his injury was almost healed and he could have brought his belongings down on his own. When he asked why she had taken it upon herself to do what he could have done unaided, she replied:

"I wanted you to rest a little longer."

"I've been resting here for more than three months," he said.

"If you stay with us any longer you'll turn into a fossil," she said. "Like us. You'll grow moss. As it is, you've aged here."

And she added:

"Three months is enough. You need to be among young people, boys and girls, students, wine, parties, fun. What you had here was some time out, which you apparently needed, but just for the winter. The winter is over. It's time for the bear to wake up."

"The bear won't forget the honey."

"The world is full of honey. And it's waiting for you."

He almost reached out to seize her shoulders, to hug her and press her body to his and feel her breasts against his chest one last time. But an inner voice reminded him that he was her guest. So he restrained himself and fought back the tears that choked his throat and almost filled his eyes. And yet there was also a vague joy that he would soon be leaving.

Shmuel's clothes, books, and toiletries were piled in disorder on the sofa. His coat and cap were here too, as well as some notebooks and cardboard folders. Atalia bent over and helped him pack everything she could into the kit bag. Suddenly she turned to her father's bookcase and plucked from it a tiny, delicate blue jug of Hebron glass, which may have been a present from one of Abravanel's Arab friends, wrapped it in several thicknesses of newspaper, tucked it between the layers of his clothes and underwear in the kit bag, and said:

"A small gift. From me. For the journey. I expect you'll break it. Or lose it. Or forget who gave it to you."

She went on squeezing more of his clothes and papers in, and even his small typewriter. But in the midst of packing she straightened herself and announced:

"Time for a break. Come to the kitchen. Let's have a coffee

together for ten minutes. I'll sit at the table and you can serve the coffee. You can make me one more paper boat. If there's one thing in the world that no one can beat you at, that's making paper boats. You can also make yourself some bread and jam or bread and cheese, so that you don't leave me hungry."

Shmuel murmured:

"I'm leaving you hungrier than when I arrived."

Atalia, choosing to ignore this hint, said:

"I have the impression that you've managed to do some writing here in these last few months, despite everything. Everybody except me spends their time here sitting and writing. They never stop writing. There must be something in the walls. Or in the cracks in the floor."

"I'd give a lot to read what your father wrote."

"He didn't leave us anything. I told you, at the end he was careful to destroy every last bit of paper. As though erasing his own life."

"You'll see—one day they'll write about him. They'll do research. Somebody will remember him, maybe years from now. I believe that somebody will dig around in the archives and unearth his story."

"But there was no story. He didn't do anything, after all. He spoke up once or twice, and they booted him out, and he felt offended, shut himself away, and never said another word. That's all. There was no story."

"I'm having trouble breathing," Shmuel said. "I'm sorry. I think I need my inhaler. But I've no idea where it is. Maybe we've packed it?"

Atalia got up, left the kitchen, and returned a couple of minutes later. She handed Shmuel his inhaler, and said simply:

"The air isn't good for you here. It's always closed. It's stifling."

She stood and finished drinking her coffee, took her cup to the sink, washed and dried it, put it back in the cupboard, approached him from behind, and covered his eyes with her hands for a moment, as in a children's game.

"That's how you've been living here with me all winter, blindfolded."

Standing at the door, she said:

"How I'd love to be blindfolded too. At least sometimes. On sleepless nights. When a man touches me. You don't need to write to us, and don't telephone. There's no need. You must turn over a new leaf."

Shmuel Ash was left sitting by himself at the kitchen table, still holding the inhaler, surprised that she had not bothered to ask him where he was going, or if he had anywhere to go. Perhaps she forgot to ask. Maybe she didn't want to know. It was as if she had simply bent down to stroke a stray cat in the street, and when it began to purr she felt pity for a moment, got out a piece of cheese or sausage and put it down in front of the creature, patted it a few times on the head, then turned and went on her way. She always stands apart.

After devouring three thick slices of bread and jam and leaving a stain on his pullover, he took his plate and cup to the sink and washed them for the last time. Then he went to finish packing.

He intended to wait in Shealtiel Abravanel's room until the old man woke up from his morning sleep to say goodbye, although he had no idea with what words the two of them could part. Then he would hoist the kit bag on his back and go on his way. He would definitely go on his way. He would not linger. He would take the stick with the fox-head handle with him without asking permission. Neither she nor the old man needed that walking stick. At least he would have a little keepsake. He had spent three months here, from the beginning to the end of winter, and the meager pocket money they had paid him might last three or four weeks. At least he would have a walking stick. He would not be leaving here entirely empty-handed. The stick, he reckoned, rightfully belonged to him.

Atalia had stuffed his clothes, some books, his notebooks, and his toiletries tightly into the kit bag. And yet he had a strong sense that he was missing something, and stood wondering what it was he'd forgotten and what might be left in the attic. He wanted to climb up to his old room and check whether Atalia had really brought all his things down, and to say goodbye to the posters and the reproduction that he had decided to leave on the wall for the benefit of his successor. Instead, he wrote a note to Atalia and put it on the kitchen table: "Please could you send whatever was left upstairs to my parents' address in Haifa? Whenever." Then he added the address.

While he was finishing his packing, Gershom Wald appeared. He pushed the door open with his shoulder, limped into the middle of the room, and stood there leaning heavily on his crutches, seeming to occupy a far larger volume of space than he really did. He fixed his gaze not on Shmuel but on the stuffed kit bag on the sofa. He was a clumsy, deformed man with broad shoulders; his strange head looked as if it had not been finished; his body resembled an ancient tree beaten year after year by the winter winds; his wide hands clasped the grips of the crutches; his twisted, hooked nose gave him the look of a sinister Jew in an anti-Semitic caricature; his white hair hung down over the nape of his neck, almost reaching his shoulders; his hoary mustache grew thick over his tightly pursed lips; and his little blue eyes pierced you so keenly you had to look away. Shmuel felt a lump in his throat, and his heart went out to this solitary man. He sought for the right words, but in the end all he said was:

"Please don't be angry with me."

Embarrassment and sorrow made him add:

"I came to say goodbye to you."

Although, in fact, he had not come. On the contrary, it was the old man who had come to Abravanel's room on his crutches to say goodbye to Shmuel.

Gershom Wald loved words, and he always used them expansively and unhesitatingly. But this time all he said was:

"I've lost one son. Come here, boy. Move closer, please. Closer. A little more." And he leaned forward and planted a single kiss in the middle of Shmuel's forehead with strong, cold lips.

51

Aₛ ʜᴇ ʟᴇꜰᴛ ᴛʜᴇ ʜᴏᴜꜱᴇ on Rabbi Elbaz Lane, he remembered to tread very carefully on the loose wooden step. He closed the iron door behind him and stopped to look at it for a moment. It was a double metal door painted green, to which was attached the knocker in the shape of a blind lion's head. In the center of the right-hand leaf of the door was the legend

ʀᴇꜱɪᴅᴇɴᴄᴇ ᴏꜰ ᴊᴇʜᴏɪᴀᴄʜɪɴ ᴀʙʀᴀᴠᴀɴᴇʟ ᴡʜᴏᴍ ɢ-ᴅ
ᴘʀᴏᴛᴇᴄᴛ, ᴛᴏ ꜱʜᴇᴡ ᴛʜᴀᴛ ᴛʜᴇ ʟᴏʀᴅ ɪꜱ ᴜᴘʀɪɢʜᴛ

He remembered the day he had arrived, how he had stood in front of this door and hesitated, wondering whether to knock or to change his mind. For a moment he wondered if there was any way back into this house. Not now. Not now. But someday maybe. Maybe years from now. Maybe only after he'd managed to write *The Gospel According to Judas*. He waited by the door for two or three minutes, knowing full well that no one would call him back, yet waiting for a call.

No call came, apart from the sounds of distant dogs barking dimly from the direction of the ruins of Sheikh Badr. Shmuel turned his back to the door, crossed the stone-paved yard, and went out into the lane without trying to close the rusty gate that always stood half closed and half open. It had been stuck like this for many years. There was no one to repair it. There may not have been any point by now. Shmuel found a vague confirmation that he had been right in the fact that the gate had been stuck for all those years. Right about what? He could not answer this question. Above the gate he saw the iron arch with those words hammered out within it:

AND A REDEEMER SHALL COME UNTO ZION
MAY IT BE SPEEDILY REBUILT 5674

He carried the kit bag on one shoulder all the way to the central bus station, holding the walking stick in his other hand. Because of the weight and the vague pain in his foot he advanced slowly, limping a little, shifting the kit bag occasionally from shoulder to shoulder and the stick from hand to hand. At the corner of Bezalel Street he caught sight of his teacher, Professor Gustav Yomtov Eisenschloss, coming toward him with a briefcase in one hand and a string bag full of oranges in the other. He was deep in conversation or argument with a middle-aged woman whom Shmuel also knew, though he could not for the life of him remember where from. While he was hesitating, he did not remember to greet his teacher until the pair had already passed him. He said to himself that the professor with his thick lenses had probably not recognized him under the big kit bag, and even if he had, what could the two of them say to each other now? How had generations of Jews seen Jesus? How had Judas seen him? What earthly use could this subject be to any living being?

At the bus station he waited for ten minutes in the wrong line. When he got to the front, the cashier told him that this counter was reserved for soldiers with travel warrants and for civilians with an order to report for reserve army service. Shmuel apologized, stood in line for a quarter of an hour or more at another counter, and wondered whether it would not be better for him to go straight to his parents in Haifa. Now that his sister was in Rome, he would not have to sleep in the sooty passage. Maybe they would give him Miri's room this time, with the nice window looking out over the bay. But his parents now seemed like strangers to him, as if they were both just a shadow of a dim memory, as if this winter he had been adopted by the elderly invalid and the widow and from now on he belonged to them alone.

When he bought his ticket, he discovered that the next bus to Beersheba left in an hour's time. He put the kit bag and the walking stick on his left shoulder so that his right hand would be free. He bought two salty bagels at the kiosk and drank a fizzy drink and suddenly felt an urgent need to ring Gershom Wald and say to him, You are dear. Would he be able to say these three words, even from a distance, on the phone, without the old man piercing him with one of his ironic looks? Or perhaps Atalia herself would pick up the phone, and he would shamelessly beg her to let him come back to his attic room right away and give her his word that from now on . . . But from now on what, he had no idea. He had meant to hang up the receiver, but instead he turned around and handed it to a thin, pale soldier who was waiting patiently behind him.

While he was sitting on a dusty bench with his kit bag between his knees, staring at the throngs of armed soldiers running around from platform to platform, Shmuel decided to use the time to jot down a few lines for himself, so as not to forget. But he couldn't find a notebook or a pen in his pockets. So instead of writing he composed in his head a short letter to the prime minister and minister of defense, Ben-Gurion. Then he canceled this letter, asked a small female soldier to keep an eye on his things for a minute, and went back to the kiosk. He drank another fizzy drink and bought two more bagels, one for himself for the journey and one for the female soldier who was looking after his belongings.

Shmuel Ash left Jerusalem at three o'clock in the afternoon on an Egged bus to Beersheba. A few months previously, he had heard about the new town that was being built in the desert on the rim of the Ramon Crater. He knew not a soul there. He intended to find somewhere to leave his kit bag and his walking stick and to look for a job as a night watchman on a building site, or as a janitor in the primary school, or as a librarian or assistant librarian in the library. There was bound to be a small library there. Every small town has a library. And if not a library, a cultural center.

Once he had found somewhere to rest his head, he would sit down and write to his parents and his sister and try to explain to them where his life was rolling to. He might also write a few lines to Yardena and maybe to Rabbi Elbaz Lane. He had no idea what he could write to them, but he hoped that in a new place it would eventually dawn on him what it was he was in search of.

Meanwhile, he sat on his own at the back of the bus, in the middle of the empty back seat. The bulky kit bag was clasped between his spread knees because he had totally failed to squeeze it into the overhead rack. He had managed to place the stick with the fox-head handle on the rack, and he had laid his coat and *shapka* on top of it, though he knew for certain that he would forget them when the time came to leave the bus at the end of the journey.

The bus left behind the gloomy stone-built houses at the end of the Jaffa Road, passed the gas stations at the exit from the city and the turn toward Givat Shaul, and emerged among the mountains. In an instant Shmuel was swept by a wave of warm happiness. The sight of the empty mountains, the young forests, and the wide sky made him feel as if he were waking up at last from a hibernation that had gone on for too long. As if he had spent the whole winter in solitary confinement and now he was free. In fact, it was not just the winter or the house on Rabbi Elbaz Lane. It was everything . . . All through his student years in Jerusalem, the university campus, the library, the cafeteria, the seminar rooms, his previous room in Tel Arza, Jewish views of Jesus and Judas' view of Jesus, Yardena, who had always treated him like an amusing but slightly ridiculous pet that made a mess everywhere, and Nesher Sharshevsky, the hard-working hydrologist she had found herself, the whole city which was always shrinking into itself as though waiting for some blow to fall at any moment, Jerusalem with its grim stone arches and its blind beggars and its wrinkled, pious old women sitting motionless for hours on end, shriveling in the sun on little stools at the entrance to their dark basements. The prayer-shawl-clad worshipers who passed at a run like huddled shadows, backward and forward from alley to alley on their way to the darkness of the synagogues. The dense cigarette smoke in low-ceilinged cafés full of students in thick polo-necked pullovers, all world reformers, all constantly interrupting each other. The heaps of rubbish piled up in the empty lots between the stone-built houses. The high stone walls enclosing churches and convents. The line of barricades and barbed-wire fences and minefields surrounding Israeli Jerusalem on three sides and separating it from Jordanian Jerusalem. Salvos of shots in the night. The stifled despair that always lay over the city.

He was happy to be leaving Jerusalem behind and to feel that every moment that passed took him farther away from it.

Outside the bus window, the hillsides were verdant. It was spring in the land, and wildflowers were blooming by the roadside. The hill country beyond the city seemed wide open, primeval, indifferent, wrapped in a great tranquility. A pale daytime moon, floating above tatters of clouds, stayed in the window of the bus. What are you doing here, Shmuel wondered, it's not your time. In Bab el-Wad the road wound between forested hills on one of which, in springtime twelve years before, Micha Wald had bled to death—alone, among the rocks all night, until he passed out and died, abandoned, before dawn. It was thanks to his death that I received the gift of this winter in his house, enfolded by his father and his wife. It was he who presented me with this winter. I wasted it. Even though I enjoyed free time and solitude in abundance there.

The bus stopped for a ten-minute break by the kiosk at Hartov Junction. Shmuel went to the restroom and bought another bagel, and he drank another fizzy drink. The air was warm and luxuriant. A pair of white butterflies chased each other in a dance. Shmuel inhaled the scents of springtime in deep drafts, filling his lungs, until he felt dizzy. When he returned to his seat, he found that new passengers had gotten on the bus, people from the nearby villages. Some were wearing work clothes and looked suntanned, though the spring had begun only a few days earlier. Some carried their tools with them, or baskets containing live chickens, eggs, or homemade cheese. On the seats in front of him two young women were carrying on a lively conversation in a language he couldn't understand. A group of schoolchildren or members of a youth movement on their way home from a trip were sitting at the front. They were singing songs from the war and the campfires at the top of their voices. The driver, a rotund middle-aged man dressed in crumpled khaki, joined in the singing. He held the steering wheel in one hand and with his other he thumped out the rhythm on the dashboard with his ticket-punch. New villages, all established since the war, flashed past the window. They were white, red-roofed villages with cypress trees in the yards and long, corrugated iron roofs of cowsheds and henhouses. Between the villages, fruit orchards and fields of young wheat and barley, clover and alfalfa, stretched as far as the distant foothills.

The bus made another ten-minute stop at Kastina Junction. People got on and off, and Shmuel, too, got out and wandered among the dusty platforms that smelled of burnt gasoline. He had a feeling that he had been expected in this place for a long time and that people were surprised at the delay and hoping that he would explain himself or apologize. He bought an evening paper at the kiosk but did not read it. Instead, he looked up to see if the pale moon was still accompanying him. He thought that that moon belonged to Jerusalem and should have stayed there and stopped following him, but it was still hovering above the wispy clouds and had merely become even paler. The driver hooted to get the passengers to board, and Shmuel returned to his seat. He did not take his eyes off the vineyards and orchards that flashed past the window. Everything made him happy and warmed his heart. On either side of the road were rows of eucalyptus trees, planted for a military purpose, to camouflage the traffic from enemy planes. As he traveled south, the new villages, here in the Lachish region, were less frequent, and only the wide fields extended along the road, until they were slowly replaced by bare low hills. These hills, too, had been painted green by the winter rains, but Shmuel knew that the green was temporary, and that in a few weeks' time the hills would once more stand parched and baking in the sun, with only a few thorny bushes, blasted by the heat, clinging to them as with sharpened claws.

When, toward evening, the bus reached the station in Beer-sheba, Shmuel left the unread paper on the seat, shouldered his kit bag, took his coat, stick, and cap down from the rack, bought another fizzy drink and downed it almost in one swallow, then set off to discover when and where he could catch a bus to the new town on the rim of the Ramon Crater. At the information desk, he was told that the last bus for Mitzpeh Ramon had already left, and that the next one would be at six o'clock the following morning. He knew he should ask something else, but he could not for the life of him think what to ask. And so he walked away from the bus station, limping slightly, with the kit bag on his left shoulder, the coat on his right shoulder, and the stick in his right hand, and wandered for a while in the little town which he hardly knew. From the ends of the new streets he could see desolate expanses of desert, low, flat sandhills on which here and there were scattered the black tents of Bedouin shepherds.

His feet led him from street to street, all resembling each other, with ugly housing developments, row upon row of uniform blocks of flats with peeling plaster, elongated boxes of three or four stories which had become shabby overnight. In the gardens were piles of scrap metal and broken furniture. In one garden, a blighted fig tree stood, and Shmuel, who loved figs, lingered for a moment to see if he could spot an early fig or two, which did not exist and could not be, because no fig tree puts forth her green figs in early spring, before Passover. Shmuel plucked a leaf off the tree and continued to carry his load slowly down the street. Processions of mostly lidless dustbins plodded along the pavements in front of the buildings. Little children were noisily chasing a yellow cat down the narrow street, but the cat escaped them and disappeared into the dark space under the crude concrete legs on which the buildings of the development stood. Thistles and weeds were growing in the unbuilt lots. Twisted scrap iron was rusting. Most of the shutters were closed, and old bicycles and prams were attached with chains to the stairwells inside the entrances to the buildings.

A pretty young woman in a colorful summer dress appeared at a first-floor window. She thrust half her body out, firm breasts pressing on the windowsill, her hair long and unkempt, and she hung a wet blouse on the clothesline. Shmuel looked up at her.

She seemed pleasant, gentle, perhaps even cheery. He decided to approach her, to beg her pardon, to ask her advice, where should he go, what should he do? But while he was still searching for suitable words, the woman finished hanging out her blouse, closed the window, and vanished. Shmuel stayed where he was, in the middle of the empty roadway. He lowered the kit bag from his shoulder. He placed it on the dusty asphalt. Carefully he laid the coat, the stick, and the cap on top of the kit bag. And he stood there, wondering.

Author's Note

In writing this book I have been greatly helped by the book *Je-sus in Jewish Eyes*, edited by Avigdor Shinan (Tel Aviv, 1999), and also by Solomon Zeitlin's *Who Crucified Jesus?* (New York, 1942; Hebrew translation, Jerusalem/Tel Aviv, 1959) and Morris Gold-stein's *Jesus in the Jewish Tradition* (New York, 1950).

Translator's Note

Direct quotations from the Old and New Testaments and most indirect biblical allusions are taken from the King James Bible.

The quotation from Josephus is from the English translation of Josephus' *Jewish Antiquities* by Louis H. Feldman, in the Loeb Classical Library, *Josephus* IX (London and Cambridge, Mass., 1969). The English translation of a poem by Yannai is from Leon J. Weinberger, *Jewish Hymnography: A Literary History* (London, 1998).